"With the cunning and verve of Gillian Flynn but with a febrile intensity all its own, Jessica Knoll's *Luckiest Girl Alive* is a debut you won't want to miss. Sly, darkly funny, and chilling to the bone, it gets under your skin and stays there."
—Megan Abbott, author of
Dare Me and *The Fever*

"*Luckiest Girl Alive* is a wickedly well-plotted page-turner that lifts back the veil of Ani FaNelli's glamour and privilege to tread among the sharp emotional thorns lying beneath. Knoll's novel dazzles with humor, cultural insight, and thematic heft."
—Alissa Nutting, author of *Tampa*

"At turns funny, shocking, violent, and heartrending, *Luckiest Girl Alive* hooks its reader and doesn't let go. Jessica Knoll's twisted, twisting debut beautifully explores reinvention, retribution, and redemption—and all the rawness in between."
—Miranda Beverly-Whittemore, *New York Times* bestselling author of *Bittersweet*

"Fresh, funny, biting, and shocking—*Luckiest Girl Alive* kept me riveted from cover to cover. I absolutely loved it."
—Lauren Weisberger, *New York Times* bestselling author of *The Devil Wears Prada*

"When Ani FaNelli wants something, she gets it: the job, the body, the man. What starts as a *Mean Girls*–seeming story line transforms into something so dark, so plot-twistingly intense that . . . well, actually, no spoilers here."
—*Marie Claire*

"[It's] *Mean Girls* meets *Gone Girl*. . . . If that doesn't sell you, I don't know what will."
—*New York Post*

LUCKIEST GIRL ALIVE

Jessica Knoll

POCKET BOOKS

New York   London   Toronto   Sydney   New Delhi

Pocket Books
An Imprint of Simon & Schuster, Inc.
1230 Avenue of the Americas
New York, NY 10020

This book is a work of fiction. Any references to historical events, real people,
or real places are used fictitiously. Other names, characters, places, and events
are products of the author's imagination, and any resemblance to actual
events or places or persons, living or dead, is entirely coincidental.

First Pocket Books paperback edition May 2018

POCKET and colophon are registered trademarks of Simon & Schuster, Inc.

For information about special discounts for bulk purchases, please
contact Simon & Schuster Special Sales at 1-866-506-1949 or
business@simonandschuster.com.

The Simon & Schuster Speakers Bureau can bring authors to your
live event. For more information or to book an event, contact the
Simon & Schuster Speakers Bureau at 1-866-248-3049 or visit our
website at www.simonspeakers.com.

Manufactured in the United States of America

10 9 8 7 6 5 4 3 2 1

"What I Know" by Jessica Knoll originally published in LENNY
(lennyletter.com) in March 2016.

ISBN 978-1-5011-9489-4
ISBN 978-1-4767-8965-1 (ebook)

To all the TifAni FaNellis of the world.

I know.

LUCKIEST
GIRL ALIVE

CHAPTER 1

I inspected the knife in my hand.

"That's the Shun. Feel how light it is compared to the Wüsthof?"

I pricked a finger on the blade's witchy chin, testing. The handle was supposed to be moisture resistant, but it was quickly going humid in my grip.

"I think that design is better suited for someone of your stature." I looked up at the sales associate, bracing for the word people always use to describe short girls hungry to hear "thin." "Petite." He smiled like I should be flattered. Slender, elegant, graceful—now there's a compliment that might actually defang me.

Another hand, the skin several shades lighter than my own, appeared in the frame and made a grab for the handle. "Can I feel?" I looked up at him too: my fiancé. That word didn't bother me so much as the one that came after it. Husband. That Word laced the corset tighter, crushing organs, sending panic into my throat with the bright beat of a distress signal. I could decide not to let go. Slip the forged nickel and stainless steel blade (the Shun, decided I liked it better) soundlessly into his stomach. The salesman would probably emit a simple dignified "Oh!" It was the mother carrying her crusty-nosed baby behind him who was the screamer. You could just tell she was that dangerous combination of bored and dramatic, that she would gleefully, tearfully recount the attack to the news reporters who would later swarm the scene. I turned the knife over before I could tense, before I could lunge, before every muscle in my body, forever on high alert, contracted as if on autopilot.

"I'm excited," Luke said, as we stepped out of Williams-Sonoma and onto Fifty-ninth Street, a gasp of icy AC curdling in our wake. "Are you?"

"I love those red wine glasses." I threaded my fingers with his to show him how much I meant it. It was the thought of the "sets" that I couldn't bear. Inevitably, we were going to end up with six bread plates, four salad plates, and eight dinner plates, and I would never get around to completing their little china family. They'd sulk on the kitchen table, Luke always offering to put them away and me snapping, "Not yet," until one day, long after the wedding, I'd get a sudden, manic inspiration to take the 4/5 uptown, storm into Williams-Sonoma like a warrior Martha Stewart, only to discover that they'd discontinued the Louvre pattern we'd chosen all those years ago. "Can we get pizza?"

Luke laughed and squeezed my side. "Where does it all go?"

My hand went rigid in his. "It's all the working out, I think. I'm starving." That was a lie. I was still nauseous from the thick Reuben sandwich, pink and overstuffed as a wedding invitation, that I'd eaten for lunch.

"Patsy's?" I tried to make it sound like I'd just come up with this idea, when in reality I'd been fantasizing about extracting a slice from a Patsy's pie, strings of white cheese stretching, but not snapping, forcing me to pinch it between my fingers and pull, a bonus glob of mozzarella sliding off someone else's slice. This wet dream had been playing on a loop since last Thursday, when we decided Sunday would be the day we finally took care of the registry. ("People are asking, Tif." "I know, *Mom*, we're getting to it." "The wedding is five months away!")

"I'm not hungry"—Luke's shoulders rose—"but if you really want to." What a sport.

We continued to hold hands as we crossed Lexington Ave, dodging packs of strong-legged women in white walking shorts and supportive shoes, toting whatever treasures the Victoria's Secret on Fifth Avenue contained that the one in Minnesota did not; a cavalry of Long Island girls, the straps of their gladiator sandals twisting up their honeyed calves like leather vines on a tree. They looked at Luke. They looked at me. They didn't question it. I'd worked tirelessly to assemble a worthy rival, a Carolyn to his JFK Jr. We made a left, walking to Sixtieth Street before making another right. It was only 5:00 P.M. when we crossed Third Avenue, found the restaurant's tables set and lonely. The fun New Yorkers were still brunching. I used to be one of them.

"Outside?" the hostess asked. We nodded and she plucked two menus from an empty table, motioning for us to follow her.

"Can I have a glass of Montepulciano?" The hostess raised her eyebrows indignantly and I could imagine what she was thinking—*that's the waiter's job*—but I just smiled sweetly at her: *See how nice I am? How unreasonable you're being? You should be ashamed of yourself.*

She turned her sigh on Luke. "You?"

"Just water." When she walked away, "I don't know how you can drink red when it's so hot out."

I shrugged. "White just doesn't go with pizza." White was reserved for those nights when I felt light, pretty. When I had it in me to ignore the pasta portion of the menu. I once wrote some tip in *The Women's Magazine*, "A study found that the act of physically closing your menu once you've decided what to order can make you feel more satisfied with your choice. So go with the pan-seared sole and snap that menu shut before you start eye-sexing the penne alla vodka." LoLo, my boss, had underlined the words "eye-sexing" and written, "Hilarious." God, I hate pan-seared sole.

"So what else do we have left to do?" Luke leaned back in his chair, hands behind his head like he was about to do a sit-up, entirely innocent that those were fighting words. Venom pooled in my brown eyes and I hurried to bat it away.

"A lot." I counted on my fingers. "All the stationery—so that's the invitations, the menus, the programs, the place cards, all of that. I have to find a hair and makeup person, and figure out a bridesmaid dress for Nell and the girls. We also have to get back to the travel agent—I really don't want to do Dubai. I know"—I held up my hands before Luke could say anything—"we can't do the whole time in the Maldives. There's only so much lying around on a beach you can do before you lose it. But can't we do a few days in London or Paris after?"

Luke's face was intent as he nodded. He had freckles on his nose year round, but by mid-May they spread to his temples, where they would remain until Thanksgiving. This was my fourth summer with Luke, and every year I watched as all that good, healthy outdoor activity—running, surfing, golfing, kite boarding—multiplied the golden flecks on his nose like cancer cells. He had me going for a while too, this obnoxious dedication to movement, to endorphins, to seizing the day. Not even a hangover could bleed this wholesome vigor. I used to set my alarm for 1:00 P.M. on Saturdays, which Luke thought was adorable. "You're so small and you need so much sleep," he would say as he nuzzled me awake in the afternoon. "Small," another description of my body I detest. What do I have to do to get someone to call me "skinny"?

I came clean eventually. It's not that I require an inordinate amount of sleep, it's that I haven't been sleeping when you think I've been sleeping. I could never imagine submitting myself to a state of unconsciousness at the same time everyone else goes under. I can only sleep—really sleep, not the thin-lipped rest I've learned to live on during the week—when sunlight explodes off the Freedom Tower and forces me to the other side of the bed, when I can hear Luke puttering around the kitchen, making egg-white omelettes, the neighbors next door arguing over who took the trash out last. Banal, everyday reminders that life is so boring it can't possibly terrorize anyone. That dull fuzz in my ears, *that's* when I sleep.

"We should aim to do one thing every day," Luke concluded.

"Luke, I do three things every day." There was a snap in my voice that I meant to remove. I also didn't have a right to it. I *should* do three things every day, but instead I sit, paralyzed in front of my computer, beating myself up for not doing three things every day like I promised myself I would. I've determined this is more time-consuming and stressful than actually doing the three goddamn things a day, and, therefore, I'm entitled to my fury.

I thought of the one thing I was actually on top of. "Do you even know how many back-and-forths I've had with the invitations person?" I'd burdened the stationer—a wisp of an Asian woman whose nervous disposition infuriated me—with so many questions: Does it look cheap to do letterpress for the invitation but not for the RSVP cards? Will anyone notice if we use a calligrapher for the addresses on the envelope but script for the invitation? I was terrified of making a decision that would expose me. I've been in New York for six years and it's been like an extended master's program in how to appear effortlessly moneyed—only now with that downtown edge. First semester, I learned that Jack Rogers sandals, so revered in college, screamed, "My small liberal arts school will always be the center of the universe!" I'd found a new axis, so into the trash went my gold, silver, and white pairs. Same with the mini Coach baguette (gross). Then it was on to the realization that Kleinfeld, which seemed so glamorous, a classic New York institution, was actually a tacky wedding gown factory frequented only by bridge and tunnelers (B & Ts—also learned what that meant). I opted for a small boutique in Meatpacking, the racks carefully curated with Marchesa, Reem Acra, and Carolina Herrera. And all those dim, crowded clubs, manned by beefy doormen and red ropes, throbbing furiously with Tiësto and hips? That's not how self-respecting urbanites spend their Friday nights. No, instead we pay sixteen dollars for a plate of frisée, wash it down with vodka sodas at a dive bar in the East Village, all while wearing cheap-looking $495 Rag & Bone booties.

I had six leisurely years to get to where I am now: fiancé in finance, first-name basis with the hostess at Locanda Verde, the latest Chloé hooked over my wrist (not Céline, but at least I knew better than to parade around a monstrous Louis Vuitton like it was the eighth wonder of the world). Plenty of time to hone my craft. But wedding planning, now that has a much steeper learning curve. You get engaged in November, and then you have one month to study your materials, to discover that the barn at Blue Hill—where you thought you would get married—has been *done*, and retooled old banks that charge a twenty-thousand-dollar location fee are now the tits. You have two months to pore over wedding magazines and blogs, to consult with your gay co-workers at *The Women's Magazine*, to discover that strapless wedding gowns are offensively middle-brow. Now you're three months into the whole thing, and you still have to find a photographer with nary a duck-face bride in his portfolio (harder than it sounds), bridesmaids' dresses that don't look anything like bridesmaids' dresses, plus a florist who can secure you anemones out of season because, peonies? What is this, amateur hour? One wrong move and everyone will see right through your tastefully tan spray tan to the trashy guidette who doesn't know to pass the salt and pepper together. I thought that by twenty-eight I could stop trying to prove myself and relax already. But this fight just gets bloodier with age.

"And you still haven't gotten me your addresses for the calligrapher," I said, even though secretly, I was relieved to have more time to torture the skittish stationer.

"I'm working on them," Luke sighed.

"They won't go out when we want them to go out if

you don't get them to me this week. I've been asking for
a month."

"I've been busy!"

"And you think I haven't?"

Bickering. It's so much uglier than a heated, dish-
smashing fight, isn't it? At least after that you have sex on
the floor of the kitchen, shards bearing the braid of the
Louvre pattern weaving an imprint on your back. No man
feels very much compelled to rip your clothes off after you
inform him, bitchily, that he left one lone turd floating in
the toilet.

I clenched my fists, flexed my fingers wide as though I
could expel the rage like Spider-Man's web. *Just say it.* "I'm
sorry." I offered up my most pathetic sigh as collateral. "I'm
just really tired."

An invisible hand passed over Luke's face, wiped away
his frustration with me. "Why don't you just go to the doctor? You really should be on Ambien or something."

I nodded, pretending to consider the idea, but sleeping pills are just button-shaped vulnerability. What I really
needed were the first two years of my relationship back,
that brief reprieve when, as I lay laced into Luke's limbs,
the night slipped away from me and I didn't feel the need
to chase after it. The few times I'd start awake I'd see that
even as he slept, Luke's mouth twisted up at the corners.
Luke's good-naturedness was like the bug spray we applied
at his parents' summer home in Nantucket, so powerful
it warded off the dread, that feeling, an alarmingly calm
omnipresence, that something bad was about to happen.
But somewhere along the way—well, around the time we
got engaged eight months ago if I'm really being honest—
the sleeplessness returned. I started shoving Luke off me
when he tried to wake me up to run over the Brooklyn

Bridge on Saturday morning, something we'd been doing almost every Saturday for the last three years. Luke isn't some pathetic puppy in love—he sees the regression, but amazingly, it's only committed him deeper to me. Like he's up for the challenge of changing me back.

I'm no plucky heroine, claiming ignorance of her quiet beauty and quirky charm, but there was a time when I *did* wonder what Luke could see in me. I'm pretty—I have to work at it, but the raw materials are there. I'm four years Luke's junior, which isn't as good as eight, but still, something. I also like to do "weird" things in bed. Even though Luke and I have very different definitions of "weird" (him: doggy style and hair pulling, me: electric shocks to my pussy with a ball gag in my mouth to stifle my screams), by his standards, we have a freaky, fulfilling sex life. So yes, I'm self-aware enough to recognize the things Luke sees in me, but there are midtown bars full of girls just like me, sweet natural blond Kates, who would get on all fours and swing their ponytails at Luke in a heartbeat. *Kate* probably grew up in a red-brick, white-shuttered home, a home that doesn't deceive with tacky siding in the back, like mine did. But a Kate could never give Luke what I give him, and that's the edge. Rusted and bacteria ridden, I'm the blade that nicks at the perfectly hemmed seams of Luke's star quarterback life, threatening to shred it apart. And he likes that threat, the possibility of my danger. But he doesn't really want to see what I can do, the ragged holes I can open. I've spent most of our relationship scratching the surface, experimenting with the pressure, how much is too much before I draw blood? I'm getting tired.

The darling hostess plunked a wineglass in front of me with sloppy purpose. Ruby liquid heaved over the edge, pooling around the base of the glass like it was a gunshot wound.

"Here you go!" she chirped, giving me what I'm sure was her nastiest smile, which wouldn't even rate on my scale.

And like that, the curtain went up, the spotlights roasting: showtime. "Oh, no," I gasped. I tapped my finger on the line between my two front teeth. "Big piece of spinach. Right here."

The hostess slapped her hand over her mouth, her face heating from the neck up. "Thanks," she mumbled and slunk away.

Luke's eyes were confused blue orbs in the lazy evening sun. "She didn't have anything in her teeth."

I took my time leaning over the table, slurped my wine from the rim to spare my white jeans. Never fuck with a rich white bitch and her white jeans. "Not in her teeth. Up her ass, on the other hand . . ."

Luke's laugh was the standing ovation. He shook his head, impressed. "You can be pretty vicious, you know?"

"The florist will charge you by the hour for next-day cleanup. You need to negotiate a flat rate on the contract." Monday morning. Of-fucking-course I had to ride the elevator with Eleanor Tuckerman, née Podalski, fellow *Women's Magazine* editor, who, when she wasn't leeching my talent in her nine-to-five, assumed her acting role as authority on everything wedding and etiquette related. Eleanor was married a year ago and she continues to discuss the event with the kind of somber reverence you would 9/11, or the death of Steve Jobs. I imagine this will continue until she gets knocked up and goes on to birth our next national treasure.

"Are you serious?" I punctuated my words with a horrified little gasp. Eleanor is the features director, someone I report to, and four years older. I need her to like me, and it doesn't take much. All girls like this want is for you to widen your eyes at them, Bambi innocent, and beg them to impart their wisdom to you.

Eleanor nodded, gravely serious. "I'll e-mail you my contract, so you can see what to do." *And so you can see how much we dropped*, she didn't add, which was totally the point.

I gushed, "That would be such a help, Eleanor," and bared my recently whitened teeth. The elevator doors dinged my freedom.

"Good morning to *you*, Miss FaNelli." Clifford batted his eyes flirtatiously. Eleanor got nothing. Clifford has been the receptionist at *The Women's Magazine* for twenty-one years and has various, absurd reasons for hating the majority of people who walk past him every day. Eleanor's crime is that she is awful, but also that one time, an e-mail went out that there were cookies in the pantry. Clifford, who couldn't leave the phones unattended, forwarded it to Eleanor asking her to bring him one, plus a coffee with enough milk that it turned the color of a camel. Eleanor happened to be in a meeting, and by the time she read the e-mail, the cookies were gone. She brought him his precious camel-colored coffee anyway, but Clifford turned his nose up at it and hasn't spoken more than five words to her since. "Fat cow probably ate the last one instead of giving it to me," he hissed to me after "the incident." Eleanor is just about the most anorexic person I know, and we fell to our knees we laughed so hard.

"Morning, Clifford." I gave him a little wave, my engagement ring winking under the farm of fluorescent lights.

"Look at that *skirt*." Clifford whistled, his eyes approving on the size two leather tube I'd stuffed myself into after yesterday's carb catastrophe. The compliment was as much for me as it was for Eleanor. Clifford loved to showboat what a peach he could be if only you never crossed him.

"Thank you, doll." I opened the door for Eleanor.

"Fucking queen," she muttered as she passed through, loud enough for Clifford to hear. She looked at me, waiting to see what I would do. If I ignored her, it was a line drawn in the sand. Laugh, and it was a betrayal to Clifford.

I held up my hands. Made sure my voice carried the lie, "I adore you both."

When the door closed and Clifford could no longer hear us, I told Eleanor I was going downstairs in a bit to do an informational interview. Could I get her a snack or any magazines from the newsstand while I was there?

"A Kind bar and the new *GQ* if they have it," Eleanor replied. She would pick at that thing all day. A nut for a mid-morning snack, a dried cranberry for lunch. But she gave me a grateful smile, and that was the goal, of course.

Most of my co-workers automatically delete those e-mails, subject line "Can I Take You to Coffee?" written by dutiful twenty-two-year-olds, at once terrified and woefully over-confident. They all grew up watching Lauren Conrad on *The Hills* and thought, *I want to work at a magazine when I grow up!* They're always disappointed to find out that I have nothing to do with fashion ("Not even beauty?" one pouted, cradling her mother's YSL bag in her lap like a newborn). I take pleasure in taunting them. "The only freebies I get in my job are the galleys of books three months before they publish. What are you reading right now?" The color draining from their faces always reveals the answer.

The Women's Magazine has a long and storied history of mixing the highbrow with the lowbrow. Serious journalism appears here and there, along with occasional excerpts from moderately prestigious books, profiles of the select few female execs who managed to break the glass ceiling, and coverage of hot-button "women's issues," aka birth control and abortion, that softer terminology really grinding LoLo's gears because, as she's fond of saying, "Men don't want a baby every time they fuck either." That said, this is not the reason one million nineteen-year-olds purchase *The Women's Magazine* every month. And my byline is much more likely to appear next to "99 Ways to Butter His Baguette" than it is next to an interview with Valerie Jarrett. The editor in chief—a chic, asexual woman named LoLo, with a menacing presence I thrive on because it makes my job feel forever in jeopardy and therefore important—seems to be simultaneously disgusted by and in awe of me.

I'd been pigeonholed into the role of the sex writer at first, I think, because of how I look. (I've learned to camouflage my boobs, but it's as though there is something inherently vulgar about me.) I ended up stuck in this role because I was actually good at it. Writing about sex is actually not an easy thing to do, and it was certainly not something most of the editors, regular subscribers to *The Atlantic*, would ever *deign* to do. Everyone here is falling all over themselves to flaunt how little they know about sex, as though knowing where your clitoris is and producing serious journalism are mutually exclusive. "What's BDSM?" LoLo asked me once. Even though she knew the answer, she gasped gleefully as I explained the difference between a sub and a dom. I play her game though. LoLo knows it's not a profile of the founder of EMILY's List that keeps the magazine flying off newsstands every month, and she needs those sales numbers in her back pocket. There have been rumors over the last year that LoLo will usurp the editor of *The New York Times Magazine* when his contract runs out. "You're the only person who can write about sex in a funny, intelligent way," she told me once. "Just tough it out and I promise you, this time next year, you will never have to write about a blow job again."

I carried around this little tease, precious to me as the shiny parasite attached to my finger, for months. Then Luke came home and announced he was in talks to transfer to the London office. There would be a significant bump to his bonus, which was already significantly fine. Don't get me wrong, I'd love to live in London one day, but not on someone else's terms. Luke was taken aback when he saw the devastation curtain my face.

"You're a writer," he reminded me. "You can write anywhere. That's the beauty of it."

I did a loop around the kitchen as I pleaded my case. "I don't want to be a freelance writer, Luke. Begging for assignments in another country. I want to be an editor here." I pointed at the ground, here, where we are now. "It's *New York Times Magazine*." I cupped my hands around this opportunity, so close, and shook.

"Ani." Luke clamped his hands around my wrists and brought them down to my sides. "I know you need to get this out of your system. Prove to everyone you can do more than write about sex or whatever. But realistically, what? You'll work there a year, then you're going to be on my back about having a kid next, and you're not even going to want to go back to work after. Let's be rational here. Should I—should *we*"—oh, he evoked the "we"—"really pass up this opportunity for a temporary whim?"

I know Luke thinks I skew Typical Kate when it comes to the kid thing. I wanted the ring and the black-tie-optional wedding and the tower of a dress, I have a rich lady dermatologist on Fifth Avenue who will inject me with anything I want, and I frequently drag Luke to ABC Carpet & Home to see sets of turquoise lamps and vintage Beni Ourain rugs. "Wouldn't those look so great in the foyer?" I always suggest, prompting Luke to flip over the price tag and feign a heart attack. I think he's relying on me to nag him into fatherhood, like all his other friends' wives have. He'll faux-complain about it over beers—"She's actually mapping out her cycle"—all of them groaning their faux-support. *Been there, man.* But deep down, they're pleased they had someone to push them into it, because they want it too, preferably a boy but hey, there's always baby number two if she fails to pop out the heir the first time around. Only guys never have to admit that. And a guy like Luke? He'd never expect he'd have to tap his watch and say, "Tick tock."

Problem is, I'm not going to push. Kids make me exhausted.

God, the idea of being pregnant, of giving *birth*, sends me into such a state. Not a panic attack exactly, more like a spin, a particular condition that surfaced some fourteen years ago, where I suddenly feel as though I'm on a whir-ring merry-go-round that has just been unplugged mid-ride. It's like I'm gradually slowing to a stop, the silence between my heart's weakening beats stretching longer and longer, as I skate the last loops of my life. All those appointments, the doctors and nurses touching me—why are his fingers lingering there? Does he feel something? Is that a cancerous lump? The spin might never stop. I'm the type of raging, obnoxious hypochondriac that can make a doctor with even the kindest bedside manner snap. I dodged fate once and it's only a matter of time, I want to explain to them, make them understand my neurosis is justified. I've told Luke about the spin, and I tried to tell him how I don't think I could ever be pregnant, because I would just worry so much. He laughed and nuzzled his nose into my neck, purring, "You're so cute you would care that much about the baby." I smiled back. Of course that's what I meant too.

I sighed and pressed the button for the lobby and waited for the elevator doors to part. My co-workers turn their noses up at meeting with these sad-sack girls the same way they turn their noses up at writing about the grundle, but I find it to be pure entertainment. Nine times out of ten, she's the prettiest girl in her sorority, the one with the best closet, the biggest collection of J Brand jeans. I'll never tire of seeing the shadow pass over her face when she sees my Derek Lam trousers slung low on my hips, the messy bun sprouting out of my neck. She'll tug at the waist of her tasteful A-line dress that suddenly seems so matronly, smooth down her overly straightened hair, and realize she played it all wrong. This girl would have tortured me ten years ago, and I fly out of bed on the mornings I get to exert my power over her now.

The girl I was meeting that morning was of particular interest to me. Spencer Hawkins—a name I would kill for—was an alumna of my high school, The Bradley School, recently graduated from Trinity College (they all are), and she "so admired" my "strength in the face of adversity." Like

I was fucking Rosa Parks or something. And let me tell you, she pushed the right button—I eat that shit *up*.

I spotted her right away when I stepped off the elevator—slouchy leather pants (if fake, good ones) perfectly balanced with a crisp white button-down and sharp silver heels, a Chanel purse dangling from her forearm. If not for her round beer face, I might have turned right around and pretended I didn't see her. I don't do well with competition.

"Ms. FaNelli?" she tried. God, I couldn't wait until I was a Harrison.

"Hi." I shook her hand so hard the chain on her purse rattled. "We have two choices for coffee—the newsstand sells Illy and the cafeteria sells Starbucks. Take your pick."

"Whatever you like." Good answer.

"I can't stand Starbucks." I wrinkled my nose at her as I turned on my heel. I heard her clicking frantically behind me.

"Good morning, Loretta!" The most sincere I ever am is when I'm speaking to the cashier at the newsstand. Loretta has severe burns all over her body—no one knows how—and she emits a strong, stale stench. When she was first hired last year, people complained—it was such a small space, and around food no less. It was just *unappetizing*. Of course it was noble of the company to employ her, but wouldn't it be better if she, like, worked in the message center in the basement of the building? I actually overheard Eleanor whining about this to a co-worker one day. Ever since Loretta started, the coffee is always fresh, the milk canisters always full—even the soy one!—and the latest issues of the magazines are artfully presented on the shelves. Loretta reads everything she touches, she skimps on air-conditioning and puts that money toward her travel fund, and she once pointed to a beautiful model in a magazine and said to me, "I thought this was you!" Her throat must have been burned too, because her voice is thick as stew. She'd pushed the picture underneath my nose. "I saw her, and thought, *This is my friend.*" The word roped around my throat, and I just barely managed to contain the tears.

I make it a point to bring these girls to the newsstand. "You were a staff writer for your college newspaper?" I'll cradle my chin in my hand, encourage them to tell me more about their exposé on the school mascot, the costume's homophobic undertones, when I've already decided how much help to provide them based on how they treat Loretta.

"Good morning!" Loretta beamed at me. It was 11:00 A.M., and the newsstand was quiet. Loretta was reading Psychology Today. She lowered the magazine to reveal pink and brown and gray patchworked all over her face. "This rain," she sighed, "as much as I hate it, I hope it rain all week so we have a beautiful weekend."

"Ugh, I know." Loretta loved to talk about the weather. In her country, the Dominican Republic, everyone danced in the streets when it rained. But not here, she said. Here the rain was filthy. "Loretta, this is Spencer." I gestured toward my fresh kill, whose nose was already twitching. Not a strike against her necessarily, you can't help how your body reacts when confronted with the stench of tragedy. I would know. "Spencer, Loretta."

Loretta and Spencer exchanged pleasantries. These girls were always polite, it would never occur to them not to be, but there was usually something strained about their demeanor that tipped me off. Some didn't even try to hide what assholes they were once it was just the two of us.

"Ohmigod was that smell *her*?" one said to me, clamping her hand over her mouth to stifle a laugh and brushing her shoulder up against mine conspiratorially, as though we were girlfriends who'd just shoplifted a pile of Victoria's Secret thongs.

"There's coffee, there's tea, take your pick." I plucked a coffee cup from the stack and pumped a dark stream while Spencer stood behind me, considering.

"The peppermint tea is very good," Loretta said, wisely.

"Is it?" Spencer asked.

"Yes," Loretta said. "Very refreshing."

"You know"—Spencer hiked her classic quilted purse higher on her shoulder—"I'm not really a tea person. But it's so hot out, and that sounds really good."

We-hel-hellll. Maybe the esteemed Bradley School was finally living up to its mission statement: "The Bradley School is committed to educational excellence and dedicated to developing compassion, creativity, and respect in each of its students."

I paid for our drinks. Spencer offered, but I insisted, like I always do, even though I have this recurring vision that my card is declined, this meager $5.23 charge the thing that obliterates the whole dog and pony show: stylish, successful, engaged, and all by twenty-eight years old, no less. The Amex bill went straight to Luke, which I felt funny about but not funny enough to put a stop to it. I make seventy thousand dollars a year. If I lived in Kansas City I'd be Paris fucking Hilton. Money will never be a problem because of Luke, but even so, there is a childhood fear of the word "declined," of Mom's bumbling excuses offered up to the cashier, her disappointed hands shaking as she forced the card back into a wallet packed fat with its maxed-out accomplices.

Spencer took a sip of her drink. "This is delicious."

Loretta sparkled. "What I tell you?"

We found a table in the empty cafeteria. Gray, rainy light crowned us from the skylights above, and I noticed that Spencer had three distinct lines across her tan forehead, so fine they could have been hairs.

"I really appreciate your meeting with me today," she began.

"Of course." I sipped my coffee. "I know how hard it can be to crack this industry."

Spencer nodded ferociously. "It's so hard. All my friends, they're doing the finance thing. They've had jobs lined up since before we graduated." She fiddled with her tea string. "I've been at this since April and I'm really starting to wonder if I should just try my hand somewhere else. Just so I have a job, it's getting embarrassing." She laughed. "And then I can actually move here and I can keep looking on the side." She looked at me questioningly. "Do you think that's a smart thing to do? I worry if my résumé shows I'm working in another industry I won't be seriously considered in magazine publishing, but then I'm also worried that if I don't get just any job, the job hunt could stretch on for so long that they're going to be more concerned that I have zero real-life work experience." Spencer sighed, frustrated by this imaginary dilemma. "What do you think?"

I was just shocked she didn't already live in the city, in an apartment on Ninety-first and First, rent and utilities all taken care of by Daddy. "Where have you interned?" I asked.

Spencer glanced at her lap, sheepishly. "I haven't. I mean, I have, but at a literary agency. I want to be a writer, which sounds so stupid and aspirational, like, 'I want to be an astronaut!' but I had no idea how to make that happen and a professor suggested I work on the business side of things to get a sense of the industry. I didn't even realize like, hey, magazines, which I love, and I love *The Women's Magazine*, I used to sneak my mom's when I was little"— this is such a common anecdote, I never know if I should believe it or if it's just become this thing people say. "Anyway, I never realized, someone is *writing* that stuff. Then I started researching the industry and this, what you do, is what I know I'm meant to do." When she finished, she was breathing hard. So much passion, this one. But it had pleased me. Most girls just wanted a job that let them play with clothes and mingle with celebrities and stroll into the Boom Boom Room because their names were permanently on the list. Those were some nice perks of the job, but they had always been secondary to seeing "By Ani FaNelli" in print. To receiving my copy back with a note: "Hilarious" or "You have the perfect voice." I'd brought that page home and Luke had hung it on the refrigerator like I'd gotten an A on a paper.

"Well, you know that as you rise up the ranks as an editor, you will write less and edit more." This is something an editor had told me once in an interview, and it had unnerved me. Who would want to write less and edit more? Now, after working in the industry for six years, I get it. *The Women's Magazine* has limited opportunities in terms of real reported pieces and there were only so many times I could advise readers to broach a difficult topic with their boyfriend while sitting next to him, rather than across from him. "Experts say men are more receptive when they don't feel as though they're being challenged head-on . . . literally." Still, there was something about telling people where you worked, their eyes lighting up in recognition, that I needed right now.

"But I see your byline all the time," Spencer said.

"Well, when you stop seeing it you'll know I'm running the place."

Spencer rolled her teacup between her palms, shyly. "You know, when I first saw your name on the masthead, I wasn't sure if that was you, *you*. Because of your name. But then I saw you on the *Today* show and even though your name is a little different and *you* look so different—not that you weren't always pretty"—a deep flush began to crawl into her cheeks here—"I knew it was you."

I didn't say anything. She was going to have to ask.

"Did you do that because of what happened?" The question quieted her voice.

Here's the little song and dance I give to anyone who asks this question: "Partly. A professor in college suggested I do that so that I would be judged on my own merits and not by what people may know of me." Then I always shrug modestly. "Not like most people really remember my name; what they remember is Bradley." Now, here's the truth: I started to realize there was something wrong with my name on the first day of high school. Surrounded by Chaunceys and Griers, the many simple, elegant Kates, not a single last name that ended in a vowel, TifAni FaNelli stood out like the hillbilly relative who shows up at Thanksgiving and drinks all the expensive whiskey. I never would have realized this if I hadn't gone to The Bradley School. Then again, if I had never gone to Bradley, if I had stayed on my side of the tracks in Pennsylvania, I can promise you right now I'd be parked outside of a kindergarten classroom in my leased BMW, drumming my French-manicured nails on the steering wheel. Bradley was like an abusive foster mother—she saved me from the system but only so she could have her twisted, meth-fueled way with me. No doubt my name raised some college administrators' eyebrows when they saw it on my application. I'm sure they half-rose from their seats, calling out to their secretaries, "Sue, is this the TifAni FaNelli from the"—stopping abruptly when they saw I attended The Bradley School and answering their own question.

I didn't dare push my luck and apply to any Ivy Leagues, but plenty of their hangers-on would have me, told me they wept as they read my essay, bursting with purple prose and histrionic declarations of all I had learned about this vicious life even though I had only just begun it. Oh, it was a tearjerker, I made sure of it. So in the end, my name and the school that taught me to hate it got me into Wesleyan, where I met my best friend, Nell, the most beautiful WASP whose stinger pierced everyone but me, and she was the one, not some sage professor, who suggested I drop the Tif and go by Ani, pronouncing it "Ahhh-nee," because "Annie" was simply too pedestrian for someone as world-weary as I was. Changing my name had nothing to do with hiding my past, and everything to do with becoming the person no one ever thought I deserved to be: Ani Harrison.

Spencer scooted her chair closer to the table, taking advantage of this intimate moment. "I hate when people ask me where I went to high school."

That wasn't a sentiment I could agree with. There were times I loved saying where I went to high school, loved the opportunity to prove how far I'd come. So I shrugged, my face stone, letting her know we weren't bound to be buddies just because we had an alma mater in common. "I don't mind. I feel like it's a part of what makes me me."

Spencer suddenly realized she was leaning in too close, that this was a point on which we couldn't see eye to eye, and it had been presumptuous of her to think we could. She drew back in her chair, giving me my space. "Of course. I would probably feel the same way if I were you."

"I'm participating in the documentary," I volunteered, to show her just how much I didn't mind it.

Spencer nodded slowly. "I wanted to ask you. But of course they would want you."

I checked the TAG Heuer on my wrist. Luke had been promising me the Cartier for the last year. "I will say that you should definitely try and get an internship, even if it doesn't pay."

"How would I afford rent?" Spencer asked.

I eyed the Chanel bag hooked over the back of her chair. On second glance, I saw that the seams were starting to unravel. Old money, this one, tied up in trusts. Good family name, decent-size house in Wayne, and not a penny to spare the panhandler on the subway.

"Waitress or bartend at night. Or, commute in every day."

"From Philly?" Not so much a question as a reminder of where she would have to come from, as though I was crazy to suggest it. My chest sizzled with irritation.

"We've had interns here who have commuted from DC," I said. I took a slow sip of my coffee then cocked my head at her. "Isn't it only two hours or so on the train?"

"I guess," Spencer said, looking unconvinced. Her dismissal disappointed me. Things had been going fairly well up until this point.

Giving her the opportunity to redeem herself, I reached up to adjust the delicate gold chain around my neck. I couldn't believe I'd left out the most important piece.

"Are you engaged?" Spencer's eyes went cartoon character wide on my pride and joy: a fat, brilliant emerald planet, flanked by two winking diamonds, the band simple platinum. It had been Luke's grandmother's—pardon me, his Mammy's—and when he gave it to me he'd offered me the option to reset the stones on a diamond band. "Mom's jewelry guy said that's the look a lot of girls go for now. It's more modern I guess."

And that's exactly why I didn't want to have it reset. No, I would wear it just the way dear sweet Mammy had worn it: at once restrained and ornate. A very clear message: This is an heirloom. We don't just have money, we *come* from money.

I stretched my fingers out, taking in the hardware as if I'd forgotten it was there. "Ugh, I know. I'm officially old."

"That is the most stunning ring I've ever seen," Spencer declared. "When are you getting married?"

"October sixteenth!" I beamed at her. Had Eleanor been there to witness this blushing bride nonsense, she would have tilted her head and smiled her "Aren't you cute?" smile. Then gone on to remind me that even though October wasn't necessarily a rainy month, weather could be unpredictable. Did I have a backup plan in case it did rain? *She'd* had a tent on standby and even though she didn't have to use it, the reservation cost her ten thousand dollars. Eleanor is bursting with neat little factoids like that.

I pushed my chair back. "I have to get back to work."

Spencer was out of her chair in half a second. She stuck her hand out. "Thank you so much, TifAni, I mean"—she covered her mouth and her whole body tittered with a geisha giggle—"*Ani*. Sorry."

Sometimes I feel like a windup doll, like I have to reach behind and turn my golden key to produce a greeting, a laugh, whatever the socially acceptable reaction should be.

I managed a tight farewell smile for Spencer. She wouldn't mistake my name again, not once the documentary aired, not once the camera narrowed in on my aching, honest face, gently dissolving any last confusion about who I am and what I did.

CHAPTER 2

I spent the summer between eighth and ninth grades listening to Mom rave about the Main Line. She said it was "*very* hoity-toity" and that I was really going to experience how the other half lives by going to high school there. I had never heard the word "hoity-toity" before but inferred what it meant based on the saucy dip in Mom's voice. It was that same throaty purr that the Bloomingdale's saleswoman used to convince her to buy a cashmere scarf she couldn't afford: "It looks *rich* on you." "Rich." The magic word. Dad did not agree when she came home later and rubbed it against his face.

I'd attended an all-girls Catholic school since kindergarten, in a town that was devoid of any Main Line aristocracy on account of the fact that it was shy of the border by about fifteen miles. I didn't grow up in the slums or anything, my surroundings were just morbidly middle class, with plenty of gaudy neighbors who mistakenly considered themselves upper. I had no idea that was the case at the time, had no idea money could show its age, and that old and worn was always superior. I thought wealth was shiny red BMWs (leased) and five-bedroom McMansions (mortgaged three times). Not that we were even fake rich enough to live in the five-bedroom travesties.

My real education started on the morning of September 2, 2001, my first day of freshman year at The Bradley School in Bryn Mawr, PA. I have marijuana (or "grass," if you want to embarrass me like my father) to thank for landing me at the mouth of the old mansion that served as the English and Humanities wing of Bradley, swiping my sweaty palms on my orange Abercrombie & Fitch cargo pants. If I'd just said no to drugs, I'd have been storming the quad of Mt. St. Theresa's upper school, my scratchy blue kilt catching between my thighs, tawny from a summer spent marinating in Hawaiian Tropic oil, day one of my mediocre young adult life that would never pan out to be anything more than a Facebook cliché. My existence defined in successive photo albums documenting my engagement weekend in Atlantic City, vanilla church wedding, and artfully arranged naked newborn.

What happened was this: My friends and I decided it was time to try pot at the beginning of eighth grade, the four of us climbing onto my best friend Leah's roof from her bedroom window, passing a soggy joint between our Bonne Bell–slicked lips. The terrifying awareness it brought to every limb—even my toenails!—was so acute I started to hyperventilate and cry.

"Something isn't right," I half-gasped, half-laughed to Leah, who tried to calm me down but ultimately succumbed to a maniacal fit of laughter.

Leah's mother came to investigate the commotion. She called Mom at midnight and said in a dramatic whisper, "The girls got into something."

I'd had a Marilyn Monroe body since the fifth grade, and the parents had no problem believing I was the mastermind of our Catholic schoolgirl drug ring. I just looked like trouble. In one week, I went from being the queen bee of our small, forty-girl class to an annoying little fly trying to avoid being squashed. Even the girl who stuck French fries up her nose before eating them wouldn't stoop so low as to sit with me at lunch.

Word traveled to the administration. Mom and Dad were called in for a meeting with the principal, an ogre of a woman named Sister John, who suggested I seek an alternative school to continue my education. Mom har-rumphed the whole car ride home, finally arriving at the conclusion that she would send me to one of these ex-clusive private schools on the Main Line, which would give me a better shot of getting into an Ivy League, which would give me a better shot of marrying into some real money. "That'll show them," she announced triumphantly, her hands choking the steering wheel like it was Sister John's wrestler's neck. I'd waited a beat be-fore daring to ask, "Are there boys on the Main Line?"

Later that week, Mom came and picked me up early from Mt. St. Theresa's, driving us forty-five minutes to The Bradley School, a coed, private, nondenominational insti-tution located in the bowels of the lush, ivied Main Line. The admissions director made sure to mention, *twice*, that J. D. Salinger's first wife had attended The Bradley School in the early 1900s, back when it was an all-girls boarding school. I stored that fun fact away, trotted it out for inter-views with prospective employers and parents-in-law. "Oh yes, I attended The Bradley School—did you know J. D. Salinger's first wife went there?" It's okay to be insufferable as long as you're aware that you're being insufferable. At least that's how I justified it to myself.

After the tour, I had to take the entrance exam. I was

seated at the head of a regal table in a formal, cavernous dining room located in a wing off the cafeteria. The bronze plate above the doorframe declared it THE BRENNER BAULKIN ROOM. I couldn't understand how anyone in the English-speaking world could be named Brenner.

I don't remember much of the exam, except the part where I had to write a description of an object without ever explicitly identifying the object. I went with my cat, and ended the passage with her diving off our back porch to her bloodied, mangled death. Bradley's boner for J. D. Salinger made me think they had a thing for tortured writers, and I was right. A few weeks later, we got word that my financial aid was approved and that I would be matriculating with The Bradley Class of 2005.

"Are you nervous, sweetheart?" Mom asked.

"*No,*" I lied out the window. I didn't understand why she had made such a fuss about the Main Line. To my fourteen-year-old eyes, the houses didn't look nearly as impressive as the pink stucco monstrosity Leah lived in. Taste, I had yet to learn, was the delicate balance between expensive and unassuming.

"You're going to do great." Mom squeezed my knee, the goop on her lips catching white sunlight when she smiled.

A row of girls, four deep, marched by our BMW, their backpacks firmly secured to their slight shoulders with both straps, thick ponytails bobbing like blond plumes on Spartan helmets.

"Mom, I know." I rolled my eyes, more for myself than at her. I was dangerously close to crying, to curling up in her arms while she ran her long pointy nails up and down my forearm until I had goose bumps. "Tickle my arm!" I used to beg when I was little, snuggling up to her on the couch.

"You're going to be late!" She planted a kiss on my cheek that left a sticky coating of lip gloss. In return, she got a sullen, new teenager "Good-bye." That morning, thirty-five steps from the front door of school, I was still only in rehearsals for the role.

First period was homeroom, and like a huge dork I was excited by this. My middle school didn't have bells or different teachers for different classes. There were forty girls per grade, divided into two classrooms, and in that classroom you were taught math, social studies, science, religion, and English by the same teacher all year long, and if you were lucky, you got the one who wasn't the nun (I was never lucky). The idea of a school where a bell rang every forty-one minutes, prompting you on to the next classroom, with a new teacher, and a new concentration of students, made me feel like I was a guest star on *Saved by the Bell* or something.

But the most exciting part of that first morning was English. Honors English, another distinction my old school never made, in which I had secured a spot thanks to that brilliant 150-word description of my cat's tragic demise. I couldn't wait to take notes in the bright green pen I'd bought at the school store. Mt. St. Theresa's made us write in pencil like babies, but Bradley didn't care what you wrote in. Didn't care if you took notes at all as long as you kept your grades up. Bradley's school colors were green and white, and I bought a pen the same shade as the basketball jerseys to display my new allegiance.

Honors English was a small class, only twelve students, and instead of desks, we got to sit at three long tables, pushed together to form the shape of a bracket. The teacher, Mr. Larson, was someone Mom would dismiss as "hefty," but those twenty extra pounds had resulted in a kind, full face: squinty eyes, a slight arch to his upper lip that made him look like he was remembering some hilarious crack one of his buddies had made to him the night before over lukewarm Bud Lights. He wore faded pastel button-downs and had the kind of floppy, light brown hair that assured us it wasn't too long ago that he was a prep school kid just like us and he, like, totally got it. My fourteen-year-old loins approved. All the fourteen-year-old loins approved.

Mr. Larson sat a lot, usually with his legs stretched out in front of him, frequently reaching one hand behind his head and resting his skull against it, while asking, "And why do you think Holden identifies with the catcher in the rye?"

That first day Mr. Larson made us all go around the room and say one cool thing that we'd done that summer. I felt confident Mr. Larson had designed this exercise for my benefit—most of the other kids, "Lifers," had been funneled from the Bradley middle school, and had probably spent the summer hanging out together. But no one knew what the new kid had been up to, and even though it was just tanning on my back porch, watching soap operas through the window like a sweaty, friendless loser, they didn't need to know that. When it was my turn, I told everyone I'd gone to the Pearl Jam concert on August 23, which hadn't happened but also wasn't a fabrication I'd created out of thin air. Leah's mom had reserved tickets for us back before the whole pot fiasco, before she finally had definitive proof that I was the bad influence she'd long suspected I was. But there was an ocean between Leah and these new people, and I had some new friends to impress, so I lied and I'm glad I did. My one cool thing I did that summer invited several approving nods and even an actual "Cool" from some guy named Tanner, which I was surprised to learn was not just a goal I set for my skin that summer but also a name.

After that game was over, Mr. Larson wanted to talk about *The Catcher in the Rye*, which had been assigned summer reading. I sat up straighter in my seat. I'd torn through the book in two days on my back porch, my thumbs leaving humid half-moon imprints on every page. Mom asked me what I thought about it, and when I told her I thought it was hilarious, she cocked her head at me and said, "Tif, he has a serious mental breakdown." This revelation shocked me so much that I reread the book, deeply concerned that this crucial element of the story had escaped me. For a moment I worried that I wasn't the literary whiz I fancied myself, but then I reminded myself how Mt. St. Theresa's eschewed literature in favor of gram-mar (less sex and sin in grammar), and so it wasn't really my fault that my observations weren't as sharp as they could be. I'd get there.

The boy closest to the marker board groaned. His name was Arthur, and that summer the coolest thing he did was take a tour of the *New York Times* office, which, based on the reactions of the classroom, wasn't as cool as seeing Pearl Jam in concert but also not as bad as seeing *The Phantom of the Opera* at the Kimmel Center. Even *I* understood it's not impressive unless it's on Broadway.

"You enjoyed it that much, did you?" Mr. Larson quip-ped, and the classroom tittered.

Arthur was close to three hundred pounds, and acne framed his face like parentheses. His hair was so greasy that when he pushed his hands through it, it stayed, an oily arc from his hairline to the crown of his head. "Could Holden be any less self-aware? Here he is, calling everyone a phony, when he's the biggest phony of them all."

"You bring up an interesting point," Mr. Larson said encouragingly. "Is Holden a reliable narrator?"

The bell rang before anyone could answer, and over Mr. Larson's instructions to read the first two chapters of *Into Thin Air*, which we would discuss later in the week, everyone swept notebooks and pencils into their book bags before storming out in a rush of Steve Madden clogs and peach-fuzz-covered legs. I didn't understand how everyone got out the door so quickly. It was the first time I noticed it, but once I did, I noticed it for the rest of my life: I was slow. What comes effortlessly to others doesn't for me.

When I realized I was alone with Mr. Larson my cheeks blushed underneath the Cover Girl Mom said I needed and I assumed the other girls would be wearing. They weren't.

"You're joining us from St. Theresa's, am I right?" Mr. Larson hunched over his desk, shuffled through some papers.

"*Mt.* St. Theresa's." I finally managed to zip my book bag.

Mr. Larson looked up from his desk, and the crease in his lip deepened. "Right. Well, the book report you did was very good. Very thorough."

Even though I would lie in bed later, replaying this moment over and over until I gritted my teeth and clenched my fists to keep from spontaneously combusting, all I wanted to do was get out of there. I've never known the right thing to say, and my face probably looked like my Irish aunt's when she has too much red wine and starts stroking my hair and telling me how much she wishes she had a daughter. "Thanks."

Mr. Larson smiled and his eyes disappeared. "Happy to have you in my class."

"Uh-huh, see you tomorrow!" I started to give a wave and changed my mind halfway through. I probably looked like I had some kind of Tourette's tic. I'd learned about Tourette's on a sick day, watching an episode of the *Sally Jessy Raphael* show.

Mr. Larson gave me a small wave back.

There was a broken desk a few steps outside of Mr. Larson's classroom, and Arthur had his book bag propped up on it. He was rummaging around in there but looked up as I approached.

"Hey," he said.

"Hi."

"My glasses," he said by way of explanation.

"Oh." I slid my hands underneath the straps of my book bag and gripped tightly.

"Do you have lunch now?" he asked.

I nodded. But I'd planned on spending it in the library. I couldn't imagine anything worse than that moment after paying for my food, looking around the room at the expanse of nameless faces and being forced to sit down where I wasn't wanted because you weren't allowed to bring food outside the cafeteria. There was so much to talk about on the first day of school, no one wanted to waste that precious gossip time by taking on the responsibility of making the new girl feel included. I got it, I would have been just as disinterested. I knew things would shift to the familiar eventually, that the curly redhead with soft blue veins in her forehead would become the girl with the highest IQ in class, who would apply early decision to Harvard and have the distinction of being the first Bradley student from the class of 2005 to be accepted. (Out of a class of seventy-one students, there would be nine overall. Main Line Magazine hadn't determined Bradley an "exemplary" college preparatory option for nothing.) That the short, stocky soccer player with actual pecs would become the guy who had gotten a blow job from Lindsay "Biz" Hanes in his best friend's basement last summer while his best friend watched. These faces and identities would eventually come together for me, and I would eventually become someone to everyone else too, with anecdotal lore to explain why I sat with who I sat with, why my allegiances resided where they did. But until then, I preferred to maintain my dignity by getting a head start on my Spanish homework in the library.

"I'll walk with you," Arthur offered.

He slung his lumpy backpack over one shoulder and led the way, his swollen, pale calves brushing against each other as he plodded down the stairs. I knew what it was like to have your body betray you—I was only fourteen and I already looked like a college student who needed to lose the freshman fifteen. Teenage boys were stupid though, and because I had relatively skinny arms and legs and a chest that looked pornographic in V-neck tees, they thought I had the perfect body. This despite the fact that underneath the clothes was a genetic mess that not even a prom dress–induced bout of anorexia could fix—a stomach that was rippled with fat, a belly button that winked like an Asian eye. It was the summer the tankini came into style, and never had I been more grateful for a piece of clothing in my life.

"Are you, like, in love with Mr. Larson like every other girl here?" Arthur grinned and pushed his glasses, which he'd found, higher on his shiny nose.

"My teachers were nuns before this. Can you blame me?"

"A Catholic girl," Arthur said, solemnly. They didn't get a whole lot of my kind around here. "Where?"

"Mt. St. Theresa Academy?" I waited for his reaction, which I didn't anticipate would be favorable. When his expression remained blank I added, "In Malvern?" Malvern was technically considered the start of the Main Line, but it was like the lowest tier of troops, shielding the generals and the captains in the cushy heart of the camp. The plebeians toeing its border prickled most storied Main Liners—Malvern wasn't *really* a member of their dynasty.

Arthur made a face. "Malvern? That's far. Is that where you live?"

And so started the years of explaining—no, I don't actually live there. I live in Chester Springs, which is even farther out, crawling with commoners, and while there are beautiful old houses that would certainly be met with approval, I didn't live in any of them.

"How far away is that?" Arthur asked after I finished my spiel.

"Like half an hour." It was forty-five minutes, fifty some days, but this was another lie I learned to tell.

Arthur and I arrived at the entrance to the cafeteria and he gestured for me to go in first. "After you."

❧

I didn't know who to be afraid of yet, so even though the cafeteria was packed and brimming with an energy that could have been interpreted as threatening, I was oblivious. I watched Arthur wave to someone and followed him when he said, "Come on."

The cafeteria was the confluence where the old mansion and the new school met. The lunch tables were wood, a worn shade of espresso, chipped to reveal their sandy skeletons in places. The dark, matching floors ended at a large entryway, which opened up into a newly constructed atrium with skylights, terrazzo gleaming underfoot, and floor-to-ceiling windows that watched the quad, middle schoolers roaming the grass like cattle. The food was contained in a U-shaped room that welcomed students from the old mansion with a deli bar and spat you out into the new atrium, shortly past the bony arms of recovering anorexics reaching into the salad bar for broccoli and fat-free Italian dressing.

I followed Arthur, who stopped at a table by an antique fireplace. It looked like it hadn't been used for years, but its soot-stained mouth suggested that the former inhabitants had appreciated it. Arthur dumped his book bag into a chair across from a girl with big brown eyes set so far apart they were practically in her sideburns. Kids called her the Shark behind her back, but her unusual eyes were actually her best feature and the thing her husband would eventually love the most about her. She was wearing bulky khakis and a white cotton sweater that gathered underneath her large breasts in a wrinkled pouch. She was flanked by another girl, chin in her hands, her long brown hair spilling over her shoulders and pooling on the table around her elbows. She was so pale I was shocked by her short skirt, that she would put her white legs on display so brazenly. Mom would have strapped me into a tanning bed before allowing me to go out with skin as blanched as that. It didn't seem to be working against her, though. The guy next to her wore a soccer jersey that seemed mandatory next to his wholesome good looks, and his hand rested on a quadrant of her lower back that only a boyfriend would touch.

"Yo," Arthur said. "This is TifAni. She went to Catholic school. Be nice to her, she's had it bad enough."

"Hi, TifAni!" the Shark said, brightly. She dragged a plastic spoon around the curves of an empty pudding cup, trying to scoop up any last remnants of chocolate goo.

"Hi."

Arthur pointed at the Shark. "Beth." Then the pale girl. "Sarah." Then her boyfriend. "Teddy."

An a cappella of hellos. I held up my hand and said hi again.

"Come on." Arthur tugged my sleeve. I hooked the strap of my book bag over the edge of a chair and approached the line forming at the deli. When it was Arthur's turn, he ordered a whopper of a sandwich, with roast beef and turkey, three different kinds of cheese, no tomatoes, just lettuce, and enough mayo that his lunch made a squishy sound every time he bit into it. I asked for cheese, mustard, and tomato on a spinach wrap (oh, the days when we thought a wrap had fewer calories than bread). Arthur tossed two bags of chips onto his tray, but I noticed that most of the girls weren't using, so I didn't either. I carried my wrap and my diet Snapple to the register and waited in line to pay.

"I like your pants." The compliment turned me around. A girl who was at once extremely bizarre looking and attractive nodded at my orange cargo pants, which I already couldn't wait to never wear again. She had strawberry blond hair that was so uniform in color it couldn't be natural, large brown eyes somehow devoid of eyelashes, and skin the color of a girl who had a pool in her backyard and no summer job. In her hot pink button-down and schoolgirl-style plaid skirt that most certainly broke

Jessica Knoll

the fingertips rule, she was dressed in a way that defied the androgynous prep style that seemed to be so dominant among Bradley girls, but she carried herself with the air of someone who ran the show.

"Thanks." I beamed.

"Are you new?" she asked. Her voice was husky, like the voiceovers in those commercials urging you to call 1-900-GIRLS now.

Off my nod she said, "I'm Hilary."

"I'm TifAni."

"Yo, Hilary!" The booming voice came from the center of the most esteemed table in the cafeteria, crowded by boys with hair on their legs—real hair, coarse and dark like my father's—and obedient girls to laugh when they accused each other of being any one of the following: pussy, 'tard, cocksucker.

"Yo, Dean!" Hilary met his call.

"Grab me some Swedish fish," he demanded. Without a tray, Hilary's hands were full. She tucked her Diet Coke underneath her chin and cradled a bag of pretzels in the crook of her elbow.

"I got it!" I was up at the register and I grabbed the sack of candy before she did, paying for it along with my wrap and drink over her protests.

"I won't forget that," she said, hooking her pinkie around the fish, somehow able to carry all of her purchases with just her hands now.

I caught up with Arthur, lingering a few feet away from the cash register. The encounter, Hilary's curiosity about me, had left my face flushed. Sometimes, a momentary truce in girlhood is much more precious than a guy you really like asking you out, sticking around even after he got the milk for free.

"I see you've met one half of the HOs."

I looked back at Hilary tossing the bag of Swedish fish onto Dean's lunch tray. Guys could use lunch trays. "Is she slutty?"

"It's an acronym for Hilary and her best friend, Olivia. That one"—he nodded to a girl with curly brown hair, laughing appreciatively as the Hairy Legs constructed a fortress out of empty French fry boats—"came up with it for their names. I don't think they even know what an acronym is." Arthur sighed, pleased by their ignorance. "Which just makes the whole thing even more brilliant."

I may not have realized that Holden Caulfield was having a mental breakdown at first, but so help me God I knew what an acronym was.

"Are they really HOs?" I'd never heard of a girl willingly co-opting a word like that before. I'd been called a slut once, the natural jump everyone makes when you have adult breasts by the time you're twelve, and I wept in Mom's lap for an hour.

"They wish they were." The skin crinkled on the bridge of Arthur's slick nose. "But they wouldn't know what to do with a dick if it punched them in the face."

❧

After lunch I had Chemistry, one of my least favorite subjects but exciting nonetheless because the HOs were both in my class. That excitement quickly faded when the teacher told us to pair up for an experiment that would prove that Chemistry can be cool. I looked desperately to my right, but my neighbor was already twisted in his seat, signaling to someone he wanted to be his partner. It was the same situation on the left. Happy twosomes meandered to the back of the room, and this migration revealed a fellow straggler, a boy with light brown hair and eyes that were visibly blue even from across the room. He gave me a nod and raised his eyebrows, a silent request to be his partner even though that was the only option. I nodded back and we made our way to the stations behind the rows of desks.

"Oh good," Mrs. Chambers said when she noticed the two of us standing next to each other, still a little unsure, "Liam and TifAni, take that last table by the window."

"Like we had any other choice," Liam muttered softly, so Mrs. Chambers wouldn't hear. "Thanks for looking out for the new people."

It took me a second to realize that he was also lumping himself into the "new people" category. I glanced at him. "You're new here?"

He shrugged, as though he assumed it was obvious.

"I am too!" I whispered excitedly. I couldn't believe my luck I'd ended up with him. New people are contractually obligated to look out for each other.

"I know." He lifted one side of his mouth into a half smile and the afternoon light caught a dimple in his cheek. Frozen like that, he could have been a poster you tear out of *Tiger Beat*. "You're too pretty to be the last one picked."

I squeezed my thighs together, trying to smother the heat.

Mrs. Chambers started in on a lecture about safety that didn't interest anyone until she mentioned that if we weren't careful, we'd walk out of here with our hair and eyebrows singed right off. I looked over my shoulder at her, realizing when I did that Hilary was watching me with her large, lashless eyes, as though she had already suffered the fate that so concerned Mrs. Chambers. I had a split second to make a decision—look away and pretend I hadn't caught her, or smile and have some kind of nonverbal exchange that could further endear me to her. The instinct that had garnered my fleeting popularity at Mt. St. Theresa's kicked in and I chose the latter.

To my delight, Hilary smiled back and nudged Olivia, whispering something to her as she leaned in close. Olivia smiled too and signaled to me. "He's hot," Olivia mouthed, stretching her lips widely around the word "hot" and giving the slightest of nods to Liam. I quickly glanced at him to make sure he wasn't looking and mouthed back, "I know."

My God, was I pleased with myself by the time the bell rang at 3:23 P.M. Only my first day, and I'd established a flirtation with the hot new guy, laid claim to him in a way that only our mutual newness could allow, and I'd bonded with the HOs. I felt like sending a flowery Hallmark card to that beast Sister John: "Dear Sister John, I'm doing so well at my new school and I found someone who I would like to take my virginity. I only have you to thank!"

CHAPTER 3

"**T**wenty-five, twenty-six—lift your chins!—twenty-eight—two more, make them your best!—twenty-nine, thirty." I rocked back and rested my butt on my heels, stretching my arms out in front of me in a bid to elongate them after "running toward the burn," the prodigal promise that I paid $325 a month to hear. I probably would have that longer, leaner body, too, if only I wasn't so desperate to get food into my mouth by the time I get home that sometimes I don't even take off my coat before I start pillaging the kitchen.

"Take your weights back to the bin and set up at the bar for calf raises." This is always the part of class that gives me the most anxiety—because I need to deposit my weights and get to my favorite spot at the bar quickly but politely, when all I want to do is elbow the slow movers out of my way. "I'm going to be on TV and I'm not here for my health, bitches!" I settle for the accidental bump, the one I typically reserve for the Singers. You know those people, just so fucking happy to be alive, bouncing down the street, buds in their ears and faces repulsive with pleasure as they belt out the lyrics to some noxious Motown classic. I've gotten bold, bumping them with my enormous bag as I pass by, savoring their outraged "Hey!" behind me. No one gets to be that happy.

I'm a little gentler in class. I wouldn't want to alter the image the instructors have of me, one carefully crafted to impress and endear: the sweet but slightly standoffish girl who will always take the most advanced option in the thigh work portion of class, no matter how intensely her legs tremble.

Fortunately, by the time I dropped my weights in the bins and turned around, I saw that my favorite spot was wide open. I looped my towel around the bar, placed my water bottle on the ground, and bobbed up and down on the balls of my feet, all the while pulling my stomach back toward my spine and pinching my shoulder blades together.

The instructor said, "Nice form, Ani."

For an hour, I tucked, sucked in, squeezed, lifted, and pulsed. By final stretch, my limbs felt like the pad thai noodles I'm always craving, and I debated scrapping the two-mile run back to my apartment. But as I stood to return my mat to the cubbyhole in the front of the room, I caught a glimpse of myself in the front mirror, specifically of the roll bulging over the back of my tank top, and reconsidered.

In the locker room after class, some girl who had phoned in all three of the abdominal sets said to me, "You were so good!"

"Sorry?" I had heard her, of course.

"During abs. That last position, I tried to let go of my legs and I couldn't hold myself up for even one count."

"Well, it's the place I need it most so I push myself as hard as possible." I patted my tummy, swollen against my

extra-small Stella McCartney for Adidas yoga pants. Ever
since wedding planning began, my binges have returned
to their high-school-level intensity. For the last few years,
I'd been able to contain them to Sundays, and the occasional Wednesday night. Overexercising and restricting
myself the rest of the week kept my weight steady at 120
pounds (willowy when you're five ten, squat when you're
five three). My goal for the wedding, and, most important,
the documentary, was 105, and knowing what I was going
to have to do—and soon—to attain that seemed to be ex-
acerbating my cravings as of late. I felt like a deranged bear
storing up for anorexia.

"No way!" the girl insisted. "You look great."

"Thanks." My eyes trailed the back of her body as she
turned from me to open up her locker. She had a long, narrow torso offset by wide hips and an expansive, flat ass.
I couldn't decide which was worse—going gentle into
that mom-jeans-wearing night, or fighting it, Botoxed and
hungry, every step of the way.

❧

I slogged home, my feet dragging along the West Side
Highway. It took me twenty-five minutes to run two miles,
which, even factoring in the stops I had to make to wait at
lights so as not get run over by a car, was pathetic.

"Hey, babe." Luke didn't bother to look up from the
iPad on his lap. When Luke and I first started dating, my
stomach used to latch on to the word "babe," hold it like
those claw games in an arcade would a little stuffed animal, a miracle they came up with anything because everyone knows they're rigged. It was all I ever wanted in
high school and college, some broad-shouldered lacrosse

player jogging up behind me and slinging his arm over my shoulder, "Hey, babe."

"How was your workout?"

"Eh." I peeled off my sweaty top, shivered when the wet hair stuck to the nape of my bare neck, no longer barricaded by the Lululemon. I went to the cabinet, located a jar of organic peanut butter, and dipped a spoon into it.

"What time are you meeting them again?"

I glanced at the clock. "One. I have to get going."

I allowed myself a single spoonful of peanut butter and a glass of water before getting into the shower. It took me an hour to get ready, much more than I spend primping for dinner with Luke. There were so many women I was dressing for. The tourists on the street (this is how it's done), the salesgirl who would kiss my ass only when she noticed the Miu Miu label nestled in the leather quilts of my bag. Most important today, the one bridesmaid, premed, who at twenty-three years old had boldly declared that if she didn't have kids by the time she was thirty, she was freezing her eggs. "Advanced maternal age is directly correlated with autism." She sucked on her vodka soda so hard it spat a bubble into the air. "All these women having kids in their thirties. It's so *selfish*. If you can't lock it down before then, adopt." Of course, Monica "Moni" Dalton was sure she'd lock it down before she was stuck with a three handle. She hasn't eaten a processed carb since the *Sex and the City* finale, and her stomach looks like it's been Photoshopped.

Except, three months from now, Moni will be the first of us to turn twenty-nine, and there will be no man next to her in bed to rouse her with birthday sex. Her panic smells chemical.

Moni also happens to be the most fun to dress for. I love catching her studying the delicate ankle straps on my

sandals, the way her eye travels in unison with my emerald. She's no stranger to Barneys herself, but that bill goes
to her parents. Not cool once you're on the wrong side of
twenty-five. At that point, the only acceptable person to
foot your bills is your man or yourself. For the record, I do
foot my own shopping bills (everything but the jewelry).
But I'd never be able to do that if not for Luke. If not for
him taking care of everything else.

"You look nice." Luke planted a kiss on the back of my
head on the way to the kitchen.

"Thanks." I tugged at the sleeves of my white blazer. I
could never roll the cuffs fashion-blog right.

"You guys are getting brunch after?"

"Yeah." I stuffed my bag with makeup, sunglasses, *New
York* magazine—which I'd purposely leave sticking half
out of the bag so everyone would know I'm reading *New
York* magazine—gum, and a rough version of the wedding
invitation our timid stationer had drawn up.

"Hey, so this week—one of my clients really wants us
to go out to dinner with him and his wife."

"Who?" I unrolled the cuffs of my blazer and rolled
them up again.

"This guy, Andrew. From Goldman."

"Maybe Nell knows him." I grinned.

"Oh God." Luke puffed out his cheeks, concerned. "I
hope not." Nell makes Luke nervous.

I smiled. Kissed him on the lips. Tasted stale coffee on
his breath. Tried not to shudder. Tried to remember the
first time I saw him, the *real* first time: at a party when I
was a freshman in college, everyone else in Seven jeans,
me smothered by the waistband of my khakis. Luke was
a senior at Hamilton, but his best friend from boarding
school went to Wesleyan. They visited each other fre-

quently over the years, but because I was only a freshman, that party fall semester was the first time I'd ever seen him. Luke wanted Nell then, before he knew what a ballbuster (his word) she could be. Fortunately or unfortunately, Nell was hooking up with Luke's best friend, so it wasn't happening. When I got home that night, smarting from Luke's perfunctory "Hello," I strategized. The guy I wanted wanted Nell, so I watched Nell closely. I ate the way she ate, leaving almost three quarters of food on the plate (she had a stockpile of blue pills to induce indifference to even the most devastating of carbs) and made Mom buy me the clothes Nell wore when I came home for Thanksgiving break. Nell taught me that I'd been playing it all wrong: Pretty girls had to appear as though they weren't trying to be pretty, which I had made the fatal mistake of doing at Bradley. There were times Nell went out in her father's polo, nasty old Uggs, and sweatpants, no makeup, just to prove her loyalty resided with her own gender. Pretty girls also had to have a self-deprecating sense of humor and point out when they had a blistering pimple and talk about their explosive diarrhea to assure other girls that they weren't interested in the role of man-eating minx. Because if the others sensed any level of deliberate prowess, they'd end you, and you could forget about the guy you wanted. The snarling force of a pack of girls could wither the most screaming boner.

By the end of freshman year I could pull those same khakis on and off without ever even unbuttoning them. I still wasn't thin *thin*, wouldn't lose another ten pounds until after college, but college standards were less rigid than New York ones. Sometime in March, a teasingly warm day, I was walking to class in a trashy tank top. The sun was like a hot hand christening my head as I passed

Matt Cody, an ice hockey player who'd humped Nell's thigh so hard his penis had left a red welt on her skin that clung on, ripening in shades of purple and blue and green, for nearly a week. He stopped dead in his tracks, marveled at the way the light exploded in my hair and eyes, and actually gasped, "Wow."

But I had to be careful. College was my first go at reinvention, and I couldn't compromise it by getting a reputation again. Nell told me I was the sluttiest tease she ever met; I made out a lot, got topless a lot, but that was as far as I'd go unless the guy was my boyfriend. And I even learned how to make that happen thanks to Nell and what she called her Hemingway theory. Hemingway used to write an ending to his novel only to delete it, asserting that it made the story stronger because the reader would always be able to intuit the ghost of that final, incorporeal passage. When you like a guy, Nell reasoned, you need to immediately find another guy, the guy you always catch staring at you in Modern American Classics maybe, the one with too much gel in his hair, bad jeans. Smile at him finally, let him ask you out, drink weak whiskey in his dorm room while he waxes poetic about Dave Eggers, Phoenix whining in the background. Dodge his kiss or don't, and keep doing it until the guy you really like gets a whiff of him—that other guy sniffing around you. He'll smell it on you, his pupils dilating like a shark inhaling a tendril of blood in the water.

After I graduated, I came across Luke again, at another party in the city. The timing couldn't have been more serendipitous because I had a boyfriend, and, *Christ*, that asshole's scent could saturate a football stadium. He was this immensely polarizing descendant of a *Mayflower* family, whom I kept around because he was the only guy who wasn't afraid to do to me what I asked him to do to me in bed. *Slap me across the face?* "Just let me know if this isn't hard enough," he'd whispered, before winding up and backhanding me so hard the nerves in my skull crackled neon and the dark blurred and twisted, a black blanket wringing above my eyes, over and over, until I came with a grotesque groan. Luke would have been appalled if I ever asked him to do something like that to me, but I was willing to trade that pulsating need to be savaged, whether a result of nature or one of nurture I could never figure out, for a last name like his, one I'd kill to put a Mrs. in front of. When I finally broke up with my boyfriend "for" Luke, the sudden freedom allotted us—to go out to dinner together and go home together like a real couple—was intoxicating. Carried us fast and far like a riptide, and we moved in together after a year. Luke knows I went to Wesleyan, obviously. Always comments on how funny it is that we never crossed paths all those times he came to visit.

"This is the Emile, in rose water." The salesgirl pulled the dress off the hanger and swung it around in front of her body, holding up the skirt and pinching the material between her thumb and index finger. "You can see it has a little bit of a sheen."

I glanced at Nell. Nell, still "a head-turner" (Mom's word) even after all these years. She'll never need to get married to feel good about herself, the way the rest of us have to. She used to work in finance, was one of two girls on the floor, the guys swiveling in their seats to catch a glimpse of Banker Barbie as she strode past. At the Christmas party two years ago, one of her meathead co-workers—married, with children, of course—picked her up, threw her over his shoulder so that her dress flipped up and exposed her elegant ass, then ran around the room making monkey noises while everyone whooped and hollered.

"Why monkey noises?" I'd asked.

"I guess that was his impression of Tarzan?" Nell's shoulders poked up into her ears. "He wasn't the smartest."

She sued the company for an undisclosed sum, and now she sleeps until 9:00 every morning, follows up a spin class with yoga, and snatches the brunch bill off the table before any of us can get to it.

One side of Nell's mouth pinched. "I'm going to look naked in that color."

"We'll have spray tans," Moni reminded her. The light streaming in from the window pointed at a monstrous pimple on her cheek, smothered in too-pink concealer. She was really stressed over this whole me-getting-married-before-her thing.

"Midnight is a very flattering shade." A Cartier Love bracelet slid loose from the salesgirl's sleeve as she returned the rose water to the rack and presented its navy cousin with a flourish. She was a natural blonde, probably made blonder by a mere one or two trips to Marie Robinson a year.

"Do people ever mix colors?" I asked.

"All the time." She went in for the clincher. "Georgina Bloomberg was in here the other week for a friend, and that's exactly what they're doing." She pulled a third option, a hideous shade of eggplant, and added, "It can be very chic when done right. How many bridesmaids are you having again?"

There were seven. All from Wesleyan and all of them

living in New York but the two who went the DC route. Nine groomsmen for Luke, all of them Hamilton grads with the exception of his older brother, Garret, who graduated magna cum laude from Duke. All of them in the city too. I once commented to Luke how sad it was that we both came here so thoroughly insulated with friends that we never really got to experience New York. All the weirdos roaming here, all the wild, mythical nights waiting for us, we didn't need them, so we never sought them out. Luke told me it's amazing how I always find a way to turn a positive into a negative.

Nell and Moni went into the back room to show me just how chic rose water and midnight can look together, and I dug around in my purse for my phone. I held it out in front of me at chin height while I scrolled through my Twitter and Instagram feeds. Our beauty director had recently filmed a segment for the *Today* show to warn viewers about the real dangers of smart phone addiction: Breakouts in the Cell Phone Zone, and Early Onset Turkey Neck, from all that looking down to see who had just gotten her butt kicked and her soul cleansed @SoulCycle.

Spencer had followed me on Instagram after we met. I didn't recognize any of the people in the filtered haze of her pictures, but I did notice a comment, asking if she would be attending the Friends of the Five event, taking place in a sad pub located next to a Starbucks in Villanova, PA. A part of me fantasized about what it would be like to go: to show up in simple cashmere, that emerald cockroach attached to my finger, Luke at my side, emanating so much unabashed confidence that through some sort of osmosis, I'd bear it too. The place I had worked so hard to fit into that was now beneath me. All those losers who never left the Main Line, who lived in apartments that probably had *carpeting*. God. There would be a whisper through the crowd, half of them outraged, half of them impressed, their "Did you see who is here? She's got balls" meaning a different thing to each of them. Maybe there would be the guy who still believed I owed him a fuck, after all these years. The event was months away. If I hit my goal weight by then, maybe.

I switched from Instagram to e-mail right as Nell glided out of the dressing room, rose water draped over her picnic bench of a body, the exposed back revealing nothing but skin and spine.

"Wow," Love Bracelet breathed, and it wasn't just to get the sale.

Nell pressed her stubby hands against her chest, flat as the thin-crust pizzas we used to order for breakfast in college. I had to look away. Nell chews on her appendages for sport, and the jagged edges of her fingertips, the raw and bloodied flaps of skin, they remind me too much of how easily the seams of the body fall apart. "If a rapist breaks into your apartment," I'd once hypothesized in the middle of a *Law & Order* episode, "how are you going to claw his eyes out with those nubs?"

"I guess I should get a gun then." Halfway through that statement Nell's blue eyes had lit up with alarm. Too late, neurons had lit a match to the thought and fired the sentence out of her mouth before she could stop it. "Sorry," she'd added, clumsily.

"Don't be." I'd pointed the controller at the TV and turned up the volume. "Sarcasm doesn't have to die for the Five."

"Ani, I look like I'm wearing a flesh dress." It may have been spoken like a complaint, but Nell was admiring the smooth expanse of her back in the mirror, the way the color blended seamlessly into the skin just above her ass worth an undisclosed sum, so that you couldn't tell where the dress ended and Nell began.

"Are you really going to make me stand next to her?" Moni whined, sweeping open the curtain to the dressing room. Moni will never be done trying to make Nell her best friend. She just doesn't get it. Nell doesn't want her ass kissed. She doesn't need it.

"That's a great color on you, Moni," I said slyly, when Nell pretended not to hear her. I'll never be done with rubbing it in Moni's pouty little face that Nell chose me, the guido, over her, the Darien princess.

Moni fussed, "I can't wear a bra though." Love Bracelet scurried over to Moni—*saggy boobs would not cost a sale, not on her watch!*—and began rearranging the jersey strands of the dress. "It's convertible, see? Flattering for all body types." She ultimately tied what looked like a sling for a uniboob. Moni hoisted the sides of the dress in the mirror, her breasts rippling beneath the fabric like an underwater bomb had gone off, thousands of feet below.

"You think the other girls will look good in this?" Moni pressed. The rest of the group couldn't make the appointment today, graciously leaving the decision in the hands of Moni and Nell. Luke had three single groomsmen—Garret, who wore polarized Ray-Bans and put his hand on your back when he spoke to you, was one of them. No one would dare jeopardize her place in the wedding party, her shot at Garret as her escort, by being combative about the dresses.

"I love it," Nell announced. It was all she had to say, and halfheartedly at that.

"It is kind of cool," Moni agreed, scowling at her body from different angles.

I went back to my phone, checking e-mail this time, forgetting all about Early Onset Turkey Neck when I came across a subject line that roiled the lone tablespoon of peanut butter in my neglected belly: FRND OF 5 SCHDL UPDATE, it read, an urgent red flag waving by its side.

"Goddamnit." I tapped on the message to open it.

"What?" Nell was holding the hemline of the dress above her knee, seeing how it looked short.

I groaned. "They want to move filming to the beginning of September."

"What was it before?"

"The end of September."

"So what's the problem?" Nell's brow would have furrowed if not for Botox ("Preventative," she'd said, defensively).

"The problem is that I've been eating like a beast. I have to go ano *now* if I want to be ready by September fourth."

"Ani." Hands on thirty-two-inch hips, Nell said, "Stop. You are so tiny right now." Nell would kill herself if she was ever this "tiny."

"You should do the Dukan diet," Moni chimed in. "My sister did it before her wedding." She snapped her fingers. "Dropped eight pounds in three weeks, and she was already a two."

"That's the diet Kate Middleton used," Love Bracelet said, and we all acknowledged the Duchess of Cambridge with a moment of silence. Kate Middleton looked so hungry on her wedding day it had to be commended.

"Let's go to brunch," I sighed. This conversation was making me wish I was alone in my kitchen, deepest night, with a stocked fridge and hours to myself to defile it. I loved the evenings Luke had clients to entertain. I'd come home with two plastic bags filled with the neighborhood bodega's finest carbs, devour every last starchy crumb, and toss the evidence down the garbage chute, Luke none the wiser. After I fed, I'd watch hours of porn clips, the kind where the men shouted at the women to bark like dogs or they would stop fucking them. I'd come again and again. It didn't take me long. Then I'd collapse into bed, telling myself that I wouldn't want to marry someone who would be willing to do that to me anyway.

❧

Moni got up to go to the bathroom after we ordered.

"What are you thinking for the dresses?" Nell shook her frosty hair out of a knot. The bartender stared.

"You looked great in the rose water," I said. "But your nipples are kind of a problem."

"What *would* Mr. and Mrs. Harrison say?" Nell placed her hand over her heart, a scandalized Victorian in a too-tight corset. My future in-laws amuse Nell to no end, what with their misleadingly modest home in Rye, New York, their summer estate on Nantucket, his bow ties and her chic white bob, held away from her face with a velvet headband. I wouldn't have blamed them for turning up their classic Nordic noses at me. But Mrs. Harrison had always wanted a daughter and I still can't believe that she's satisfied with the likes of me.

"I don't think Mrs. Harrison has ever seen her own nipples," I said. "It would probably be a good anatomy lesson for her."

Nell held up an invisible monocle to her left eye and squinted. "So these are what you call areolas, dear?" she said, her voice wobbly as elderly tourists standing on the subway. It was a stereotypical old lady impersonation, and she sounded nothing like Mrs. Harrison. I could picture the look on my future MIL's face if she could hear us, roasting her over the cayenne pepper in our fourteen-dollar Bloody Marys. She wouldn't get mad—Mrs. Harrison never gets mad. Instead her fine eyebrows would pinch, the skin there collapsing in a way Nell's cannot, her lips parting in a soft "Oh."

She had been so patient the first time Mom visited the Harrison home, prowling the handsomely decorated rooms, turning over candlesticks and other totems to decipher their origins ("Scully & Scully? Is that a store in New York?" "Mom, *stop*."). Most important, Mr. and Mrs. Harrison were contributing 60 percent to the wedding. Thirty percent was coming from Luke and me (okay, Luke), and the remaining 10 percent from my parents, despite my protestations that they didn't have to, despite the fact the check would never clear even though they insisted. As the main investors, the Harrisons were fully within their rights to veto my fabulously hipster band and dominate the guest list: more sixty-year-old women in headbands, fewer twenty-eight-year-olds in skanky party dresses. But Mrs. Harrison had only held up her never-manicured hands and told me this is *your* wedding, Ani, and you should plan it as you see fit. When the documentary people first reached out to me, I'd gone to her, fear lodged in some secret pocket in my throat, like I'd swallowed a bulging time-release Adderall with no water. My voice so husky I was embarrassed by it, I'd told her how they were digging into the incident at Bradley, that they wanted to portray the untold story, the real story, the one the media had gotten wrong fourteen years ago. It would be worse if I didn't agree to be a part of it, I reasoned, they could paint me any way they wanted and at least if I had the opportunity to speak for myself I could—"Ani," she'd stopped me, her expression bewildered, "of course you need to do it. I think this is a very important thing for you to do." God, I am a shit.

Nell acknowledged the shine in my eyes by diverting the conversation. "So midnight? I liked the midnight."

"Me too." I twisted my napkin into a villainous mustache, the ends pointy and hard, curled into a wicked smile.

"Stop worrying about the new film date," Nell said, her read on me as sharp and as worrisome as Luke's is not.

I came across Nell like you would a Robert Mapplethorpe at a street art fair, gobsmacked that something so valuable would be lumped in with a bunch of other crap like that. She'd been slumped against the bathroom wall in Butterfields, a dorm we later took to calling Butterfingers, for the lacrosse team residents who manhandled girls made Gumby-legged by Popov vodka. Even with her mouth hanging open, her tongue dry and pebbled white from all the medically sanctioned stimulants, there was no question that she had a movie star face.

"Hey," I said, my hand on her tanning-bed-tan shoulder—easy to crawl into those fluorescent coffins when you're so young you think twenty-four sounds ancient—and I shook her until she opened her eyes and I saw that, of course, they were as brilliant blue as the sky on the cover of the Wesleyan brochure mailed to prospective students.

"My bag," Nell kept wailing, even as I pulled her to her feet, wrapped my arm around her dagger ribs, and dragged her back to my room. I had to throw her into the brush twice, leaping on top of her as Officer Stan from campus security ambled by in a golf cart, out for freshman blood with an alcohol content of .001 or more.

I woke up the next morning to find Nell scrambling about on my floor, digging under my futon, her frustration sounding in quiet grunts.

"I tried to find your bag!" I said, defensively.

She looked up at me, panic freezing her on all fours. "Who are you?"

We never found her bag, but eventually I figured out why it was so goddamn important to her. The bottle of pills—to help her sleep, to help her not eat, to help her stay up all night studying in the library—clanking together like a baby's rattle as she walked. It's the only thing we don't really talk about.

Nell reached across the table and her ugly fingers pushed into the crevices of mine. She squeezed, and I felt the tiny bug between our hands; hers stained blue when she drew it back. I put the discipline on my tongue. Took a gulp of my bloody, swallowed, and waited. Even if this documentary did nothing to clear my old name, even if no one believed me, the least I could do was take away their ammo: She's disgusting, nothing but a fat, bitter slam pig. The pill left a residue on my tongue that tasted the way money smells—musky, powdery—and I willed myself to believe that redemption was the only possibility.

CHAPTER 4

It was only my second week at Bradley and already I had to replace my entire wardrobe, with the exception of the orange cargo pants from Abercrombie & Fitch. Ostentatious as they were, Hilary had graced them with her seal of approval. I had a vision of her in my room, complimenting the mid-level-mall collection in my walk-in closet. Nestled between a stack of khakis, she'd spy a flap of orange, sticking out at her like a candy-coated tongue. "Do you want them?" I'd say. "They're yours. No, seriously. They're yours!"

Mom took me to the King of Prussia Mall and we spent two hundred dollars at J. Crew on piles of tweedy, cable-knit things. Next we went to Victoria's Secret, where I picked out a rainbow selection of tank tops with built-in shelf bras. Mom suggested I wear them under everything to smooth out my "baby fat," which puckered stubbornly around my belly button. The last stop was Nordstrom, for a pair of Steve Madden clogs, the same ones all the wrap and salad girls wore. You heard them thwacking down the hall before you saw them, the soles of the shoes sticking and unsticking from their heels. "I just want to glue them to their feet," I overheard a teacher say.

I begged Mom to round out our purchases with a Tiffany Infinity necklace, but she said Dad would have her head.

"Maybe for Christmas," she teased. "Get good grades."

The other major change involved my hair. Dad's side of the family is 100 percent Italian, but Mom is sliced with Irish, and with my coloring Hilary determined I could handle even blonder highlights. She told me the name of the salon she went to and Mom booked the first available appointment with the cheapest stylist on staff. The place was all the way out in Bala Cynwyd, which was even closer to Philadelphia and, therefore, farther from us. Mom and I got atrociously lost on the way to the appointment and we arrived twenty minutes late, which Mom said the snotty receptionist didn't have to remind us of three fucking times. I was worried the salon would turn me away and tried to reassure myself that we'd been seen climbing out of a BMW—that had to count for something, right?

Thankfully, the cheapest stylist on staff found it in her heart to pardon our tardiness and painted my head in thick stripes of yellow, orange, and white, each one at least an inch from my scalp so that I already needed a touch-up before I even walked out the doors. Mom did not care for the final product and threw an embarrassing fit, which at least managed to get us 20 percent off the salon's crappy services. Then we drove straight to the drugstore and purchased a light brown hair dye for $12.49, which, when blended with the expensively bad bleach job, resulted in a gorgeous golden hue that faded into the same color as Mom's exhausted brass candlesticks as quickly as my star rose and fell at school. I found it fitting that my perfect shade of blond lasted as long as my popularity, really.

Even though Hilary and Olivia were warming to me,

they were still cautious. So I kept my head down and spoke
only when spoken to, usually in passing in the hallways or
on the way out of the classroom. I was a while off from
being invited to eat lunch with them, further still from
being invited to one of their houses on the weekend, and I
didn't push my luck. I understood this was the assessment
period. I could be patient.

In the meantime, Arthur and crew kept me company,
and it wasn't bad company by any means. Arthur cherished his gossip, and I don't know how he did it, but he
was always the first to report on a mortifying incident he
had no business knowing about. He was the one to break
the story that Chauncey Gordon, an icy junior with a
sneer perpetually tattooed on her face, had been so drunk
at a party that when the student president tried to finger
her she peed all over his hand. Teddy had actually been at
that party, and even Teddy didn't know that. Teddy had
the kind of pebbled red cheeks that all blond, sporty boys
seem to have, and his summer tan came all the way from
Madrid, where he'd attended a prestigious tennis camp
for promising and rich young athletes. Without a football
team, Bradley students chose soccer as the sport to revere,
and they didn't care about tennis. Still, I always felt Teddy
could have leveraged himself better, made a play to sit
at the table with the Hairy Legs, but he seemed content
where he was. Arthur, Teddy, Sarah, and the Shark had
known each other for years, and not even Arthur's sudden, worrisome weight gain ("He wasn't always this big,"
the Shark whispered once when he went back for a second
sandwich) or the halo of acne around his face could en-
danger his seat at their lunch table. I guess it was sort of
sweet.

Then the Shark made my year when she clued me in to

the fact that we could get out of PE if we played a sport. None of the wrap and salad girls took PE, and those were the thirty-nine minutes of my week I loathed the most.

"But then the downside is . . . you have to play a sport," the Shark said, assuming we were in agreement when it came to a sport being worse than PE, which we were not.

I had played field hockey at Mt. St. Theresa's, but I wouldn't say I was athletically inclined. However, I was the only one who didn't mind mile-time day in gym. I never finished first, but it seemed like I could just go and go and go without ever getting tired (Mom said I'd gotten my good wind from her), so I opted to join the cross-country team. The fact that it was coached by Mr. Larson had nothing to do with my decision. Nothing at all.

I couldn't wait for all the running to carve all that baby fat off my frame. My flirtation with Liam was burgeoning, and trimming down could only help whatever it was we were building to. Liam played lacrosse, which was a spring sport, so at the moment he didn't have a team to join, and without all that sweaty boy bonding he was also residing in popular kid limbo right along with me. You could tell he had been cool at his old school, and it was obvious he belonged with that table of Hairy Legs. It seemed he would get there eventually, the sharks already circling him, smelling him, trying to decide if he was prey or playmate.

Even though Liam and I were in the same chem class, he was a sophomore. He'd moved to the area from Pittsburgh over the summer, his father a sought-after plastic surgeon with cheek implants that made him look a little like a Star Trek gul (source: Arthur). Liam had gone to public school in Pittsburgh, which was appalling even to me, and from what I'd gathered, the administration refused to transfer a lot of his credits because they weren't "applicable," which is administrationspeak for, "gross, public school." He'd already slept with two seniors at his former alma mater, which made him seem dangerous to girls like the HOs. And dangerous was good. We'd all seen Leonardo DiCaprio lose his shit for Claire Danes in *Romeo + Juliet* just a few years ago, and we were waiting for our own tortured heartthrob who would risk life and limb to climb between our legs.

You may think that because I went to Catholic school, I would have reservations about premarital sex, and I did, but none of them included the fear that fornication would send me to the fiery depths of hell. I had the opportunity to see firsthand what raging hypocrites nuns and priests could be. Preaching about kindness and acceptance and showing none of it. I'll never forget how my second-grade teacher, Sister Kelly, warned the class not to speak to Megan McNally for the rest of the day because she'd wet her pants. Megan just sat at her desk, in a pool of her own rotten-tooth-yellow urine, hot tears of humiliation curling down her droopy red cheeks.

I came to the conclusion that if a woman of the cloth could be so sure she was going to heaven despite being such a massive asshole, God must be more lenient than I'd been led to believe. What was a little impurity of the mind and body?

My reservations had more to do with the technical— will it hurt, will I bleed everywhere and embarrass myself, how long until it stops hurting and starts feeling good, and the biggie, what if I get pregnant? Secondary to those concerns were STDs and the threat of acquiring a bad reputation. I was learning from Arthur that lots of girls slept around at Bradley, but only a handful of them were shamed for it. Chauncey was a prime example. Even though she pissed on the student president's hand, she generally had a boyfriend, and therefore didn't seem to be judged harshly. It seemed to me that as long as I was having sex with a boyfriend, I could escape any social ire too. And that was preferable to me anyway. I didn't want sex to get off (I'd figured out how to do that on my own long ago anyway). No, I wanted the cool sheets against my back, to cradle his body with my knees as he whispers, "Are you sure?" A nod, the expression on my face frightened but wanting, the push that would change it to pain, signaling to him how much I was giving to him, him wanting me even more for my sacrifice. I could have an orgasm any day of the week—underneath my covers, in less than a minute—but there was something about this, about a guy wanting my pain, that strummed me deep inside.

❧

Bradley required that all students take a two-hour annual computer seminar, and when Liam walked into the tiny lab he chose to sit next to me, even though there was a seat wide open next to Dean Barton and Peyton Powell, both juniors, both flashing idols on the soccer field.

The computer science teacher led us through a series of complicated instructions in order to set up our school e-mail address. I was deciding between the name of my suicidal cat and "lithium" as my password when Liam nudged me and motioned to his screen. I squinted at the page. "The Purity Test: 100 Questions to Determine if You're a Prude Who Needs to Get Laid or if You're a Dirty Whore Who Needs to Close Her Legs."

Liam aimed his mouse at the first question, "Have you

ever French-kissed someone before?" and looked at me, like, "Well?"

I rolled my eyes. "I'm not in the fourth grade."

Liam laughed quietly and I thought, *Good one, Tif.*

And so this went on, ninety-nine more times—Liam pointing to a question, looking to me for my answer. When we got to the part that asked how many people you've slept with, Liam hovered his arrow over the answer "1–2." I shook my head, and he inched to the right, "3–4." I shook my head again, and, grinning, he moved it again, "5+." I punched his arm lightly. Dean's head swiveled.

"We're going to have to change that," Liam said softly as he swept the arrow all the way to the left and clicked on a button, the word "Virgin!" blinking in bubblegum pink.

The lab ended and Liam quickly exited out of the page, but not before Dean and Peyton paused at our table and Dean asked, "What's her score?" A big grin stretched his homely face wide. I got Peyton's appeal—with his fluffy blond hair and cerulean eyes, he was prettier than any Bradley girl. But Dean. Sure, he was tall and had a good body, but with his large ears and flat face, his coarse muddy hair, he looked like the middle monkey from the March of Progress illustrated in our biology books.

"Low, man." Liam laughed. "Low."

No one bothered to consult me, even though I was sitting right there and it was my test and my score, but even so, an inexplicable thrill shimmied through my body. My purity score mattered, for whatever reason, and that meant I mattered too.

After that, Liam started sitting with the Hairy Legs and the HOs at lunch.

My invitation came a couple weeks later, nearly October by then, after thunder and lightning drove all sports teams to the gym. Mr. Larson claimed the stairs, the ones that ran from the locker rooms in the basement to the basketball court, which the soccer team had immediately monopolized.

"Two steps," Mr. Larson said. His thick thighs split wide as he demonstrated the drill. He jogged back down and blew his whistle, and we hiked the stairs in sets of two, again and again, sweat coiling the hairs at the napes of our necks.

"Two-foot hops." Mr. Larson glued his legs together and bounced up the stairs like a pogo stick. He turned around at the top and looked down at us as if to ask if we had any questions. When no one spoke, he blew the whistle looped around his neck and shouted. "Go!"

I still had another flight of stairs before me when I looked up and saw Dean and Peyton and a few other members of the soccer team, their backs against the wall, their gazes menacing. With each step I cleared, my huge breasts slammed against my rib cage, forcing my breath out in a fat-kid grunt. This was not an activity I wanted anyone to witness, let alone an assemblage of prep school Adonises.

It seemed like an eternal agony, but then I heard "All right, guys," and watched as Mr. Larson jogged up the rest of the stairs, all the way to the landing until his wide back blocked Dean and Peyton from my view. He was saying something to them, impossible to hear over the noisy protest of my lungs, but I caught Dean's "*Awww*, come on, Mr. Larson."

"Pat!" Mr. Larson yelled, waving the boy's soccer coach over. "Sic your dogs."

"Barton! Powell!" Coach Pat's voice launched like a cannonball from across the gym. "Get your butts over here!"

I was a few steps from the top now, and I heard Dean's words clear as if they were spoken into my own ear. "Someone's marked his territory."

Mr. Larson's shoulder blades pinched together in outrage, and then he was inches from Dean, hand wrapped so tightly around his arm I could see the white halo of his fingertips in Dean's skin.

"Hey!" Dean raged, twisting.

Then Coach Pat was there, his mouth hot in Mr. Larson's ear, and the whole scene dissipated as quickly as it had escalated.

"What was that?" I tripped over the last step and smacked my shin into the concrete. "Ow," I moaned.

Mr. Larson turned to look at me with such concern that for a moment I thought I'd cut myself when I fell and just didn't realize it. I patted down my legs, but there was no sign of injury or blood.

"Tif, you okay?" Mr. Larson reached for my shoulder but quickly drew his hand back, scratching the back of his head instead.

I wiped sweat off my upper lip. "I'm fine. Why?"

Mr. Larson dropped his head, revealing the perfectly centered crease in his thick slab of hair. "Nothing. No reason." He put his hands on his hips and looked out at the soccer players dancing around the ball, spinning wildly on the polished hardwood floors. "Girls, let's move this into the weight room."

I found out later that Dean got detention for what he said to Mr. Larson. The next day, Hilary asked me to eat lunch with her. Somehow, these events were connected. I didn't know what that connection was, and I was too impatient to claim my rightful spot at their table to care.

Arthur was distraught over my new cafeteria zip code.

"You're playing organized sports and now you're breaking bread with the HOs," he lamented after English class. "What's next, Dean Barton is your boyfriend?"

I made a gagging noise, more for Arthur than for myself. "Never. He is truly a grotesque human being."

Arthur took the stairs faster than I did, his breathing troubled at the top. He got to the cafeteria first and gave the door a two-handed shove. It gasped open, clanging sharply against a metal folding chair. "Well, *I* could rip his cock off and choke him with it." The door swung back, slamming my shoulder and cutting Arthur off for a moment. I nudged it open to see him still standing there, grinning nastily. "I hate pretty much everyone, you know?" He let that linger there for a moment before walking away. I stooped with hurt but pretended it was just so I could prop a chair in front of the door, because Mr. Harold, the history teacher, was always jiggling with the latch and huffing, "Goddamnit!" when he let go, thinking he had fixed it, only to have the door snap shut with a defiant clap. "This is a fire hazard!" he warned the students not listening all around him, pinning the chair against the door to hold it open. When I looked up Hilary was waving at me from across the room. "Finny! Finny!" What they'd all started calling me. Delight bloomed on my face, and I followed the sound of my new nickname like the nascent little lemming that I'd become.

"I'll be back at nine thirty to pick you up." Mom pushed the gear stick into park, and the car rocked back on its heels with a wheeze. The check engine light had been on for a month. The mechanic told Mom it would cost eight hundred dollars to turn it off, and when she asked him if he thought she'd been born yesterday he just repeated himself. "You really need to get it fixed," he said, and it was Mom who flushed red as the car.

Never, in my life, had I arrived at a dance alone, and the idea of walking into the gym without a friend flagging my side made me nauseous for Leah. But just a few short hours ago at lunch, Hilary and Olivia had asked if I was going to the Fall Friday Dance.

"I wasn't planning on it, but . . ." I held my breath. Waited for one of them to fill in my sentence, to invite me to her stately home, thousands of ivy arms hugging its brick body, so we could try on outfit after outfit, vetoing each one until there were clothes strewn all over the floor, sweater arms and legs twisted at excruciating angles, a series of dead body chalk outlines.

"You should." Hilary managed to make it sound like a warning. "Ready, Liv?" They rose from the table and I did too, even though I had half a wrap in front of me and my stomach was writhing for more.

I couldn't go to the dance in what I was wearing, and it would be tough to manage cross-country practice and then get home, change, and get back to Bradley in time. I told Mr. Larson I wasn't feeling well and he said, so kindly I had to look away from him, that I should just go home and get some rest. I didn't want to lie to Mr. Larson, but I also thought that it was unfair I had no one to approve my tank top and jean skirt except Mom, and that I had a right to do everything within my power to change that.

"You look very nice, sweetheart," Mom added, when

my fingers stilled on the handle of the door. For a moment, I wished we could just peel out of the parking lot, go
and split a mushroom and artichoke quesadilla at Chili's.
We always ordered honey mustard sauce to dip it in, and
the waiter always looked at us funny when we asked him
to bring us a side.

"I think I'm too early though." I forced a tone of confidence so Mom would see I knew what I was talking about,
and I wasn't just stalling. "Maybe we should circle around
one more time."

Mom shook her watch free from her sleeve. "It's seven
forty-five. I'd say fifteen minutes is just the right amount of
fashionably late."

It will be worse if you don't go. The handle clicked before
I even realized I was pulling, and I nudged the door open
with the fat wedge of a Steve Madden.

❧

The world inside the gym vibrated with *TRL's* top ten and
strobe lights, shifting rhythmically in shades of pink and
blue and yellow. I just had to locate a group to slip in with
quickly, I strategized, before anyone realized I was here
alone.

I saw the Shark, hanging outside the rainbow glow of
the dance floor with a few theater kids.

"Hey!" I shouldered my way into the fold.

"TifAni!" The Shark's pupils were predatory in the perimeter's shadow.

"What's up?" I shouted.

The Shark launched into a tirade against dances ("Just
an excuse to dry-hump") but added that she came because
Arthur might be able to get us pot. I found myself wishing

I had eyes located on the sides of my head, like her, so that I could scan the bodies on the dance floor without making it glaringly obvious that I was only talking to her until I didn't have to anymore.

"How can you not like dances?" I gestured to the room, an excuse to take inventory of the crowd. In the five seconds this afforded me, I didn't see Hilary or Olivia, or Liam, or any of the Hairy Legs.

"I'd like dances if I looked like you." The Shark's eyes lingered on the dangerous hem of my jean skirt. I'd lost six pounds in the three and a half weeks since I'd joined the cross-country team, and all my clothes were smiling low on my hips.

"I'm still so fat." I rolled my eyes, thrilled.

"Well, well, well." Arthur's frame blocked the dance floor from my view, and this made me angry enough to forget how much his rant had hurt earlier. "Are you going to show us all how to slow-dance with enough room for the Holy Spirit?"

I snapped, "They don't actually do that, you know." At first, I'd been relieved by Arthur's fascination with Mt. St. Theresa and all its holy contradictions. It gave us something to talk about. Now I wished he would just let it go. Only he never would. It seemed like innocent ribbing, but I saw it for what it was: his way of keeping the curtain up on me, reminding everyone—reminding *me*—who I really was and where I really came from.

"Were you even allowed to dance?" Arthur kept at it. In the neon belly of the gym, he looked like he was sweating droplets of fruit punch. Arthur was always sweating. "Isn't that the devil's pastime?"

I ignored him, shifting my weight to the right to peer around him.

"The HOs aren't coming." Arthur said.

I reared back as though he'd hit me. "How do *you* know?"

"Because only losers come to these things." Arthur grinned, his swollen cheeks glowing triumphantly with facial oil.

I canvassed the room for evidence to prove him wrong. "Teddy's here."

"Because Teddy wants to get his dick sucked." I followed Arthur's eye line to Teddy and Sarah, dancing as though their pelvises had been sewn together in home ec.

Not wanting Arthur to see me cry, I mumbled that I had to go to the bathroom, ignoring him calling after me, insisting that he was just kidding. I rounded the corner of the gym, pep-talking myself the whole way. *They would come. They would.*

I froze at the top of the stairs to the locker room, when I saw who was ascending them, having just returned from the bathroom.

"Feeling better?" Mr. Larson was wearing jeans. I'd never seen him wear jeans before. He looked like a guy in a bar. A guy with grown-up intentions. I crossed one leg over the other, concerned he could see up my skirt from where he stood, a few steps below me.

"A little." I took the reach out of my voice like a sick person would, so that he saw only my lips moving around the words.

"Come on, TifAni." Mr. Larson's voice was so chastising, so typically adult, that my body tightened in teenage outrage: How dare he turn on me like that? "You know you can't skip out on practice. What happened?"

I knew if I lied and told him I'd gotten my period that he'd leave me alone, but the idea of talking about my period with Mr. Larson made me want to throw up. "I wasn't feeling well. But it passed. I swear."

"Well then." Mr. Larson smiled, and not sincerely. "I'm happy for your miraculous recovery."

"Finny!" The voice behind me turned the night on its side. Hilary's skirt was so short that I could see a flash of cherry red underwear. Hilary dressed the way I was trying to train myself not to dress, but because she did it as a form of rebellion, rather than out of habit, it worked for her rather than against.

"Come on." She curled a hot pink fingertip at me.

"If you girls leave school property I have to alert your parents." Mr. Larson's voice was closer now, and I turned back to see him just one step below me.

"Mr. Larson." I bulged my eyes at him. "Please. Come on."

For a little bit there was just a beat of some horrible song, and then Mr. Larson sighed and said he never saw me.

❧

A navy Navigator idled by the curb. The door swung open to reveal three rows of Hairy Legs, Dean and Peyton included, Olivia perched gleefully on Liam's lap. Jealousy corkscrewed in my chest. *It's just because it's a full car.*

Hilary settled in and smacked her hands on her thighs. "Sit on my lap," she sing-sang. We could have fit if we just scrunched up next to each other but as I folded myself in the L shape of her body, I smelled the gin, and understood her affection.

I addressed the group. "Where are we going?"

"The Spot." The driver met my eyes in the rearview mirror. Dave was a senior with arms so thin and devoid of body hair this rabid Italian girl envied him. They called Dave the Hammer behind his back, he was such a tool, but cars are currency in high school, and he had one.

The Spot was nothing but a lone patch of land, fenced in by resting dogwoods, their fleeting bloom still three quarters of a year away, and voluminous, untamed maples clustered close enough together to block the road in the front and the Bryn Mawr College dorms in the back. Bradley kids had claimed the property years ago as a place to drink Natty Ice and give the occasional blow job.

It would have been faster to walk. Cut through the brush behind the squash courts, cross the sleepy, one-way street, and we would have been there in five minutes. But Dave circled the perimeter of the Bradley campus, found a spot to park on an active street several hundred feet from the rough opening in the forest. We filed out of the car, clumsily, giggling, and gathered by the curb. Dean took the lead, helping me navigate the path even though it was clear and well-worn. The trail ended at the base of a miniature vista, and in the far corner, I made out a sawed-off stump. I wove toward it, patting my hand on the surface, making sure it was dry before I sat.

Dean reached into his pocket and held out a beer. "I can't," I said.

It was too dark to make out Dean's face, but his form loomed, challenging. "You *can't*?"

"My mom's picking me up in an hour," I explained. "She'll smell it."

"Lame." Dean snapped the can open for himself and sat next to me. "My parents are away next weekend. I'm having a few people over."

The prong of a car's headlights illuminated our pen, just long enough for Dean to see me smile. "Cool."

"Don't tell the HOs," he warned.

I wanted to ask why, but Peyton sauntered over. "Dude, you know you're like sitting in the same place that Finnerman blew that little faggot."

Dean released a wet burp. "Fuck off."

"I'm serious. Olivia saw them here." Peyton redirected his voice. "Liv, didn't you see Arthur giving Ben Hunter a blow job right here?"

Her words carried over in the dark. "It was nasty!"

I traced my finger over the smooth wood surface, considering how sharp the chain saw must have been for the amputation to be this clean. There were a lot of questions I wanted to ask, but I didn't want to draw attention to my connection with Arthur if he was more marginalized than I thought. This was a serious accusation. "Who's Ben Hunter?" I asked, trying to stall while I worked out this new piece of information.

Dean and Peyton laughed at each other, and Dean slung his arm around my shoulder. "Some little faggot who used to go here. Slit his little fairy wrists."

Peyton leaned forward. My eyes had adjusted to the dark, and his face was even more striking up close. "Sadly, he did not succeed in killing himself."

"Sadly." Dean shoved Peyton with one hand. He stumbled, dropping his beer. The can rolled, hissing, on its side. Peyton muttered a curse and chased after it.

"What happened to him?" I asked, hoping I didn't sound as stricken as I was.

"Aw, Finny." Dean gave me a shake, harder than I was prepared for, and I bit down on my tongue. "You feel bad for him?"

I swallowed, tasted the tin of my blood. "*No*. I don't even know him."

"Well, I'm sure his boyfriend is devastated." Dean sucked on his beer. "Watch out for that guy. Arthur. He's a fucked-up kid." His fingers dangled over my shoulder, absentmindedly brushed my nipple. "Don't forget Friday"—our secret made his voice low and private—"and don't tell Hilary and Olivia."

I was stupid enough to do as he said.

The cabdriver who drove me to Dean's party, unlike the ones who would later whip me up and down the West Side Highway on mornings I was late for work and nights I stayed past 8:00 so I could expense the ride, was a patient man. He watched in silent amusement as I piled a ten, nine ones, eleven quarters, six dimes, and one nickel into his palm. $22.40. That's how much it cost to chauffeur me from school to Dean's house in Ardmore. That's how much I paid to lose my dignity.

The sun was slinking behind the trees when I climbed out of the cab, my sports bag pulling one shoulder low. I was still wearing my sweaty running clothes, but Dean said I could shower at his house. I was terrified someone would burst in and discover the secret of what my body actually looked like, so once Dean led me inside and showed me the guest bedroom, the one with its own bathroom, I was in and out in record time.

I ran a brush through my new blond hair and aimed a blow-dryer at it for a few minutes. I was years away from understanding how to "do" my hair, which was thick and wavy but would have answered obediently to a round brush and a straightener, had I known those were tools I needed to have. Fortunately, the look of the early millennium was a messy half loop high on the head, so I threw my hair into a damp knot and patted my chin and nose with Clinique concealer. Some mascara and I was ready. I'd begged Mom for money to buy new underwear specifically for this occasion, taking scissors to the pairs I owned and telling her that running was causing them to unravel at the seams. In the lingerie department in Nordstrom I purchased the sexiest thing I saw: three pairs of silk, leopard print bikini briefs. When I got home and tried them on I discovered the waistband came all the way up above my belly button—it was pre-Spanx control top, really—but I just shrugged and rolled them down to my hips, figuring the material and the print were all that mattered. Nothing sadder than the adolescent rite of passage to have sex before understanding what sexy is.

"Hey-o!" Dean gave me a high five as I entered the kitchen. He was crowded around the granite island with Peyton and a few other guys, all soccer players, dinging quarters into cups of beer. I was the only girl in the room.

"Finny, make a cameo for me." Dean kissed the quarter. "You're my good luck charm."

Peyton whispered something to his partner and they laughed. I knew it was about me. Probably something rude and sexual, and I burned with pride.

I had no technique, just the momentum of the moment, and I angled the quarter, the edge closest to me facing down, slamming it against the sticky marble of the countertop. It bounced high, spun in a dizzy blur, and thunked into a glass, the beer erupting into angry bubbles.

A roar from the crowd and Dean slapped my hand again, this time clamping his meaty fingers around mine when our palms met, pulling me toward him and hugging me so hard I could smell the spicy deodorant he'd generously applied in lieu of taking a shower after soccer practice.

"Fucking awesome," Dean bellowed at the opposing team.

Peyton cast those blue eyes on me, approval warming me from the inside out. "That was pretty sweet, Tif."

"Thanks." My smile reached my ears. Dean handed me a beer, and I took a pull, relished the sourness fizzing in my empty stomach. I wasn't in the habit of skipping meals yet, but that night I was so giddy, so hot to the touch with excitement, that it didn't take any effort to forgo dinner.

I felt two hands on my shoulders, squeezing the muscles just a beat too long. Liam smiled and wrapped his arm around my shoulder. I was barefoot, and I fit perfectly into his armpit, which thank God smelled nothing like Dean's. "Look at what a midget you are," he said.

"I am not!" I protested giddily.

Liam took a sip of his beer and fixated on a spot above my head, contemplating something. He looked back down at me. "There's a table on the porch that would be perfect for beer pong."

"I'm really good at beer pong," I said, putting more of my weight on him. The side of his body was hard with lean teenage boy muscle.

Liam took another sip, a long one this time that emptied out the contents of his beer. He made an *ahhh* sound when he brought the can away from his lips. "No girl is good at beer pong," he declared. He walked me to the sliding glass door. The deck was damp and slimy beneath my naked feet, but I didn't want to go back in the house and find a pair of shoes, risk Liam asking someone else to be his partner in my momentary absence.

Dean and a few others trailed us outside. Teams and rules were set. Liam and me against Dean and Peyton. Hoes could blow and a bounce knocked out two cups. Five minutes in, Liam and I were winning.

It didn't take long for Dean and Peyton to catch up to us. I lost a little bit more of my touch every time it was my turn to raise the red Solo cup to my lips. When Peyton and Dean beat us, I thought that was it and we could just walk away from the table, but Liam said that where he came from, it was good sportsmanship to drink the last cup. It was my turn and I obediently swallowed the remaining contents in small, sickening waves.

"Holy shit!" Dean clapped his hands. The stern October air caught a few words before releasing them into the night—"Never seen a girl take it down like that"—their effect as good as an A in English class, as the pride I felt years later when I landed a desk in that glossy honeycomb tower. *Who are the pussy girls they're hanging out with?* I smiled smugly, knowing it was Hilary and Olivia. I accepted the cocoon of Liam's odorless armpit again, leaning into him so heavily he stumbled.

"Easy there," he said, but he laughed.

Then we were inside, sitting cross-legged around the living room table, playing quarters again. Only this time whiskey scorched my throat when it was my turn to drink. Dean said something so funny I fell over from laughing. Liam—no, wait—Peyton was next to me and he propped me back up, telling me maybe I should sit this next round out. I looked past him, searching for Liam. I wanted Liam.

"She's fine." Dean tipped the bottle over the glasses again.

Someone called Peyton a pussy, and he said, "Look at her. I'm not taking advantage of her like that."

That must have been when I fell asleep. Because the next thing I knew, I was lying on the floor of the guest bedroom, my gym bag by my side. I groaned and lifted my head and so did the boy between my legs. Peyton. He stroked my thigh and went back to doing whatever he was doing that he thought was making me feel good. I couldn't feel a thing.

There was activity by the door, someone poking his head in and urging Peyton to do something, go somewhere. I was too tired to cover myself.

"I'm coming," Peyton snapped. A laugh and then the door closed.

"I have to go." I looked at his beautiful face in the valley of my legs, meticulously shaved on the off chance something like this would have happened with Liam. "Let's hang out for real, okay?"

I fell asleep.

"Ow, ow," I was moaning this before I opened my eyes, before I could locate the source of the pain. Liam. There he was. And there was his face above mine, also twisted in pain, his torso immobile but his hips pressed close to mine, pressing closer still in an agonizing rhythm.

I was hunched over the toilet in the guest bathroom, the tiles cool beneath my knees. Was I throwing up blood? Why was there blood in the toilet?

A few months after this, when I stopped lying to myself long enough to admit that I'd become the cautionary tale mothers told their daughters, I pretended like I was asleep when the train lurched to a stop at the Bryn Mawr train station. I rode the R5 the rest of the way into Philadelphia and called the school when I arrived. "Oh my God! I fell asleep on the train and ended up in the city."

"Oh dear," croaked Mrs. Dern, Headmaster Mah's long-time assistant and an exceedingly committed smoker. "Are you all right?"

"I am, but I'll probably miss first two periods," I said.

Mrs. Dern made the mistake of sounding concerned rather than suspicious, so instead of boarding the first R5 winding back through the Main Line, I wandered around Thirtieth Street Station. I found a Chinese food buffet, and even though it was not even ten in the morning, the undisturbed rows of glistening meat and vegetables were too beautiful to resist. I made a plate, and with the first plastic forkful I shoved into my mouth, I bit into some mysterious pocket that exploded, a burst of salty, gritty chemicals that made me gag.

That's what I tasted in my third and final round that night. A foul, bitter blob on my tongue deposited in tandem with a boy's euphoric groan.

When I woke up it was morning and I was in a bed and in a room I didn't recognize, the sun unraveling like flight lines, welcoming and warm, as initially oblivious to the night's tragedy as I was.

There was movement behind me and before I turned over to see who it was, I accepted that I wanted it to be Liam so badly that it couldn't be. But of all people, it had to be Dean. He was shirtless, his lean torso exposed, and, for a moment, I thought I would throw up on it.

He groaned and rubbed his face. "How you feeling, Finny?" He propped himself up on his elbows and looked down at me, curiously. "Because I feel like shit."

I realized I was still wearing my Victoria's Secret tank top, but only that. I sat up, clutching the duvet cover to my chest, looking around the room. "Um, do you know where my pants are?"

Dean laughed, like it was the funniest thing he'd ever heard. "No one does! You were walking around without them for half the night."

The way Dean told it, this was just another innocent anecdote from our wild party, the same way some senior announced he was going home and everyone found him passed out in his car in the driveway the next morning, never even having fit the key into the ignition. Or the way another guy from the soccer team had forgotten to put any turkey on the sandwiches all the guys made late night, so he ended up eating a mayonnaise sandwich. It was a story so funny it deserved to be told again and again: TifAni was so hammered she walked around without pants for a few hours!

Life had shifted drastically while I slept, but Dean was looking at me like we were comrades in this post-party apocalypse, and it was so impossibly tempting to accept that reality over the other one that I did with a weak laugh.

Dean gave me a towel and dispatched me to the guest room. There, on the floor by the dresser, were my enormous panties crumpled into a little leopard ball. I shoved them in my gym bag, ignoring the blood.

CHAPTER 5

Oh come on. *No* one?" The editor in chief of *The Women's Magazine* spun around her office like a Phillip Lim–outfitted lazy Susan, presenting a tray of macaroons to a circle of painstakingly malnourished editors in an unsuccessful bid to get one of us to eat.

"I'm off sugar," I said, defensively.

Penelope "LoLo" Vincent dropped the tray on her desk and plopped into her chair. She waved her hand at me, her nails painted the color of gangrene. "Of course. You're getting married."

"Oh, fine. I'll bite the bullet!" Arielle Ferguson was our associate editor, very sweet and very clueless in her size eight dress. She lurched forward and selected a cookie, so pink it concerned me, between her fingers. *Ugh, Arielle*, I wanted to telecommunicate to her, *LoLo only wants the anorexic editors to eat.*

LoLo watched Arielle, aghast, as her jaw worked through the two hundred empty calories. Everyone held their breath, frozen in secondhand fear for her. Arielle brightened when she swallowed. "So good!"

"Right." LoLo lingered on the word, her tongue

snapping on the *t*, a deranged mother hen cluck. "So! What does everyone have for me?" She dug the heel of her YSL Tribute sandal into the floor and spun half an inch in her chair, her eyes holding Eleanor in their laser gaze. "Tuckerman, go."

With a flick of her wrist, Eleanor transferred a pile of blonde hair from the front of her shoulder to the back. "So I was talking to Ani the other day and she mentioned how her friend used to work in finance, and how sexual harassment is still shockingly commonplace in that industry." She nodded at me. "Right, Ani?" I was slow to smile at her. Only when I did, did Eleanor continue. "So Ani and I were talking, you know, it's like we've come so far in terms of recognizing that sexual harassment is a problem and educating people about it. Which is great. But it's like we've gotten really black and white and earnest about issues like this at the same time that raunchy humor—particularly from women—dominates pop culture. It's bled over to how women speak and joke around, and that blurs the line in terms of what women are comfortable with, so how do you know what is unacceptable, or even *illegal* behavior in your professional life? I'd love to do a piece that examines what is sexual harassment in 2014 when nothing is sacred anyway."

"Fascinating." LoLo yawned. "What's the hed?"

"Well, um, I thought, 'What Is Sexual Harassment in 2014?' "

"No." LoLo examined a chip in her nail.

"The Funny Thing About Sexual Harassment."

LoLo spun in my direction with a gay little laugh. "Clever, Ani."

I glanced at the notepad on my lap, bearing the words "THE FUNNY THING ABOUT SEXUAL HARASS-

MENT" in all caps, skimming all the research I'd collected underneath it. "Also, there's this great book coming out and we could time it to our story. It's by these two Harvard sociology professors. Specifically about how pop culture has influenced the workplace much more so than we realize." The galley was sitting at my desk. I'd requested it from the publicist so I could read it before pitching this very idea to LoLo.

"Excellent." LoLo nodded. "Be sure to pass that to Eleanor and help her with *anything* she may need." The vein in her forehead throbbed like an angry heart over the word "anything." I always wonder if LoLo knows more than she lets on. That she sees what a talentless hack Eleanor is, what an obvious kiss ass. Eleanor is from some Podunk town in West Virginia. But oh, the places she's gone since she's moved to New York. She's tenacious, I'll give her that much. We have so much in common that it took me a while to understand why we didn't get along. Infighting. We both defeated the odds to get to where we are now, and we're terrified there isn't room enough for the both of us.

"Now"—LoLo drummed the armrests of her chair— "what have *you* got for me, Mrs. Harrison?"

Shifting in my seat, I gave her my backup option, the one I wanted to present as a fun little aside, a great cover line, once I'd wowed her with a pitch that actually had some gravitas. Eleanor makes me meet with her before we go into these meetings so we can discuss the issue as a whole, make sure the lineup is just the right amount of smart and skanky. She tends to pluck my sharpest idea and present it as this half-baked nugget I was struggling to make something out of until she swooped in and reshaped the whole thing into ASME-winning material.

"The American Council on Exercise recently adjusted the calorie burn for a few activities," I began, "and sex is one of them. It's almost double what they assigned it twelve years ago. I thought it would be funny if we had some writer do the Sex Workout or something. She could wear a Jawbone and a heart rate monitor and actually evaluate her efforts in terms of calories burned."

"Brilliant." LoLo turned to our managing editor. "Can we bump 'Dirty Talk' from October and replace it with 'The Sex Workout'?" Without waiting for her response, she barked at the digital director, "Let's get that cover line up online and testing immediately." She lowered her chin at me. "Well done."

Eleanor trailed me back to my desk, a contrite little gnat. No, she was too gangly to be a gnat. More like a mosquito who had gotten a taste of my blood and wanted more. "I hope you don't mind that I brought up your friend's situation in the meeting. I know that's a personal thing."

My desk phone was lit up red with a voice mail. I hiked up my pants before sitting down—I'd been following the Dukan diet for the last seven days, and the waistbands of my skirts and pants were starting to pucker away from my stomach as I sat. It was so soothing that when I couldn't sleep, the gnawing in my gut and the memories on an insomniac Tour de France, I would grab a pile of pants from my closet and model them for myself in the bathroom mirror, marveling at the way I could pull on size twos without ever unbuttoning them. This small, private victory almost made up for the fact that when I crawled back into bed, Luke flinging his sleep-heavy arm over my size twenty-six waist, I'd have to smell his searing middle-of-the-night breath. Did his breath smell this bad when we were dating? It couldn't have. I couldn't have ever been that in love with someone who had breath that bad. Something had happened. His tonsils maybe. I'd mention it to him in the morning. This was fixable. Everything was fixable.

I cooed, "Of *course*, I don't, Eleanor."

Eleanor perched on the edge of my desk. She was wearing a pair of white, wide-legged pants. "Love those trousers," LoLo had said when she walked into her office for the meeting, and now I have the misfortune of knowing what Eleanor's face looks like when she squirts. "Maybe she'd want to talk about her experience for the story?"

"She might," I said. There was my green ballpoint pen, cap off, idling on my desk. I nudged it with my elbow, inch by inch, until the inky head grazed the seam of Eleanor's pants. I maintained eye contact with her as I dutifully promised I would ask her that very afternoon.

Eleanor rapped her knuckles on my desk, and the corners of her mouth dug into her jowls. Not a smile, a conciliatory smirk. "Maybe we can arrange to get you an additional reporting byline. That would be so great for you." Additional reporting bylines go to interns. My piece on birth control and blood clots had been nominated for an ASME the year before, and Eleanor would never forgive me for it. She removed her ass from my desk, and I admired my handiwork, the way the oily squiggles took on the appearance of green varicose veins on her outer thigh.

"So great for me," I agreed, my smile finally genuine, and Eleanor mouthed "Thank you," and pressed her hands together in prayer, like I was such a dear, before walking away.

I picked up my phone, triumphant, and dialed into my

voice mail. After listening to the message from Luke, I hung up and called him back.

"Hey, you."

I loved the sound of Luke's voice on the phone. Like he was busy but having fun and stealing away to tell me something in confidence. I'd been the one to push for the engagement—obnoxiously push. The HBO producers had e-mailed me almost a year ago now, asking if I would want to participate in a documentary loosely titled *Friends of the Five*. I was no friend of the five, but the opportunity to redeem myself, to tell my side of the story—it made my mouth water. But if I was going to do this, I would do it right. There was no way I was mugging for the camera if I hadn't checked off all the boxes in the hotly contested "having it all" category: cool job, impressive zip code; hungry body, and the kicker—dreamy, loaded fiancé. An engagement to Luke would make my rise unassailable. No one could touch me if I was marrying Luke Harrison the IV. How many times had I fantasized telling my story to the camera, bringing my hand to my face, the emerald that would soon be mine gloating as I wiped away a dainty tear?

Luke and I had been dating for three years before the engagement, I loved him, and it was time. It was time. This was how I put it to Luke, solemnly over dinner one night. "I wanted to wait until next year's bonus," he said. But he caved, had Mammy's ring reset for my tiny finger, and I happily agreed to participate in the documentary. I know I shouldn't fall into the old trap that I'm not someone, that I haven't really "made it," until I have a ring on my finger. Fucking *Lean In* and all that. I'm supposed to be better than this, a more confident, independent woman than this. But I'm not. Okay? I'm just not.

"What if we do that dinner with my client tonight?" Luke asked. He'd been trying to set this thing up for a week. I still had two more days left on the "attack phase" of Dukan. After that, I would be allowed to eat a few select vegetables. Don't even think about broccoli, fat ass.

I held the phone tighter. "Can we do it in a few days?"

The only sound was frat-boy hollering from Luke's floor.

Back when we first started dating, I was terrified for Luke to meet my mother. Her nostrils would twitch—yup, that's the smell of the *real* deal—and she would call me Tif, would ask Luke how much money he made, and it would all be over then. Luke would come to his senses, realize I'm the girl you meet in a bar and bang a few times until you fall in love with a natural-ish blonde with an androgynous first name and a modest trust fund. Instead, to my utter amazement, when we returned to his apartment after dinner with Dina and Bobby FaNelli, he bundled me in his arms, rolled me onto the bed, and said in between kisses, "I can't believe I'm the one who got to save you." Like I had a slew of blue blood Dumpster divers lined up before me, vying to wife away my garbage scent.

"Never mind," I said. "I can do it tonight." Maybe some broccoli would help.

❧

I stopped by the fashion closet before dinner. The outfit I was wearing wasn't ugly enough. The uglier and trendier the outfit, the stronger I emanate intimidating magazine editor.

"This?" I pulled out a baggy Helmut Lang dress and leather jacket.

"Is it 2009?" Evan snipped. Come on, there has to be a requisite bitchy gay fashion editor.

I grumbled, "You pick something."

Evan drummed his fingers along the racks of clothing, tapping each hanger like a key on a piano, finally landing on a Missoni striped top and polka-dot shorts. He looked over his bony shoulder and stared crossly at my chest. "Never mind."

"Oh, fuck you." I leaned against the accessories table and nodded to a floral print shirtdress, the lower back cut wide open. "That?"

Evan regarded the garment, brought his fingers to his lips, and *hmm*ed. "Derek usually cuts for straighter figures."

"Derek?"

Evan rolled his eyes. "Lam."

I rolled my eyes right back at him and snatched the dress off the hanger. "I'm seven pounds down, I think I can handle it."

The dress pulled slightly across my chest, so Evan unbuttoned it a notch, slipped a long pendant over my head, and studied me. "Not bad. What diet are you doing again?"

"Dukan."

"Isn't that what Kate Middleton did?"

I started to apply eyeliner in the mirror. "I chose it because it was the most extreme. It's not going to work unless it feels like the worst thing in the world."

❧

"*There* you are," Luke greeted me, crossed between relief and irritation. On time is late for Luke, and his militant punctuality annoys me so much it's something I actively rebel against by running a few minutes behind, always.

I made a big show out of checking the time on my phone. "I thought you said eight?"

"I did." Luke's kiss was either oblivious or placating. "You look nice."

"It's eight oh four though."

"They wouldn't seat us until we're all here." Luke pressed the palm of his hand into the naked small of my back and guided me further into the restaurant. That was a chill, right? That was us, still electrified by each other?

"God, I hate that," I said.

Luke grinned. "I know."

I had vaguely noticed the couple standing by the hostess station, looking on as though they were waiting to be introduced. The client and his wife, body mean with Equinox muscles, cheery blond hair swept away from her face in a ninety-dollar blow-out. I always eye the wife first; I like to know what I'm up against. She was wearing the typical Kate uniform: white jeans, nude wedges, and a silky, sleeveless top. Hot pink, I'm sure she spent a few minutes debating it—was she tan enough, maybe the navy silky sleeveless top instead, can't go wrong with navy—and over her shoulder, a cognac Prada the exact same shade as her shoes, the perfect match more age revealing than the skin starting to pucker in her neck. She had at least ten years on me, I determined, relieved. I don't know how I'm going to live with myself when I turn thirty.

"Whitney." She gave me her hand, sporting that afternoon's manicure, and shook so weakly it was like she wanted me to know that being a stay-at-home mom was the most important thing in the world to her.

"Nice to see you," I replied, which I'd traded in for

"Nice to meet you" ever since Mr. Harrison first introduced himself to me like so. I was horrified, wondering how many people I'd tipped off to my pedantic rearing with all my lewd "Nice to meet you's" over the years. The beauty of good breeding—for those lucky enough to enter this world with the golden rib—is that it's almost impossible to authentically replicate, and poseurs will always out themselves, usually in some spectacularly embarrassing way. Every time I think I've climbed out of the bourgey pit, I realize something I've been doing wrong and my people pull me back in. *You're not fooling anyone.* Take oysters, for example. I thought it was enough to pretend to love those salted loogies, but did you also know you're supposed to place the shell exterior-side down once you've slurped them back? Something that small is that telling, the danger always in the details.

"And this is Andrew," Luke said.

I slipped my hand into Andrew's enormous paw, but my smile stalled when I finally bothered to take in his face. "Hi?" I said, and he cocked his head and looked at me funny too. "Ani, is it?"

"If you'll follow me," the hostess said, taking off into the restaurant and pulling the four of us with her like a magnet. I trailed Andrew, studying the back of his head, pickled with gray (now?), and wondering turned into hoping he was who I thought he was, the want practically Harlequin.

There was a traffic jam while we decided which couple should take the banquette, Luke suggesting that it go to "the girls" because we were both small (Whitney laughing, "I think that's a compliment, Ani") and the table, like so many things in New York, was playhouse size. This is why everyone leaves, eventually. The babies come and

there are limping shopping bags and perspiring snow
boots and boxes of cheap Duane Reade Christmas orna-
ments piled up in the foyer, and one day someone trips on
the handle of a Medium Brown Bag and just breaks, and
so begins the slow crawl to Westchester or Connecticut.
Luke whistles—"Easy"—when I say this, but good fucking riddance. The Mrs. Monsters, lying in wait for their
husbands at Dorrian's and Brinkley's, luring them to the
suburbs when the lease runs out, the birth control not
long after that. I was no stranger to Dorrian's in my day,
but I also wanted to *be* here, in the cramped, overpriced
restaurants, the subway simmering with rude weirdos,
the glossy tower that housed *The Women's Magazine*, the
misleadingly ambitious lady mag editors pushing pushing for less lust, more substance. "You don't think I want
to strangle myself with the scrunchie we told readers to
wrap around their boyfriend's dick?" LoLo roared once,
when not a single editor came to the September lineup
meeting with a blow job idea. "This is what *sells*." Maybe
everything in New York wouldn't feel so playhouse size,
like such a struggle to just get anywhere, if the husband
hunters stayed away. But that's the thing about New York
that I think I love the most—it makes you fight for your
place. I'd fight. There was no one I wouldn't hurt to stay.

I ended up across from Andrew and Luke across from
Whitney. There was talk of switching, vetoed by Luke
and his corny joke that he could always eat dinner across
from me. Andrew's grapefruit knee kept kissing mine,
even though my butt was pushed as far back into the banquette's fold as possible, and I just wanted everyone to
stop with the small talk, the bad jokes, so that I could find
a quiet moment to narrow my eyes on Andrew and ask,
"Are you?"

"I'm sorry," Andrew said, and at first I thought he meant for invading my space. "You just look so familiar to me." He stared, his lips parting as he slowly picked apart my disguise: the cheekbones—sharp now!—the honey highlights there to complement my Stygian hair, not force it into blond submission. "Oh *sweetie*," Ruben, my colorist, clucked when I first came to see him. He pinched a chunk of yellow straw between his fingers and scowled at it like it was a cockroach.

Luke had been unraveling his dinner napkin, but he stopped and stared at Andrew.

It was one of those rare moments where you have the wherewithal to understand that something important, life altering even, is about to happen. I've experienced it twice before, the second time when Luke proposed. "This is going to sound crazy"—I cleared my throat—"but, are you . . . Mr. Larson?"

"Mr. Larson?" Whitney murmured, and she let out a giddy yelp as everything came together for her. "Was he your *teacher*?"

He must have cut off his floppy hair sometime after he left Bradley, but pop off the finance-guy mop like a Lego part, take a Photoshop pen to blur his lines and build out his jaw, and there he was: Mr. Larson. Most people, you could cover their mouths and guess if they're smiling or not based on the shapes of their eyes. Mr. Larson's seemed to have gotten stuck crinkled after an especially boisterous laugh.

"What a small world." Mr. Larson laughed, amazed, his Adam's apple shimmying in his throat. "And you go by Ani now?"

I glanced at Luke. We may as well have been at different dinner tables, part of different conversations. His expression was as sour as Mr. Larson's was delighted. "I just got sick of people asking me how many 'f's in TifAni."

"This is just crazy," Whitney said, glancing among the three of us. She landed on Luke and seemed to realize something. "I guess this means you were at Bradley"—there was an abrupt, panicked pause as her brain completed the loop—"oh, I see, you're *TifAni*."

No one could look at each other. The waitress appeared, oblivious to the relief she offered, and asked if tap water was okay. It always is.

"Isn't it funny how New York has some of the cleanest drinking water in the world," Whitney said, expert hostess, skilled in maneuvering an awkward turn in the conversation. "A filthy city like this?"

We all agreed. Yes, it was funny.

"What subject?" Luke asked, suddenly, and when no one answered he added, "Did you teach?"

Mr. Larson brought an elbow to the table and leaned on it. "Honors English. Did it for two years right after I got out of college. When I couldn't imagine not having the summers off. Remember, Whit?"

They shared a wounding, conspiratorial laugh. "Oh, I remember," she said, shaking her napkin out. "Couldn't wait for you to get that out of your system." Well, I couldn't fault her for that. I would never date a teacher either.

Andrew looked at me. "Ani was my best student though."

I busied myself smoothing my napkin on my lap. "You don't have to say that," I mumbled. We both knew how epically much I'd disappointed him.

"And now she's one of the best writers at *The Women's Magazine*," Luke said, fatherly, proudly. What a crock. Like Luke doesn't think my "career" is just some cute filler phase before we have kids. He reached across the table and put his hand over mine. "She's come a long way." That was his warning shot. Luke doesn't like it when people bring up Bradley. I used to think it was because he was trying to protect me, felt so moved by that. Now I realize, Luke just wants everyone to get over it already. He still doesn't want me participating in the documentary. He can't quite explain why, or he can, but he doesn't want to offend me, but I know what he's thinking: *You're embarrassing yourself.* In the Harrison world, nothing is more admirable than rimy stoicism.

"*Hmmm.*" Whitney tapped her nail, pink as a ballet slipper, on her lower lip. "*The Women's Magazine?* I think I've heard of that one." Husband hunters always say this when they find out where I work. It's not a compliment.

"I didn't know that's where you ended up," Mr. Larson said. "That's fantastic." He gave me the nicest smile.

Whitney noticed. "It's been forever since I've picked it up. But I used to read it like it was my Bible before I met Andrew. Isn't that what they call it? The Women's Bible?" Her laugh was dainty. "I imagine I'll be confiscating it from my daughter's room at some point, the way my mother used to!" Luke laughed politely, but Mr. Larson didn't.

I found the smile I use when children are the topic of conversation and put it on. "How old?"

"Five," Whitney said. "Elspeth. We have a boy too, Booth. He's almost one." She made googly eyes at Andrew. "My little man."

Oh, Jesus. "Great names," I told her.

The sommelier appeared by Luke's side and introduced himself. Did we have any questions about the menu? Luke asked if everyone was okay with white, and Whitney said she couldn't imagine drinking anything else in this heat.

"Let's do this Sauvignon Blanc." Luke pointed to an eighty-dollar spot on the menu.

"Oh, I love Sauvignon Blanc," Whitney said.

Dukan didn't permit wine, but I had to drink to socialize with women like this. That first glass, the endorphins ballooning in my stomach, it was the only way I could realistically feign an interest in her world. Her kid's piano lessons, her Van Cleef push present. I couldn't believe Mr. Larson had succumbed to a woman whose greatest aspiration in life was to do the supermarket glide. When the waiter came by with the bottle, I accepted his pour gratefully.

"To finally meeting your lovely wife." Luke raised his glass. *Lovely*. What a gross word. I used to love these dinners, used to love working for the wives' approval. What an accomplishment it was when it finally blasted across their faces. Now, I was just bored. Bored, bored, bored. Is this what I'm killing myself for? Is this what I really thought would fulfill me? Twenty-seven-dollar roast chicken dinner and a fiancé who sweetly fucks me when we get home.

"And yours." Andrew clinked his glass against mine.

"Well, not yet." I smiled.

"Now, Ani." Whitney was doing that thing I hate, pronouncing my name "Annie" instead of "Ah-nee." "Luke says the wedding is in Nantucket. Why there?"

Because of the privilege inherent in the location, Whitney. Because Nantucket transcends all classes, all areas of the country. Go to South Dakota and tell some sad smug housewife you grew up on the Main Line, and she doesn't know she's supposed to be impressed. Tell her you summer on Nantucket—be sure to verb it like that—and she knows who the fuck she's dealing with. That's why, Whitney.

"Luke's family has a place there," I said.

Luke nodded. "Been going since I was a kid."

"Oh, I'm sure it's going to be gorgeous." Whitney leaned an inch closer to me. She had that hungry breath. Hollow and stale, like nothing had passed through her lips for some time. She asked Andrew, "Didn't we go to a wedding on Nantucket a few years ago?"

"Martha's Vineyard," Andrew corrected. His knee brushed mine again. The wine coated my throat like cough syrup, and I realized how much better he looked older. There were a million things I wanted to ask him, and I was agitated and resentful that Luke and Whitney were here, hijacking this moment from us. "Is your family from Nantucket?" he asked Luke.

Whitney laughed. "No one is *from* Nantucket, Andrew." Nantucket's ten thousand locals would disagree, but what Whitney meant was that people like *us* weren't from Nantucket. It used to thrill me when a woman like this assumed I was cut from her cloth. It meant my mask was that convincing. When did that assumption start to strum the rage? Once I got the ring, the Tribeca zip code, the Waspy white knight on one knee, once I wasn't so distracted by *trying* to get my formerly French-manicured hands on all these things, I was able to take a step back and reassess. There is very little that is noble about me, and even I'm finding it hard to believe that anyone could be satisfied, really satisfied, by this existence. Either every member of the tartan club is just walking around, spiritually bereft, and not talking about it, or this truly is enough for them. I thought the end game must be pretty fucking spectacular if they were willing to protect it like they were. Luke and his entire family, his friends, their wives voted for Mitt Romney in 2012. His pro-personhood bullshit could prevent rape and incest victims, women whose lives were in danger, from having safe abortions. It could shut down Planned Parenthood.

"Oh, that will never happen," Luke had said with a chuckle.

"But even if it doesn't," I said, "how can you vote for someone with a stance like that?"

"Because I don't care, Ani." Luke sighed. My silly feminist wrath had been cute once. "It doesn't affect you, it doesn't affect me. What does affect you and me though? Obama taxing the shit out of us because we're in the highest bracket."

"That other stuff *does* affect me, though."

"You're on birth control!" Luke bellowed. "What do you need an abortion for?"

"Luke, if it weren't for Planned Parenthood I could have a thirteen-year-old right now."

"I'm not doing this," he declared, and lunged at the light switch on the wall. He stalked to the bedroom, slamming the door behind him, leaving me crying alone in the dark kitchen.

I told Luke about *that night* at a time when he was enamored with me, which is the only time you should ever tell anyone something shameful about yourself—when a person is mad enough about you that disgrace is endearing. Each nasty detail made his eyes bigger and yet somehow sleepier, like it was all too much to really take in, he'd process the rest later. If I were to ask Luke right now what happened to me that night, I don't think he could tell me. "Jesus, Ani, I don't know, it was bad, okay? I know something bad happened to you. I get it. You don't have to remind me every fucking day."

He knows it's bad enough that it shouldn't be talked

about, at least. That was a major point of contention when I was first considering the documentary. "But you're not planning on talking about that night, right?" "That night," such comforting synecdoche. I actually had been toying with the idea of speaking into the camera, brazenly recounting what Peyton, Liam, and Dean (God, especially Dean) had done to me, but there was a problem. I didn't have the emerald yet. And I wanted that dazzling green brag on my finger by the time we started shooting. So I twisted my mouth like I'd bitten into a lime after a tequila shot and said, "*Of course* not."

"I grew up in Rye," Luke said.

Whitney rushed to swallow her sip of wine. "I'm from Bronxville!" She dabbed a napkin at her mouth. "What high school did you go to?"

Andrew laughed. "Honey, I don't think you were in high school at the same time as Luke was."

Whitney threw her napkin at Andrew in mock outrage. "You never know."

Luke laughed. "Well, actually I went to boarding school."

"Oh." Whitney deflated. "Never mind." She opened her menu, and, like a yawn, everyone else had to too.

"So what's good here?" Andrew asked. The candlelight twisted in his glasses, so that I couldn't tell if he was asking me or Luke.

"Everything," Luke said at the same time I said, "They do a great roast chicken."

Whitney wrinkled her nose. "I just can't ever bring myself to order chicken at a restaurant. And all that arsenic." Stay-at-home mom who was also a fan of *The Dr. Oz Show*. My favorite kind!

"Arsenic?" I held my hand to my breast, the concern on my face an indication for her to go on. At Nell's recommendation, I'd read Sun Tzu's *The Art of War*. My favorite strategy is to feign inferiority and encourage my enemy's arrogance.

"Yes!" Whitney seemed very alarmed I didn't appear to have heard this before. "Farmers feed it to the chickens." She pursed her lips, disgusted. "It makes them grow faster."

"That's horrible," I gasped. I'd read that same study— the *actual* study, not the scaremongering translation made viral by the *Today* show. This place wasn't serving fucking frozen Perdue chicken breasts. "Well, I will definitely not order the roast chicken then."

"I'm terrible!" Whitney laughed. "We've just met and I've already ruined your dinner." She smacked her forehead with her palm. "I need to stop talking. But when you're around a one-year-old all day, you just chatter chatter the moment you have some adult company."

"I'm sure your kids love having you around." I smiled, like I couldn't wait for the day that would be me. No way she got that body by any fewer than three hours a day in the gym. No way she was going at this alone. But God help you if you asked about the Dominican nanny. They can make snide little digs about *The Women's Magazine* all they want, but rearing children is real work, and you'd better duck if they so much as suspect that you're dismissing *all their real work*.

"I'm so lucky I get to be with them every day." Whitney's lips were glossy with wine. She rubbed them together and put her chin in her hand. "Did your mother work?"

"She didn't." But she should have, Whitney. She should have let go of her little kept-housewife fantasy and contributed to our household. I can't say it would have made her happier, but we didn't have the luxury of considering happiness. We were broke, Mom signing up for new credit cards every other month to finance her Bloomingdale's excursions, while the shoddy Sheetrock walls of our dramatic McMansion went rank with mildew we couldn't "afford" to have removed. But you're right, Whitney, she was so lucky she got to be with me every day.

"Mine either," Whitney said. "It makes such a difference."

I kept smiling. Like in the last push of a race, if you stop and walk now, you'll never find your stride again. "*Huge* difference."

Whitney tossed her hair gleefully. She loved me. Her shoulder brushed mine and her voice was low and flirty as she said, "Ani, you have to tell us. Are you doing that documentary?"

Luke draped one arm over the back of his chair and fiddled with his silverware. I watched the white slivers of light dance on the low ceiling.

"I'm not supposed to say."

"Oh, that means you're doing it." Whitney swatted my arm. "That's what they told Andrew to say too—right, Andrew?"

I have this recurring dream, where something bad has happened and I need to dial 911, but I've lost all control over my fingers. They keep slipping across the buttons (it's always an old-fashioned landline I'm dialing from), and every time I realize, *You're having this dream again, but this time you're going to outsmart it. Just take it slow*, I think. *You can't mess this up if you take it slow. Find the nine. Push. The one. Push.* The agony of needing something so immediately but the ask has got to be patient. I needed to know immediately why Mr. Larson was doing the documentary. When? Where? What would he say? Would he talk about me? Would he *defend* me? "I had no idea you were doing it too," I said. "What do they want from you? Just to weigh in as kind of an observer, or something?"

The arch in Mr. Larson's lip deepened. "Now, Ani, you know I'm not supposed to say."

Everyone laughed, and I had to force myself to join in. I opened my mouth to push some more, but Mr. Larson said, "We should get coffee or something and talk about it."

"Yes!" Whitney chimed in, her excitement so genuine she disabled my own. Any woman who is that keen on her husband getting coffee with another woman, ten years younger to boot, has a rock-solid marriage.

"You should," Luke added, and I wished he hadn't said anything at all. Because his endorsement sounded so glaringly insincere following Whitney's.

❧

Whitney tripped on her way out the door. She caught herself and giggled that she didn't get out much. That wine had gone straight to her head.

Mr. Larson had ordered an Uber after dessert, and a black SUV was waiting for them at the curb, ready to take them back to their sitcom-set home in Scarsdale. Whitney kissed me on the cheek and sung into the air, "So nice to have met you. Really, what a small world." Andrew shook Luke's hand and clapped him on the shoulder. Then Luke stepped away, opening a space for me to slip into and say good-bye. I stood up on my tippy-toes to press my cheek against Andrew's and feign a kiss. He pressed his hands against my back, and when he felt the bare skin there, he pulled away as though I had electrocuted him.

We watched their car nose into traffic, and I ached for

Luke to wrap his arms around me and hold me against his Turnbull & Asser shirt. If he'd done that, he would have felt that I was trembling.

Instead, he just said, "That was weird, huh?" and I smiled my agreement like I hadn't just spun off my center and knew there was no going back now.

CHAPTER 6

The morning after Dean's party I climbed into his Range Rover with Liam and two sophomores from the soccer team. Dean's license was suspended (there was a fat stack of unpaid parking tickets in the glove compartment), but that didn't stop him from whipping around town, tires squealing, DMX warning joggers to leap into the brush if they didn't want to be mowed down on their evening run. Nausea boiled in my stomach when Liam got into the car and blatantly ignored the empty spot right next to me, choosing instead to sit in the front seat next to Dean. I'd tried to talk to him in the kitchen before we left to get breakfast and it hadn't gone well.

"I don't really know how I ended up in Dean's room and I feel like I should say I'm sorry or something because I didn't want to hook up with—"

"Finny"—Liam laughed at me, my nickname just one more thing of Dean's he'd co-opted in his effort to assimilate—"come on. You know I don't care you hooked up with Dean too."

Dean called to him then, and he brushed by me, and I

was glad for the moment alone to collect myself, the tears I forced back finding another channel in my throat, dissolving into a thin salty drip that left me feeling raw and burned in the torturous days that followed. When that finally cleared up, I was left with something much worse. Something that to this day seems to lie in wait, pouncing right at a moment that joy or confidence dares to dance. The memory that I had apologized to my own rapist, and he had laughed at me. *You think you're happy? You think you have anything to be proud of?*—it always taunts—*Ha! Remember this?* That usually sets me right. Reminds me what a piece of shit I am.

When we arrived at Minella's Diner, Liam also made the point of sitting next to Dean, and not me. For forty-five minutes I feebly laughed at everything the boys said and did, yes, those two pancakes that got stuck together sort of do look like balls—swallowing and swallowing to keep from vomiting into my short stack. It felt like hours before we paid, before it was safe for me to call my parents and tell them, perkily, that I'd grabbed breakfast with Olivia and Hilary in Wayne, and could they come pick me up? Then I sat on the curb between Minella's and the Chili's next door, my head cradled between my knees. I could smell something sour in the narrow gap there, and that's when the paranoia really started to set in. Did I have AIDS? Was I going to get pregnant? I was racked with this feeling like I needed water, only I wasn't thirsty, had drank an entire pitcher of water at the diner trying to quench a thirst that wasn't really physical. Years later, I still experience this same sensation. I'll slam water, liters of it, my agitation swelling along with my bladder as relief isn't found at the bottom of the Fiji bottle. I once asked a psychiatrist about it—I always volunteered for our monthly rape-scare story ("A man on the street offered to help me carry my groceries home and then he assaulted me!"), slipping in my own questions and concerns as though they were pertinent to the article, turning it into my own personal therapy session—and she pointed out that thirst is a basic, biological instinct. "If you feel thirsty when you're not actually thirsty, it could indicate that an important need isn't being met."

Forty minutes passed before Mom's car slowed in front of the Minella's sign. I waited for her to circle the parking lot and settle to a stop next to me. When I finally opened the door, heard her Celine Dion CD whining and smelled her putrid Bath & Body Works vanilla lotion, I practically crumbled into the front seat. At least there was something comforting in this, her annoying choices in music and grooming, their safe familiarity.

"Is Olivia's mother here?" Mom asked, and I actually looked at her and realized she was fully made up and ready to socialize.

"No." I slammed the door shut.

Mom stuck out her lower lip. "How long ago did she leave?"

I put my seat belt on. "I don't remember."

"What do you mean you don't—"

"Just drive!" The hot rage in my voice was as much a surprise to myself as it was to Mom. I covered my mouth with my hand, heaving one silent sob into it.

Mom wrenched the gearshift into reverse. "You're grounded, TifAni." She peeled out of the parking lot, her mouth set in that thin, hard line that always terrified me, that I would find myself mirroring in my fights with Luke, realizing I probably looked pretty scary too.

"Grounded?" I laughed sarcastically.

"I'm so *sick* of this *shit* attitude! You are so *ungrateful*. Do you even *know* how much this school is costing me?" She slapped the steering wheel with an open hand on the word "know." I began to gag. Mom's head snapped in my direction. "Have you been *drinking*?" She took a hard right and swerved into an empty parking lot, slamming the brakes so hard the seat belt stabbed me in the stomach and I finally vomited in my hand. "Not in the BMW!" Mom shrieked, leaning across me and pushing my door open and me along with it. I emptied the contents of my stomach right there in the parking lot of Staples. The beer, the whiskey, Dean's salty semen—I couldn't get it out fast enough.

By Monday morning, there was nothing in my stomach but acid, scalding my innards like the surprise whiskey in that late-night round of quarters. I'd been up since 3:00 A.M., when my own heartbeat, pounding like an angry parent's fist on his teenager's locked door, woke me. A small, pathetic part of me hoped that what I'd done would just be dismissed as run-of-the-mill party antics. Mark ate a mayonnaise sandwich and TifAni made the rounds with the soccer team! But even then, I wasn't that naive.

It was subtle—the crowds didn't part and no one pinned a scarlet letter on the lapel of my shirt. Olivia saw me and pretended she didn't, and some older girls flew past in a giggling huddle, laughing loudly once they were a safe enough distance away. Yes, they'd been talking about me.

When I walked into homeroom, the Shark clutched the edge of her desk and swung her round bottom out of the seat. She caught my neck in her arms before I could sit down. Everyone in the classroom pretended not to hear, even managed to carry on their conversations, as she said, "Tif, are you okay?"

"Of course I'm okay!" It felt like there was dried clay on my face when I smiled.

The Shark squeezed my shoulder. "If you need to talk, I'm here."

"Okay." I rolled my eyes at her.

Once I was at my desk, in my seat, dutifully jotting down everything the teacher said in my notebook, I was fine. It was the moment the bell rang, when everyone scattered like bedbugs from the light, that the panic stretched its arms and yawned big, rousing from its fitful sleep. Because then I was roaming the hallways, a wounded soldier on enemy territory, aware of the red light between my eyes, that I was injured and slow, could do nothing but keep moving and pray they'd miss.

Mr. Larson's classroom was like finding the trenches. Arthur had been salty with me lately, but surely given these extenuating circumstances, he would have some compassion for me. He had to.

Arthur nodded at me as I sat down. A solemn nod, an "I'll talk to you about what you've done in a moment" nod. This somehow made me more nervous than lunch, which was next period. I'd been sitting with the HOs regularly for the last few weeks, and I couldn't decide which would be worse—showing my face in the cafeteria and claiming my chair at their table only to have them refuse me, or chickening out and going to the library, sealing my expulsion from their company when there was the off chance that if I could prove I had a pair of balls, they might forgive me. Welcome me back, even.

But if Arthur thought this was bad, then it was far, far worse than I originally thought.

When the bell shrieked, I gathered my things slowly. Arthur paused by my side, but before he could say anything, Mr. Larson did. "Tif? Can you stick around a moment?"

"I'll talk to you later?" I asked Arthur.

He nodded again. "Come over after practice." Arthur's mom was the art teacher at the middle school, and together they lived in a ramshackle old Victorian catty-corner to the squash courts, where the headmistress used to reside in the fifties.

I nodded back, even though I knew I couldn't. I didn't have time to explain that I was grounded.

The English and Humanities wing settled into its late-morning nap as the students stampeded to the cafeteria for lunch. Mr. Larson leaned against the edge of his desk, crossing one leg over the other, the cuff of his khakis hitching up, revealing one tan, fuzzy ankle.

"TifAni," he said. "I don't want to make you upset, but I've been hearing some things this morning."

I waited. I understood, intuitively, not to speak until I knew what he knew.

"I'm on your side here," he promised. "If you've been hurt you need to let someone know. That person doesn't have to be me, by any means. But someone. An adult."

I rubbed my palms on the underside of the desk, feeling the relief blossom like a budding flower, sped up to reveal the petals unfurling, multicolored, on a Discovery Channel commercial. He didn't want to call my parents. He didn't want to involve the administration. He was giving me the best gift a teenager could ever ask for: autonomy.

I chose my words carefully. "Can I think about it?"

I heard the Spanish teacher, Señora Murtez, in the hallway. "Yes, diet! If they don't have Dr Pepper then Pepsi!"

Mr. Larson waited until she slammed her door shut. "Have you seen the nurse today?"

"I don't need to see the nurse," I mumbled, too embarrassed to tell him about my plan. The R5 train barreled by a Planned Parenthood on my way to Bryn Mawr every day. I just had to get there after school and everything would be fine.

"Whatever you tell her will be confidential." Mr. Larson jabbed his finger into his chest. "Whatever you tell *me* will be confidential."

"I don't have anything to tell you." I strained to inject my words with attitude. With all the dark, tortured teenage angst that I actually had now.

Mr. Larson sighed. "TifAni, she can make sure you don't get pregnant. Let her help you."

It was like that time my dad came into my room and said he was doing laundry, reaching for a pile of dirty clothes in the corner. I was lying in bed, reading *Jane*, but when I saw what he was doing I shot upright. "Don't!"

Too late, he was holding a pair of my underwear stained maroon with period blood. He froze like a bank robber holding a bag of bills and stuttered, "I'll, uh, get your mother." I don't know what *she* was supposed to do. Dad never wanted a daughter, never really wanted kids I don't think, but probably could have dealt with a boy. He married Mom five months after they met, a few weeks after she found out she was pregnant. "He was furious," my aunt told me once, her lips purple with Merlot, "but he came from a traditional Italian family and his mother would have had his head if he didn't do the honorable thing."

Apparently, he perked up when the doctor told them they were having a boy. Anthony, they wanted to name me. I don't like to imagine the look on Dad's face when I was actually born, when the doctor chuckled. "Whoops!"

"I'm taking care of it, don't worry," I told Mr. Larson. I pushed back my chair and slung my book bag over my shoulder.

Mr. Larson couldn't even look at me. "TifAni, you are one of my most talented students. You have a very promising future. I would never want to see that compromised."

"Can I go now?" I put my weight on one hip, and Mr. Larson nodded sadly.

❧

The HOs and the Hairy Legs were piled up at their usual table, which had never been big enough for them. A few outliers always ended up at the adjoining table, their chairs angled at a sharp diagonal so that they could catch every word of the conversation they weren't really a part of.

"Finny!" To my immense relief, Dean held his hand up for a high five. "Where have you been?" Those four words—"where have you been?"—chased all but one fear out. Liam was sitting far too close to Olivia, the lunchtime sun brilliant on her slick nose, spotlighting the fray in her beer brown curls. She was someone who, years later, I could have seen as beautiful. A little oil control powder, regular keratin treatments, her whippet limbs made for loose, drapey, bra-adverse pieces by Helmut Lang. I would have hated myself next to her, come to think of it.

"Hey, guys." I stood at the head of the table, clutching the straps of my book bag like it was a life jacket attached to my back, like I'd float away without it.

Olivia ignored me, but Hilary lifted one lazy corner of her mouth, lashless eyes regarding me with an amused glaze. I expected this when I agreed to Dean's terms. It may seem like it wasn't the smartest move to betray the HOs, but Dean was a powerful force. Get in with him and the rest of the guys, and it didn't matter if Olivia and Hilary secretly hated me. They would hide it, and that was all that mattered.

Dean shifted left in his seat, patting the open sliver next to him. I sat down, my thigh pressing against his thigh. I swallowed a scorching mouthful of acid, wishing it was Liam's leg next to mine.

Dean leaned in, his French fry breath in my ear. "So how you feeling, Finny?"

"Fine." A film of sweat was collecting between our legs. I didn't want Liam to see this, I didn't want Liam to think that out of the three, I'd chosen Dean.

"What are you doing after practice?" Dean asked.

"Going right home," I said. "I'm grounded."

"Grounded?" Dean practically shouted. "What are you, like, twelve?"

I flushed when everyone laughed. "I know. I hate my parents."

"It doesn't have anything to do with. . . ." Dean trailed off.

"Bad grades."

"Phew." Dean wiped his brow. "Because I mean, I like you, but if my parents find out about that party, well, I don't like you *that* much." He laughed aggressively.

The bell rang and everyone stood, leaving their greasy paper plates and candy wrappers on the table for the janitor to collect. Olivia made a beeline for the quad, which she would cut across to get to Algebra II before anyone else. She was a good student, a nervous student—breaking down in tears over a B+ on a pop quiz in Chem that pretty much everyone else failed. She didn't notice when I hurried after Liam.

"Hey." My head lined up perfectly with Liam's shoulder. Dean was too tall, too big, a circus gorilla who would rip you limb from limb if you didn't hug him back.

Liam looked at me and laughed.

"What?" I laughed back, uneasily.

He wrapped his arm around my shoulder, and, for just a brief moment, I entertained the relief. Maybe he hadn't been acting aloof, maybe it really was all in my head.

"You're crazy, girl."

The cafeteria had emptied out. I paused in front of the door, anchoring Liam to me. "Can I ask you something?"

Liam tilted his head back and groaned. The way he said "Whaaaat?" was how I imagined he spoke to his mother, when he sensed the thing she had to ask him about was when he would ever get around to cleaning his filthy room.

I dropped my voice to a conspiratorial whisper. We were in this together. "Did you use a condom?"

"That's what you're worried about?" His bright eyes rolled in a complete circle, like a ventriloquist had given him a stern shake. For a moment, his eyelids hooding the blue, he wasn't nearly as attractive as I'd thought he was. There was something about his eyes, you could have named a Crayola crayon after them, that made him extraordinary.

"Should I be?"

Liam put his hands on my shoulders and brought his face close to mine, our foreheads almost grazing. "Tif, you only have a twenty-three percent chance of getting pregnant."

Oh, how this random number has stuck with me

through the years. The stodgy old head of the fact-checking department at *The Women's Magazine* won't even accept stats lifted from an article in *The New York Times*. "YOU MUST PROVIDE ORIGINAL SOURCE," her all-staff e-mails remind us, at least once a month. Yet I was willing to accept this number, espoused by the person who I later learned found me on the floor of the guest bedroom, the square of my body from my belly button to my upper thighs naked (Peyton made a halfhearted attempt to pull my pants up for me). He dragged me into bed, wrestled my pants off my dead weight legs, and plunged inside of me without even bothering to take the rest of my clothes off. He said I woke up and moaned when he did that, and that's how he knew I was okay with it. I lost my virginity to someone who's never seen my breasts.

"Well." I shuffled my feet. "I was thinking maybe I should go to Planned Parenthood. Get the morning-after pill."

"But"—Liam grinned at me, his sweet little idiot—"it's not the morning after."

"It works for up to seventy-two hours." This is how I'd spent the rest of my weekend, researching the morning-after pill on the family computer in the basement, then researching how to hide my search history.

Liam read the clock on the wall above my head. "We had sex around midnight." He closed his eyes, his lips moving as he did the math. "So you can still make it."

"Right. I was going to get it after school. There's a Planned Parenthood in St. Davids." I held my breath as I waited for his reaction. To my great surprise he said, "I'll figure out a way to get us there."

Liam secured us a ride with Dave, Bradley's very own personal chauffeur, even though we could have easily taken the train, could have avoided one more person knowing about the humiliating turn my life had taken in the last sixty-four hours. Sixty-four hours—I still had eight hours left.

The trees were just starting to shed, and through their spare limbs I caught a glimpse of Arthur's house as the car hiccuped over speed bumps, before making a right onto Montgomery Ave. I wasn't so desperate for him now, not with Liam glancing back at me from the front seat, asking not once but twice how I was doing. Some very small, frenzied part of me wished that we were too late, that my period wouldn't come next month, that the drama, the "What should we do?" that connected us now could last a little bit longer. I understood that, when it was gone, Liam would be too.

We maneuvered onto Lancaster Ave, and from there it was a straight shot. Dave made a right into the parking lot, but, instead of finding a spot, he just pulled up to the entrance of the clinic and unlocked the doors.

"I'm going to drive around for a bit," Dave said as I climbed out of the backseat.

"No, man," Liam said, nervously, stepping onto the pavement and next to me. "Just wait."

"No way." Dave pulled the gear stick into drive. "Crazy people always want to bomb this place."

Liam slammed the car door shut much harder than he meant to, I'm sure.

The waiting room was mostly empty, save for a few sets of women scattered among the chairs along the walls. Liam found a seat furthest away from the nearest occupant, wiping his palms on his khakis and glancing around, accusingly.

I approached the receptionist and spoke through the opening in the glass divider. "Hi. I don't have an appointment or anything, but is there someone here I could see?"

The woman pushed a clipboard through the opening. "Fill this out. Indicate the reason for your visit."

I plucked a pen from an old 76ers McDonald's cup and settled into the seat next to Liam, who peered over my shoulder at the form.

"What did she say?"

"I'm just supposed to write down the reason I'm here."

I started to fill in the boxes. Name, age, DOB, sex, address, and signature. In the space next to the words "Reason for your visit today," I scrawled, "Morning-after pill."

When I got to the part that asked me for my emergency contact, I looked at Liam.

He shrugged. "Sure." He removed the clipboard from my lap and settled it in his. Next to "Relationship to the patient," he wrote, "Friend."

I got up and passed the clipboard back to the woman at the front desk, now blurry behind the filmy pane of tears. The word "friend" was lodged in my stomach like a knife, like the paper-thin Shun I'd envision splicing my fiancé's kidneys one day.

Fifteen minutes passed before the white door opened and I heard my name. Liam crossed his eyes at me and gave me a thumbs-up, a goofy expression, like he was distracting a small child from the tetanus shot she was about to get. I managed a brave smile for him.

I followed the nurse into an examining room and scooted onto the table. Another ten minutes passed before the door opened and a woman entered, blond hair fine and cropped close to her neck, a stethoscope draped leisurely around her neck. She frowned at me. "TifAni?"

I nodded and the doctor placed my file on the counter and paused over it, her eyes walking back and forth across my information.

"When did you have sex?"

"Friday."

She looked at me. "Friday when?"

"Some time around midnight." Apparently.

She nodded, lifting the stethoscope off her shoulders and pressing it to my chest. While she examined me, she explained what the morning-after pill was. "Not an abortion," she reminded me, twice. "If the sperm has already implanted the egg, it won't do anything."

"Do you think it has?" I asked, my heart pumping harder for her to hear.

"There is no way for me to know that," she apologized. "We do know that it's most effective when taken as close to the intimate encounter as possible." She glanced at the clock above my head. "You are on the cusp of the cutoff, but you did make it." She slipped the stethoscope underneath my shirt and pressed it into my back. With a soothing sigh, she said, "Deep breath." In another life, she could have been a hipster yoga instructor in Brooklyn.

She finished examining me, told me to hang tight. There had been a question burning in my throat for the last ten minutes, but it was her reaching for the handle of the door that forced me to say it.

"Is it rape if you can't remember what happened?"

The doctor opened her mouth, as though she was about to gasp "Oh no." Instead she said, so quietly I almost

didn't hear it, "I'm not qualified to answer that question."
She slipped out of the room soundlessly.

Several more minutes ticked by before the nurse, her
peppiness especially noticeable in the wake of her cool,
serene superior, returned, a brown paper lunch bag full of
brightly colored condoms bunched underneath her arm,
a prescription bottle in one hand and a glass of water in
the other.

"Take six right now." She shook six pills into my clammy
palm and watched me chase them down with water. "And
six twelve hours from now." She looked at her watch. "So
set your alarm for four A.M." She shook the paper bag at
me, teasingly. "And being careful can be fun! Some of
these even glow in the dark." I took the bag from her, all
that careful fun rattling around inside, mocking me with
its fluorescent futility.

Liam wasn't in the waiting room when I returned, and
the paper bag went damp and flimsy in my hand as it occurred to me that he might have taken off.

"I was here with someone," I said to the woman at the
front desk. "Did you see where he went?"

"I think he stepped outside," she replied. I caught a
glimpse of the doctor behind her, the blond hairs gnarled
around her neck like a claw.

Liam was outside, sitting on the curb.

"What are you doing?" It came out shrill. I heard Mom
in it.

"I couldn't be in there any longer. I felt like they thought
I was gay or something." He stood and brushed dirt off his
butt. "You get what you need?"

I would have welcomed some crazy's bomb going off
in that moment. One last tragedy that would anchor Liam
to me. I pictured him rushing me, covering my body with

his as fiery shards of building sphered through the air. No screams at first, everyone too stunned, too singularly focused on just surviving. That would be the most surprising lesson I'd learn at Bradley: You only scream when you're finally safe.

CHAPTER 7

feel like I'm in the south of France!" Mom lifted her champagne flute.

I almost didn't, but I couldn't help myself. "It's Prosecco," I sneered.

"So?" Mom set her glass on the table. A lipstick mark, so pink it was embarrassing, printed the rim.

"Prosecco is Italian."

"Tastes like champagne to me!"

Luke laughed, and his parents joined in gratefully. He was always doing that, saving Mom and me from ourselves.

"And with this view you certainly can't tell the difference between France and the States," added Kimberly, our wedding planner, who corrected Mom every time she called her Kim, which was every time. She swept her hand out in a grand gesture, and we all turned to look at the Harrisons' backyard as though we hadn't seen it a million times before, the lime green grass that ended sharply at the ocean's horizon, so that after a few Dark and Stormys, it appeared as though you could waltz straight out onto the water even though it was a thirty-foot drop to the sand.

There was a splintered staircase embedded in the side of the earth, twenty-three steps to the bitter tongue of the Atlantic. I refused to wade in any deeper than my knee-caps, convinced it was churning with great whites. Luke thought this was hilarious and loved to swim deep, his perfect stroke taking him further and further out in the frosty water. Eventually, he'd turn, his head bobbing like a blond apple, raising one freckly arm in the air and beckoning to me. "Ani! Ani!" Even though terror was ripping my insides apart, I'd be a good sport and wave—he would only go out further and stay out longer if I revealed one iota of fear. If a shark got him, held him under until blood formed a film on the surface of the water like a magenta oil spill, I would be too afraid to go in after him. Afraid for my own life, sure, but just as much afraid of the carnage of his body, the leg missing beneath the knee, a jagged edge of bloody muscles and veins, the sweet, musky odor the body emits when it's been opened like that. I smell it still, even though fourteen years have gone by. It's like a few molecules have been trapped in my nasal passages, the neurons reminding my brain any time I almost forget.

Of course, it would be even worse if Luke survived, be-cause I'd be a real bitch if I abandoned my legless fiancé. I couldn't imagine anything worse than spending every day of my life with a physical reminder of the terrible things life can do, of the ever-present reality that no one is safe. Luke, beautiful Luke, with his friends and family who were so good at being normal, the way a restaurant quieted a little as we walked to our table, his hand on the small of my back . . . it had dulled the dread in the beginning. Luke was so perfect, he made me fearless. Because how could anything bad happen around a person like that?

Right after we got engaged—Luke on his knee when we

crossed the line of the New York City Marathon, running to raise money for leukemia, which his father had beaten ten years ago—we took a trip to DC to visit his pocket of Hamilton friends stationed there. Most of them I had met at various weddings over the years. But there was one I hadn't, Chris Bailey. Bailey they called him—a wiry guy, snaggletoothed, limp hair parted down the middle. He didn't look like the other Aryan gods in Luke's posse. I met him at the bar we went to after dinner—he hadn't been invited to dinner.

"Bailey, get me a drink," Luke said, a little bossy, but playful too.

"Whadya want?" Bailey asked.

"The fuck does this look like?" Luke pointed to his Bud Light, the label wrinkly with perspiration.

"Whoa." I laughed. A real laugh, at first. It was all in good fun. "Easy." I put my hand—the one weighed down by the emerald—on Luke's shoulder. He strapped his arms around my waist and pulled me into him. "I love you so fucking much," he said into my hair.

"Here you go, man." Bailey handed Luke a beer. Luke stared at it, threateningly.

"What's wrong?" I asked.

"Where's my fiancée's drink?" Luke demanded.

"Sorry, man!" Bailey smiled, his snaggletooth catching on his lower lip. "I didn't know she wanted anything." To me, "Whadya want, my dear?"

I did need a drink, but not from Bailey, not like this. Luke always messed around with his buddies—really, these guys were tan ex-athletes, healthy and jokey, the very definition of a buddy. But there was an inequality in this exchange with Bailey that I'd never seen before. Bailey had the look of a kid brother, desperate to fit in, desperate to please, willing to take whatever abuse necessary. It was something I recognized all too well.

"Bailey, please excuse my asshole fiancé." I looked at Luke, a cutesy, pleading look. *Come on, tone it down.*

But on it went for the rest of the night—Luke barking orders at Bailey, cutting him down for carrying them out wrong, my horror swelling the drunker and meaner Luke got. I was picturing Luke in college, tormenting this hanger-on, maybe even taking advantage of a girl passed out on the lumpy fraternity couch. Luke knew it was rape if she wasn't coherent enough to say yes, right? Or did he think it counted only if the boogeyman jumped out of the bushes and ravaged some sober, unassuming freshman on her way to the library? Oh my God. Who was I marrying?

Luke demanded Bailey drive us home, even though Bailey was drunk, even though we were in a bustling area of DC with plenty of cabs. Bailey was happy to do it, but I refused to get in the car. Caused quite the to-do on the street screaming at Luke to go fuck himself.

Later, back at the hotel room, tears in his eyes, all traces of the snarling bully he'd been for the last few hours gone, Luke said, "Do you know how much it kills me when you tell me to fuck off? I would never speak that way to you."

I raged, "When you treat someone the way you treated Bailey, it's your own way of telling me to go fuck *my*self!" Luke gave me the look he always gives me when he thinks I'm being ridiculous. Like I need to get over high school already.

Even though that incident seemed out of character for Luke, even though he woke up the next morning and "felt sick" over how he'd behaved the night before, it was that weekend that I stopped seeing Luke as so perfect and pure. Stopped thinking nothing bad could happen to me while I was with him. Now I was scared all the time again.

I popped a lobster-mac-and-cheese bite into my mouth; it was my third. I'd finally settled on a caterer, the one Mom suggested after reading that she was a Kennedy favorite. Sometimes even she knew the right buttons to push.

I almost waited until just a few days before the tasting to invite my parents. This way it would have been too late and too expensive to make arrangements to get up to Nantucket. There are three ways to get here—a direct JetBlue flight from JFK, which is almost never less than five hundred dollars; a JetBlue flight to Boston followed by a forty-five-minute flight in a plane similar in size to the one JFK Jr. crashed into the Atlantic; or a six-hour drive to Hyannis Port (eight for my parents in PA), where you could take an hour-long ferry ride or a small plane to your final destination. But I knew if I waited, Mom would find a way to come, and the thought of her driving her rickety old BMW all the way to Hyannis by herself, having to figure out which ferry to get on and where to park and hauling her fake Louis Vuitton bags on board, was so sad I couldn't stand it.

Dad had no interest in coming, which was no great surprise. He hadn't had an interest in my life, in any life, his own included, ever since I could remember. For a time I wondered if he was cheating on Mom, if he could be the type who had a secret family on the side, his *real* family, whom he actually loved. One time, when I was in high school, he told Mom he was going to get the car washed. About half an hour after he left I called out to Mom that I was making a run to CVS. Halfway there, I realized I'd forgotten my wallet. I had to turn around in an empty lot, circling the crudely flattened land, the thick forest pulverized to make room for a brand-new housing development, and I discovered Dad, sitting behind the wheel of his car, just staring at the sticky mud. I backed out quick, before he could notice me, and gunned it back home, my heart racing with what I'd just seen, my mind trying to make sense of it. Eventually I realized, there was nothing to make sense of. Dad was ambivalent, simple as that. There was no second family he loved more than us. He might not have loved *anyone*.

Luke generously offered to pay for Mom's JetBlue ticket—it was no trouble, really, especially since it was just her—and Mom drove into the city on Friday, using our guest pass to park her car in our garage.

"Will it really be safe here?" She fretted with her keys and pressed lock, the car chirping in response.

"Yes, Mom," I groaned. "This is where we keep our car."

Mom ran her tongue over her glossy lips, unconvinced.

I give the Harrisons credit for the patience they have with my mother, for her idiotic attempts to impress them. *I'm not that great*, I want to tell them. *Why do you put up with her?*

"Thank you for the tip," Mr. Harrison had said just that morning, when Mom told him that he should really keep an eye on his portfolio because interest rates are going up. Mr. Harrison was the president of Bear Stearns for nine years before he retired; how that man didn't tell Mom which way was up I have no idea.

"Anytime." Mom beamed, and I widened my eyes at Luke, standing behind her. He made the universal relax gesture, pressing his palms down, as though he was trying to shut the full trunk of a car.

We settled on the lobster-mac-and-cheese bites, the mini lobster rolls, the wasabi steak tips, the tuna tartare spoons, the Gruyère bruschetta ("The 'ch' in bruschetta is actually pronounced like a 'k,'" Mom said knowledgeably, even though I was the one who taught her that after I studied abroad in Rome my junior year), the oyster bar, the sushi bar, and the antipasto bar. "That's for my husband's side of the family!" Mom joked. Italians who don't even know how to pronounce "bruschetta." We are the worst kind.

We would do the tasting for the main course and the cake on Sunday. "It's simply too much food to take in all at once," Kimberly declared breathlessly, her thighs spilling over the sides of one of the Harrisons' lawn chairs. Oh, she could have taken it, all right.

"Can you believe they're getting married?" Mom gushed to Mrs. Harrison, clasping her hands together, girlishly. I hated when Mom pulled this cutesy shit with my future mother-in-law, who is a simple, serious tomboy, not prone to syrupy displays of affection. The problem is that Mrs. Harrison is too polite not to reciprocate. When Mom gets sentimental with her, it's excruciating having to watch Mrs. Harrison struggle to keep up, which only intensifies my fury toward Mom.

"It *is* exciting!" Mrs. Harrison tried.

It was 3:00 P.M. when Kimberly left, when Luke stretched his arms up to the ceiling and suggested we go for a run.

Everyone else was "having a lie-down" at Mr. Harrison's suggestion. It was all I wanted to do. When I was off the Dukan diet, I was off. No exercise. Wine until I dragged myself to a sleepless night in bed. As much food as I could fit into my shrinking stomach until it was time to starve again.

Mom and the Harrisons retired to their rooms to have their lie-downs while I begrudgingly laced up my sneakers next to Luke. "Just three miles," he said. "Enough to feel like we've done something."

Luke and I made a left out of the driveway. I was already breathing hard as we broke over the small incline on his street, the ragged dirt road opening up in front of us, sun beating relentlessly on the thin slit of exposed skin splitting the middle of my scalp. I'd meant to grab a hat.

"You happy?" he asked.

"I'm annoyed they didn't have a better crab cake," I gasped.

Luke shrugged without breaking his gait. "I thought it was pretty good."

We kept on. Before I started working out twice a day—barre class in the morning and four-mile run at night—I felt strong as I ran and ran and ran. Now it was like the muscles failed me, my legs heavy when my legs were the one thing that had never been heavy. I knew I was over-exercising, grinding myself into exhaustion, but the scale was moving, and that was all that mattered.

"You okay, babe?" Luke asked about half a mile in. He had set the pace, hadn't slowed when I tried to, when the stitch braided the muscles in my lower left side. I rebelled by falling behind him, wondering how big the distance between us would have to get before he realized something was wrong.

I stopped and stretched my arm over my head. "Cramp."

Luke jogged in place in front of me. "It gets worse when you stop."

"I ran cross-country. I know that," I snapped.

Luke's hands were balled at his sides—which is the

wrong way to run, it wastes energy. "I'm just saying." He grinned and smacked my butt. "Come on, you're a survivor."

This is Luke's favorite thing to say about me, to remind me. I'm a survivor. It's the finality of the word that bothers me, its assuming implication. Survivors should move on. Should wear white wedding dresses and carry peonies down the aisle and overcome, rather than dwell in a past that can't be altered. The word dismisses something I cannot, will not, dismiss.

"You go." I flung my arm accusingly at the road. "I'm heading back."

"Babe," Luke said, disappointed.

"Luke, I don't feel good!" I made my hands fists now, held them over my eyes. "I haven't been eating! And now I just shoved eight fucking pounds of lobster-cheese into my system."

"You know what?" Luke stopped running in place, shook his head at me like a disappointed parent, and laughed bitterly. "I don't deserve to be treated like this." He took a few steps away from me. "I'll see you back at the house."

I watched him sprint off, plumes of dust billowing at his heels, lobster cheese curdling in my intestines as his stride propelled him farther away from me. I'd never been on Luke's bad side before, ostensibly because I'd never dared to do anything but charm him. It must sound stupid, but it was the first time I realized that for the rest of my life, till death do we part, it was on *me* to maintain this veneer's sparkly, streak-free shine. If Luke noticed so much as a pinkie's smudge, he would punish me for it. The spin came on so fast, a vibrant swirl of white-hot sun, I actually sat down in the dirt.

❧

After dinner, Luke's cousin Hallsy came over for a nip of bourbon. *"Hallsy?"* I'd echoed, incredulously, the first time Luke mentioned her to me. He'd looked at me like I was the one who needed to get a grip.

Hallsy's parents have a house down the same dirt road Luke and I had just run, and Mrs. Harrison's parents both have houses on the other side of the island, in Sconset. You can't ride your sweet little Sunday bike into town without running into a pearled member of Luke's bloodline.

Hallsy had brought with her a Tupperware container of pot brownies she'd gotten from the busboys, twenty years her junior and still not off limits, at Sankaty Head Golf Club, where all the Harrisons were members. It's weird, how some people like Mrs. Harrison can grow up with all the money in the world and it's just so normal to be rich that she doesn't even realize she has something to flaunt. Then others, like Mrs. Harrison's very own niece, are so insecure that they have to wear it in contempt on their faces, in the tacky diamond watches on their wrists. Hallsy is only thirty-nine, and already her face is pulled tight as a pair of Lululemon yoga pants across a plus-size girl's rear. She's never been married, which she'll tell you she never wants to be even though she hangs all over every remotely fuckable guy after a single drink, while they gently untangle her Marshmallow Man arms from around their stiff necks. It's no wonder the only ring on her finger is the Cartier Trinity, what with the way she's ruined her face and the fact that she spends more time sunning on the beach than she should running on a treadmill. But it's not just her sunspot-speckled chest and stocky, lazy frame. Hallsy is the type of person others describe as "whacky" and "kooky," which is just the civilized way of saying she's a nasty cunt.

Hallsy she loves me.

Women like Hallsy are my specialty. You should have seen the expression on her sci-fi-looking face the first time I met her, when I had the audacity to say that while not everyone in the room may support Obama's politics, I think we can all agree that he is a supremely intelligent man. The conversation between Mr. Harrison and Luke and Garret waged on without anyone really paying my comment much attention, but I happened to look over at Hallsy to find her glaring at me, waiting for me to notice. "*This family* doesn't care for Obama very much," she said through her teeth. There was a moment between us where Hallsy saw more of me than I will ever show Luke, but I recovered quickly and gave her a nod, like I was grateful. I kept my mouth shut for the rest of the conversation, only swiveling my head from Luke to Garret to my future father-in-law and back again to show how enraptured I was with all the fine points the Harrison men were making. Later, when we went into town for drinks, Hallsy chose to sit next to me in the cab, and at the bar she asked me where I got my hair cut because she was looking for a new stylist. I told her to ask for Ruben at Sally Hershberger, and the corners of Hallsy's plumped-up lips fought their way upward, against the tide of the Botox. You might think someone like Hallsy would only be inclined to torture someone like me, but if she did that, it would be an admission of her own aesthetic short-comings. As long as I deferred to her, it was in her best in-terest to embrace me. It sent the message that there was no need to be jealous or intimidated—she was every bit as desirable as an overaerobicized twenty-something.

Hallsy has a brother named Rand, who is two years

younger than Luke and five years younger than Garret, and her parents call him the Boy and say things like "It's a miracle the Boy graduated from college at all," even though it's the furthest thing from a miracle because there is a new dormitory at Gettysburg bearing the Harrison name. Rand was currently following a big-wave tour with his surfer friends in Tahiti. Nell hooked up with him once but couldn't go any further than making out because she said he kissed like a drunk five-year-old. "He has the fattest tongue," she said, flattening hers and wiggling it around to show just how disgusting it is. I silently savor this piece of knowledge any time Hallsy lodges a crocodile complaint regarding the twenty-one-year-old model/actress Rand is dating whenever he lands in New York for a few months. She couldn't be prouder to have a perfectly weathered playboy brother. It raises her stock.

I was sitting at the table on the back porch when Hallsy walked in. Hallsy picked my hair up off the back of the chair and threaded her fingers through it, saying, "It's the beautiful bride!" I tilted my head up, and she kissed me on the cheek with her lips pumped full of poison. I never let Mom kiss me, and it would have bothered her to see how affectionate I am with Hallsy, even Nell. Fortunately, Luke and I had driven her to the airport not long after he came back from the run I so callously aborted. Mom would have loved to stay—she'd met Hallsy once and the next time I saw her she was wearing a fake diamond horseshoe necklace, a mall stand replica of Hallsy's—but Luke and I had been the ones to buy her ticket and it cost three hundred dollars more for her to fly back on Sunday. Controlling the purse strings is an empowering feeling right up until I remember it wouldn't be possible without Luke.

Mr. Harrison came outside with a bottle of Basil

Hayden's and put it on the table next to the bourbon glasses and the brownies. The first time Hallsy brought over the help's brownies no one told me they were fudgy with pot, and I ate three and had to be put to bed with the spins, one of the loops finally landing me into a sticky spell of sleep that I fought and fought until I woke up at 2:00 A.M. shrieking about a spider dangling right over my head (there was no spider). The whole dream frightened me so much it triggered a charley horse that tore apart my calf. I was howling and gripping my leg, and Luke just stared at me like he'd never seen such a scene in his life. In the morning Mr. Harrison grumbled into his coffee, "What was all that commotion about last night?" It's the only time he's ever been annoyed with me, and I haven't touched a Hallsy brownie since.

So tonight, I caught the corner of Luke's eye when I stuck my hand in the Tupperware container. "I'm just having one," I said under my breath.

Luke sighed in a way that made his nostrils look like sideways triangles. "Do whatever."

Luke hates drugs. He tried pot once in college and said it made him feel dumb. He did go on this weird ecstasy bender with an ex-girlfriend his junior year, where they popped a pill every night for four nights in a row, but that's where Luke Harrison's fast life ended. Garret had arrived at the house that afternoon, and he was already on his second brownie. (I did coke with him in the bathroom at the Harrison Christmas party the year before. We both swore ourselves to secrecy from Luke.) Mr. Harrison and Hallsy were nibbling, but Mrs. Harrison kept right with her vodka. I get the feeling Mrs. Harrison has the same attitude about drugs as Luke does—she's fine with others doing them in moderation, they're just not for her.

"Did you finally get the honeymoon itinerary all squared away?" Hallsy asked.

"Finally," Luke groaned, giving me a jokey, reproachful look. Is it really so much to fucking ask that he plan one thing for the wedding?

"Thank you for putting me in touch with your friend," I said to Hallsy.

"Oh, so you *are* going to go through Paris now?" Hallsy swallowed the last bite of brownie and burped loudly. Hallsy loves to joke about having no manners, thinks it makes her seem reckless and carefree, like one of the guys. A lot of good that strategy has done for her.

"On the way back," Luke said, "we fly into Abu Dhabi, spend one night, fly to the Maldives for seven days, then back to Abu Dhabi and then Paris for three more days. It's not really 'on the way,' but Ani really wants to go to Paris."

"Of course she wants to go to Paris!" Hallsy rolled her eyes at Luke. "It's her honeymoon."

"Dubai just seems like Las Vegas to me," I said, trying not to sound defensive. "I need some culture."

"Paris will be the perfect foil to the beach vacation." Hallsy sank back in her chair and rested her head in her hand. "I'm just so glad you didn't decide on *London*." She timed the roll of her eyes to the word "London." "Especially since you might end up living there, which"—she snorted crudely—"good luck with that."

I started to say how no decision had been made yet, but Luke cocked his head at his cousin, confused. "Hallsy, you lived in London after college."

"And it was the worst!" she wailed. "Sand niggers fucking everywhere. I thought I was going to be kidnapped and sold into white slavery." She jabbed a finger at her hair, the color of six-hundred-dollar highlights.

A laugh gurgled low in Garret's throat, and Mrs. Harrison pushed her chair away from the table. "Oh dear. I'm getting another vodka."

"You know I'm right, Aunt Betsy!" Hallsy shouted after her. The brownies were making my brain feel like warm wet soil, ripe for a seed to plant. It clung to that sentence "You know I'm right, Aunt Betsy!" and regenerated it over and over.

"Your mom agrees with me, she'll just never say it," Hallsy said haughtily to Luke, who chuckled at her. "Speaking of things she'll never say." She swiveled in her chair so she was facing me. There was one lone brownie crumb stuck to her lip, trembling like a hairy mole. "Ani, you have to promise me something."

I pretended my mouth was full of brownie so I didn't have to answer her. This refusal was some pathetic attempt to show that her language offended me. Hallsy didn't pick up on it.

"Don't seat me with the Yateses at your wedding. For the love of *God*."

"What did you do this time?" Mr. Harrison quipped. The Yateses were family friends of the Harrisons, though much closer with Hallsy's parents as they had a son around her age. A son I'd heard she'd harassed, drunkenly and sloppily, on many occasions.

Hallsy held her hand over her heart and pouted in a way she thinks makes her look cute. "Why would you assume it was something *I* did?"

Mr. Harrison gave her a look, and Hallsy laughed. "Okay. I sort of did something." Luke and Garret groaned, and Hallsy rushed to say, "But my heart was in the right place!"

"What was it?" I said, much more rudely than I'd meant to.

Hallsy turned to me, something like a challenge smol- dering in her eyes. "You know their son, James?"

I nodded. I'd met him once. Some drinks thing. I asked him what he did, and the prick told me it was a rude ques- tion. I didn't even care what he did, I just wanted him to be polite and return the question so I could brag about what *I* did.

Hallsy tucked her chin into her neck and muddled her voice. "I mean, I'd always sort of suspected"—she limped her wrist and looked around the table, making sure every- one caught her drift—"and someone recently told me it was true. He'd come out." She shrugged. "So I sent Mrs. Yates flowers and my condolences." She continued out of the corner of her mouth. "Course, then it turned out that he wasn't actually gay."

Luke barked a laugh, dragging his hands over his face. He separated his fingers so that all you could see were his eyes. "Who else would this happen to?" he moaned, in- citing laughter from everyone but me. The brownie had distracted me, made me alert to the wondrous and spooky, and I was mesmerized by what they call the Gray Lady, the thick blanket of dusty fog that rolls in when the sun sets on Nantucket. At that moment, the Gray Lady was everywhere.

Hallsy swatted Luke's shoulder. "Anyway, now she's not speaking to me or my mom and it's this whole thing. It's like, I was just trying to be supportive!"

Luke was laughing. Everyone was laughing. I thought I was, too, but my face felt numb in the fog. Maybe it wasn't even a fog, maybe it was a poisonous gas and we were under attack, and I was the only one who realized it. I found my legs and stood, picking up my glass of wine as though I was going into the kitchen for a refill, which is what I should have done. Should never have said what I said next, which was "Don't worry, Hallsy." The laughter died down and everyone turned to look at me, standing, obviously about to say something of importance. "We'll stick you at the flabby singleton table with the rest of your kind." I didn't ease the back door into its hinges, like I usually do. Just let it clap shut, sudden and mean as a Venus flytrap.

❧

Luke waited a few hours before he came and found me in bed. I was reading a John Grisham paperback. There were John Grisham paperbacks all over the Harrison house.

"Um, hi?" Luke hovered over the bed, a golden ghost.

"Hi." I'd been reading the same page over and over for the last twenty minutes. The fog had cleared, and now I wondered how bad it was. What I'd done.

"What was that about?" Luke asked.

I shrugged. Kept pretending to read. "She said 'sand nigger.' She told one of the most ignorant stories I've ever heard. That didn't bother you?"

Luke snatched the book out of my hands, and the rusty springs in the bed crunched as he sat. "Hallsy is batshit crazy, so no, I don't really let anything she says bother me. You shouldn't either."

"I guess you're just a cooler customer than I am then." I glared at him. "Because that bothered me."

Luke groaned. "Ani, come on. Hallsy made a mistake. It's like"—he stopped and thought for a moment—"it's like if you heard someone had cancer and you sent that person flowers and it turned out not to be true. Like she said, her heart was in the right place."

I stared at Luke, slack-jawed. "The issue isn't that she got her information wrong. The issue is that she thinks being gay is such a horrible 'diagnosis'"—I bunny-eared the word, calling out Luke's offensive analogy—"that it warrants flowers and her *condolences!*"

Luke folded his arms across his chest. "You know. This is what I'm talking about. When I say I'm getting really fucking sick of this."

I scooted up on my elbows, the sheets rising, a white cotton drawbridge unlatching with the bend in my knees. "Getting really fucking sick of what?"

Luke gestured at me. "Of this. This . . . this . . . *poutiness.*"

"I'm fucking pouty for taking offense at blatant racism and homophobia?"

Luke brought his hands to his head, like he was protecting his ears from a loud noise. He shut his eyes, opened them. "I'm sleeping in the guesthouse." He tore a pillow from the bed and left the room.

❧

I didn't expect to sleep at all, so I settled in on *The Last Juror*. I finished it by dawn, the sun filtering through the blinds in lazy yellow strands. I opened *The Runaway Jury* next, had read almost one hundred pages before I heard the shower start next door, Luke shouting to Mrs. Harrison that he wanted his eggs sunny-side up. He'd done that for my benefit, I could tell. He wanted me to know only a single wall separated us now, that he'd chosen to come in from the guesthouse and start his day without speaking to me. I hated myself a little as I bent the corner of the page, running my finger over the crease to seal the fold. Then a little more as the humid shush of the shower sounded closer. I pushed the curtain all the way to the right and stepped in, felt his hands forgiving on my hips, the hair around his erection wet and coarse.

"I'm sorry." Beads of water gathered on my lips. It was a hard thing to do, apologize, but I've done harder things. I pressed my face into the crook of his neck, hot and steamy as a New York City sidewalk helplessly exposed in the thick of summer.

CHAPTER 8

Mom grounded me for two weeks after Dean's party. She's fond of timing the statement, "That's a riot," to the corny punch lines of *Friends*, and that's exactly what my punishment was, a riot. With the performance I'd given at Dean's party, I'd grounded myself.

Still, I was tolerated at the lunch table, and that was mostly thanks to Hilary and Dean. Everyone else just seemed relieved when I announced I was under house arrest for the rest of the month. Quarantined, they had time to decide: Were my missteps contagious?

For whatever reason, Hilary had really taken a shine to me. Maybe because I aided and abetted her trashy teenage rebellion, maybe because she asked me to read her theme paper on *Into Thin Air* and I basically rewrote it into an A+ assignment. I didn't care. Whatever it was she needed from me, I would give her.

Olivia tried to act like she didn't care when she found out about Dean's party, like it didn't bother her that I'd been invited and kept it secret, or that I'd hooked up with Liam, which she'd made clear was something she wanted to do. "Was it fun?" she asked brightly. Her blinking went rapid, as though it powered the phony smile on her face.

"I think?" I turned my palms up, and that got a real laugh, at least.

In the movies and on TV, the most popular girls in school are always gorgeous, with buxom curves scaled to impossibly Barbie proportions, but Bradley and other schools with a similar milieu defied this law. Olivia was pretty in the way that a grandmother would notice: "My, what a lovely young lady." She had hair so curly it puffed up, frizzier and angrier when she turned a blow-dryer on it. Her cheeks got too pink when she drank, and black-heads pooled in the pores on her nose, collecting more oil as the day wore on. Liam wouldn't come around to her on his own, the attraction had to be painstakingly manu-factured.

Nell later taught me to tone down my beer commercial potential rather than capitalize on it. Actively striving for the traditional markers of beauty and status—the blond hair perfectly styled, the tan skin perfectly even, the bra-zen logo stamped all over your bag—why, it's downright shameful. This was something that took me years to learn, because Mom had been catching my chin in her hand and applying "a little color" to my lips since I was eleven, be-cause preening was celebrated, never mocked, at Mt. St. Theresa's.

Like me, Liam was learning to see Olivia's curls as charming, rather than kinky, and did her flat chest actually have more of a curve than he thought? I didn't interfere with this. All my life, I've found it difficult to advocate for myself, to ask for what I want. I fear burdening people so much. I'd like to blame it on what happened that night, on what happened in the ensuing weeks, but I think it's just part of my blueprint. Asking Liam to go with me to get the morning-after pill was about the boldest thing I'd ever done, and with that single word, "Friend," scribbled slowly on the page like a fourth grader's reminder to himself of the rule " 'i' before 'e' except after 'c,' " I remembered why I so rarely do it.

Olivia just needed a little time to be sure that my retreat wasn't a maneuver. To accept it was sincere. Almost three weeks after Dean's party, I saw her in the distant end of the Math wing. She paused as I advanced on her and said, "You look skinny." It came out as more of an accusation than a compliment, the way even fourteen-year-old girls know to do. How did this happen? How did *you* do this?

I lit up inside and chirped, "Cross-country!" But the truth was that ever since that night, the only thing I could stomach was cantaloupe. I slogged through my runs, my mile time worsening rather than improving, Mr. Larson shouting, "Come on, TifAni!" Not encouraging. Exasperated.

When Hilary invited me to sleep over at Olivia's house on Saturday, the last Saturday of my sentence, Mom said yes, like I knew she would. She said I'd been so helpful and well behaved that she would shave one day off my grounding. That was also a riot. She was obsessed with Hilary's and Olivia's parents, particularly Olivia's mom, Annabella Kaplan, née Coyne, who was a descendant of the Macy's family and drove an antique Jaguar. Mom knew not to interfere with that burgeoning friendship, the tuition's true payoff the connections, not the education, the same way I knew to just look away when Liam looped his arm over Olivia's ballerina shoulders, the acid charging up my throat like a linebacker.

Mom deposited me at the mouth of Olivia's house at 5:00 P.M. on Saturday. It didn't look like much from the front, you would certainly expect more from the granddaughter of the Macy's guy. But it was just that it was so obscured by trees and vines and ivy, and once you walked through the back gates you realized that the house continued on and on, the yard opening up into an acre of land with a swimming pool and a guesthouse where Louisa, the Kaplans' maid, lived.

I knocked on the back door. Several seconds passed before I saw the top of Hilary's berry-tinted bleached head bobbing toward me. I never once saw the Kaplans when I came to Olivia's house. Her father had a ferocious temper, which Olivia wore in moody bruises on her wrists, and her mother was usually recovering from some kind of plastic surgery. This parental amalgam—abusive and vain—only further solidified Olivia in my mind as the glamorous, poor little rich girl I longed to be for so many years after I knew her. Not even what she did to me, not even what happened to her later, was enough to quench my bloodlust.

Hilary swung open the door. "Yo, girl." Hilary and Olivia called everyone girl. It took me years to break the annoying habit.

My eyes lingered on the slit of Hilary's flat stomach, exposed by her cut-off T-shirt. Behind her back, the guys called her HIMary, for her broad shoulders and athletic frame. But I found her toned muscles fascinating. She wasn't Olivia thin, but there was not an ounce of fat on her body, and Hilary did not play a sport and her mother forged a letter from her "squash coach" to get her out of gym class. It was like she had a Pilates body before Pilates was even a thing.

I'd been nervous to come. Olivia hadn't invited me—Hilary had. Over the last two weeks, Olivia had really upped her game with Liam. I let him go without a fight. If it was between him and Olivia and Hilary as friends—we'd realized that with my name, our acronym was now HOT—well, I knew which one had more long-term potential.

"Come on." Hilary charged up the stairs two at a time, her hamstring muscles flexing with each push against gravity. Hilary always had to do everything a little bit weirder than everyone else. It was part of her schtick.

Olivia had an entire wing of the house all to herself—a large, loft-like space with a bathroom separating her room from that of her little sister, who was away at boarding school. Hilary told me once that Olivia's sister was the pretty one, the favorite one. It was why Olivia barely ate.

Olivia was sitting cross-legged on the floor, propped lazily against her bedpost. Bags of Swedish fish and Starbursts, a bottle of vodka, and an overturned liter of Diet Coke surrounded her like sweet casualties of war.

"Hey, girl." Olivia pulled a Swedish fish between her teeth until the body snapped in half. She reached for the bottle of vodka. "Drink."

We chased the vodka with Diet Coke, sinking our teeth into the candy, wincing, trying to absorb the bite. The sun tiptoed away from the window, our pupils ballooning, but we still didn't turn on the lights.

"Let's get Dean over here," Olivia said, only when we'd put a safe enough dent in the vodka. When the goal is to get fucked up, Dean's greediness must be considered.

I was woozy with hunger and sugar. Olivia grinned at

me, the seams between her teeth Christmas red. "He'll come if he knows you're here."

If only I could have liked Dean back, if his mere presence, the sensory memory of his sperm on my tongue didn't make me heave, maybe everything would have turned out differently.

"He'll come!" Hilary rolled onto her back with a laugh, holding her knees to her chest and rocking back and forth. I could see her underwear. Radioactive green, this time.

"Shut up." I wrapped my lips around the opening of the vodka bottle and shuddered as the liquid trickled into my stomach, lava hot.

Olivia was on the phone, saying, "Just wait until it's dark, or Louisa will see."

If I had been with girls from Mt. St. Theresa, we would have all clamored to the mirror, feverishly rubbing our cheeks with blush, so much mascara on our eyelashes they'd look like hairy spider legs. But Olivia just pulled on the messy loop on top of her head, securing it closer to her scalp. "They have forties."

"Who is it?" I waited, hoping to hear Liam's name.

"Dean, Liam, Miles." She worked her jaw through a Starburst. "And Dave. Ugh."

"Fucking Dave," Hilary agreed.

I said I had to go to the bathroom. I stumbled down the hall and locked the door behind me, what I was about to do more shameful than clogging the toilet: make myself up. My cheeks were ruddy when I looked in the mirror; I splashed water on my face, trying to cool down, trying to ready my canvas. I scavenged around in the drawers for eyeliner, lip gloss, something. I found some crusty old mascara and plunged the brush into the tube over and over, trying to scrape as much out of it as I could.

I heard the guys pounding up the stairs, and I locked eyes with myself in the mirror. "It's okay. You're okay." I hadn't bothered to turn on the light, and the sun's last remaining thread fell across my face, bleaching any semblance of confidence I'd hoped to see.

When I returned to Olivia's room, I saw everyone sitting in a circle, drinking those forties out of sweaty paper bags. There was an open spot between Liam and Dean. I took it, edging as close to Liam as I dared. Dean passed a bottle to me. I didn't understand the difference between a regular beer and a forty, and I pushed the paper bag down to read the label: malt liquor beer. I drank it without asking what malt liquor was.

After an hour of brain-dead conversation, the words going wobblier and wobblier in my mind, Olivia announced it was safe to go outside and smoke.

We crept down the stairs, filing through the kitchen and out the door one by one, like the most well-rehearsed fire drill. We huddled in a circle by the privacy garden shielding the kitchen's windows, the arms of a small, plush maple tree stretching toward us, waiting for a hug. I hadn't realized that was only the second kitchen. "The maid's kitchen," Olivia explained, which was bigger than the one in my modest McMansion. Olivia's parents rarely used this side of the house, she said, and we would remain undetected so long as we stayed quiet.

Dean extracted a joint from a pack of cigarettes, running a lighter underneath its belly before bringing one end to his lips and firing up the other.

We passed to the left, Olivia and Hilary going before me, neither of them able to hold the smoke in, erupting into spastic coughing fits, the guys rolling their eyes and urging them in hushed whispers to hurry up and pass before it burned out.

I hadn't smoked pot since that night in the eighth grade, at Leah's house. I was terrified of that feeling, the way the high slunk up from behind and closed its cape around me without any warning. Every vein in my body had engorged and pulsed, and I'd been convinced it would never go away, that I would never feel normal again. But the desire to do better than Hilary and Olivia was greater than the fear. I pulled on the joint, the end flaring like a lightning bug on the first day of summer. I held the smoke in my lungs for a long time to impress Liam, blowing it out in a slow, graceful ribbon that curled around his face.

"I need to meet more Catholic girls," Liam said, his eyes sleepy.

"I hear they use teeth," Olivia murmured, low, as though nervous to see how the joke would land. It invited a robust laugh, which Olivia shushed frantically, her fear of her father temporarily overriding pride—she'd steered correctly.

Dean clapped me on the back. "Don't worry, Finny, you were pretty out of it."

It was one of those awful moments where you have no control over your reaction, when the pain is too exposed to hide. I laughed, the sharp contrast between the sound and the look on my face only making it worse.

Once we wore the joint down to a nub, Liam said he had to use the bathroom and retreated into the house. I wondered if I should follow him as the conversation hummed on. I felt the consequences of what I'd just done, of my bravado in trapping the smoke in my chest for so long, close on my heels. My heart was marching in my ears when I realized Olivia was gone too, had slipped off without my even realizing it. I peered through the maple's ruby leaves and over the flat green hedges guarding the windows, but the kitchen was empty.

"I'm cold," I said, panicking when I realized just how cold I was. I was shivering. "Let's go inside." I needed to move, needed to focus on putting one foot in front of the other, on my hand on the cool doorknob twisting, anything but the way my body was shuddering, like one of those plastic windup toys, candy red gums and stark white teeth on a pair of feet, chattering across the table, a cardigan-wearing uncle's idea of a gag.

"Let's just hang for a while." It was Dean speaking. It was Dean's arm pulling me into him. Dean was the only one there. Where had everyone gone?

"Wait." I dipped my head low, my forehead against Dean's chest, anything to avoid his mouth, the angle at which it was coming at me.

Dean wiggled his finger into the crevice between my chin and my neck, applying an upward pressure.

"I'm really cold," I protested even as I gave in to it. I swallowed when I felt Dean's wet lips on mine. Just for a little bit, I thought. You only have to do this for a little bit. Don't be rude.

I toyed with Dean's fat tongue, realizing my palms were on his chest, still pushing him away. I wrapped them around the back of his hairy neck obediently.

Dean's fingers were stumbling over the button of my khakis. It was too soon to stop, Dean wouldn't believe me if I put an end to it now. As calmly as I could, I broke the kiss.

"Let's go inside." I tried to make it sound breathy, se-ductive, but we both knew there was nowhere to make

good on my promise inside the house. Too late, I realized
my play was dangerously transparent, that I'd fatally mis-
calculated Dean. He seized the button on my pants with
such gusto my pelvis thrust forward and my feet flew off
the ground. I stumbled backward, landing on my wrist at
a ruthless angle, and I let out an injured-puppy yelp that
reverberated through the yard.

"Shut up!" Dean hissed. He dropped to his knees and
slapped me.

Even before I'd come to Bradley, even before all the evidence proved I was the one not like the others, I was still
not a girl you slap. The hot hand on my cheek undid me. I
was screaming, the sound guttural and ancient, something
I'd never heard before. There is so rarely an occasion in this
modern life when your body takes over, when you find out
what it will do, the smells and sounds it will release when
it's trying to survive. That night, on the ground with Dean,
clawing and screeching, a starchy sweat collecting in my
armpits, I found out, and not for the last time.

Dean had the button undone and my pants low on my
hips when the lights in the front of the house popped on,
when we heard Olivia's father hollering. Olivia burst out
the back door and screamed at me to go and never come
back. I heard Dean gasping behind me as I ran to the gate
and my hands shook over the latch.

"Move!" He shoved me out of the way and released the
hook, the gate swinging open. Dean charged through but
paused, inexplicably holding the gate open behind him so
I could escape as well. The dark driveway was shortening
ahead of me when I heard the patter of more footsteps
behind me, the other boys, heading for Dave's Navigator
parked on the street.

At the road, I turned right. I didn't know where I was

going, just that right was away from Dave's car, away from
the direction its nose pointed. I kept going until the light
from Olivia's house faded completely, and it was dark and
I could collapse on the side of the road, my lungs sharp
with the cold night air, my heart cartwheeling madly, as
though I'd never run a mile straight in my life, as though it
wasn't the school sport I chose of my own accord.

I was deep in the bowels of the Main Line, the mansions
set far back from the road, burning bright and smug in the
trees. I slipped into the brush at the mere vibration of a car
on the road, peering through the lingering red and yellow
leaves and exhaling only when I saw that it wasn't Dave's
Navigator. Adrenaline had purged my body of any high,
but by the way I zagged on the road, I could tell it would
be hours before the vodka and Diet Coke wore off, hours
before I realized my wrist was swollen to two times its size,
that it was throbbing in sync with my heart.

A plan had formulated in my mind: Get to Montgomery Avenue, then walk the straight line to Arbor Road,
where I would turn right to get to Arthur's house. I'd
chuck pebbles at his window the way boys do when they
like a girl in the movies. He would take me in. He had to.

I kept turning on different roads, each time so sure that
was the one that would lead me to the main strip. At one
point I grew so desperate that I didn't flee when a set of
headlights appeared at the top of a steep hill, the vehicle
to which they belonged low and sleek, definitely not Dave.

As it rolled to a stop at the bottom of the hill, I jogged
up to the window to ask how to get to Montgomery. The
mom face in the window panicked, her mouth dropping

open in horror and the car squealing beneath her foot. Her Mercedes shot out ahead of me, tearing into the night, in fast pursuit of the dinner party where she would no doubt regale her flaccid friends with the tale of her narrow escape of the hooligan carjacker who appeared like the boogeyman on Glenn Road.

After what somehow felt like both forever and a second, I found a turn that opened up into a long row of streetlamps, a Wawa anchoring the curve of the last quarter mile. I was so impatient I broke into a run, my hands loose at my sides the way Mr. Larson taught us. "It takes energy to make a fist," he explained, showing us his own, clenched tight. "And you want to conserve as much of it as possible."

I jogged under the gas station's fluorescent lighting, shielding my eyes against their sudden, razor brightness, as though it were the sun that just burst free from the clouds. I pushed the door open with my shoulder, discovered how warm it was inside, realized just how raw I smelled now that I was in a contained space. I stopped a few inches short of the counter to keep the stench from reaching the cashier.

"Montgomery Avenue is further up on the right, right?" I was horrified to realize I was slurring my words.

The cashier looked up from his crossword puzzle, irritably. He blinked, and it was like it reset his entire face.

"Miss." He covered his heart with his hand. "Are you all right?"

I touched my hand to my hair and felt dirt. "I just tripped."

The cashier reached for the phone. "I call the police."

"No!" I leapt forward, and he took a step back, still holding on to the phone.

"Don't do that!" he yelled. I realized for the first time that he was scared too.

"Please," I said. His finger had hit only the number nine. "I don't need the police. I just want you to tell me how to get to Montgomery Avenue."

The cashier paused, both hands clutching the phone so tightly that the skin on his knuckles turned white. "You are very far away," he said, finally.

I heard the door open behind me, and I froze. I didn't want to create a scene with another customer in the store. "Can you just tell me how to get there?" I whispered.

The cashier slowly hung up the phone, looking unsure as he reached for a map.

I heard my name.

It was Mr. Larson behind me. It was Mr. Larson's hand on my shoulder, guiding me out of Wawa, clearing the take-out bags from the passenger seat and urging me to get in his car. There was a surrender in being found that made me lose my grip on all my secrets. All my lies—the ones I told everyone, even myself. Tears shivering on my cheeks, one split with a cut so thin and midnight dark it could have been a pen mark, I started to tell him what had happened. And then I couldn't stop.

❧

Mr. Larson gave me a blanket and water and an ice pack for my face. He wanted to take me to the hospital, but I became so hysterical at the suggestion that he agreed to bring me back to his apartment. The fact that he knew exactly how to handle the situation—get me to a safe place, calm me down, sober me up—didn't surprise me then, but it does now. He was an adult, of course he knew what to do, but what I couldn't have realized then is how new to it he was, how young twenty-four is when you're not fourteen. Not two years earlier Mr. Larson had been skinny-dipping in Beebe Lake at Cornell with his fraternity brothers, was the only one to score with the freshman they all called Holy Shit because she was so beautiful you gasped "holy shit" when you saw her. We didn't even look so far apart in age; if I'd been wearing makeup and a dress, we could have been going back to his apartment after a first date gone exceedingly well.

I had made it to Narberth, had walked at least seven miles from Olivia's house. It was almost one in the morning, and Mr. Larson had been driving home from the bars in Manayunk, where most of his friends lived, where he would live if it wasn't such a hike to Bradley in the morning. He had stopped at Wawa for a snack, he told me. Then he patted his middle and said, "I've been eating too many snacks lately." He was trying to get me to smile, so I did, politely.

Mr. Larson didn't look fat to me, but when we got to his apartment and I was able to trace the perimeter of the living room, studying the pictures on his walls, the blanket he'd given me loosening around my shoulders, I saw that he used to have that same slim, muscular build that Liam and Dean had. Muscled shoulders worked hard for in the gym, but the slender waist revealing what would be there without the bench press. I'd stopped thinking of Mr. Larson as the best-looking guy I'd ever seen in real life after he'd become my coach, after he'd started getting on my case, but these pictures reminded me of what I'd seen on my first day of school. I pulled the blanket tighter around my shoulders, suddenly feeling like the V-neck of my sweater was too low.

"Here you go." Mr. Larson appeared in the doorframe, a soggy slice of Tombstone pizza on a plate for me.

I ate obediently. I had insisted Mr. Larson not make anything for me, I had no appetite, but as I bit into the microwaved pizza, the center still doughy and cold, a rabid hunger overcame me. I ate that slice, then three more before I finally leaned back on the couch, spent.

"Feel better?" Mr. Larson asked, and I nodded, grimly.

"TifAni," he began, hunching forward in the La-Z-Boy chair next to the couch. He had been careful to take that seat. "We need to talk about next steps."

I dropped my face in the blanket. The pizza had given me the energy to cry again. "Please," I whimpered. *Please don't tell my parents. Please don't tell the school. Please just be my friend and not make this any worse than it already is.*

"I probably shouldn't be telling you this." Mr. Larson sighed. "But we've had, problems, like this, with Dean before."

I used the blanket to wipe my face and raised my head. "What do you mean?"

"This isn't the first time he's physically assaulted another student."

"*Tried* to," I corrected him.

"No," Mr. Larson said, firmly. "What he did at his house three weeks ago wasn't trying, what he did tonight wasn't trying."

Even after everything was said and done, after the ashes fermented the grass, after I moved on to college and then New York City and got everything I thought I wanted, Mr. Larson was the only person who ever told me that this, none of this, was my fault. I saw the momentary hesitation even in Mom's eyes. You give a blow job, it can't be done *to* you. How can it be what you say it is? How could you go to the party, be the only girl, drink that much, and not expect to have what happened happen?

"My parents will never forgive me for ruining this," I said.

"Yes," Mr. Larson promised. "They will."

I leaned back, resting my head against the couch and closing my eyes, my legs aching with all the Main Line roads I'd wandered. I could have fallen asleep right there, but Mr. Larson insisted I take his bed, the couch was fine for him, really, it was.

He closed the door with a gentle click, and I climbed beneath his duvet, dark red and scratchy with wear. Mr. Larson smelled like a grown-up, like a dad. I wondered how many other girls had slept in this bed before me, if Mr. Larson had kissed their necks while he moved on top of them, slow and labored, like I had always pictured sex would be.

I woke up in the middle of the night screaming. I never actually heard it myself. But it must have been pretty bad to send Mr. Larson panting into the room. He heaved the light on, standing over me and pleading with me loudly to wake up from my bad dream.

"You're okay," Mr. Larson shushed when he saw my eyes focus on him. "You're okay."

I gathered the blanket underneath my chin, everything covered except my head, the way Mom used to do with heaps of sand at the beach. "Sorry," I whispered, embarrassed.

"You don't have to apologize," Mr. Larson said. "It was just pretty bad. I thought you might want to wake up from it."

My bodyless head nodded. "Thanks."

Mr. Larson was wearing a T-shirt, snug around the impressive slope of his shoulders. He turned to go.

"Wait!" I held the blanket tighter. I couldn't be in this room alone. My heart hiccuped threateningly in the cavity of my chest, the first sign of the spin. It couldn't go on like this for much longer, and if it stopped, I needed someone there to call for help. "I can't . . . I'm not going to be able to sleep. Can you stay?"

Mr. Larson looked over his big shoulder at me in the bed. There was a sadness in his face I didn't understand. "I could sleep on the floor."

I nodded, encouragingly, and Mr. Larson continued on to the living room, returning with a pillow and a blanket. He arranged his materials on the ground next to the bed before turning off the light and crouching low, rearranging them to fit his form.

"Try to sleep, TifAni," he said drowsily. But I didn't try. I stayed up all night, listening to his soothing breath assure me everything would be okay. I didn't know it then, but I had a lifetime of sleepless nights waiting for me after that.

❦

In the morning, Mr. Larson microwaved me a frozen bagel. He didn't have cream cheese, only a crusty stick of butter with bread crumbs clinging to the ragged end.

Even though the swelling in my face had gone down during the night, I still had that thin red line etched into my cheek. But it was my wrist that was really concerning me, so Mr. Larson offered to go to CVS and get me an Ace bandage and a toothbrush. After that, he wanted to drive me home, and he promised he would help me tell my parents what had happened. I agreed reluctantly.

When he left, I picked up his phone and dialed home.

"Hi, sweetie!" Mom said.

"Hi, Mom."

"Oh!" she said. "Before I forget, Dean Barton called for you a few minutes ago."

I clung on to the kitchen counter to steady myself. "He did?"

"He said it was important, um, hold on, let me find the message." I heard Mom rustling around, and it was all I could do not to scream at her to hurry up. "What, honey?"

"I didn't say anything," I snapped, before I realized she was talking to Dad.

"Yes, in the freezer in the garage." Pause. "It's *in* there."

"Mom!" I barked.

"TifAni, relax," Mom said. "Your father, you know how he is."

"What did Dean say?"

"I have the message right here. Call soon as possible, about chemistry project. He left his number too. He sounded very nervous." There was the dainty tinkle of her laugh. "He must like you."

"Tell me the number?" I found a Post-it and a pen in Mr. Larson's drawer and wrote it down.

"I'll call you right back," I said.

"Wait, TifAni, when should I pick you up?"

"I'll call you right back!"

I hung up the phone and hurriedly dialed Dean's number. I needed to know what this was all about before Mr. Larson got back from CVS.

Dean answered on the third ring. His hello was hostile.

"Finny!" His tone changed completely when he realized it was me. "Where the hell did you go last night? We tried to find you."

I fed him a lie about how I ended up at the house of one of my teammates, who lives not far from Olivia.

"Good, good," Dean said. "So listen, about what happened last night. I'm really sorry." He laughed sheepishly. "I was really fucked up."

"You hit me," I said, so quietly I wasn't even sure if I'd said it or not until Dean responded.

"I'm really sorry, Finny." Dean's voice caught in his squat throat. "I feel sick that I did that. Can you ever forgive me? I won't be able to live with myself if you don't forgive me."

There was a desperation in Dean's voice that I felt too—it would be so much easier if this never happened, and only we have the power to make it so.

I swallowed. "Okay."

Dean's breath sounded heavy on my ear. "Thank you, Finny. Thank you."

I called Mom back after we hung up and told her I would take the train.

"And, Mom?" I asked. "Do you have any Neosporin? Olivia's dog scratched my face while I was sleeping." Olivia didn't have a dog.

When Mr. Larson returned I was dressed and ready with my lies. I insisted on taking the train, insisted he didn't understand my parents, that it would be better if I told them on my own.

"Are you sure?" Mr. Larson asked. His tone made it clear that he didn't believe one shred of it.

I nodded apologetically. "There's an eleven fifty-seven from Bryn Mawr. We can make it if we leave now." I turned away from the disappointment in his face so he couldn't see my own. I sometimes wonder if this was the decision that set everything into motion. Or if it would have happened anyway, if, like the nuns at Mt. St. Theresa's said, God has a plan for all of us and he knows the outcome before we're even born.

CHAPTER 9

didn't lie to Luke. I told him I was going to e-mail Mr. Larson a few days after we returned from Nantucket. I hadn't been able to stop thinking about him, hadn't been able to stop picturing the two of us shoulder to shoulder in a dim bar, a mixture of concern and lust on his face when I confessed my second dark secret to him: I'm not sure I can go through with this. The way he would kiss me—the restraint he would try to have at first because of his wife. Booth. Elspeth. But then he'd remember, it's me.

Then the credits of this little fantasy roll. Mr. Larson would never do *that* with me. I didn't even really want to do that with him either. I was getting married. This was just cold feet doing the same shuffle they do for every bride. And it's normal to have cold feet, Mom reminded me when I felt her out, let it drop that maybe I wasn't as ready to get married as I thought I was. "Guys like Luke don't come along every day," she warned. "Don't mess this up, Tif. You'll never get anyone as good as him again."

Mr. Larson's appeal was that he was there for it all. He saw me at my stray dog lowest and still he stood behind me, did everything he could to help me. He imagined the future I could have before I even wanted it for myself, and he was the one to push me toward it. That's faith. Growing up, I thought faith was about believing Jesus died for us, and that if I held on to that, I'd get to meet him when I died too. But faith doesn't mean that to me anymore. Now it means someone seeing something in you that you don't, and not giving up until you see it too. I want that. I miss that.

"Why do you need it?" Luke argued when I asked for Mr. Larson's e-mail address. Not suspicious. But not thrilled either.

"What do you mean why?" I spat at him, like I would at an intern who questioned the assignment I'd just given her. What about this *don't* you get? "It's insane that we ran into each other like that. He's doing the documentary. I want to know if we're filming at the same time. What he's going to talk about." Luke's face wasn't giving, so I went for melodramatic. "Everything, Luke. I want to talk to him about everything."

Luke thumped his arm on the couch and groaned. "He's my client, Ani. I just don't want things getting . . . messy . . . like that."

"You just don't get it," I sighed. Walked forlornly into the bedroom and quietly shut the door. When I asked for the e-mail address again the next day, Luke wrote me back with just that and nothing else.

With Mr. Larson's address in the To field, I channeled my inner Prom Queen and wrote him a sweet, spirited e-mail. "I can't believe we ran into each other the way we did! Small world, right? I'd love to catch up sometime, I feel like we have so much to talk about."

I clicked refresh eight times before Mr. Larson's reply appeared. I opened the e-mail, my cheeks hot with hope.

"How about coffee?" he wrote back. "Would you be comfortable with that?" My eye roll must have burned off the calories in the grapes I'd snuck. Coffee? He was still treating me like his student.

"I believe drinks would make both of us more 'comfortable,'" I wrote.

"You had that bite even when you were a kid" came his reply, the word "kid" making me bristle. But he agreed.

On the day we were to meet, I wore an oversize leather T-shirt dress and peep-toe booties to work, thinking, *This is what someone with "bite" wears in the middle of summer.*

"You look fantastic," LoLo said when she passed me in the hallway. "Did you get Botox in your forehead?"

"That's the nicest thing you've ever said to me," I said, and LoLo cackled with laughter the way I knew she would. I thought we were just exchanging pleasantries, but LoLo slowed to a stop and took a few steps backward, beckoning me into a corner. "So that 'Revenge Porn' piece of yours is brilliant. Really brilliant."

I'd lobbied hard for that idea, for six pages in the feature section to report on the women who had been made victims by vindictive ex-boyfriends, on the way privacy and sexual harassment laws hadn't caught up with technology, so that, technically, there was nothing law enforcement could do to help them.

"Thank you." I beamed.

"It's amazing, you really can do anything," LoLo continued. "But I think it will have more of an impact at the *you know what* than it will here." Her eyebrows struggled to go higher on her forehead, then gave up.

I would play. "It's a timely article. I wouldn't sit on it for long."

"Oh, I don't think we'll have to." Her smile revealed a

row of coffee-drinker teeth behind a coat of Chanel lipstick.

I matched my expression to hers. "That's *fantastic
news.*"

LoLo wiggled her darks nails at me. "Ciao."

It felt like a good omen.

❧

Through the Dionysian fog of the bar, Mr. Larson's
Clydesdale back appeared as if a mirage. I wove through
the happy hour release of Theory pencil skirts and bank-
ers with wedding rings in their pockets, heels sounding a
chant, "Be real. Be real. Be real."

I tapped his shoulder. He either had removed his tie or
hadn't worn one that day, and his shirt opened in a little V
right at his throat, the small sliver of skin there as shocking
as the first time I saw him in jeans. A reminder of all the
ways I still didn't know him. "Sorry!" I lifted one side of
my mouth in a contrite smile. "I got stuck at work." I blew
a strand of hair out of my mouth to prove how frazzled I
was. *I'm so busy but I made time for* you.

This was not true, of course. I'd started getting ready in
The Women's Magazine bathroom at approximately 7:20.
I'd put on deodorant, brushed my teeth, held mouthwash
in my cheeks for so long my eyes watered. Then it was on
to the makeup, the pains I took to appear as though I wasn't
wearing much at all. It was 7:41 when I left the office. One
minute behind schedule, the schedule I'd determined
would place me at the bar in Flatiron at 8:07. "The perfect
late to show he doesn't hang the moon for you," Nell says.

Mr. Larson's lips hovered at the edge of his tumbler.
"I should make you run laps." He took a little sip, and I

noticed how low his scotch was, realized he was already warm.

The idea of Mr. Larson telling me what to do now, screaming at me to run faster, pick up the pace, don't phone this *in*, TifAni, prickled the skin at the nape of my neck. I busied myself settling into the stool next to him. I couldn't let him see me prickled. Not yet.

I tucked a panel of hair behind my ear. "You know I still do your hill workout at least once a week?"

Mr. Larson sniffed out a little laugh, and even though the skin bunched around his eyes, his face had remained boyish, unfazed by the gray hair at his temples. "Where? The one thing about this city—it's so flat."

"I know, nothing can hold a candle to the hill on Mill Creek. I'm in Tribeca, so I have to make do with the Brooklyn Bridge." I sighed, glibly. We both knew that living in a sleek one-bedroom by the Brooklyn Bridge was superior to living in some threadbare mansion in Bryn Mawr.

The bartender took notice of me and asked me what I wanted with a nod. "Vodka martini," I said. "Straight up." That was my glossy editor drink. I don't crave martinis the way I do, say, an economy-size bag of chocolate-covered pretzels, but when I need a warm blur to descend on me, and fast, it's my elixir of choice. Sometimes it even tricks me into thinking I'm the kind of tired that will lead to sleep.

"Look at you." Mr. Larson leaned away to take in everything I'd put together for him. The wicked leather dress, the bar of black diamonds in the ear I had purposely exposed to him. I caught a spark, amusement and approval fusing together in his eyes. It was only a slap shot of a moment, but it was unbearable in a way, like touching a hot stove by accident. The response in your body overwhelming all systems. "I always knew this is who you would be."

I could have burst, but I clung to deadpan. "A lush?"

"No, this." He sliced his hands sideways at me. "You're one of those women that people look at on the street and wonder who they are. What they do."

My drink slid in front of me and I took a blazing sip. I needed it in case I didn't stick the landing of what I was going to say next. "What I do is write a lot of blow job tips."

Mr. Larson looked away. "Come on, Tif."

The sound of my old name, the disappointment in Mr. Larson's voice, it was like Dean's hand across my face all over again. I took another big sip that left my lips slippery with vodka and tried to recover. "Too much from your old student?"

Mr. Larson rolled his glass between his palms. "I hate hearing you cut yourself down like that."

I dug my elbow into the bar, swiveling on the stool so I could face him and he could see I was entertained by the whole thing. "Oh, I'm not. If I can't have my journalistic integrity, then at least I can have a sense of humor about it. Believe me, I'm fine."

Mr. Larson turned his eyes on me, and I could hardly stand the knowing there. "You certainly seem fine. I guess I'm just trying to figure out if you really are."

The martini hadn't taken hold yet, and I wasn't quite ready to get into this. I thought we'd start out slow, a few sexually charged, self-deprecating jokes from me about my job, Mr. Larson seeing through my aw-shucks routine to the ambition, the savvy that I had and his wife lacked. Did I feel that Luke was lacking in some way too? *I do, I do*, I would say, sadly, maybe spring a few tears to my eyes. *He just doesn't understand. So few people do.* A pointed look at Mr. Larson—assuring him he was one of the few.

"Okay, okay," I laughed. "This documentary thing, it has me out of my mind."

Mr. Larson matched me with his laugh and I was relieved. "I know what you mean."

"I'm wary of it," I said. "But I'm still dying to do it."

Mr. Larson didn't appear to understand. "Why would you be wary?"

"Because I don't know what the bent is. I know what the editing process can do." I dropped my voice and leaned in closer, like I don't admit the next thing to very many people, but for Mr. Larson I would make an exception. "I mean, I manipulate the hell out of what I write. I know exactly how I want something to turn out before I even do the research and call up Dr. Hack from the *Today* show. If what he tells me doesn't fit, I just ask the question a different way. Or"—I tilted my head, remembering the other option—"I try Dr. Hack from *Good Morning America* and get him to give me something that will fit."

"So that's how that works." Mr. Larson's eyes tapered in at the corners, carefully, like he was squinting through the peephole in my entire facade. That direct line he had, it was the spider crack that would eventually make the windshield cave in.

I smirked at myself. "I'm just saying. I can't hang all my hopes on this."

Mr. Larson's shoulder sloped down lower, right by mine. His breath was on fire with Lagavulin. "No, you can't. But I don't think you have anything to worry about. I think they're interested in the story no one's heard, which is yours. That said"—he leaned away, taking all his peaty heat with him, and it was like I waded into a cool pocket in the ocean—"nothing's a guarantee. You have to know that no matter what they say about you, all that matters is what you know about yourself here." He covered his chest with his hand. It was such an earnest, after-school-special thing to say I would have mocked it had it come from anyone else. But it had come from Mr. Larson, and I would remember it fondly, repeat it whenever I questioned if I'd made the right decision, for many years to come.

I fiddled with the wet corner of a cocktail napkin. "Mr. Larson, there isn't much to comfort me there."

Mr. Larson sighed, like he had just received some really bad news. "Tif, my God. That wrecks me."

I was furious with myself for the way my face puckered up, wrinkled and hideous. I slapped my hand to my forehead, shielding the carnage.

Mr. Larson hunched down low, got underneath the visor of my hand. "Hey," he said, "come on. I didn't mean to upset you." And then there was the perfect pressure of his hand on my back, a little lower than it needed to be, that feeling between my legs, so desperate I craved a swift end, so delicious I would miss it when it was gone.

I gave him a wobbly smile. Everyone loves a trouper. "I swear I'm not a mess."

Mr. Larson laughed, and his hand went higher on my back, rubbed encouragingly, fatherly. I cursed myself for playing it wrong again, but I made a mental note too. *He likes me broken.*

"So what's the deal?" Mr. Larson asked, removing his hand entirely and straightening up. "You going back there in September to film?"

A logistical question. Not much opportunity to unravel there. "I am. Are you?"

Mr. Larson shifted on his barstool and grimaced. It was too small for someone like him to sit comfortably. "Same."

The bartender came by and asked if we wanted another.

I nodded, eagerly, but Mr. Larson said he was fine. I slunk in a little and tried not to show it. "Is Whitney on board for it?" I exhaled, irritably. "Because Luke isn't."

"Luke doesn't want you to do it?" I could see this bothered Mr. Larson, and I was glad.

"He just felt like it would take me back to a very dark place. And while we're planning our wedding, no less."

"Well, he's concerned about you. I can see that."

I shook my head, excited for the opportunity to expose the great St. Luke. "He just doesn't want to deal with me and my silly hysteria. Nothing would make him happier than if I were to never mention Bradley again."

Mr. Larson traced his finger along the rim of his glass, tenderly, and I could *feel* him smoothing a Band-Aid over the tear in my face that night in his apartment. Saying, "There," once it latched tight on to my skin. He spoke into his empty glass. "Moving on doesn't mean you don't talk about it. Or hurt about it. It's always going to hurt, I imagine." He glanced at me, almost shyly, to see if I agreed, which is a courtesy Luke never pays me. No, Luke just gets up on his soapbox, purports to tell me exactly how I should metabolize that cruel slice of my life. Why do I need to do the documentary? I shouldn't care so goddamn much about what everyone thinks of me. Easy to say when everyone fucking loves you.

"I don't mean to speak for you," Mr. Larson said, "I'm sorry." His apology made me realize I was scowling.

"No." I blinked Luke away. "You're exactly right. Thank you. For saying that. No one ever says stuff like that to me."

"I'm sure he does his best." Mr. Larson reached for my hand, and I was so surprised all my limbs stiffened and he had to fight a little to get it, to hold my hand up in the air like a man leading a woman to a dance floor in Victorian times. "He obviously loves you." He pressed his thumb to the evidence on my finger, twisted the stone just a little, and raised his eyebrows at me.

It was the perfect moment to be bold. "But I want someone to get me."

Mr. Larson placed my hand on the bar, carefully. I wondered if he had picked up on it, the pulse of every last nerve he had hit. "That's a two-part deal, Tif. You have to let yourself be got."

I leaned my head on my hand. Spoke the line I'd rehearsed in my head so many times ever since our meet-cute. "Mr. Larson," I said, "you really don't want to call me Ani, do you?"

"Is this your way of asking if you can call me Andrew?" His lip curled into the arch that's always there whenever I picture him at the front of the classroom. This man really could not be hustled, and I was inflamed with a need for him, as basic and savage as thirst. "Because you can."

Andrew's shirt pocket suddenly lit up bright like Iron Man's heart. He removed his phone, and I caught "Whit" on the screen. The absence of the last three letters of her name read like a betrayal. "Sorry," he said. "I'm meeting my wife for dinner after this. I didn't realize the time."

Well, of fucking course he's meeting his wife for dinner after this, Ani. What did you think? That the two of you were going to declare your true love for each other at a soulless, charmless wine bar in Flatiron and go and get a hotel room? You're disgusting.

"I just want to tell you something quickly," I said, and it dragged Andrew's eyes away from his phone, at least. "Something I've wanted to say for a long time. I'm really sorry. About what happened in Headmaster Mah's office. How I backed out on you like that."

"You don't have to apologize, Tif."

"Ani" wasn't going to stick with him, but I didn't mind it. "I do, though. And I never told you this, but"—I hung my head—"I spoke to Dean on the phone that morning at your place. When you ran out to CVS."

Andrew sat on that for a moment. "But, how did he know you were at my apartment?"

"He didn't." I explained how I called home to tell my parents I was on my way, how I found out Dean was trying to track me down. "I actually thought I could go in to school on Monday and everything would be okay." I snorted scornfully. "God, I was an idiot."

"Dean was the idiot." Andrew placed his phone on the bar top and steadied his eyes on me. "It was all Dean's fault. Never yours."

"And I let him get away with it." I released a disgusted breath. "Because I was scared I wouldn't be popular anymore if I didn't. I'm so *mad* at myself for that." In college, when rumors swirled that some freshman had been taken advantage of by some lacrosse player, I'd found myself furious with her for not reporting him. *Don't just let them get away with it!* I'd wanted to scream, standing next to her in line for the salad bar. But then something about the way she piled the cauliflower florets on top of her salad—no one ever put cauliflower in her salad—swung like a wrecking ball at my heart. Made me wonder if that had been her favorite vegetable as a child, if her mom cooked it especially for her even though her brothers and sisters groaned their hatred for cauliflower. I wanted to reach out and wrap my arms around her from behind, press my face into her soapy-smelling blond hair, say, "I know."

Because I couldn't do it either. Mr. Larson had poked

his floppy-haired head into Headmaster Mah's office first thing Monday morning, like we planned, and told him there had been another issue with Dean Barton and also with the new student Liam Ross. I didn't even make it to homeroom. Mrs. Dern found me in the hallway and said I was needed in Headmaster Mah's office immediately. I trudged past the Junior and Senior Lounge, through the cafeteria yawning with the few students who relied on it for breakfast, and up the stairs to the administration wing. Mr. Larson was standing in the corner of Mah's office, politely leaving the one lone seat open for me. I refused to look at him; I could just feel the expectation of his encouraging smile. As I denied everything, the only place I could stand to look was at my Steve Madden clogs, the soles ringed white with rainwater. I wondered if Mom knew how to get that out.

"So you don't have an incident to report?" Headmaster Mah practically panted, not even bothering to hide his relief. The Bartons had financed the new addition to the cafeteria, after all.

I smiled and said I didn't. The cut on my face was just barely covered in concealer. Headmaster Mah noticed it and did a poor job of pretending not to.

"What happened?" Mr. Larson demanded in the hallway.

"Can we just let it go?" I pleaded. I didn't stop walking. I could tell he wanted to put his hand on my arm and stop me, but we both knew he couldn't. I walked faster, trying to escape his disappointment. It filled up the hallway like cheap cologne.

Now, all these years later, Andrew examined me like you would a new freckle on your chest. When did that appear, exactly? Could it be dangerous? "You need to give yourself some more credit, Tif," he said. "You were just trying to get through." Under the smooth bar lights, I could not detect a single flaw in his wide, handsome face. "You made something out of yourself, and you did it *honestly*. Unlike some people we know."

I seethed, "Dean," even though sometimes I think we're more similar than I'd like to admit.

We sat in a dreamy silence for a few moments, the lights softening all our edges, filling in our holes. I watched, out of the corner of my eye, as the bartender noticed us again. Tried to will him away, but he asked, "Can I get you anything else?"

Andrew reached into his pants pocket. "Just the bill." My new martini glimmered at me, mockingly.

"Maybe we can get lunch or something?" I tried. "When we're both in town that weekend."

Andrew found the card he was looking for and passed it across the bar. He smiled at me. "I'd like that."

I smiled too. "Thanks for getting this."

"I'm sorry I can't stay for another." Andrew shook his watch free of his sleeve and raised his eyebrows at it. "I'm really pushing it here."

"It's cool, I'll just sit here, drinking alone"—I sighed majestically—"enjoying people staring at me and wondering who I am and what I do."

Mr. Larson laughed. "So I got a little saccharine. I'm proud of you, Tif."

The windshield cracked a little deeper.

❧

The bedroom door was shut, a shard of dark running parallel to the floor. Luke must have gone to bed early. I peeled off my leather dress and stood over the AC unit for a few moments.

I washed my face and brushed my teeth. Locked the door and turned off the lights. I left my clothes on the couch and crept into the bedroom in my bra and underwear—I had worn the nice ones. In case.

Luke stirred as I opened a drawer.

"Hi," he whispered.

"Hi." I unclasped my bra and let it fall to the floor. Luke used to tell me to just come to bed after I'd done that, but he didn't anymore. I slipped into boxer shorts and a tank top.

I climbed underneath the covers. The air in the room was arctic and artificial, the window unit growling aggressively in the corner. The lights were off, but everything was visible thanks to the residual lights of the Freedom Tower, the Patrick Batemans cursing off their computers at Goldman Sachs's sprawling headquarters, and I could see Luke's eyes were open. You can't find a pitch-black room in New York, another reason I love it here—the light from the outside world streaming in at all hours, assuring me there is someone awake, someone who could help me if something bad were to happen.

"Did you get what you want?" Luke asked, his voice flat as the running path along the West Side Highway.

I chose my words carefully. "It was good to talk to him."

Luke rolled over, his back a judgment passed on me. "I'm going to be so glad when this whole thing is over and everything can go back to normal."

I know the normal Luke misses, I know the Ani he wants to come to bed. It's the Ani after a night at the Chicken Box, the Nantucket bar famous for its long line of shivering girls in Easter-egg-colored Calypso shift dresses.

There is a bartender there, Lezzie. Her name is really Liz, but when you resemble a younger, only slightly thinner Delta Burke, dress in camo, and sport a ring through the fleshy partition of your nostrils, douche bag blue bloods think it's Louis C.K. levels of comedy genius to nickname you Lezzie.

Luke's friends' wives get all twitchy and uncomfortable around Lezzie, but not me. It's become the running joke in our group—send Ani up to get the drinks, she'll come back with at least one free Life Is Good (a disgusting combination of raspberry vodka, Sprite, cranberry juice, and Red Bull) because Lezzie loves her. Luke loves her too—inasmuch as she exposes the vast difference between me and the other girls, with their swollen pearl earrings and Patagonia fleeces, pretty but smugly sexless. Luke got the girl who doesn't squirm in the presence of a tough box muncher, the girl who actually gets a kick out of flirting with her.

"It's my little Ani Lennox," Lezzie says whenever she sees me. "How many diets?"

I'll hold up my fingers to indicate the number of girls who want their Life Is Goods with diet Sprite and light Red Bull, and Lezzie will laugh knowingly and say, "Coming right up."

While Lezzie assembles the drinks, Luke's nose will brush the humid clump of my hair, and close to my ear he'll ask, "Why does she call you Ani Lennox again?"

And I always tilt my head, giving him more of my neck as I say, "Because Annie Lennox is gay. And if I'm gay then she can fuck me."

By the time Lezzie puts the cocktails on the bar, Luke is hard in his Nantucket red shorts, and I have to strategically walk in front of him as we carry the drinks over to the Booths and Griers and Kinseys.

"Ones with lemons are diet," I say to the girls, the lie bringing a sadistic smile to my face. Lezzie loves to serve "diet" calorie bombs to high-maintenance bitches in size twenty-six white jeans.

We slurp a few down, enough to take the bite out of the air outside. Nantucket can get down to fifty, even forty degrees when the sun drops out of the sky, even in the fiercest crush of summer. Then we call up a cab and make our way back to the Harrison estate, where there are enough bedrooms to sleep the entire graduating class of Luke's fraternity. Some people stay up to smoke pot, play beer pong, or microwave odd drunk person food combinations in the kitchen, but not me and Luke. No, we always go right to bed, my dress bunched around my waist before we even mangle the sheets. We decided long ago that I would always wear a dress to the Chicken Box, no matter how cold it is outside. Makes for easy access once we get home.

I'm always fascinated by Luke's face as he grunts above me, the veins that appear, the way the blood rushes to his cheeks, filling in the spaces between his freckles so that it appears he has none at all. He never tries to make me come on these nights—it's like he's decided this ritual is purely for him—but I always do anyway. And that's because I'm remembering the night, almost two years ago now, when Lezzie followed me into the bathroom and backed me into the wall, her lips surprisingly delicate and nervous on mine. The way she pushed her meaty thigh between my legs as I started to kiss her back, giving me something to press into, a place to dull the ache.

I debated telling Luke about it. Not because it was the

right thing to do or any self-righteous bullshit like that, but because I couldn't decide—would he be turned on? Or disgusted? Finding the freak sweet spot, that's always been the perennial struggle with Luke.

Ultimately I decided against it. Maybe I would have told if Lezzie looked more like Kate Upton, maybe if she hadn't chosen to kiss me right around the time I began to spoil like a forgotten carton of milk in the back of the refrigerator.

Still, I'm right there with Luke when he squeezes his eyes shut and howls his final call. I like when a guy stays inside of me after, but Luke shrivels up fast. Rolls on his back and gasps how much he fucking loves me.

I may never fully make my way out of the bourgey pit, but that doesn't mean I'm not a trophy wife too. I'm just a different kind.

CHAPTER 10

I felt very still and purposeful after I'd been excused from Headmaster Mah's office. I may have let Mr. Larson down like he would never let me down, but I couldn't dwell on that now because the next step was clear. Get to Olivia. Apologize for causing a scene and getting her into trouble at home. Do whatever was necessary to get back into her good graces. I felt this was possible because it served Dean's interests to keep me happy. Olivia would follow Dean's lead, I was sure of it.

I tried to track her down before lunch. Looked under the door of her favorite bathroom stall, even. But no luck. My next opportunity was lunch. Which meant I had to get to her before the others sat down, which would be easy because Olivia was usually the first person holding court at the table on account of the fact that she never walked the lunch line. I found her in her usual seat, performing her favorite disordered ritual: shredding a Swedish fish apart at the tail, rolling the pieces into balls before popping them in her mouth. A half-moon bruise saddled the right corner of her mouth, and I felt sick. I wish I could say it was because the thought of what her father did to her roiled my stomach, but I was fourteen and selfish. That bruise was my funeral.

"Liv," I said, hoping the sound of her nickname would soften her to me.

"Huh?" she asked, as though she'd thought someone had said her name but she wasn't sure. I sat down next to her.

"I'm so sorry about Saturday." I remembered what Dean said to me and added, "I should never smoke after I drink. It makes me so fucked up."

Olivia turned toward me and gave me a smile so eerie, so detached from human emotion that I still sometimes start awake in the middle of the night, haunted by the memory. "I'm fine." She pointed at my cheek, at the cut covered clumsily with concealer. "We're twins."

"There you fucking are, Finny." Dean was next to me, holding a lunch tray overflowing with sandwiches and chips and soda. He slammed it down next to me. "What the fuck? I thought we had a deal?"

I said I didn't understand.

"I just came from fucking Mah's office," he said. Then announced, loudly, to the group gathering at the table, that he had gotten a warning about an "incident" that had occurred over the weekend and that he might not be able to play in the big Haverford game this week. This aroused a scandalized gasp from all.

"That's fucking bullshit," Peyton fumed, and Liam nodded ferociously even though he didn't play soccer.

"Well," Dean mumbled. "I can play if nothing else happens between now and then."

(I always wished I'd said, *Then, just don't rape anyone in the next two days.*)

Dean gave me a withering look. "I thought we were cool?"

"It wasn't me," I whimpered.

"So you *weren't* in his office earlier this morning?" Dean demanded.

"I was, but I didn't go there on my own," I said. "Mr. Larson and him called me in. I didn't have a choice!"

Dean narrowed his beady eyes at me. "But how did they know to call you in if you didn't *say* anything?"

"I don't know," I said, lamely. "I think they just assumed."

"Assumed what?" Dean's chest heaved with a mean laugh. "They're not fucking David Copperfield fucking mind readers." Dean crossed his arms over his chest to the chorus of group laughter. It was something I would have joined in on if the barb hadn't been directed at me. There was something so bizarrely charming in the fact that Dean knew who David Copperfield was, referenced him like that. "Just get out of here, TifAni. Go bite Mr. Larson's dick or something."

I looked around the table. At the smirks on Olivia, Liam, and Peyton. Hilary didn't do that to me, but she didn't look at me either.

I turned and walked out of the new cafeteria, beneath the plaque on the last beam that bragged, THE BARTON FAMILY, 1998.

I thought Mr. Larson would take it easy on me at practice later that day, after all I'd been through, but he was more ferocious than ever. I was the only one who couldn't complete the mile test in under seven minutes and thirty seconds, and everyone had to run laps because of me. I hated him. Walked out on final stretch even though Mr. Larson once proliferated that old wives' tale that our muscles would get bulky if we didn't stretch them taffy thin after we ran. He called at me to come back, but I just said my mom was picking me up early and I had to go.

I usually took the train home from school, but that day Mom was picking me up so we could shop the presale at Bloomingdale's in the King of Prussia Mall.

I never used the showers in the locker room after practice. No one did. They were gross. But that day I had to make an exception because I didn't want to spend the next few hours shivering in my sweaty clothes while trying on wool peacoats. I quickly washed up under the water, which smelled neglected, like it had been sitting in the pipes since the place was a boarding school. Wrapped in a towel, I walked to my locker on the sides of my feet, trying to limit the amount of skin the gummy floor could contact. As I rounded the corner, Hilary and Olivia came into view. Neither of them played a sport or had to take PE, and I'd never seen them in the locker room before.

"What are you guys doing?" I asked.

"Hey!" Hilary said, her odd throaty voice peppier than usual. She'd thrown her hair into a high half loop since I'd seen her in Chem. One strand of bleached berry blond hair escaped, so brittle and overprocessed it pointed straight up in the air, a sharp spoke in her crown. "We were looking for you."

"You were?" My voice went up.

"Yeah," Olivia chimed in. Under the sallow laboratory-like lights, her nose appeared seeded with tiny black kernels. "What are, um. What are you doing tonight?"

Anything you ask me to. "I'm supposed to go shopping

with my mom. But I can do it another night if something is going on."

"No." Olivia glanced at Hilary, nervously. "It's fine, we can do it another time." She started to walk away, and I panicked.

"No, really," I called after her. "It's not a big deal. I can just tell my mom we'll do it another night."

"Don't worry about it, Tif." Hilary turned, her profile practically samurai. There was something like remorse in her alien eyes. "Another time."

They hurried away. Damnit. I'd been too eager. I'd scared them off. I pulled my clothes on angrily, fought a brush through my wet hair.

I was sitting on the curb outside the gym, waiting for Mom, when Arthur dropped his book bag on the ground next to my feet and sat down. "Hey."

"Hi," I said, almost shyly. It'd been a while since we'd spoken.

"You okay?"

I nodded, and I meant it. That interaction with Olivia and Hilary had revitalized me. There was a chance still.

"Really?" Arthur glanced up at the sun, his eyes turning to slits behind his glasses, the lenses smudged sloppily but somehow with intent, like graffiti on an abandoned building wall. "Because I heard what happened."

I twisted my head to look at him. "What did you hear?"

"Well." He shrugged. "I mean *everyone* already knows about the party at Dean's house. What happened with Liam. And Peyton. And Dean."

"Thanks for listing them all like that," I muttered sullenly.

"And the morning-after pill," he added.

"Jesus Christ," I groaned.

"They all think you busted up Olivia's party because you were jealous she and Liam were hooking up."

"People think that?" I buried my head between my knees, strands of wet hair sliding over my arms, snakelike.

"Is it true?" Arthur asked.

"Don't people wonder how I got this?" I pointed at my cheek, which I hadn't even bothered to cover up with concealer after my shower.

Arthur shrugged. "You fell?"

"Yeah." I snorted. "And Dean caught me."

I spotted Mom's red BMW pulling into the drive. It stood out like a sore thumb among the somber black and tan sedans and SUVs. Of course TifAni FaNelli's mother drove a whore red car, her skank was genetic.

"I have to go," I said to Arthur.

❧

The morning arrived, brittle and bright. Fall in earnest, and I excitedly strapped myself into the new black peacoat Mom had bought me the night before. I'd found it at Banana Republic, and it wasn't on sale like the ones at Bloomingdale's. But Mom said I looked so sharp that she would get it for me anyway. She had to split the purchase between a credit card and cash and then told me not to tell Daddy. God, it grossed me out when she called him Daddy.

On the train ride to school, hope was still a fat shiny balloon in my chest. Hilary and Olivia weren't done with me yet. The air held a new charge, and I looked "sharp."

When I walked into school, I felt something else. A pulse. The hallways pumping, alive with it. That morning, a small crowd of freshmen and sophomores, outcast upperclassmen, clumped together at the entrance, rubber-necking something epic. I neared the Junior and Senior Lounge, a place where only juniors and seniors were allowed, a deadly serious rule that even parents and teachers respected. They'd hover in the doorway, calling the name of the student they were looking for rather than step inside and see for themselves.

This time, when I approached, the crowd did part. A wide berth that formed in slow-motion-movie time.

"Oh my God," said Allison Calhoun, another freshman who'd snubbed me on my first day but started kissing my ass when she saw that Olivia and Hilary had taken me on. She giggled maliciously into her hand.

When I fought my way to the lounge's state line, I discovered what had drawn the crowd. My running shorts—the ones I'd worn yesterday for practice—were tacked to the bulletin board on the far wall beneath a handwritten sign that read, SNIFF A SKANK (AT YOUR OWN RISK . . . SHE STANKS!). The words were written in bright bubble letters, their color and shape as happy as a message for a bake sale to raise money for kids with cancer. Only a girl could have written them. A realization hardened in me as I remembered Hilary and Olivia, acting so oddly nice in the locker room the day before.

I pushed back out of the crowd the same way I came in. There was a bathroom right across the way, and I locked myself into a stall, remembering how I'd gotten my period yesterday, had been so relieved when it arrived because it meant the morning-after pill had worked. The run had jogged it all loose. When I'd taken off the shorts, they'd been stained a brownish red. I couldn't even imagine how dirty and gross they looked, how the terrible combination of sweat and period blood must smell. I'd been so distracted by Hilary's and Olivia's sudden kindness I hadn't even noticed the shorts were missing when I packed my bag.

The door opened and I heard the tail end of a spirited debate: "Deserves it."

"C'mon, it's pretty mean, don't you think?"

Silently, I climbed on top of the toilet, tucking my legs underneath me.

"Dean takes it too far," another said. "It's all fun and games until she tries to kill herself like Ben."

"Ben can't help being gay," the first girl said. "She can help being a whore."

Her friend laughed, and I swallowed a thick sob. I heard the water run and the sound of paper towels crunching in their hands. Then the door yawning shut behind them.

I had never cut school in my entire life. I can't even call in sick to work now, all that good Catholic girl obedience milled into my bones, but the day had broken me, bulldozed any fear about what might happen if I didn't follow the rules. All that mattered was honoring the humiliation, so crushing, it left me short of breath. I waited right where I was, working a section of hair between my fingers over and over ("self-soothing behavior" according to *The Women's Magazine*'s body language expert), until the first-period bell stopped ringing. I gave it another five minutes to ensure I wouldn't run into any stragglers in the hallways. Then I climbed off the toilet seat, silent as Spider-Man, pushed open the door to the bathroom, and walked briskly down the hallway and out the back entrance. I'd take the train to Thirtieth Street Station. Wander around the city for the day. I was halfway out the parking lot when I heard someone calling my name behind me. It was Arthur.

"I think we have some leftover lasagna in here." Arthur peered into the refrigerator, buzzing noisily.

I glanced at the display on the stove: 10:15. "I'm fine."

Arthur bumped the door shut with his hip, a casserole dish in his hands, the top crusted yellow with cheese. He cut a generous slice and slid the plate into the microwave.

"Oh." He licked tomato sauce off his finger and dropped to his heels, rummaging around in his backpack. "Here." He flung my shorts at me.

They were light as paper, but when they landed in my lap I emitted a baritone "oof" as though someone had kicked me in the stomach.

"How did you get these?" I smoothed them out on my lap like a dinner napkin.

"They're not the fucking *Mona Lisa*," he said.

"What does that mean?'

Arthur zipped his backpack shut and rolled his eyes at me. "Haven't you ever been to the Louvre?"

"What's the Louvre?"

Arthur laughed. "Oh, dear."

The microwave beeped, and Arthur got up to test his dish. With his back to me, I took a quick whiff of my shorts. I had to know what everyone else had smelled.

It was bad. The odor was sharp, primeval, inhabited your lungs like a disease. I stuffed the damp mesh ball into my backpack and propped my head on one hand, the tears snaking a silent, diagonal path across my nose.

Arthur sat down across from me, letting me cry while he shoveled piles of steaming red-sauced meat into his mouth. Between bites he said, "When I'm done with this

I'm going to show you something that's going to make you feel a lot better."

Arthur polished off the loaf of lasagna in minutes. He took his plate to the sink and dropped it in there, not even bothering to rinse it. With a little wave of his hand, he started for the door in the corner of the kitchen. I'd assumed it was a door to a pantry or closet, but Arthur opened it to reveal a cold black rectangle. I'd later discover that Arthur's old house had no shortage of doors—leading to back stairwells; closets; rooms mountained with books and papers, lumpy, floral-print couches sagging in the corners. At one point, Arthur's mother's side of the family had money, but it was so tied up in trusts, complicated legal decisions made of their past, that no one would ever spend it. Mr. Finnerman had walked out on Arthur and his mom eight years earlier, which had destroyed Mrs. Finnerman but which she tries to pretend didn't. "Just one less mouth to feed!" she's fond of saying whenever she's feeling pitied. Mrs. Finnerman had gotten a job at Bradley not long after Arthur was born, knowing Mr. Finnerman was never going to wake up before noon, would never pull his own weight, that her position would ensure her son a spot, and a break, financially. Not everyone is flush on the Main Line, but the priorities are certainly different than the kind I'd grown up with. Education, travel, culture—this is what any pennies pinched should be used for, never flashy cars, loud logos, or personal maintenance.

Still, on the Main Line, coming from a family that used to have money was infinitely more acceptable than coming from a family with money that was new as could be. It was part of the reason Arthur despised Dean. Arthur had property that would yield a much higher return than the latest Mercedes S-Class: He had knowledge. He knew mysterious things like to pass the salt and pepper together and that steak should always be cooked medium rare. He knew Times Square was the most despicable place on earth and that Paris was divided into twenty arrondisse-ments. Soon enough, with his connections and his grades, he would be accepted into Columbia, where his mother's side had legacy.

His hand on the doorknob, he turned to me. "You coming?"

Closer, I made out a few dingy steps before the dark swallowed them whole. I'd always hated the dark. I still went to bed with the hallway light on.

Arthur patted along the wall until he found the light switch, and one lone bulb shuddered on. A cloud of dust puffed up beneath his foot with his first step. He'd kicked off his shoes when we first walked into his house, and his feet were swollen, the skin ripe and shiny like a baby's.

"This is not what my basement looks like," I said, trail-ing not far behind. The floor was gray concrete, the walls ripped open, orange fluffy innards exposed. An army of clutter anchored one side of the basement—discarded furniture, boxes of scratched records, dusty paperbacks, old *New Yorkers* slumping with mildew.

"Let me guess." Arthur grinned at me over his shoul-der. Beneath the jaundiced bulb, his acne purpled. "It has *carpeting.*"

"Yeah, so?" Arthur continued toward the mess against the far wall and didn't answer. I made my voice carry across the room. "What's wrong with carpeting?"

"It's *tacky*," he declared, wading through the boxes. For the rest of my life, I would live only in places with hard-wood floors.

Arthur squatted to the ground, so that for a moment I

could see only the greasy swell of his hair. "Oh my God"—then came his laugh—"look at this." When he stood he was holding a dead deer head high in the air, like a sacrifice.

I wrinkled my nose. "Please tell me that isn't real."

Arthur stared into the animal's gentle eyes for a moment, as if trying to decide. "Of course it's real," he concluded. "My dad hunts."

"I don't agree with hunting," I said, tartly.

"But you agree with hamburgers." Arthur dumped the deer into an open box. One sculptural antler curled into the air, a bony beanstalk that led to nowhere. "You just let other people do your dirty work."

I folded my arms across my chest. I meant I didn't agree with hunting for *sport*, but I didn't want to argue with him and prolong this little field trip. We'd been downstairs just a few minutes, and already I felt pruney and cold, like skin that's been resting for hours underneath a damp bathing suit. "What do you want to show me?" I pushed.

Arthur doubled over, digging through another box, examining whatever he exhumed and tossing it aside when he determined it wasn't what he was looking for. "Aha!" He held up what looked like an encyclopedia and waved me over. I sighed and followed the path he'd forged through the junkyard, realizing once I was by his side that it was a yearbook he had in his hands.

Arthur flipped to the back inside cover, tilting the page so I could read the note next to his pink fingertip.

Art-man,
    I'm not going to get all gay and shit and tell you what a good friend you are, so fuck off!

                                                    Bart-man

I read the note three times before I understood. Bart-man was Dean, a play on his last name, Barton. "What year was this?"

"Nineteen ninety-nine." Arthur licked his fingertip and began to turn the pages. "Sixth grade."

"And you were *friends* with Dean?"

"He was my best bestie friend." Arthur giggled nastily. "Look." He stopped on a collage of candids. Students joking around at lunch, making funny faces on Super Saturday, posing with a giant green dragon, the Bradley mascot. There was a photo in the lower-left-hand corner, fuzzy in the way all photos appear after a few years, so that our past selves seem quaint and old world, and we realize, a little disdainfully even, all we know now that we didn't then. Arthur and Dean were winter white, their crackled smiles in desperate need of a swipe of Chap Stick. Arthur was a hefty kid, though nothing like he was hulking next to me now. But Dean. He was so puny, his arm around Arthur's bulldog neck so slight and fragile, he could have been someone's kid brother.

"That was right before the summer he had his growth spurt," Arthur explained. "He got big and turned into an asshole."

"I just can't believe you were ever friends." I brought my face closer to the yearbook page and squinted. I wondered if girls at Mt. St. Theresa's upper school said that to Leah now. I just can't believe you were ever friends with *TifAni*. They'd laugh their disbelief—*that's a compliment, Leah*. If they weren't saying it now, they would be soon.

Arthur snapped the yearbook shut, nearly nipping my nose. I let out a soft yelp, startled. "So don't act like you're the first to encounter the wrath of Dean Barton." He thumbed the cover's heavy gold font thoughtfully. "He will do anything to make people forget that he used to sleep over at the fag's house."

He tucked the yearbook under his arm. I thought we would go then, but something in the corner caught his attention. He pushed deeper through the boxes and stooped, trading the yearbook for his new discovery. His back was to me so that I didn't see what he had in his hands at first, just heard his giddy little laugh. When he turned, the body of a long, lithe rifle pointed at me. He brought the gun closer to his face, resting his fleshy cheek against the handle and hooking his finger around the trigger.

"Arthur!" I shrieked, stumbling back. I lost my balance, and my hand came down hard on an old swimming trophy. It was my bad wrist, the one I'd landed on when Dean slapped me, and I bellowed something incoherent.

"Oh my God!" Arthur doubled over with fierce, silent laughter, leaning on the rifle like a cane. "Relax"—he gasped, his face flushed a furious red—"it's not loaded."

"You're really not funny." I hobbled to my feet and squeezed my wrist, trying to blunt the pain.

Arthur wiped his eyes and sighed, exorcising the last ripples of his laughing fit. I glared at him, and he rolled his eyes mockingly. "Seriously"—he flipped his grip, holding the rifle by its muzzle and extending it to me—"it's not loaded."

I released my wrist reluctantly, taking the handle, a little slick from Arthur's grasp. For a moment we were both holding it, a pair of track runners caught on camera passing the baton. Then Arthur let go and the rifle's full weight was in one hand. It was heavier than I realized, and the barrel swung to the ground, scraping the concrete floor. I slipped my other hand under its cool belly and hoisted it upright again. "Why would your dad leave this here?"

Arthur stared at the steel nose of the gun, his glasses foggy and smudged in the trembling light. I almost snapped my fingers, yodeled, "Anyone home?" but in an instant he jutted out his hip and made his wrist go limp. "Why," he said, his voice gone light as a feather, "to make a man out of me, silly." He lisped the last word, "sthilly," popped his hip more, and I laughed, not sure what the appropriate reaction was, only that laughing was what he wanted from me.

It was nearly November when the temperature turned on us, drove out the last lingering warm pockets of summer. Even so, drops of perspiration roiled beneath my sports bra as I rang Arthur's doorbell. The assistant girls' field hockey coach, who had been subbing for Mr. Larson for weeks, had no idea what she was doing and just told us to run five miles every day. Anything to get rid of us for an hour so she could flirt with the Bradley athletic director, who was married with two kids in the lower school. I'd taken to cutting through the woods and smoking at Arthur's for miles three through five. Either Coach Bethany didn't notice that I didn't come back with the rest of the team or she didn't care. I'm thinking the latter.

Arthur cracked open the door just enough to wedge a square of his face in the frame, a pimpled Jack Nicholson in *The Shining*.

"Oh, it's you," he said.

"Who else would it be?" I'd been coming by after cross-country practice for the last few weeks, ever since the day I cut class. The school caught me, no big surprise, and Mom and Dad grounded me, also no big surprise. When my parents asked why I did it, what was "so important" that I had to leave school grounds in the middle of the day, I told them I'd had a craving for the penne alla vodka slice at Peace A Pizza. "A craving?" Mom shrilled. "What are you, pregnant?" The corners of her face slouched in as she realized high schoolers get pregnant all the time and how humiliating it would be for her to have to take her fourteen-year-old daughter shopping at A Pea in the Pod.

"Mom!" I huffed, indignant even though I had no right to be. She hadn't hit that far from the mark.

I think Bradley suspected something had happened in the lounge that day, something that had violated the Bradley code of moral excellence, but Arthur had removed my shorts before they figured out exactly what, and I certainly wasn't going to be the one to tell them.

Worse than the sudden drop in my stock—Mr. Larson was gone, without explanation. "He's left us to embrace a new opportunity" was all the administration would say. I confided in Arthur, only Arthur, about the night I spent at Mr. Larson's house. His eyes bulged behind his filthy glasses when I told him how we'd slept in the same room. "Holy shit!" Arthur gasped. "Did you have sex with him?"

I gave him a disgusted look, at which Arthur laughed. "I'm just kidding. He has a girlfriend. A hot one. I heard she models for Abercrombie & Fitch."

"Who told you that?" I snapped, instantly feeling thick and squat, a fat little loser Mr. Larson took pity on once.

Arthur shrugged. "That's just what everyone says."

Even though I was grounded, my parents had only a vague sense of when cross-country practice ended, so I could easily hang out with Arthur most days. For the first time, I was grateful I lived so far away that I had to take the train home. "Sometimes practice is an hour and a half, other times two," I told Mom. "It depends on the mileage of the day." She took me at my word, and so all I had to do was call her from the germy pay phone at the Bryn Mawr station and say, "Getting on the six thirty-seven." By then, practice had been long over and the initial blast of my high had mellowed into thick, warm sludge. I'd place the phone in the receiver, watch the creaky 6:37 come to a stop with an exhausted white puff. Either I was moving more slowly or everything else just appeared to be.

Arthur's eyes darted over my shoulder, to the squash courts behind me and the parking lot behind that, nannies waiting to pick up kids from practice, their beat-up Hondas pulsing with a commercial-free stretch of Y100. "People have been coming by, ringing the doorbell, and running away."

"Who?" I asked, feeling sick.

"Who do you think?" He looked at me accusingly, like I'd brought them to his door.

"Can you just let me in already?" One quivering bead of sweat escaped my sports bra. Took its time snaking into my underwear.

Arthur swung open the door, and I ducked in underneath his arm.

I followed Arthur up the stairs, three flights that moaned noisily beneath our weight. He had moved out of his bedroom and into the attic over the summer, he'd explained to me the first time he brought me up there. "Why?" I'd glanced around the bare-bones room uneasily, rubbing away the goose bumps on my arms. There was no insulation in the walls, and as a bedroom it felt makeshift, vulnerable. Nothing homey about it. Arthur had stuck his hand out the window and tapped the crusty belly of the pipe against the ledge. Some black ashes fluttered away, like charred snowflakes. "Privacy," he'd said.

He'd taken very few possessions with him when he moved, even his clothes remained in his old bedroom, so that every morning before school he used it as a sort of dressing quarters. But one very important object had made the journey north with him, was granted a prime position on a stack of textbooks that served as his night-stand: a picture of him as a child with his father. It was summer, and they were at the shore, laughing and looking out at the mucky brown ocean. Someone had glued pastel-colored seashells all over the picture frame. I'd picked it up once, quipped, "This looks like a kindergartner's arts and crafts project," and Arthur had snatched it back. "My mom made it for me. Don't touch it."

Beneath this cherished picture was the Bradley middle school yearbook, which played an integral role in one of our new favorite pastimes: defacing the class pictures of the HOs and the Hairy Legs. It was more fun to destroy them in their middle school form—braces, frizzy hair, lanky limbed, and ugly.

We would do this after we'd smoked and stumbled down the stairs, jelly legged and giggly, to raid the kitchen. Mrs. Finnerman held office hours in her classroom until five, then stayed another hour or two to catch up on paper-work, so the place was ours until then. It was the perfect arrangement she didn't know about.

Some people lose weight, can't eat, when they're stressed. I thought I'd be one of those when everything first happened, but once the acid-flavored anxiety of what would become of me dissolved to reveal what *had* become of me, the hot new girl already washed up seven weeks into the semester, food had never tasted so good.

Arthur had figured this out years ago, and he was an enthusiastic partner in crime. Together, we came up with all kinds of concoctions to feed our emotional voids—nuke Nutella and it becomes a hard chocolate cookie. This was pre-Nutella ubiquity, and I'd asked, "What the hell is this?" when I first came across it in the cabinet. "Some weird European shit," Arthur had said and shrugged, and I'd made a face at it, impressed. Or we'd plop a roll of cookie dough on a baking sheet and shove it in the oven without even breaking it up, roasting it as a log until the outer ends were golden and the inside was raw, eggy mush that we ate with a spoon. All the clothes Mom had bought me at the beginning of the semester were rebelling against me, the opening of my khakis spread like my legs with Peyton's head between them, refusing to close no matter how hard I ran.

Today, after we clattered down the stairs into the kitchen, the yearbook tucked underneath Arthur's arm like my future mother-in-law's vintage Chanel clutch, Arthur announced that he wanted nachos. He held the doors to the kitchen cabinets out wide, a conductor directing his symphony.

"You're a genius," I said, the corners of my mouth pinching hungrily.

"You mean a genachos." Arthur gave me a sassy look over his shoulder, and I laughed so hard my knees buckled. Then I was lying on the tiles of his old kitchen, tiles Mom would have called "fuddy-duddy." The word "fuddy-duddy" made my sides itch even harder with laughter.

"TifAni, come on," Arthur scolded. "You don't have much time." He pointed at the display on the stove. It was 5:50.

The thought of not getting my fix centered me. I

climbed to my feet and began to pull toppings from the fridge—a shiny block of orange cheese, blood-red salsa, a watery container of sour cream.

We arranged our nachos in silence, stoned and sloppily dressing the chips. We took the plate to the linoleum breakfast table and sat, still not speaking, too competitive for the chips with the most cheese. When not one tortilla crumb remained, Arthur got up from the table and retrieved a gallon of mint chocolate chip ice cream from the freezer. He found two spoons, staked them through the pastel surface, and placed the carton on the table between us.

"I'm so fat," I moaned, exhuming a large chunk of chocolate.

"Who cares." Arthur stuck his spoon in his mouth, pulling it out slowly, sucking all the meat off the bone.

"I bumped into Dean in the hallway today. He said, 'You really are a wide load, aren't you?'" I liked the ice cream in the corners best. It melted first, obeyed when I coaxed it around the edge of the carton.

"Fucking rich white trash." Arthur stabbed the ice cream with his spoon. "You don't even know the half of it."

I tongued a back molar, chiseling away its thin chocolate coating. "What don't I know?"

Arthur furrowed his eyebrows at the ice cream. "Nothing. Never mind."

"Okay"—I stopped eating for a moment—"*now* you have to tell me."

"Trust me." Arthur dropped his chin to peer at me over his glasses, and an extra layer of skin gathered in his neck. "You don't want to know."

"Arthur!" I demanded.

Arthur sighed heavily, like he was sorry he ever brought it up, but I knew he wasn't. The more sacred a piece of information, the more desperate the gatekeeper is to reveal it, the harder you have to work to relieve her of the burden. That way she doesn't feel horribly guilty about betraying confidences—what could she do? She was browbeaten into it! I say "she" because it's an inherently feminine game, and when I look back on all of this now, at the way Arthur was a natural at navigating the ball on the field, I realize it's much more telling of his sexuality that his own declarations so theatrical, so over the top, that I could never figure out if he was just messing with everyone. Playing the role assigned to him, and brilliantly.

"I think I deserve to know," I said, my voice full of meaning. "Of all people."

Arthur held up his hands, the universal "stop" sign. *He couldn't take it anymore!* "Okay," he acquiesced. He speared his spoon in the ice cream and flattened his hands on the table, considering how to tell me what he was about to tell me. "There was this kid. Ben Hunter."

I remembered the name from the night of the Fall Friday Dance, when I'd snuck away with the HOs and the Hairy Legs to watch them all drink at the Spot. Olivia's gleeful disgust over seeing Arthur giving Ben a blow job, Peyton's addendum that Ben had tried to kill himself, his mean conclusion that he hadn't succeeded. I never really believed the first part of the story, it reeked of an Olivia lie, told to assemble a curious crowd with her in the center. Even so, something stopped me from telling Arthur what I knew. There was a small part of me that believed it could be true, and didn't want to know if it was. I couldn't stand the idea that Arthur had been on his knees in the Spot, weirdo number one sucking weirdo number two's dick. Arthur was my intellectual compass, not another raging, lusty animal in heat. Not like me.

I pretended I'd never heard the name Ben Hunter before. "Who is he?"

"Dean made him kill himself. Well"—Arthur pushed his glasses further up his nose, adding another fingerprint to the left lens—"try to kill himself, at least."

I abandoned my spoon in the ice cream, so warm and gooey now the handle sunk, slowly, as the green quicksand absorbed the tip. "How? How do you make someone try and kill themselves?"

Arthur's eyes went dull. "You torture them for years and then you degrade them by—" He grimaced. "It's disgusting. Are you sure you want to know?"

Ice cream gurgled in my throat as I groaned. "Will you just tell me?"

Arthur sighed, and his linebacker shoulders dropped further down his back. "You know Kelsey Kingsley?" I nodded. We had history together. "She had this graduation party in eighth grade. She lives on, like, three acres—pool, tennis courts, all that, but just a lot of land too. Anyway. Dean and Peyton and some other soccer douche bags showed up. They were already in upper school at this point so that was creepy, but Peyton had some boner for Kelsey. He likes 'em young." Arthur tipped his chin at me, as though I were a prime example. "They convinced Ben to go with them in the woods, they said they had pot." Arthur spooned up a golf-ball-size lump of ice cream. His mouth was strung green when he opened it again. "I don't know why Ben believed them. I never would have. Peyton and those guys? They held Ben down and pulled his shirt up, and Dean—" Arthur swallowed and shivered away a brain freeze.

"Dean, what?"

Arthur pressed his fingers to his temples. Exhaled.

He raised his eyebrows at me. "Dean took a shit on his chest."

I leaned back in my chair and steepled my hands over my mouth. "That's disgusting."

Arthur piled more ice cream onto his spoon. "Told ya. Anyway"—he shrugged—"when they let him go he ran. He was missing for almost twenty-four hours before someone discovered him in the bathroom of some Rite Aid by Suburban Square. He'd bought a razor and—" Arthur flipped his right hand over and mimed slicing the skin open, gritting his teeth as though the pain was real.

"But he didn't die?" I realized I was holding my own wrist in my hand, applying pressure to an imaginary wound.

Arthur shook his head. "People generally don't cut deep enough to nick the major artery." He seemed proud of knowing this.

"So where is he now?"

"Some institution." Arthur shrugged. "It was only six months ago, if you think about it."

"Do you talk to him?" I asked, watching closely for his reaction.

Arthur scrunched up his whole face and gave a little shake of his head. "I like the kid, but he has problems." With that he slid the yearbook to the center of the table, nudging the ice cream carton out of the way. My spoon toppled over and disappeared from view.

"Let's play with Dean in honor of Ben," he suggested, flipping to our favorite page. We'd drawn monkey ears on Dean, written, "Monkey see, monkey die," above his smiling face. I'd written that, originally, as "Monkey see, monkey do," but Arthur had crossed out "do" and written "die."

We had other regular pages too. Olivia's received

plenty of attention. I'd decorated her nose with black polka dots. Written, "I need Bioré strips." "And a boob job," Arthur had added.

Arthur preferred Peyton over Olivia though. The yearbook was three years old, and we had been in the sixth grade and Peyton in eighth. It was a real accomplishment, but Peyton had been even prettier when he was in middle school. We'd drawn pigtails on either side of his temples, and, even though I'd been the one to do it, I had to blink every time we opened the yearbook to his picture, remind myself that he wasn't really a girl. "Fuck me in my pretty ass," Arthur had written. "Choke me while you do it," he'd added, recently, explaining that one time on a bus ride Peyton had wrapped his scarf around Arthur's neck and held it there until a purple ring formed. "I had to wear a turtleneck for a fucking month," Arthur had harrumphed. "And you know how easily I overheat."

Arthur drew a thought bubble out of Dean's mouth: "What is Gentleman Dean Barton thinking today?" Before he could decide, the door opened and we heard Mrs. Finnerman calling out a hello. Arthur snatched the bowl off the table and tucked it into his pocket.

"In the kitchen, Mom!" he called. "TifAni's here."

I twisted in my seat to see Mrs. Finnerman enter the kitchen, unwrapping a stringy scarf from around her neck. "Hi, honey," she said to me.

"Hi, Mrs. Finnerman." I smiled, hoping it didn't look lazy and drugged.

Mrs. Finnerman removed her glasses, fogged over in the transition from the cold to the warm house, and wiped them on the hem of her shirt. "Are you staying for dinner?"

"Oh, no, I can't," I said. "But thank you."

"You know you're welcome anytime, dear." She put her

glasses on, and her eyes were bright behind the Windexed pane. "Anytime."

Mr. Larson had warned us it would happen. Two weeks of grammar, immediately following our discussion of *Into Thin Air*. This announcement had elicited a dramatic groan from the class and a playful grin from Mr. Larson, one I imagined he gave all his dates, right before slipping his hand underneath the blond weight of their hair and leaning in for a soft kiss.

Given the grueling grammar course I'd suffered through at Mt. St. Theresa's, this news was disappointing but also, to my surprise, fueled me with a sort of territorial adrenaline. *Try me*, I'd thought back in September. Gerund phrases, the present participle, noun modifiers—I'd wipe the floor with these amateurs. Now, with Mr. Larson gone and my competitive spirit blunted, I was just grateful for the opportunity to coast.

The substitute they'd brought in to replace Mr. Larson, Mrs. Hurst, had the body of a ten-year-old boy and bought her clothes—khakis and pastel-colored button-downs— at GapKids. From behind, she easily could have been an upper schooler's annoying little brother. Her daughter was a senior at Bradley, and because she had gotten into Dartmouth early decision and had a large, sharp nose and eyes ringed with purple commas, I'd assumed she was a harmless book nerd. But years of dismissal from pretty girls and boys who weren't that horny had turned her into a bitter gossip. Her mother, seated at the head of the classroom, one bony ankle draped over the other, had my number from the get-go.

She started on me the day somebody brought in doughnuts—left over from the yearbook meeting earlier that morning. Mrs. Hurst cut the remaining Krispy Kremes in half, even though there were eleven doughnuts and only nine students, more than enough for everyone to have a whole. I assumed she did it so that we could sample other flavors, and took half of a Boston cream and half of a powdered sugar.

"TifAni," Mrs. Hurst clucked disapprovingly. "Geez. Leave some for the rest of the class."

Her insults landed softly like that, enough to arouse a cautious titter from some students, hesitant to get involved with social politics. Honors English, which was filled with the children of Ivy League stage mothers, wasn't her ideal audience (she would have had better luck with the mean degenerates in Chem), but she would take what she could get.

My friendship with Arthur had not escaped Mrs. Hurst. That combined with the fact that Arthur was the smartest person in the room—head of the table included—and not exactly modest about it, and he may have had an even bigger bull's-eye on his forehead than I did.

One morning, a particularly convoluted explanation of the appositive phrase prompted Arthur to scribble his own example on the note the two of us had been passing back and forth, something we did all the time, even in the cafeteria, when we could speak freely. "Mrs. Hurst, the dumb-ass new teacher . . ." I slapped my hand over my mouth to catch my laugh, but a high-pitched sliver escaped. The class froze along with Mrs. Hurst, who took her time looking over her ski pole of a shoulder, her red marker bleeding into the board like a leaky gunshot wound.

"You know what?" She extended the marker in my direction. "I want you to help me with this."

Any other student would have sensed the humiliation that was imminent, would have crossed her spoiled, privileged arms across her chest and refused. Better to take your chances in the dean of students' office than to receive your punishment in front of your peers. But I was still saddled heavily with that Catholic girl fear, and when a teacher told you to do something, you did it. I felt Arthur's sidelong glance as I stood and trudged to the front of the classroom, a dead man walking the plank.

Mrs. Hurst pressed the marker into my hand and stepped away from the board, clearing a space for me to step into.

"Maybe an example will help?" she offered much too sweetly. "Write this down."

I hovered the marker over the board and waited.

"TifAni."

I looked under my raised arm at Mrs. Hurst, waiting for the rest of the phrase.

"Write that down," Mrs. Hurst cooed. "TifAni."

I wrote my name, dread lining the seams of my stomach. As I dotted the "i," Mrs. Hurst continued, "Comma."

I anchored my name with the punctuation and waited for my next set of instructions.

Mrs. Hurst said, "A cheap mall rat. *Comma.*"

Whether the gasp in the classroom was in reaction to what Mrs. Hurst had said or to Arthur's vicious "Fuck you," I'm not sure. But then Arthur was standing, coming around the corner of the table and approaching Mrs. Hurst, who was having a pretty tough time maintaining the cunt look on her face with a six-two, three-hundred-pound bull charging at her.

"Arthur Finnerman sit right back down in your seat this instant." Mrs. Hurst's words rambled together, and she shrunk back as Arthur stepped in front of me, a dog protecting his master from an intruder.

Arthur pointed his finger in Mrs. Hurst's face, and she gasped. "Who the fuck do you think you are, you dumb bitch?"

"Arthur." I put my hand on his arm, finding the skin beneath his polo shirt hot to the touch.

"Bob!" Mrs. Hurst suddenly shrieked. Then again and again, with manic regularity. "Bobbb! Bobbbbb! Bobbb!"

Bob Friedman, fellow English teacher across the hallway, burst into the room, looking dazed, an apple bitten down to its core lodged between his thumb and forefinger. "What's happened?" he gasped through a mouthful of Fuji.

"Bob." Mrs. Hurst took a shaky breath, but she straightened up, emboldened by his skinny presence. "I need your help in escorting Mr. Finnerman to Mr. Wright's office. He is *physically* threatening me."

Arthur laughed. "You're one crazy bitch, lady."

"Hey!" Mr. Friedman pointed the carcass of his apple at Arthur and strode to the front of the classroom, tripping on a book bag and stumbling the rest of the way there, almost losing his glasses in the process. He pushed them back up the bridge of his nose before hovering his hand above Arthur's back. We'd all heard the rumors about the annual sexual harassment seminar teachers were required to take. They were terrified to touch us. "Let's go. Mr. Wright's office, *now*."

Arthur made a disgusted noise and shrugged off Mr. Friedman's phantom hand on his back. He stomped out of the room, well ahead of Mr. Friedman.

"Thank you, Bob," Mrs. Hurst said, all prim and formal, pulling at the hem of her shirt and puffing out her flat chest. Mr. Friedman nodded and scurried after Arthur.

Several students were holding their hands over their mouths; two nerds were biting back tears.

"I apologize for the disturbance," Mrs. Hurst said, trying to sound stern. But I saw the tremble in her hand as she wiped my name away with the eraser and told me to take my seat. At least she stopped bothering me after that.

❧

I didn't see Arthur around school for the rest of the day. After practice, I walked the well-worn path to his house, the leaves on the ground so thin and stale that they just crumbled beneath my sneakers.

Arthur didn't come to the door when I knocked. I pounded and pounded, the shutters shaking on the windows, but he wouldn't answer my call.

❧

Arthur wasn't in school the next day either, and I assumed he had been suspended for the rest of the week, but when I sat down at the lunch table, my old lunch table, which was now my permanent home, the Shark's eyes filled with tears as she whispered to me that Arthur had been expelled.

The word "expulsion" filled me with the same kind of dread that "cancer" or "terrorist attack" did. "How could they expel him? He didn't even *do* anything. Not really."

"I think it was just the final straw for them." The Shark blinked, and a tear formed. I watched in amazement as it rolled down not her cheek but the side of her face. She flicked it away, like you would an ant scurrying along your thigh. "After the fish."

She may as well have been speaking Spanish, which I was just barely holding on to with a C. "The fish?"

"Oh." The Shark shifted in her seat. "I thought he told you about that."

"I have no idea what you're talking about." Impatience makes me loud, and the Shark brought her finger to her lips, shushing me.

She lowered her voice. "I don't know, I wasn't there. But he was suspended last year for stomping on a fish in biology class."

I could picture this, I realized. I could picture the way Arthur bared his teeth and popped his eyes at Mrs. Hurst, that face, his large foot coming down on the slippery blue body, flapping and gasping for breath on the wet floor, knowing he had to deliver as much force as possible or the thing would just slide away. "Why would he do that?"

"Those guys." The Shark shook her head, a mother dismayed by the violence in music videos already. "Dean. They dared him to." She brought her fingers to her temples, stretching the skin so that she became an Asian shark. "Poor Arthur. He'll never get into Columbia with this on his record. Not even with legacy."

Later that afternoon, I pretended like I had a cramp a mile into the five-mile loop and motioned for the other girls to run on without me. Then I doubled back toward school and covered the same ground in seven minutes.

This time, I held the doorbell down and didn't let up

until I felt the house shake with Arthur's footsteps. He swung open the door and gave me a flat look.

"Arthur!" I barked at him.

"Calm down already." He turned and started up the stairs. "Come on."

We sat on his bed and he passed the bowl to me.

"Is it really final?" I asked.

Arthur opened his mouth wide and exhaled a fat tube of smoke. "It's really final."

"It's fucking Dean who should be expelled," I muttered.

"There's a reason the cafeteria is named after his family." Arthur tapped the side of the bowl against the bed frame, loosening up the contents. He offered it to me again and I shook my head.

"Well, maybe he would have been expelled if I'd had some balls," I said.

Arthur groaned and launched himself off the bed. I caught my balance as the mattress shifted in my favor. "What?" I demanded.

"But you didn't," Arthur said. "You didn't! So stop with this self-loathing *bull*shit."

"You're mad at me for that?" I clutched my stomach; I couldn't take anyone else being mad at me ever again.

"*You* should be mad at you!" Arthur roared. "You had the chance to take him down and you didn't because you"—he launched a hearty laugh straight from his gut—"actually thought you could redeem yourself." That made him laugh more. "Oh my God, oh my God," he kept repeating, like it was the funniest fucking thing he'd ever heard.

I felt everything go still and quiet in me. "Oh my God, *what*?"

Arthur sighed, pityingly. "It's just, don't you see? Don't you get it? You were injured out the gate. And you're just—" He grabbed his hair. When he released it, tufts stood wildly at all angles. "You're just such a stupid cunt that you couldn't see it."

I would have taken Dean's hand a million times across my face over this. At least what he wanted, what he was angry he couldn't have, was the most basic, primal thing in the world, which was in no way a reflection on me as a human being. The realization that Arthur saw me as something completely different than how I thought he saw me was devastating. We weren't friends, peers, united in our disdain for the Hairy Legs and HOs, above it all. I was a reject that Arthur had kindly taken in. Not the other way around. I hit back the only way I knew.

"Yeah, well," I sputtered, "at least Dean wanted me. I had a chance. Unlike you. Fucking walking around with a three-year-old boner for him."

Arthur's face crumpled, ever so slightly, and for a moment I thought I would cry too. He had defended me, had been the only one to do that besides Mr. Larson. Before I could stop this train from shrieking to life, Arthur's features settled comfortably into a mean, cold stare. And then it *was* too late. "What are you even *talking* about?"

"You know what I'm talking about." I flipped my blond ponytail off my shoulder. My hair, my boobs, everything about me that had gotten me into so much trouble was suddenly my only weapon to defend myself here. "You're not fooling anyone." My eyes darted around the room. I spotted the yearbook on Arthur's desk. I sprung off the bed and seized it, flipping to our favorite page.

"Uh, let's see." I found Dean's picture. "'Fuck me in the ass. So hard it bleeds.'" There was so much scribble on Dean's picture that Arthur had drawn an arrow from Dean's face to the bottom of the page, where he'd written more. "Oh! And this gem: 'Chop my cock off.'" I looked up at Arthur. "You'd probably stuff it and sleep with it every night like a blankie, you fucking faggot."

Arthur lunged at me. His paws were on the book, yanking it out of my hands. I tried to wrench it back, and when I did, I lost my balance. I stumbled backward, slamming my head against the wall. Like a toddler, I was infuriated by this boo-boo. I wailed and held the place where it hurt.

"Did you ever stop to think," Arthur huffed, our little scuffle inciting his heart, buried under all those layers of fat, "that I don't want to fuck you not because I'm gay but because you're disgusting?"

I opened my mouth to defend myself, but Arthur cut me off. "What you should do is hack those off—no one who's ever done anything important has a rack like that." He cupped his own man boobs and shook them violently.

If I'd continued on the run I'd have been climbing the hill on New Gulph Road at the moment, but I still wouldn't have been breathing as hard as I was then. I had my fingers around the picture on Arthur's nightstand, the one of him and his father, laughing at the water, and before Arthur could grab me, I fled. I heard him on the stairs behind me, but unlike in a horror movie, the murderer was obese and slow and stoned. I was by the door, hauling my backpack over my shoulder, before Arthur had even made it to the second floor. Then I was outside, and I just kept going until I knew Arthur was well behind me, bent over and braced on his knees, gasping and furious. I didn't stop for almost half a mile, realizing I was going for the

Rosemont station now, which was further but wouldn't be a place Arthur would think to look for me. When I finally slowed to a walk, I looked at the picture in my hands, saw the happiness Arthur wanted there, and considered turning back. But then I thought how his dad was a dick. I was probably doing him a favor by taking that picture. Maybe it would help him move on, stop being such a fat asshole. I paused on the side of the road and found a safe place for it anyway, tucking it into a folder to protect all the stupid shell decorations on the frame.

I found out a few days later that Arthur enrolled in Thompson High, a public school in Radnor. In 2003, Thompson High sent only two students out of its graduating class, 307 total, to Ivy League universities. Arthur wasn't destined to be among them.

CHAPTER 11

t was an e-mail that, had I been twenty-two years old, fresh out of college, desperate for a job, I would have called up Nell to read aloud. "Oh my God, listen to this!"

> Dear Ms. FaNelli,
>   My name is Erin Baker, and I'm the HR coordinator for Type Media. We have an opening for the Features Director at Glow magazine, and we'd love for you to come in and interview if you are interested. Could I take you to coffee to discuss this week? Pay is competitive.
>   Warmly,
>   Erin

I closed the e-mail. I was in no rush to respond because I was not interested in the least. Yes, features director was a major step up from senior editor and I could make more money, but I didn't have to worry about money, not really. No matter how much they offered me, it would never be enough to make a move to a magazine exactly like *The Women's Magazine*, only not nearly as iconic, when LoLo had dropped the fucking *New York Times Magazine* on my doorstep like a house cat does a headless mouse.

Even though I had written the words "his member" far too many times in my tenure at *The Women's Magazine*, there was a recognition in the name that offered me protection, much like my engagement to Luke did. When I tell people I'm in magazines, and they ask where, I never, ever get tired of cocking my head modestly and answering in my best uptalk, "*The Women's Magazine?*" That inflection in my voice—have you heard of it? Like those smug Harvard bastards—"Oh, I went to school in Cambridge." "Where?" "Harvard?" Yes, we've all fucking heard of Harvard. I got off on that instant recognition. I did enough explaining in high school, to justify my peasant presence among kings—"I live in Chester Springs. It's not too far. I'm not too poor."

I signed out of my e-mail. I'd write this Erin Baker back later, some bullshit, "Thank you so much for thinking of me but at this time I'm very happy in my current position."

I tapped my moss green fingernails on the tabletop, wondering where Nell was. Several minutes ticked by before I knew she had arrived. The heads turning by the entrance to the restaurant were the first sign. The second was the top of Nell's head, the most shocking shade of blond steering her right at me.

"I'm sorry!" She folded into the seat. Nell is so tall her spindly legs never fit under the table. She crossed them in the aisle, one bootie dangling over the other, the heel sharp and thin as a talon. It was one of those nights. "I couldn't get a cab."

"This place is a direct shot on the one from your place," I said.

"Subways are for people who work." She grinned at me. "Asshole."

The server came by, and Nell ordered a glass of wine. I already had one, half down. I'd been trying to make it last, since I was only allowing myself two, essentially dinner.

"Your face," Nell said and sucked in her cheekbones.

Finally. "I'm starving."

"I know. It sucks." Nell opened her menu. "What are you getting?"

"The tuna tartare."

Nell looked confused as she scanned the menu, small as a prayer book in her hands. "Where is that?"

"It's under appetizers."

Nell laughed. "I'm so fucking glad I'm never getting married."

The server returned with Nell's wine, asked what he could get for us. Nell ordered a burger because she's a sociopath. She wouldn't even eat the whole thing anyway. The Adderall would have her disinterested after a few bites. I wish that worked for me, but whenever I took one of Nell's blue pills, even the occasional night that coke turned into morning in the blink of an eye, my appetite always clawed its way to the surface. The only thing that worked for me was pure, hard discipline.

When I placed my order the waiter said, "Just so you know that's a very small dish." He made a fist to show me.

"She's getting married." Nell batted her eyes at him.

The waiter made an "ahh" noise. He was gay, tiny and pretty. Probably had a beefy bear he'd hook up with after his shift was over. As he took my menu he said, "Congratulations." The word was like an ice cube held to an exposed nerve in a tooth.

"*What?*" Nell gasped. My forehead had creased into that V shape, which it always does right before I cry.

I covered my eyes with my hands. "I don't know if I want to do this." There, it was said. Out loud. The admission like the one tiny pebble that dislodged, tumbled down the mountainside, so insignificant it didn't seem possible the thrashing white avalanche that followed.

"Okay," Nell said, clinically, her pale lips pursing. "Is this a recent thing? How long have you felt like this?"

I exhaled through my teeth. "A long time."

Nell nodded. She hovered her hands on either side of her glass of wine, staring into the red depths. In the dim restaurant there was no sign of blueness in her eyes. Some girls need that light, those two bright pools, before you can decide, yes, she's pretty. But not Nell.

"How would you feel," she said, and there was a quick flare of her nostrils, "if you called it off. If Luke was one day just some guy you used to know?"

"Are you actually quoting Gotye?" I snapped.

Nell tilted her head at me. Her blond hair slid off the side of her shoulder and dangled, glinting like an icicle on the edge of a roof.

I sighed. Thought for a moment.

There was this one night, not too long ago, when some belligerent guy had called me an ugly whore because he thought I'd cut him in line at the bar.

"Fuck you!" I'd sneered at him.

"You could be so lucky." The chain around his neck was dancing silver in the lights, and his reptilian skin folded in places it shouldn't have at his age. If only he had resisted the local Hollywood Tans like I had.

I'd held up my most important finger. "You're adorable, but I'm engaged."

The look on his face. That ring's almost magical powers in the way it emboldened me, protected me from the
hurt.

I said to Nell, "It would make me really sad."

"What about it makes you sad?"

Because when you're twenty-eight and you live in a
doorman building in Tribeca, step out of a cab, Giuseppes
first, and are planning a Nantucket wedding to someone with the pedigree of Luke Harrison, you're thriving.
When you're twenty-eight, single, and look nothing like
Nell, hawking those same pumps on eBay to pay the electric bill, Hollywood makes sad movies about you.

"Because I love him."

The next two words sounded innocent enough, but I
knew Nell, and they'd been chosen for maximum impact.
"How sweet."

I nodded an apology at her.

The silence that followed seemed to hum, like the highway behind my house in Pennsylvania. I grew up so used
to it I mistook it for quiet. Only noticed it when I hosted
a sleepover for the first time with my Mt. St. Theresa
friends. "What is that *noise*?" demanded Leah, wrinkling
her nose at me accusingly. Leah was married now. Had a
baby she dressed in head-to-toe cotton candy pink for her
Facebook albums.

Nell brought her hands together in one last plea. "You
know, people don't care about you as much as you think
they do." She laughed. "That sounded bad. What I meant
was it might only be in your head that you have something
to prove."

If that was true, it meant deposits returned, a Carolina
Herrera gown sulking in my closet. Doing this documentary without my four-carat tumor, evidence that I was

worth more than my previously determined value. "It's not."

Nell bore into me with her ink-colored eyes. "It is. And you should think about that. Hard. Before you make a big mistake."

"This is rich." I laughed aggressively. "Coming from the person who taught me how to operate *every single person in my life*."

Nell's lips slipped open, moving around words she wasn't saying. I realized she was repeating what I had just said, back to herself, trying to make sense of it. In a moment her expression changed from frustration to amazement. "Because I thought this"—she circled her hands frantically, calling up all "this" I'd mustered for myself—"was what you wanted. I thought you *wanted* Luke. I thought this little charade made you *happy*." She clapped one hand to the side of her face and sputtered, "Jesus, Ani, don't do this if this doesn't make you happy!"

"You know?" I layered one arm over the other. Each a carefully placed barrier to keep her out from where it mattered most. "I asked you here hoping you'd make me feel better. Not worse."

Nell sat up, cheerleader perky. "Okay, Ani. Luke's a great guy. He sees you for exactly who you are and accepts you for it. He doesn't expect you to be someone you're not. By golly, you should really thank your lucky stars for him." She glowered at me.

Our adorable waiter reappeared with a basket in his hands. "Sorry," he mumbled. "You probably don't want this. But, bread?"

Nell gave him a dazzling, infuriating smile. "I'd *love* some bread."

He visibly cheered in her spotlight, the blood dashing

to his cheeks and his eyes brightening, sharpening, the way everyone's do when Nell tosses out a handful of her fairy dust. I wondered if he felt it when his arm bisected the space between the two of us, when he placed the basket in the center of the table. The way the air crackled there, warning.

~ ❧ ~

The weeks passed, pushing New York further from the summer, September only halfheartedly fighting the heat. Filming was scheduled to start, whether I was ready or not. I had a dress fitting, and the seamstress marveled at the gap between my waist and the size six bodice. I'd balked when I first ordered it. A size six? "Wedding gown sizing is completely different from the sizing of regular clothes," the salesgirl had assured me. "You may be a two or even a zero at a place like Banana Republic, but that makes you a six or an eight in a wedding gown."

"Don't order the eight," I'd said, hoping my horrified expression also explained that I would never shop at Banana Republic.

I was driving "home" to the Main Line on Thursday evening. First day of filming was Friday. The documentary team hadn't received permission to shoot inside the school, something that brought me relief, but not for obvious reasons. Bradley wouldn't want any negative press, and my story would certainly give it to them, so that implied the angle the documentary was taking was more in line with my own. I wondered who else the team had gotten, besides Andrew. I'd asked, but they wouldn't tell.

I'd pillaged the fashion closet the day before I left: Dark waxed jeans, Theory silk tops, suede booties that were neither too high nor too low. I got the accessories editor to lend me a lovely little necklace: delicate rose gold chain, a small bar of diamonds glinting in the middle. It would pick up nicely—tastefully—on camera. I had a professional blow out the messy, trendy waves in my hair that afternoon. The goal was to look simple and expensive.

I was folding a charcoal-colored blouse into my weekend bag when I heard Luke's key in the door.

"Hi, babe," he called.

"Hi," I said, not loud enough that he could hear me.

"You in there?" Luke's Ferragamo shoes clicked closer, and soon his frame filled the open doorway. He was wearing a spectacular navy suit, narrow pants sewn from a fabric so rich it shone. He put his hands on either side of the frame and leaned forward, his chest expanding.

"Nice loot," Luke said, nodding to the pile on the bed.

"I didn't have to pay for it, don't worry."

"No, that wasn't what I meant."

Luke watched me transfer piles of clothes from the bed into the gaping hole of the bag.

"How are you feeling about this?"

"Good," I said. "I feel like I look good. I feel good."

"You always look good, babe." Luke grinned.

I wasn't in the mood to joke. "I wish you could come with me," I sighed.

Luke nodded sympathetically. "I know. Me too. But I just feel bad because I don't know when I'll get a chance to see John again." Luke had been all set to go with me this weekend, but a few weeks ago he'd found out his friend John, who's been feeding orphans in India or some shit that makes me feel like a plastic bitch for what I do, was coming to New York. He would be here only two days and then he was back in India for another year. He couldn't even come to our wedding. He was bringing his fiancée, another volunteer named Emma, who was twenty-five. I was instantly wounded by her beautiful name and her perfect age. I still couldn't believe I was going to be thirty in two years. "Twenty-five?" I'd snorted to Luke. "What is she, a mail-order child bride?"

"Twenty-five's not that young," he'd shot back. He'd heard himself and added, "I mean, to get married."

I understood how important John was to Luke. Even though things were chilly between Nell and me right now, if she moved across the world and came back to New York for two nights, I would drop everything to see her too. That didn't bother me. What did was Luke's palpable relief that he was off the hook. That was a pain I couldn't lie away. I e-mailed Mr. Larson, thinking, *You drove me to this.* "Want to get that lunch on the Main Line?"

"I love you though," Luke said. It came out like a question: "I love you though?" "You're going to do so great, babe. Just tell the truth." He laughed, suddenly. "The truth shall set you free! Man, I haven't seen that movie in so long. Whatever happened to Jim Carrey anyway?"

I wanted to tell him that's a line from the Bible, not *Liar Liar.* To just take this fucking seriously for once. I was going into the lion's den with nothing to protect me but a few old green carats on my finger. How could that possibly be enough? Instead, I said, "He did that Burt Wonderstone movie. It was actually pretty funny."

When I'd asked the director, Aaron, what hotel he'd booked me, his eyebrows had jumped halfway up his forehead in surprise. "We just assumed you would stay with your family."

"They live pretty far out," I'd said. "It would probably be more convenient if you got me a hotel in the area. The Radnor Hotel is pretty reasonable, I think."

"I'll have to check to see if that's in our budget," he'd said. But I knew it would be. No one had said this to me, but I suspected my story was the pin holding this whole thing together. There was no new light to shed on the incident without my version of events. Also helpful was my chest, which Aaron's eyes seemed to flick to involuntarily.

I hadn't slept in my childhood bedroom since college, and even then it was only sporadically. I interned every summer, in Boston the summer of my freshman year, and then in New York after that. I tried to spend the holidays with Nell's family as much as possible. My sleep was heavenly at Nell's house.

It was an entirely different experience at my parents' place, where I would oftentimes lie awake almost all night, gripping a silly tabloid magazine in terror. I didn't have a TV in my room, and this was before colleges dealt out laptops like free condoms at the health center, and the only way I knew how to distract myself from the galloping anxiety, from the disgust that this room, this house, dredged up from the shadowy mine of the past, was to read about the Jennifer Aniston–Brad Pitt–Angelina Jolie love triangle. For me, the only worthy competitor of bleak, starless memory is superficial fluff. The two are successfully and mutually exclusive.

As I got older, and as I made more money, it was like an epiphany—I can actually afford to get a hotel. It was easy to blame on the fact that, when I came home, I brought Luke, and my parents wouldn't allow us to sleep in the same room. Not even now that we're engaged. "I just don't feel comfortable with the two of you sleeping in the same bed under my roof until you are married," Mom said, demurely, narrowing her eyes at me when I laughed.

I didn't tell my parents that Luke had backed out of the trip until the very last minute. And over Mom's hollow insistence that I stay at home, I calmly explained that the production company had already paid for the Deluxe Guest Room at the Radnor Hotel, and it was more convenient for me anyway since it put me only five minutes from Bradley.

"It's more like ten," Mom pointed out.

"It's better than forty," I snapped. Then felt bad. "Why don't we go out to dinner on Saturday night? Luke's treat. He's sorry about canceling."

"That is so sweet of him," Mom gushed. "Why don't you pick the place?" Then she added, "I do love Yangming though."

And so I tucked my withering body into Luke's Jeep (*our* Jeep, he keeps correcting me) on Thursday evening. Proud of the New York plate. Proud of my New York license. The streetlights caught the bauble on my hand every time I spun the wheel, the collision creating a burst of jade light so sharp it could blind. "Philadelphia. Just a hop, skip, a cab, a Metroliner, and another cab away" from New York City, Carrie Bradshaw said once. It felt so much farther than that. Like another dimension, like a life of someone else who I felt sorry for now. She had been so naive and unprepared for what was to come, it hadn't just been sad. It had been dangerous.

❧

"So what we'll have you do first is state your name, age, and how old you were at the time of the"—Aaron fumbled for a word—"the, uh, incident. Let's refer to it as the date it happened, maybe. So how old you were on November twelfth, 2001."

"Do I need more powder?" I fretted. "I get really shiny on my nose."

The makeup artist approached and scrutinized the stage layer of foundation. "You're good."

I was sitting on a black stool. The wall behind me was black too. Friday was the day we filmed in the studio, a cavernous room above a Starbucks in Media, PA. The whole place smelled like the burnt, overpriced fuel of diabetic Americans. I would tell my story here, and on Saturday morning, when the students were sleeping off the previous night's antics, we'd get some shots of me around the outskirts of Bradley. Aaron said he wanted me to point out "places of interest." The navigational points at which my life became an average before and rarefied after were places of interest now, I supposed.

"Just pretend like it's you and I, having a conversation," Aaron said. He wanted to get this all in one take. I should keep going, from start to finish, without any break. "The emotional continuity of the story is important. If you feel yourself getting teary eyed, that's okay. Just keep going. I may jump in here and there to keep you on track if I feel like you're digressing. But we want you to just go."

I wanted to tell him I wouldn't get teary eyed, but I might get sick. Heaving clear syrupy bile into the toilet, my hand, out the car window had been my way of coping for a long time. ("It's normal and nothing to be concerned about," the grief counselor had assured my parents.) I took a deep breath. The buttons pulled on my silk blouse as my chest expanded and retracted.

"So we're just starting with the basics, like I said." Aaron pressed the bud in his ear and said in a low voice, "Can I get quiet on the set?" He looked at me. "We're just doing a thirty-second sound check. Don't say anything."

The crew—about twelve of them—fell silent as Aaron counted on his watch. I noticed for the first time he was wearing a wedding ring. A gold one. Much too thick. Did his wife have a flat chest and that was why he couldn't keep his eyes off mine?

"We get it?" Aaron asked, and one of the sound guys nodded.

"Awesome." Aaron clapped his hands together and backed out of the shot. "Okay, Ani, when we say, 'Take,' I want you to state those three things—your name, your age—oh! And this is important. It should be the age you will be when this airs in eight months—"

"We do that in magazines too," I babbled nervously. "Use the age someone will be when the issue hits the newsstands."

"Exactly!" Aaron said. "And then don't forget to add how old you were on November twelfth, 2001." He gave me a thumbs-up.

In eight months I would be twenty-nine. I could hardly take it. I realized something that made me brighten. "My name will be different in eight months too," I said. "Should I go by that?"

"Yes, absolutely," Aaron said. "Good catch. We'd have to film that all over again if we didn't get it right." He backed away from me and gave me another thumbs-up. "You're going to do great. You look *gorgeous*."

Like I was there to shoot a fucking morning talk show.

Aaron nodded to one of the crew members. The room was solemn as he said, "Take one." He cracked the clapboard, and Aaron pointed his finger at me and mouthed, "Go."

"Hi, my name is Ani Harrison. I'm twenty-nine years old. And on November twelfth, 2001, I was fourteen years old."

"Cut!" Aaron shouted. Softening his voice, he said, "So you don't need to say 'Hi.' Just 'I'm Ani Harrison.'"

"Oh, right." I rolled my eyes. "Yeah, that sounds stupid. Sorry."

"Don't apologize!" Aaron said, much too forgivingly. "You're doing great." I swear I caught one of the crew members roll her eyes. The woman had a bouquet of frizzy curls framing her narrow face, the cheekbones probably more pronounced in adulthood, the way Olivia's might have been.

When they yelled cut this time, I got it right. "I'm Ani Harrison. I'm twenty-nine years old. On November twelfth, 2001, I was fourteen years old."

Cut. Aaron falling all over himself to tell me what a great job I did. That woman definitely rolling her eyes.

"Let's do a few where you just state your name, okay?"

I nodded. Quiet on the set, Aaron pointing at me to go. "I'm Ani Harrison."

Aaron counting on his fingers to five, pointing at me to do it again.

"I'm Ani Harrison."

Cut.

"You feel good?" Aaron asked, and I nodded. "Great. *Great.*" He was all fired up. "So now you're just going to talk. Just tell us what happened. Better yet, tell me what happened. You don't have to look directly into the camera either. Just pretend like I'm your friend and you're telling me this story about your life."

"Got it." I fought hard for the smile I gave him.

Quiet on the set. The clapboard came down like a guillotine. Nothing left to do but to tell.

CHAPTER 12

I f it hadn't been for the Swedish fish, I wouldn't have been there, right in the blue-red, palpitating heart of it. I didn't even like Swedish fish before I came to Bradley, but they were among the only things Olivia ate, and she was skinny. Rationally, I understood Olivia was skinny not because Swedish fish were an addition to her diet but because they *were* her diet. It didn't matter. The urge for that chew, that tang stinging the corners of my mouth, sent me through the cafeteria a second, sometimes third time. Nothing could deter me. Not the table of my former friends located precariously close to the cash registers, not my pants now so tight that I'd taken to using a large clothespin as a button. (It gave me another inch or two.)

I made my way through the food atrium. Passed the deli line, the hot meal of the day, the salad bar, and the fountain soda station—Teddy there, cursing about how the ice machine was always broken—and got in line to pay. Just like at a pharmacy, candy and chocolate and gum were available by the cash register. There were two lines, and there was an awkward moment when I almost ran into Dean, when we both stepped forward to try to get into the shorter line. I gave it to him without a fight—it was the one closest to his table, the one I tried to avoid anyway. I watched Dean shuffle to the front, dragging his feet like the wait was annoying him. There is something about seeing someone from behind, something about the way people walk away, that I've always found unnervingly intimate. Maybe it's because the back of the body isn't on guard the way the front is—the slouch of the shoulders and the flex in the back muscles, that's the most honest you'll ever see a person.

The quad drove the high noon sun in from the left; tendrils coiled around the woolly patches of hair on Dean's neck. I was thinking, how strange that it's blond, baby thin, when the hair everywhere else was coarse and dark, when Dean went sideways in the air.

Why is Dean jumping? It was the first thing I thought, continued to think even as a dense smoke charged the new part of the cafeteria, the part where I was no longer welcome, my excommunication my saving grace, really.

I was on the ground, my bad wrist irate. I howled as someone rushed past and stomped on my finger. Physically, I had the sensation that I was screaming. I felt the ragged edges of my throat, but I couldn't hear anything. Someone seized my gimpy wrist and pulled me to my feet, and I felt the pressure of a scream in my chest again, but the release was cut short as my lungs hitched on the smoke. I was racked with a wicked cough, that feeling like you'll never get a good breath again.

It was Teddy who had my wrist. I followed him in reverse of the way I'd just come, exiting by the entrance into the old part of the cafeteria, where the deli line started for the first lunch shift at 11:51 A.M. I felt something warm and gooey in my palm and I looked down, expecting to see blood, but it was just the bag of Swedish fish, still secure in my hand.

The cafeteria bulged with black smoke. We couldn't get out the way we usually came in, and Teddy and I pivoted in unison, like we were rehearsing a dance for the talent show. We stumbled up the flight of stairs behind us toward the Brenner Baulkin Room, where I had only been once, to take my entrance exam.

When I recall this moment now, it's a silent memory. In reality the fire alarm was piercing an unbearably high note overhead, and there was screaming, moaning. Later I was told that the husky voice Hilary took such pains to curate fell away, and she was just a little girl, whimpering, "Mom, *Mom,*" as she shuddered on the floor, broken glass glinting like diamonds in her pale, parched hair. Her left foot, still in its Steve Madden clog, was no longer a part of her body.

Olivia lay next to her, not asking for anyone. Olivia was dead.

Teddy flung the door open. Beneath the important oak table, where Headmaster Mah hosted steak dinners for the parents who donated at the platinum level, were others. The Shark, Peyton, Liam, and Ansilee Chase, a senior who overacted in every school play she starred in. This random representation of year and social standing, this was it. This was the awful tie that would always bind us.

My first memory of sound is Ansilee panting, the way she sputtered, "Oh my God, oh my God," as he came into the room not thirty seconds after we did, the gun dangling playfully at his side exactly at our eye level. I didn't know it at the time, but he was holding an Intratec TEC-9 semiautomatic handgun. It looked like a scaled-down submachine gun. We silently pleaded with Ansilee to shut up, holding our trembling fingers to our mouths.

He would have found us anyway. It was hardly a great hiding spot.

"Boo!" His face appeared between the chair's elegant claw legs. A tiny, pale face, garnished with fluffy black hair that looked as soft and new as an infant's.

Ansilee broke, blubbering and crawling away from him, knocking a chair over as she wiggled out from underneath the table and shot to her feet. His face disappeared and then all we saw were his legs from the knees down. He was wearing shorts, even though it was November, and his calves were white and shockingly smooth. I'd like to say one of us went after her, tried to save her—she'd been accepted early decision to Harvard, she couldn't die—but instead, here is where I always say, "We were in shock! It all happened so fast!"

The sound the gun made was nothing compared to the sound of Ansilee's body hitting the floor. "Jesus fucking Christ," Liam gasped. He was next to me, and he grabbed my hand, looked at me like he *loved* me. The hardwood floor was covered with a large Oriental carpet, but by the sickening crack Ansilee's head made when it connected with the ground, it wasn't nearly as thick and lush as it appeared.

The Shark clutched me to her chest, and I felt her large bosom heaving like on the cover of a romance novel. His face appeared between the chair legs again.

"Hi." He smiled. It was a smile totally unconnected to all the things in life that bring us joy: a spectacular spring day after a bleak winter, the first time the groom sees his bride, her excited face buoyed by layers of white. He aimed the gun at us, swinging his arm from right to left so, for a moment, it was trained on each of us, and a low groan rippled through the group. I stared at the ground when it was my turn, willing myself not to shake, not to be the most obviously scared, which I somehow understood would make me the most interesting to him.

"Ben," the Shark whispered. "Please." I felt her fingers dig into my skin, her armpit sweaty on my shoulder, and I remembered the name Ben.

"Fuck you." It wasn't aimed at any of us. There was a long moment where he wore us down. Then his expression softened like the flame of a candle descending on wax. "Oh, goody. It's Peyton."

"Ben"—Peyton was shaking so hard the floor picked up the tremor—"man, you don't have to—" Peyton never said anything after "to." What a stupid little word to be your last. His beautiful face took the brunt. One Peyton tooth skittered right in front of me, white and perfectly shaped as a piece of Chiclets gum.

This time the gun had been low and close. The sound sent Liam behind the Shark and me, as far away as he could get from Peyton without abandoning the hood of the table. Teddy was all the way at the other end, holding on to a chair leg like it was his mother's and he was begging her not to go out on a Saturday night. My ears felt like they were turning in on my skull. I brought a finger to one and felt the wet. A drop of blood hit the carpet, spread red in the fibers like a sonic boom. It was the only drop that was mine.

Ben rested on his haunches a little longer, admiring his work. The chairs had caught Peyton, and they held his body upright, arms flung wide scarecrow-like. There was nothing left of his face below the nose. A great gust of steam billowed all around him, like laughter on a freezing cold night.

Liam was burrowed in my back, his mouth a humid

kiss on my shoulder, so he didn't see the miraculous thing that happened next. But the rest of us watched in disbelief as Ben stretched out, and then all that was visible of him were his smooth white calves moving further and further away from us, turning left, in the direction of the back stairwell that led to the ground floor, where the Language wing was located. Above it were the abandoned dorm rooms left over from Bradley's boarding school days. They only used them for in-school suspensions now.

I didn't even realize I'd been holding my breath until I was gasping like it was the finish line at a cross-country race. "Who is he?" I heaved into the Shark's chest. "Who was that?" I asked again, even though I knew.

"Is Ansilee okay?" Liam whimpered, his voice high and pathetically foreign, this abrupt shift in power stripping him of all his cool new-guy bravado. All he had to do was look behind him to answer his own question. Because I did, and Ansilee's head was open like a casket.

"This is like fucking Columbine," Teddy mumbled from the other end of the table. We'd all been in middle school when that happened. I don't know about Bradley, but at Mt. St. Theresa's, we stood around the lone, crackly TV in the library, watching the coverage, until Sister Dennis unplugged it and threatened all of us with demerits if we didn't go back to class immediately.

Smoke was slithering in from the cafeteria. I was aware that we had to leave, but also that the only way out was to follow His path.

"Does anyone have their cell phone?" Not every teenager owned a cell phone back then, but everyone in that room did. It didn't matter, because no one had had time to grab their book bags before they fled.

"What do we do?" I looked at the Shark, certain she

would have the answer. When she didn't speak, I said, "We have to get out of here."

None of us wanted to crawl out from underneath the table. But the smoke was wafting in, putrid with human hair and melting man-made materials: polyester book bags, plastic lunch trays, rayon purchases from Abercrombie & Fitch. I pushed out the chair to our right and Teddy did the same at his end, and the four of us scrambled to our feet. There was a heroic-looking buffet in the corner, and it became the place where we met. Its body blocking us from the waist down felt like some small measure of protection.

We argued. Liam wanted to stay put and wait for the police, who surely had to be on their way. Teddy wanted to leave. The fire was too fast. There was a large window high on the wall, beaming sunlight onto the table, beneath which Peyton and Ansilee waited. That was a compromise for a bit. Teddy stood on a chair, bumping Ansilee's shoulder as he positioned it beneath our maybe escape. Teddy pushed and grunted, but he couldn't get the window open, and he was the strongest one left in the room.

"We have to get out of here!" Teddy insisted.

"He could be waiting out there for us!" Liam said. "That's what those Columbine kids did!" He slammed his hand down on the buffet. "Faggot! Fucking faggot!"

"Shut up!" I yelled. You had to yell to hear over the fire alarm, sizzling in our ears. "That's why he's doing it!" Liam looked at me like he was afraid of me. I didn't understand how important that was at the time.

"He won't hurt us if we're with her." Teddy pointed to the Shark.

Liam laughed viciously. "He won't hurt you either! That's why you're willing to leave."

"No"—Teddy shook his head—"Ben and I were never friends. He loved Beth though." It had been so long since I'd heard the Shark's real name that I didn't even know who Teddy was talking about at first.

"I haven't seen Ben in a long time." The Shark sniffled, dragging her forearm across her nose. "And that . . . that was not Ben."

A chair toppled over, and the ruckus brought all four of us together in a nervous clamor of bodies. It was the moan that broke us apart.

"Oh my God," the Shark said. "Peyton."

The air sounded wet as he tried to breathe it. The Shark and I crept around the buffet and crouched by Peyton's side. He'd managed to drag half his body out from underneath the table, and he was clawing at the air, his fingers so set in their gnarl it was as though he'd sunk them into plaster before it dried. He tried to speak, but only blood gurgled up where his lips should have been.

"Get a towel or something!" the Shark shrieked at Teddy and Liam, both still as photographs in the corner.

They started into action. I heard silverware jangling as they raided the buffet, finally coming up with linens emblazoned spring green with THE BRADLEY SCHOOL. They tossed them at us.

The Shark and I pressed a napkin on either side of Peyton's beautiful, ravaged face. Blood and sticky muscle tissue sealed the cloth to where his jaw had been, turned it red as completely and quickly as a magic trick. It was a horrifying thing to look at, his face shred of features and skin, but it was like saying the word "the" over and over until you don't even recognize it, the power of repetition to transform the ordinary to the exotic. Semantic satiation, is it? With Peyton, it was the converse: Look at his face long enough and it was less grotesque than if you'd never seen it at all, if you'd only imagined how bad it could be.

Peyton managed a moan. I took his hand, still signaling madly, and guided it to the floor, squeezing his fingers gently.

"It's okay," the Shark said. "You have that big game next week." She started to cry harder. "You're going to win that big game next week."

Everyone knew Bradley didn't stand a chance. Peyton sobbed and squeezed my hand back.

I don't know how long we sat there. Talking to Peyton. Telling him that his parents loved him and they needed him to come home, so just fight. Keep fighting, you're doing great, you're so strong, we told him, even as his hand chilled in my own, even as it stopped being so laborious for him to breathe, because soon he was barely breathing at all.

And all the while, the flames in the cafeteria bounced up the stairs, until we could make out their sharp peaks, threatening to dance down the hallway, trap us in the Brenner Baulkin Room and never let us out.

"Where the fuck are the police?" Liam wailed. We'd all cried with relief when we heard their sirens at least ten minutes ago.

"We have to go," Teddy said. He looked at Peyton and immediately looked away, digging the heels of his hands into his swollen eyes. "I'm sorry, you guys, but we have to go."

"But he's still breathing." I looked down at Peyton. I'd eased his head into my lap when he started to gag on his own blood. My crotch was soaked and sticky, and some wild, grisly corner of my mind turned on the memory of the last time his head had been between my legs, like a sudden, jarring flick of a light switch in the middle of the night, shocking you out of the thickest stage of sleep. At least in that vision, Peyton's eyes were open, crystal and ignorantly kind, thinking he was doing something good.

"TifAni, we are going to die in here if we don't go now!" Teddy said.

The Shark pleaded, "Can you carry him or something?"

Teddy tried, and all of us tried to help him, even Liam, but Peyton was as final and as heavy as a block of cement.

The room smelled hot and sick. Teddy begged us one last time.

Before we slunk into the hallway, holding the hands of the person ahead of us and behind us, four tough teenagers linked together like kindergartners crossing the street, Liam pillaged the buffet. He was looking for something, anything, to protect us. The best he could do was to offer each of us a steak knife.

"My mom told me to never fight off a rapist with a knife," I said, so woozy from the heat it didn't even occur to me the morbid hilarity of saying that to Liam. "Because he can overpower you and turn it on you."

"He's not a rapist," the Shark said, softly.

"Oh, I'm sorry," Liam said. "Should she have said 'psycho faggot murderer'?"

We also took the fine linen napkins, what was left of the ones we'd piled onto Peyton's face, tying them around our mouths like bandits.

I looked at Peyton one last time before we left. His chest sighed a good-bye, a final plea: I'm still alive. I felt the agony of leaving him alone and alive like a pregnancy, so full and all encompassing it had the power to change my entire life.

The fastest we moved was down the hallway, to the left,

until we got into the stairwell. We burst through the door, our neat little line breaking as we became a whirlwind of arms and legs clutching at each other in a tight circle—no one knew what we would find in there, no one wanted to be at the front of the line.

To our immense relief, the stairwell appeared empty. We tore off our face masks, gratefully.

"What do you think?" the Shark asked. "Up or down?"

"I say up," Teddy said. "He wouldn't have gone up." The old boarding rooms bled out to another stairwell, which would loop us down to the Mathematics wing. There was an exit in the Mathematics wing.

"Good call," Liam said, and Teddy smiled. He was still smiling as the bullet dovetailed into his collarbone, blood splashing the wall behind him like the Jackson Pollock paintings we were learning about in Contemporary Art.

I only knew that the bullet had come from up. And I was running down the stairs, skidding around the turns, bumping into the Shark and Liam as bullets met the railing, the sharp clang of metal on metal unlike anything I'd ever heard.

The door on the first floor led to the Language wing, and the longest moment of my life was the time it took for the Shark to turn the handle and swing it open, those seconds enough for Ben to close in on us. The door was old and slow, and it remained open behind us after we dashed through. Ben didn't have to slow down to open it again, he simply ducked through right after us. He was skinny and quick, would have been a great cross-country runner.

Liam hooked right, mistaking an empty classroom for cover. It was an inadvertently noble, intentionally self-preserving turn (not that I blame him for that), and it saved me.

"Why didn't you follow him?" I'm usually asked, at this point in the story.

"Because," I say, irritated that I've been interrupted, that whatever moron interrupted me couldn't understand that Ben was so close I could hear that his breathing was different than our breathing. Sharp and quick, like that of an animal whose lungs have evolved to chase. "He was right behind us. I knew he would have seen and followed us, and then we'd have been cornered, which is what happened."

"To Liam?" Aaron asked.

"To Liam."

"Let's get back to what happened next."

The Shark and I tore through the Language wing. We pounded up the stairs, and when we cleared the last step, there was the door to the cafeteria. Shut tight, it should have created the fire hazard Mr. Harold was always warning us about, only it hadn't. It had contained the fire in the old part of the cafeteria, tucked it deeper in, so that it had advanced on the Brenner Baulkin Room where we had just been, where Peyton and Ansilee remained. There was a clear path from the door, through the new addition, where the overhead sprinklers had gone on, drenched the fire into submission. There was an exit to the quad there. The Shark and I never broke our stride, just plunged in.

But it was in the spot where the Hairy Legs and the HOs used to sit where we both stopped, water up to our ankles and still coming down, plastering our hair to the sides of our faces. Where I thought I would vomit up my own heart when I saw Arthur.

Arthur, blocking our exit, standing in the rubble of building and bodies, his face pebbled with water and holding his father's hunting rifle across his body like the bar a tightrope walker uses to keep his balance. Dean was slumped against an overturned cash register, his right arm, the arm that had been closest to the blast, marbled with white muscle and blood that had come from a place so deep it could have been tar.

"There you are," Arthur said to me. His smile scared me most of all.

The Shark said, "Arthur," and began to cry.

Arthur looked at her, disapprovingly. "Get out of here, Beth." He pointed the rifle at her and waved it behind him, at the quad. Her freedom.

The Shark didn't move, and Arthur hunched down, so he was level with her peculiar eyes. "I mean it, Beth. I like you."

The Shark turned to me and sobbed, "I'm sorry." Then she tiptoed cautiously around Arthur, broke into a run when he screamed at her, "Don't you fucking apologize to her!" I watched her feel the dry grass beneath her feet. She went left, one final sprint toward the middle school parking lot. Then I couldn't see her anymore, just heard her rabid scream when she realized she was still alive.

"Come here." Arthur used the gun to beckon me like a long, witchy finger.

"Why?" I was ashamed that I was crying. I hate that I know how I will react when it's all over. That I know I won't be brave.

Arthur pointed the rifle at the ceiling and shot, and both Dean and I screamed in alliance with the fire alarm, still wailing, furious it hadn't been attended to yet. "Come here!" Arthur snarled.

I did what I was told.

Arthur pointed the rifle at me, and I begged. I was so sorry I took that picture of his dad, I said. I would give it back. I had it in my locker. (I didn't.) We could go. It was his. Anything to delay what I knew he was about to do.

Arthur glared at me, his wet hair hanging in his eyes, not even bothering to push it away. "Take it," he said. At first I thought he meant "take it," like just take what's about to happen to you, a call for me to man up. But then I realized Arthur wasn't pointing the gun at me, he was *handing* it to me.

"Don't you want to be the one to do it?" He looked to Dean. Fear had misshapen his ape-like features into someone new, someone I'd never met before and who had never hurt me. "Don't you just want to blow this cocksucker's cock off?" Closer to Arthur now, I saw that a white crust had hardened in the corners of his mouth.

I made the mistake of taking the bait, of reaching out and trying to take the gun. "Nah-uh." Arthur pulled it back. "Changed my mind."

Then he pivoted, surprisingly graceful, and shot Dean between his legs. Dean made an inhuman noise as blood and water shot straight up in front of his face like a fountain at Epcot Center.

The steak knife slipped underneath Arthur's shoulder blade. But it was a shallow puncture, a sideways slice, the way you'd run a letter opener underneath the flap of an envelope. It came out the same way it went in with almost no effort at all. Arthur turned toward me, arched his lip, and actually said, "Huh?" I shifted my weight back, the way my dad taught me to do before I threw a ball, the only useful thing the man has ever taught me in my life. I slammed the knife into the side of his neck, and Arthur stumbled sideways, making a noise like he was trying to clear out phlegm in his chest. I went with him, pulled the knife out again, and lunged once more. I knew I'd hit sternum, heard the crunch as I submerged the blade in his chest, and this time I wasn't able to pull it back out. But that was okay, because I didn't need to. Arthur managed to gargle something like "I was only trying to help," and the bright blood spilling over his lips rushed faster.

That's where I always end the story, and it's where I ended it for Aaron.

But there's one more thing, the part I never tell anyone. Which is that I actually thought, *They have to forgive me now*, as Arthur landed on his knees, the weight of his upper half propelling him forward. At the last second survival instinct kicked in, some flickering circuit in the brain realizing that if he landed on his chest it would only drive the handle deeper into its resting place. He tipped backward, but the tight muscles in his thighs caught him, and he ended up on his side with a large splash, one arm stretched out underneath his head, one leg stacked over the other, a soft bend at his knees. I always think of Arthur when I get to the thigh work portion of barre class, when I assume that exact same position to tighten my saddlebags. "Give me ten more!" the instructor demands, perkily, as I lift my leg, the muscle failing me and the desire to give up so great. "You can do anything—anything!—for ten seconds!"

CHAPTER 13

ncredible." Aaron clapped his hands and broke the room's still spell. Crew members stretched and roamed. I heard "Grab a drink?" and wiped my face.

Aaron came at me, his hands steepled together. "Thank you for being so open and vulnerable with us."

I hurried to erase the story written all over my face. "Sure," I mumbled.

"You probably need a drink or something." Aaron dipped low and squeezed my arm, tenderly. I made sure he felt me stiffen in his grasp. He drew away.

Aaron reminded me of an ambulance chaser I dated in college. This emo fucking break dancer who'd ask me about the tendons in Peyton's neck and the slow drop of the curtain on his blue eyes—had the sparkle gone out slowly or had he known? Accepted? I thought this was love, too, once, this vested interest in all that was gory in my life. Now the pendulum had swung the other way.

Aaron cleared his throat. "So, get yourself a drink!" He laughed stiffly. "But remember, seven A.M. call time in your hotel room tomorrow." That was for the hair and makeup people. Then they'd pack up their round brushes and eyelash curlers and we'd all drive over to Bradley for the "location shots."

"Got it." I rose and brushed myself off. I'd almost made it to the door when Aaron stopped me.

"*Argh*, okay," he said. "I've been debating asking you this all afternoon."

I glared at him so he wouldn't.

But then he leaned forward and told me something I hadn't expected at all. Something that put that familiar acid taste on my tongue. When he finished with his proposition, he held up his hands—*Don't shoot!*—and said, "Only if you're comfortable, of course."

I let him squirm in my silence for a moment. "Is this a trick?" I folded my arms across my chest. "To get your money shot or something?"

Aaron appeared startled. Hurt, even. "Ani, oh my gosh, of course not." His voice dipped low. "You know I'm on your side, right? We are all"—he gestured around the room—"on your side. I can understand why you wouldn't think so, after what you've been through. Heck, I'd be suspicious of everyone too." The word "heck" felt warm on my ears, like something a granddad would say. "But I hope you come to trust me. This is not a trick. I would never trick you." He backed away and gave me a little bow. "Why don't you think about it? We have all weekend."

I pressed my lips together and studied his wedding ring again. Recast Aaron as kind, rather than leering. Wondered if that had been the reality all along, and, if it was, what else I'd read wrong.

❧

I opened the studio door and stepped into the cool belly of September. I was so glad summer was over. I hated it, always had. It may seem odd, given the memories that are tied to fall for me, but whenever I catch the first edge in the air, notice the leaves flushing, I shiver with joy. Fall will forever be an opportunity to reinvent myself.

I waved good-bye to some of the crew heaving cameras and equipment into the back of a primitive black van. For a moment I considered taking a picture of it, texting it to Nell with the caption "Rapiest rape van ever?" But I remembered the way she'd stared me down at dinner, the combination of disappointment and disgust ruining her perfect face, and decided against it. I plugged the Radnor Hotel into the Jeep's GPS. I hadn't come this way much in high school, and I'd been "home" so infrequently since then that the roads I used to frequently travel now gave me a vague sense of déjà vu. *I've been here before, but when?* This confusion swelled in me as pride. It meant this was no longer home. New York was. *You didn't reject me, I rejected you.*

I backed out of the parking lot slowly. I was a tentative driver now that I didn't do it often. Clutching the wheel like some blue-haired old lady, I maneuvered onto Monroe Street. I heard my phone buzz in my bag, but I wouldn't check it until I could pull over. A few years ago, LoLo made us all sign a pledge, some partnership with Oprah, that we wouldn't text and drive. It wasn't my word that kept me from reaching for my phone but the stat I'd looped my name beneath: Texting and driving increases your risk of a fatal car crash by 2,000 percent. "That can't be right," I'd demanded of Martin, one of our fact-checkers. Martin is so strict we once got into a fight over a line I wrote, "You *need* this lip gloss in your life."

"Maybe we should put this another way?" he suggested. "It's not food or water, so technically you don't 'need' it in your life."

"You're kidding me, right? It's facetious."

"Well, at least remove the emphasis on the word 'need.'"

But when I'd questioned the accuracy of that 2,000 percent stat, he'd only nodded solemnly. "It's right."

There was a crack, and I started so intensely the car swerved. I swept my hand over the back of my head, a quick check for injury. Over the violent pulse of my heart, I realized it was only the construction workers on my left, slowly assembling what would be a sprawling McMansion. Sometimes, when I'm waiting for the subway, or crossing the street, a phantom pain will appear in my head, or shoulder, and I'll touch my hand to it, pull it away expecting to see blood. The last person to realize he's been shot is always the person who's just been shot.

A Wawa loomed to my right. I wrenched the wheel, confusing the GPS woman as I pulled into the parking lot. "Continue to your left, continue to your left," she berated me. I stabbed at the buttons until she went silent.

I reached into my bag and pulled out my phone. No texts from Luke. I opened my e-mail. Found the one from Mr. Larson—Andrew—about our lunch on Sunday. "Today was harder than I expected," I wrote. "Any chance you could meet for a quick." I paused. Knew I was pushing it, so I wrote, "slice at Peace A Pizza?" I would eat carbs for Andrew.

Peace A Pizza was the residential hangout when we were in high school. Headmaster Mah was such a fan he was always the customer of the month, giving the camera an embarrassing thumbs-up in the picture that hung next to the fountain soda machine. Dean once wrote, "Me love pizza long time" across Mr. Mah's face. Of course he didn't get into trouble for it, even though everyone knew he was the one who did it.

I hit send and waited five minutes, even though I doubted I'd get a response anytime soon. I decided to go back to my hotel. Maybe by the time I got there he would call.

The Radnor Hotel is one of those places that advertises itself as a boutiquey beauty in the heart of the Main Line—a wedding destination—when really it's just an overworked Marriott with sprawling parking lots and the roar of the highway not far behind it.

Whoever had stayed in the room before me had smoked, and hadn't been discreet about it. Our beauty director had wrung her hands over thirdhand smoke on the *Today* show—that's the kind that's embedded in ugly couch fabric and apparently does the most damage to your skin. Normally, I would call downstairs to the front desk and request to move like a demanding little bitch, but there was something about the room's stale breath that I found soothing. I pictured a girl, an outlier like me, curled up in the floral armchair by the window, narrowing her eyes as she pulled on her cigarette, the tip blazing in response. She was back in town for a funeral, I decided. She didn't get along with her parents either, and that's why she was staying here instead of at home. I felt a delicious camaraderie with her that made me feel less alone. Which was exactly what I was, at six o'clock on a Friday evening, the last act of *Never Been Kissed* playing out on TBS. I held a coffee mug full of warm vodka between my hands, trying to ignore the M&M's in the minibar beckoning me like a prostitute in the part of

Philadelphia where Hilary once got a butterfly tattoo on her lower back.

It had been an hour since I'd written Andrew, and the only e-mails I'd received were from Groupon, alerting me to deals for liposuction, keratin, Swedish massage, fractional skin resurfacing, dating. There was another from Saks, which had selected a pair of snakeskin Jimmy Choo booties for $1,195 just for me. I wasn't that flush.

I checked the call sheet for tomorrow, trying to calculate if I had enough time to go for a run before the hair and makeup people arrived. I never expected to sleep, but I certainly didn't expect to here of all places. A thought suddenly dawned on me, and I set my coffee mug down. I dug around in the nightstand table, and—aha—there it was, a phone book, yellow and ancient in my hands.

Larsons, Larsons, Larsons, I thought, flipping to the L section, tracing an oxblood fingernail over the names once I got to "Lar."

There were three Larsons, but only one lived on Grays Lane in Haverford. Andrew had once pointed out his folks' house on a run, used that word, "folks," which was such a sweet Andrew word, so I knew that was it.

I eyed the phone in its receiver. If I called from this number, I could just hang up if anyone but Andrew answered. Whitney might be there, his parents certainly would be. But, Christ, what were those systems where the caller ID shows up on the TV screen they have now? I'd told Andrew I was staying here. What if I called and the Radnor Hotel blinked in plain sight, interrupting whatever PBS program the family was probably watching? He'd know it was me who hung up on his mother, if she got to the phone before he did. I knew nothing about Andrew's parents, but I pictured them as former academics, both with soft white tufts of hair, glasses of red wine in their hands as they discussed the energy crisis through the lens of the Obama administration in low, respectful tones. These kind intellectuals responsible for turning out a person like Andrew Larson, with all his emotional intelligence that drew me to him, desperate as a groupie.

The vodka opened up some clear channel of memory, because in an instant I recalled a trick from middle school sleepovers. *67 before the number and it blocks the caller's identity. I decided to test it out with my cell phone first, punching in the secret code followed by my 917 area code. I worshiped my 917 area code. Not a PA girl anymore. A New Yorker.

My screen read "Unknown number" and I gasped a laugh. I couldn't believe it actually worked.

I gathered a little more courage from my coffee cup. You know, maybe I didn't even have to hang up if his parents answered. This was a perfectly innocent request. Production had changed my call time on Sunday and I couldn't do lunch anymore, and I just wanted to try to catch him while we were both here. It wasn't a lie yet. My call time would change, if I agreed to do what Aaron had asked me to do.

I punched in *67 first. There was a pause, and then the gentle purr of the dial tone in my ear, the shrill ring in the Larson household, several miles away.

"Larson residence." The voice that answered could have cracked your skull in half.

"Hi." I stood and began to pace. But I'd forgotten about the cord, how short it was, and the receiver crashed to the floor behind me, wrenching the phone out of my hand. "Shit!" I hissed, dropping to the ground to grab it.

"Hello?" the voice demanded from the floor. "Hello?"

"Hi," I said again, "sorry. Is Mr. Larson there?"

"Speaking."

"Sorry, Andrew Larson."

"This is he. To *whom* am I speaking?"

I wanted to hang up. It would have been easier if I had. But muscle memory took over and my knuckles went white on the phone. "This is Ani FaNelli. I'm trying to get ahold of your son." Adding, so this request didn't seem *indecent*, "I was one of his students."

There were a few surly blasts of Mr. Larson Senior's breath. Then, "My God, girl, I thought you were one of those crank callers." The connection crackled with his laugh. "Just a second."

He put the phone down. There were muffled voices in the background. Agonizing moments of silence before Andrew Larson Jr. was saying, "TifAni?"

I forgot all about the posturing and the excuses. I just told him the truth. Today was hard, and I was alone.

Andrew hadn't brought Whitney with him for the weekend. When I heard that, I caught my breath, hoping he would suggest we grab a drink instead of meeting at Peace A Pizza, my idea, but he just said, "Peace A Pizza. I haven't been there in years. Forty minutes?"

I placed the phone in its receiver with an accusing click. Pizza. At a time so early the sun still taunted me in the sky. There wasn't anything indecent about this. Relief and disappointment went to battle. I felt the gritty determination of both.

I'd washed off the camera makeup the moment I entered the hotel room, averting my eyes from the places the fluorescent lights pointed out, the powder and foundation gathered in creases around my eyes and mouth. Twenty-eight, and, thanks to my slick olive skin, I was often mistaken for just out of college, but it was impossible to tell how much longer that would last. I'd seen aging overcome people like a fast-growing cancer. Not enough antioxidants in the world to ward it off.

I went to work again—tinted moisturizer, concealer, bronzer, mascara, lip stain. Luke is always amazed at the weight of my makeup bag. "Do you actually use all of this crap?" he asked me once. It was a compliment because yes, I did.

It was 6:50 when I climbed into Luke's Jeep. Fourteen minutes. That's how long it took to drive just two miles into Bryn Mawr. That terrified crawl—it wasn't just so I could be the right amount of late. I was genuinely afraid that I'd pushed my luck too far now. That the universe had no choice but to intervene, point its finger at a mean-eyed luxury-make SUV and drag it into my lane, pinning me between its polished body and the median, the steering wheel cracking my sternum into bony splinters, one of which would puncture a heart or a lung. Proving what a falsehood it was that I got out of that cafeteria because great things were ahead for me, things the five were never meant to accomplish anyway. Which is what I sometimes tell myself when I fall into a depressed slump, when all I can see is the open nut of Ansilee's head in my mind's eye, and the day doesn't seem like it will ever turn to night.

I didn't know what kind of car Andrew drove, so there was no way for me to scan for it in the packed parking lot before I entered. That one drink on an empty stomach had induced a brave haze, but anxiety was still stronger. The place was teeming with teenage limbs, gangly legs too long and restless to squash underneath the table, and, like Nell's, they sprawled into the open aisles, a series of overturned pogo sticks. No Andrew. I backed into a corner and waited.

I had that feeling like I didn't know what to do with my arms—fold them, hold one elbow with one hand?—when the doors opened and a whoosh of crisp air ushered Andrew in. He was wearing a fine knit sweater and good jeans, jeans picked out by a magnificently thin stylist at Barneys.

I gave him a little wave, and he made his way over to me.

Andrew whistled. "This place is packed." I agreed, hoping again he would suggest we go somewhere else, but then he said, "I guess we should get in line."

When I was in high school, novelty pizzas were still high concept. Macaroni and cheese pizza, bacon cheeseburger pizza, penne alla vodka pizza—it had been so wild to me. Now all I think is carbs on top of carbs. No wonder I was such a porker.

I said as much to Andrew, and he laughed. "You were never a porker." He patted his brawny middle. "This guy on the other hand." It was true. There had been a playful, frat boy roundness to him back then. I still can't believe Andrew was twenty-four years old when he was my teacher. Twenty-four that night in his bedroom, when he woke me up from my bad dream and I begged him to stay. There had been so much sadness in his face before he agreed. For a long time I thought it was because he felt sorry for me, but now I wonder if it was something else. If maybe he was mourning the great divide between us, what could have been if our age difference was just five years less.

Through the glass partition, the pies gleamed high with toppings that, on their own, were more than I was eating at my meals these days. My stomach yawned.

I ordered a slice of margarita. A safe choice, I reasoned, because no flair meant no flair caught in my teeth. Andrew ordered a slice of the Mediterranean salad.

There were no open tables, only open chairs, and if this was all the time I had with Andrew, I wasn't about to waste it next to a pair of rawboned gigglers, napkins over their laps in the event of an untimely erection. I nodded at the door. "Want to sit outside?"

There were two benches in the front, but those were occupied, so Andrew and I went around the side and sat on the curb, paper plates balanced gingerly on our thighs, the gravel pocking our skin through our jeans.

I took a bite. "Oh my God," I moaned.

"Not better than New York," Andrew said.

"Better than anything." I held up my finger. "Wedding diet."

Andrew nodded. "Whitney went crazy with that too." A portly artichoke rolled off his slice and hit the ground with a wet thud. I thought about Ansilee's head and had to place the paper plate on my lap. Like that, the tomato sauce had taken on the consistency of blood. This happens to me occasionally with ketchup too, usually when I go through a bout of thinking about Peyton. There are times I see the mangled destruction on his face all day and no red food is safe. Neither is meat. Just the thought. I held a napkin to my mouth and forced myself to swallow the last bite I'd taken.

"So today wasn't easy, huh?"

Andrew was sitting close to me but not so close that there could be an innocuous brush of our thighs. He hadn't shaved that morning, and his scruff was golden over the summer tan that clung on. He was heartbreaking to look at.

"Not because I had to talk about it," I said. "That I don't care about. I care about people believing me." I leaned back on my hands, something I never would have done on a New York City street corner. "I looked around at the crew after we were done, and I just wondered, *Do they really believe me?* I don't know what to do to make people believe me." I watched the cars pass each other on the road. "I'll do anything." I took a deep breath, that old desperation flaming in me like a pull on a cigarette. It makes me capable of things I don't want to be capable of, and if I don't watch myself with militant supervision, my blade could very easily slip, cut Luke too deep, sever me from the life I've worked so hard to assemble. But when I stand next to Andrew and see how my head just barely reaches the place where his shoulder starts to pitch, when I think how big he is and how hard it must be to control himself, I wonder if he would be the one thing that's worth my exile from the tartan tribe.

"You're doing it," Andrew said. "Right now. By telling your side. If people still don't believe you afterwards, you did all you could do."

I nodded, obediently, but I was unconvinced. "You know what drives me crazy most of all?"

Andrew bit into his slice, releasing a shiny rivulet of oil that trickled all the way to his wrist. He caught it in his mouth before it disappeared under the cuff of his sweater, sinking his teeth into his flesh. I watched the white bite marks recede from his skin.

"The Dean Stalwarts," I said. "I think I hate them more than I hate Dean. Especially the women. You wouldn't

believe the crap they send me. *Still.*" I adopted the stern
voice of a midwestern church lady with multiple chins and
hairy knees. "The Lord knows what you did and you will
answer to him in your next life." I ripped apart the crust
of my pizza. "Fucking inbred Jesus fuckers." I cowered at
my own words, immediately regretful. Luke might laugh
when I said stuff like that, but that was not what Andrew
wanted from me. *Broken,* I reminded myself, *that's what
works on him.* "Sorry. It's just, if they even knew what Dean
did to me."

Andrew took a sip of his soda. "So why don't you tell
them?"

"It's the one thing . . ." I sighed. "It's the one thing my
mom doesn't want me to talk about. Luke doesn't either.
He knows what happened with those guys, of course, but I
don't want his parents to know about that night. It's humiliating." I found a piece of crust without any red and nib-
bled on it. "It's not just for my mom or Luke though. I'm
hesitant to go on the record about this too, especially when
it comes to Liam. It's a serious allegation to make against
someone who is always going to be fifteen in everyone's
minds." I watched a group of teenagers tease each other on
the sidewalk, Starbucks cups in their hands. Coffee tasted
like gasoline when I was that age, now it's lunch. "A fifteen-
year-old who was chased into a classroom and shot in the
chest. Something about it sits funny, even with me. I don't
know. Haven't his parents been through enough?"

Andrew sighed. "That's a tough one, Tif."

I wrapped my hands around my shins. "What would
you do, if you were me?"

"If it were me?" Andrew dusted crumbs off his lap and
shifted so that his knees pointed at me. "I think there is a
way you can be honest but not speak ill of the dead. And

I certainly wouldn't pass up the opportunity to expose
Dean for what he really is." The edge of his knee grazed
my thigh by accident, and he quickly pulled it back.
"There is no one in this world who deserves that honor
more than you."

I let the tears rise to the surface and turned to him to
let him see. It didn't take much. My chest felt like a wash-
cloth, wringing, wringing. "Thank you."

Andrew smiled at me. He had arugula in his teeth, and
I loved him more.

I took my shot. "Want to drive by Bradley and see if
anything's going on tonight?" I had pictured us doing this,
of course, I just didn't think I would actually ask. But the
sky was losing its fight against the dark and there was only
the crust left on Andrew's pizza and I couldn't let him go
yet. Andrew said yes in a way that made me think he had
been waiting for me to ask, and my heart extended its beat
to every limb in my body.

Andrew offered to drive. He had a BMW, but it was the
perfect amount of weathered to convey that old money
nonchalance I will never naturally project. There were
golf clubs in the backseat and an empty Starbucks cup
in the center console. Andrew reached for it. "Hand me
that, would you?" he asked. As I passed the cup his way
I caught 'Whitney' scribbled on the side. There was a
line struck through the boxes for latte and nonfat milk.
I couldn't think of a more apt description for Andrew's
nothing-burger wife: Whitney is the type of woman who
drinks Starbucks nonfat lattes.

Andrew chucked the coffee cup in a nearby trash can

and climbed behind the wheel. He turned the car on, revealing he had been listening to the nineties station on Pandora. Third Eye Blind wailed, eerily. How many times had I driven these same streets, listening to these same songs? So long ago that this situation, Andrew and I next to each other in his car, would have aroused concern. It still did now, just for different reasons.

It wasn't a long drive to Bradley. A left onto Lancaster Avenue, another left onto North Roberts Road, and a right onto Montgomery. Bradley kids frequently walked to this Peace A Pizza before they passed their driving tests. I used to do it with Arthur all the time.

The soccer field stretched out on our left, empty and stubborn summer green. Andrew's large hand flicked the turn signal, and we waited patiently for an opening in traffic. Then we were blazing alongside the soccer stands, passing the opening to the path I used to take to Arthur's house. Mrs. Finnerman never moved away, remained visible as the mother of the boy who gleefully plotted the death of his classmates at the prestigious Bradley School. The media lamenting, "How could it happen here?" and, for once, really meaning it. School shootings belonged to the Midwest middle-class, strip-mall towns where there was no Ivy League legacy and guns were given as stocking stuffers. The car sputtered at the curb, and Andrew turned to me. "Wanna break in?"

I looked out the window at the school's black eyes. More times than not, I had entered Bradley with vomit roasting in my throat. I should have felt it now, a sort of Pavlovian response to the place, but Andrew was like a net, keeping the dread out. I was vaguely aware that this was something Luke had done for me once, when we first met—reminded me that hope and warmth resided in me, so that even sleep was possible—when Andrew reached for me and I started out of my seat. "Sorry." He smiled, and his fingers fiddled with my seat belt buckle. "This sticks sometimes."

"No, sorry, you just surprised me," I stammered. I heard a click, and the pressure on my chest lessened.

❧

The Athletic Center was unlocked. "Way to go, Bradley," I muttered, and Andrew murmured his agreement as he held the door open. Bradley should have better security measures in place after what happened, but the school stood strong against state and media pressure to erect metal detectors and hire armed security guards. As far as the administration was concerned, this was a one-time incident and there was no reason to further terrorize students by infringing on their privacy and subjecting them to random pat downs by trigger-happy rent-a-cops. They had the support of the parents too, as so many of them were graduates of Bradley themselves, and no one wanted to see the institution that *J. D. Salinger's first wife attended* held to the same security standards as an inner-city public high school.

We descended the stairs into the basketball courts. "Pretty sure shoes like that are not permitted on these floors." Andrew nodded at my suede flats, the ones with the clunky silver heels, and started for the carpeted flooring that ringed the court.

I ignored him, stepping onto the polished maple. My shoes ticked off a few beats, and Andrew stopped and watched me drag my heel along the surface, drawing a fuzzy white line that ended with an ear-piercing squeak.

He stepped off the carpet next to me, grinding the heel of his loafer into the floor, matching my mark.

The gym deposited us in the Science wing, where a brass framed poster of the periodic table of elements made me smile. "You know Mr. Hardon?" Mr. Hardon was the Honors Chemistry teacher. He had a mustache that twitched involuntarily, and due to his unfortunate name and odd disposition, he was mostly known as a pervert and referred to as Mr. Hard-On.

"You mean Mr. Hard-On?" Andrew grinned, and it wiped the fourteen years off his face.

I stopped walking. "You knew that's what we called him?"

"Tif, the entire teaching staff called him that. His name was *literally* Mr. Hard-On." He tipped his chin at me, an ask for more credit. "It was a logical leap to make."

My laugh somersaulted down the empty hallway, hit the seven steps to the old mansion. Ascend them and the cafeteria was to the right and the English wing was to the left. I thought about that sound ricocheting in the space the Shark and I had crossed, after we'd lost Liam, and immediately wished I could reel it back.

The computer lab appeared on our right, once such a throwaway room, now stocked with iPads mounted on futuristic looking stands. The dark room held our image in the glass, looking in.

Andrew pressed his knuckles into the pane. "I can't even imagine what everyone said about me."

"They didn't say anything. Everyone loved you. We were all crushed when you left."

The glass caught Andrew dropping his head to his chest. "Those Bartons, they play dirty." He eyed me in our reflection. "It would have been my last year anyway. Teaching was always a layover for me until I grew up a little. I just wasn't ready to get a real job after I graduated. Though"— he swished his mouth side to side, considering—"I probably would have stayed on longer after what happened. At least another year to help you guys out."

This had never even occurred to me, that I could have had him for more time than I did. Anger tightened my chest as I realized how Mr. Larson was just one more thing Dean had taken from me.

We continued down the hallway, arriving at the entrance of the Junior and Senior Lounge. I stepped inside, the space still intimidating in its unfamiliarity. I'd rarely spent time there, not even as a senior. There was an exclusive code to the place even when you were of age, and it wasn't a spot where the marginalized could enjoy a free period. It wasn't like I was completely friendless for my remaining years at Bradley. I had the Shark. We'd been really close, but we lost touch once we got to college. I still regret that. I also had some of the girls on the cross-country team, which I continued to sign up for every year. I really did love running before I made it into something torturous and hard, something I did to impress Luke. There was a solace that settled in me as I collected the miles beneath my feet, a total absence of self-doubt.

Andrew lingered in the open doorway. He was so tall he could rest his hands against the arch in the ceiling. He leaned forward, his broad chest stretching even wider, his body blocking the way. I used to play this game when I first began to toe the line of adolescence, when my boobs came in and I was hungry for the boys my age to catch up:

I'd scan the damp basement room containing whatever seventh-grade party I was attending, and wonder which boy was strong enough to overtake me. Whoever he was, no matter how pimpled and squeaky, if he was big enough to hurt me, I wanted him. It's something I've come to understand about myself—I want someone who can hurt me but won't. Luke has failed me there. I know Andrew wouldn't.

"Do you think about Arthur ever?" I asked him.

Andrew slipped his hands—all but his thumbs—into his pockets. The body language expert at *The Women's Magazine* told me that when someone puts his hands in his pockets, he's feeling shy—unless he continues to reveal his thumbs, in which case it's a sign of confidence. "A lot actually, yes."

I nodded. "I do too."

Andrew took a few steps into the lounge, closing the distance between us and setting off all my signals like an airplane in distress. If he wanted to cross this line, he could, this place had ground what remained of my steely resolve fine as flour. There was nothing left of the day but gray, and with the white of the room bruising all around us, we could have been in a black-and-white movie. "What do you think about when you think about him?"

I traced the arch of his rib cage with my eyes while I considered the question. "I think about how smart he was. *Savvy* smart. Arthur understood people in a way I never will. He could really read them. I wish I could do that."

Andrew took a few more steps closer, until he was right in front of me, resting his elbow on the high ledge of the window. There was just the slightest curl to his top lip. "You don't think you can read people?"

"I *try*." I smiled, pleased. Was this flirting?

"You're very grounded, Tif." He pointed right at my gut. "Don't ever doubt this."

I looked down at his finger, inches from my body. "You know what else?" I asked.

Andrew waited for me to continue.

"He was *funny*." I looked out the window, at the low frame of the quad. "Arthur was funny." I said that to Luke once, and he recoiled from me.

Andrew's eyes crinkled at an old memory of Arthur. "He could be very funny."

"But I don't feel bad," I said, quietly. "Is that bad? I don't feel bad about what I did to him. I feel nothing." I slid my hand from left to right—this is how flat it all is. "I feel neutral when I imagine killing him." I sucked in a breath and released it, the sound like blowing on a hot bite of food. "My best friend thinks I'm still in shock over it. That I've blocked out any emotion to spare myself the trauma." I shook my head. "I wish that was it, but I don't think it is."

Andrew pinched his eyebrows together and waited for me to say more. When I didn't, he asked, "So what do you think it is then?"

"That, maybe"—I sunk my incisors into my lip—"I'm a cold person." I rushed out the next part. "That I'm selfish and that I'm only capable of *feeling* about things that benefit me."

"Tif," Andrew said, "you are *not* selfish. You're the bravest person I know. To go through what you went through at your age—and not just go through it, but survive it and thrive like you have—it's remarkable."

I was holding back tears now, terrified I would scare him off with what I was about to say next. "I can stab my friend to death but I can't admit I'm about to marry the wrong guy."

Andrew looked sick. "Is that true?"

I thought about it before I did it, there was still time to take it back and excuse away all the doubt, like I always did to myself, but I nodded.

"Then what are you doing? Why not just walk away?" Andrew sounded so disturbed it only made me feel worse. I thought everyone, on some level, felt some reserve about the person they were with.

I shrugged. "Isn't it obvious? I'm scared."

"Of what?"

I fixed on a spot beyond Andrew's shoulder and tried to think of a way to explain. "With Luke, I feel this . . . this crushing loneliness sometimes. And it's not his fault"—I swiped a finger under my eye—"he's not a bad person, he just doesn't get it. But then I think, *Well, who would? Get this nasty piece of my life?* I'm not easy, and maybe this is the best I can hope for. Because there are a lot of good things there too. Being with him is insurance in its own way."

Andrew's face pinched. "Insurance?"

"I have this thing in my head"—I brought my fingers to my temple and tapped—"no one can hurt me if I'm Ani Harrison. TifAni FaNelli is the type of girl who gets squashed, maybe, but not an Ani Harrison."

Andrew hunched down so that he was eye to eye with me. "I don't remember anyone squashing TifAni FaNelli."

I held my thumb and index finger an inch apart. "But they did. To this small."

Andrew sighed, and then his smart-looking sweater was scratching my face, his fingers curled into the back of my head. We had touched so few times in our lives, and it broke me, really, that I didn't know his smell and his skin better than I did. An inexplicable sorrow swelled up at Luke, at Whitney, at his beautifully named children, all the hearts invested that would keep us apart, caught them all in its pit and came crashing down.

The setup in Andrew's old classroom hadn't changed; there were still those three long tables pushed together to create a bracket, the teacher at the front of the room in its clutches. But sleek metal tables and stools had replaced the old linoleum tables and the janky, mismatched chairs. It was very Restoration Hardware, a set that wouldn't look entirely out of my place in my own apartment, the style I've curated something Mrs. Harrison describes as "eclectic." I hovered above the table and examined my distorted image: the long pointy chin, one eye here and one eye there. Whenever I had a pimple in high school, I would assess its severity in anything remotely reflective—the glare in the classroom window, the glass panel between me and the deli meats in the cafeteria. I would never have been able to concentrate in class with so much opportunity before me.

Andrew wandered over to his old desk and examined a few of his successor's knickknacks.

"You know Mr. Friedman still works here," Andrew said.

"Really?" I remembered the day he hauled Arthur out of the classroom, Mrs. Hurst trying to pretend like she wasn't as frightened as she should have been. "He was always kind of dopey."

"Actually"—Andrew turned and leaned against the desk, folding one ankle over the other exactly like he used to do when he taught class—"Bob is very smart. Too smart to be a teacher. It's why he doesn't connect with the students." Andrew touched his hand to his forehead. "On another level than the rest of us."

I nodded. It was more dark than dusk outside now, but the English and Language wing faced a main street, ablaze with streetlights and the Bryn Mawr College art building.

"That's why everyone loved your class so much," I said. "You were on our level. More like a peer."

Andrew laughed. "I don't know if that's a compliment."

I laughed too. "No, it is." I glanced down at my fun house reflection again. "It was good to have someone so young. Only a few years removed from it all."

"I don't know how much help I was," Andrew said. "I'd never seen this kind of viciousness before. I don't know, maybe it did happen when I was in high school and I just wasn't paying attention." He thought for a moment. "But I think I would have noticed. There was something very cut-throat about Bradley that I picked up on right away. And you"—he gestured at me—"you never even had a chance."

I didn't like that. You always have a chance. I just screwed mine up. "I wasn't very sharp when I was here," I said. "But if I have to find a positive in it, it's that I learned how to fend for myself." I brushed my knuckles over the table's metal scales. "Arthur taught me a lot, believe it or not."

"There are better ways to learn," Andrew said.

I smiled sadly. "I would have welcomed them. I did the best with what I got."

Andrew tucked his chin into his neck, like he was gathering his thoughts to make an important connection between the Museum of Natural History and Holden Caulfield's fear of change. "You've been honest with me, so"—he cleared his throat—"I want to be honest with you."

There was a perfect plot of light illuminating the space

behind him. It was so bright that he appeared to be nothing but a figure, faceless, expressionless. My heart boomed in my chest, sure he was about to admit something of importance. Our connection, our exquisite chemical reaction—it wasn't just in my head. "About what?"

"That dinner. It wasn't just a matter of us living in a small world." He took a noisy breath through his nostrils. "I knew Luke was your fiancé. I pushed for him to set up dinner so I could see you."

Hope rose in me like a temperature. "How did you know that?"

"I can't even remember who told me, one of my co-workers who knew I'd taught here, though. Told me that Luke was engaged to a Bradley girl. Luke had mentioned your name to me before—Ani—but I couldn't remember any Anis from Bradley. I did the Facebook thing." Andrew mimed typing, then covered his face with his hands, a sweetly girlish gesture, and laughed. "God, that's embarrassing, but I looked Luke up on Facebook. Saw you in his pictures. I couldn't believe that was you."

The sky was done changing and the room went still, complete with the shadows it had collected for the night. But now something cut the street light, and, for a second, without that blinding blast of yellow behind him, I saw Andrew's face entirely. He looked terrified.

We watched out the window as a little silver bullet of a car parked in front of the old mansion's entrance. The word "Security" broke in half when the driver opened his door and stepped out, walking with an official stride toward the school.

My heart seemed to drop down and back, the thing it always does right before I start to spin and spin. I refuse to call it a panic attack. Panic attacks are for nervous fliers, hipster neurotics. Their demons, whatever they are, can't even compare to the terror of knowing it's about to happen, the something bad I've been waiting for ever since I got out of the cafeteria. My turn. "Is he here for us?"

Andrew shook his head. "I don't know."

"What is he doing here?"

Again, Andrew said, "I don't know."

The security guard disappeared into the building, and in the distance we heard a door bang shut and a shout's echo. "Hello?" Andrew put his finger to his lips and motioned for me to come close to him. He was pushing the chair away from the desk, and then, I couldn't believe it, we were climbing underneath the desk together, Andrew bending and arranging his enormous limbs to make room for me.

When we were knee to knee Andrew pulled the chair in behind us, really squishing us in, and then he *grinned* at me.

I couldn't feel my heart beating anymore, another characteristic that separates the spin from a panic attack—no brave palpitations, only a sad white flag—and in a few minutes I felt the sureness of a presence in the room. Had that really been the car of a security guard we'd seen? *The Women's Magazine* had run a slew of articles over the years warning women about predators who dressed up as police officers, plumbers, even deliverymen in order to gain access to your car, your house, *you*. Always you they wanted, to rape, to torture, to kill. My vision seemed to narrow to a pinprick, like when you turn off an old TV, that one dot that lingers until the screen goes totally blank. I wasn't breathing, I was sure of it. My heart had stopped, and these were just the last few moments of consciousness, the neurons in the brain still burning embers, before I dipped off into the dark.

A light swept over the front of the room, and someone cleared his throat. "Anyone in here?"

He sounded low and uniform, the way Ben had. "Boo." So flat, it could have been any word. "Hi." "No." "Sure." Mr. Larson covered his mouth, I could tell by the extra crow's-feet gathering around his eyes that he was trying not to laugh, and a tremble began in my hips—why my hips? Maybe because I wasn't standing; it would have been in my legs, but my hips were supporting me now.

The light disappeared, and we even heard footsteps retreat, but I knew he was still there, I could feel him. He had exaggerated his exit, then crept back, waiting for us to crawl out, two dumb idiots thinking they were safe. A copycat. Bradley had tried to pretend like we didn't need to worry about that. But we would. We always would. Mr. Larson whispered, "I think he's gone," and I shook my head, widening my eyes at him desperately.

"What?" Mr. Larson whispered again, and he pushed the chair back.

I seized his thick wrist and shook my head at him, begging him not to go.

"TifAni." Mr. Larson looked down at my hand, and I saw the horror on his face, knew we were done for. "You're like ice."

"Still. Here," I mouthed.

"TifAni!" Mr. Larson shook me off and crawled out onto the floor, ignoring my manic signaling to come back. He used the chair to hoist himself to his feet, and I slunk back deeper underneath the desk, readying myself for the hot pop of the gun, the soggy inside of Mr. Larson's head. But I just heard "He's gone."

Mr. Larson dropped to his knees and peered under the desk, at me, a feral cat in a cage. His brow splintered, and he seemed contrite, ready to cry for me. "He's gone. We're okay. He couldn't have done anything to us." When I didn't move, he dropped his head and sighed. The sound was full of remorse. "Tif, I'm so sorry. Shit, I wasn't thinking . . . the desk . . . I'm sorry." He held out a hand and pleaded at me with his eyes to take it.

All this time with Andrew, I've worn my victim's mask, thinking this was what he wanted from me. But there was no performing in my arms, gelatinous and quivering, as I reached for him, the limbs themselves so useless he had to take hold of my elbows, the only sturdy points he could find, the only way he could get me to my feet. My lower half wasn't doing much better, and he propped me up against his chest. We stayed pressed together much longer than we needed to, well after I got my legs back, the not doing anything the most dangerous part. Eventually, his hand asked the question on the tender small of my back, and then we were kissing, the relief that much greater for all the terror that came before it.

CHAPTER 14

n my memory the hospital is green. Green floors, green walls, gangrene hollows under the officers' eyes. The retching even produced a dull chartreuse substance that sunk to the bottom of the toilet. I flushed, thinking about all those times Mom told me to wear clean underwear, "because, TifAni, what if you're ever in a car accident?" Not that the underwear I was removing at the moment wasn't clean, but it was old and there was a hole above the crotch, big enough for a few pubic hairs to wiggle through. It would be many years before I regularly spread out for the Indian women at Shobha. "Everything?" "Everything."

I stuffed the ratty underwear in the leg of my khakis before stuffing those in the clear evidence bag and handing it off to the female officer, the one who looked more like a man than Officer Pensacole. In there already was my J. Crew cardigan and Victoria's Secret tank top, both ombréed with blood that hadn't completely dried yet. The smell of it so nostalgic and familiar to me. Where had I smelled that smell before? In cleaning supplies, maybe. Or at the Malvern YMCA, where I first learned to swim.

Whoever received that plastic evidence bag, with clothes that held the DNA of several dead teenagers, would no doubt find the underwear in the leg of the khakis. It wasn't some brilliant hiding place. But there was something about my underwear bouncing around in that plastic bag, on display for all it passed, that filled me with despair. I was so tired of everything that was embarrassing about me being on display.

I wrapped myself in the flimsy hospital gown and tiptoed across the hospital room to sit down on the hospital bed, holding my arms across my chest, trying to contain my breasts. They seemed enormous and unpredictable without a bra. Mom was in the chair next to the bed, under strict orders from me not to come near me or touch me or anything, and she was weeping. It was infuriating.

"Thank you," Officer She-Man said to me, and she didn't sound like she was grateful at all.

I folded my feet underneath me. It had been weeks since I'd shaved, and I didn't want anyone to see the black prickles around my ankles. The doctor, also a woman (no man shall pass. Even Dad was in the hallway) came toward me to do the examination. I insisted I wasn't hurt, but Dr. Levitt said that sometimes we're in so much shock that we don't realize we actually are hurt, and she just wanted to make sure that wasn't the case. Would it be okay if she did that? I wanted to scream at her to stop talking to me like I was a five-year-old about to receive a tetanus shot. I'd just stuck a knife in someone's chest.

"I'm sorry"—Officer She-Man stepped in Dr. Levitt's path—"but I have to swab her first. You could destroy evidence in the examination."

Dr. Levitt backed away. "Of course."

Officer She-Man came at me with her little evidence

collecting kit, and I suddenly realized how good I'd had it when it was just pretty Dr. Levitt who wanted to examine me. I still hadn't cried yet. I'd seen enough *Law & Orders* to know this was probably because I was in shock, but that didn't make me feel any better about it. I should have been crying, not thinking about dinner, how Mom would probably let me eat wherever I wanted after a day like this. Where should we go? My mouth watered as I considered the possibilities.

Officer She-Man swabbed the skin beneath my fingernails and that part was fine. But then she went for the opening of my hospital gown, and the tears came steady and fierce and I gripped Officer She-Man's sausage wrists. "*Stop!*" I heard that word over and over again, and at first I thought it was Officer She-Man telling *me* to stop, but then I realized it was me and I was fighting her off like she was Dean, kicking, thrashing, biting. My gown opened and my titanic breasts spilled everywhere and when I realized Mom was over me now too and she was seeing my naked body I rolled on my side and threw up again. Some of it got on Officer She-Man's dykey black slacks, and that almost made me smile.

When I came to I felt like I'd gone back in time. I thought that I was in the hospital because I'd had a reaction to the pot I'd smoked at Leah's house. I thought, *There must be so many people who are mad at me.*

I patted my body down before I even opened my eyes, relieved to feel that someone had retied my hospital gown and pinned me in on both sides with a thick white blanket.

The room was empty and still, dusk shading the windows. Dinnertime. I wanted to go to Bertucci's, I'd decided. Their focaccia and cheese bread was exactly what I was in the mood to eat.

I pushed myself onto my elbows, my triceps shaking in a way that made me realize how involved they were in everyday moments that I took for granted. There was a film coating my lips that my tongue couldn't crack. It was stuck on good and I had to rub it off with a fist.

Suddenly the door swung open and Mom walked in. "Oh!" She took a step back, startled. There was a coffee cup and a stale pastry in her hand. I didn't even drink coffee yet, but I wanted both I was so hungry. "You're up."

"What time is it?" I sounded raw. Like I was sick. I swallowed to make sure, but my throat didn't hurt.

Mom shook her fake diamond Rolex out of her sleeve. "It's six thirty."

"Let's go to Bertucci's for dinner," I said.

"Sweetie." Mom hunched to sit on the edge of the bed but remembered my warning and snapped upright. "It's six thirty in the morning."

I looked out the window again, this revelation making me see the light outside as blossoming, rather than waning. "It's morning?" I repeated. I was starting to feel woozy and weepy again. I was just so mad that I couldn't understand anything. "Why did you let me sleep here?" I demanded.

"Dr. Levitt gave you that pill, remember?" Mom said. "To help you relax?"

I squinted, trying to see back through my memories, but I couldn't. "I don't remember," I wailed. I covered my face with my hands. I was crying silently for something and I didn't know what.

"Shhh, TifAni," Mom whispered. I couldn't see her, but I imagined she reached out before remembering again. Her sigh was resigned. "Let me get the doctor."

Mom's footsteps receded, and then I remembered Ben's calves, so white they nauseated me, disappearing into the smoke.

Mom returned, but not with Dr. Levitt. This doctor was wearing not scrubs but faded jeans cuffed to reveal slender ankles and white sneakers, brand new. She wore her hair in a shiny silver bob. She looked like a woman who had a garden, who wore a floppy straw hat while she tended to her tomatoes, rewarding herself with a glass of lemonade on her front porch afterward.

"TifAni," she said. "I'm Dr. Perkins. But I want you to call me Anita." Her request was quiet and firm.

I pressed my hands against my cheeks, mopping up facial grease and tears. "Okay," I said.

"Is there anything I can get for you?" Anita asked.

I sniffed. "I'd really like to brush my teeth and wash my face."

Anita nodded solemnly, like this was an important thing for me to do. "Hang tight. I'm going to work on that for you."

Anita was gone for all of five minutes before she returned with a travel-size toothbrush, children's fruit-flavored toothpaste, and a bar of Dove soap. She helped me out of bed. I was okay with Anita touching me, because she didn't seem like she was about to break down in hysterics at any moment, forcing *me* to comfort *her*.

I turned on the water so I couldn't hear Anita and Mom talking about me while I used the bathroom. I peed and scrubbed my face, brushed my teeth next, spitting one long sticky line of the sweet-tasting toothpaste into the sink. It refused to break away from my lips, and I had to cut it off using my fingers.

When I reemerged, Anita asked me if I was hungry, which I was, viciously. I asked Mom what happened to the coffee and pastry, and she said Dad had eaten it. I glared at her as I climbed back into bed.

"I'll get you whatever you want, sweetheart. The cafeteria has bagels, orange juice, fruit, eggs, cereal."

"A bagel," I said. "With cream cheese. And orange juice."

"I'm not sure if they have cream cheese," Mom said. "They may just have butter."

"Anyplace that has bagels has cream cheese," I snapped.

It was the sort of rude response that would usually incite Mom into calling me an ungrateful bitch, but Mom didn't dare in front of Anita. Just put on a big fake smile and turned on her heel to go, revealing the dent in the back of her hair she'd gotten from sleeping in the stiff hospital chair.

"Is it okay if I sit down here?" Anita pointed to the chair next to the bed.

I shrugged like it didn't matter to me. "Sure."

Anita tried to sit with her legs tucked underneath her body, but the chair was too small and too uncomfortable. She settled for the normal way, one leg crossed leisurely over the other, hands cupping her knee. Her nails were light purple.

"You've been through quite a lot over the last twenty-four hours," Anita said, which wasn't entirely true. Twenty-four hours ago I was just getting out of bed. Twenty-four hours ago I was just a bratty teenager who didn't want to go to school. It was eighteen hours ago that I discovered what the slimy inside of a brain looks like, what a face looks like without skin and lips and the odd pimple.

I nodded, even though her calculation was incorrect, and Anita said, "Do you want to talk to me about it?"

I liked that Anita was sitting next to me, rather than across from me, staring me down like I was a pickled cadaver awaiting dissection. Years later I learned this is a psychological trick to get people to open up. I wrote a tip in *The Women's Magazine* that if you have to have a difficult conversation with "your guy"—how I loathe that term—do it while you're driving, because he will be more open to what you have to say when you're side by side rather than if you were to broach the subject of moving in together head-on.

"Is Arthur dead?" I asked.

"Arthur is dead," Anita answered, very matter-of-fact.

I knew the answer already, but it was shocking to hear those words coming from a person who had never even met Arthur. Had no idea Arthur existed until just a few hours ago.

"Who else?" I dared.

"Ansilee, Olivia, Theodore, Liam, and Peyton." I never even realized Teddy's real name was Theodore. "Oh, and Ben," she added.

I waited for her to remember more names, but she didn't. "What about Dean?"

"Dean is alive," Anita said, and I stared at her, slack-jawed. I was positive he had been dead when I left him. "But he's very badly injured. He may not walk again."

I brought the blanket to my mouth. "Might not walk?"

"The bullet entered his groin and severed a vertebra in his spine. He's getting the best care possible," Anita said, adding, "He's lucky to be alive."

I swallowed at the same time a hiccup jumped up my throat. The impact ached in my chest. "How did Ben die?"

"He killed himself," Anita said. "It was the plan all along

for both of them. So you mustn't feel bad about what you've done." I was afraid to tell Anita that I didn't feel bad. I didn't feel anything.

Mom appeared in the doorway, a plump bagel in one hand and a container of orange juice in the other. "They had cream cheese!"

Mom had taken it upon herself to fix up the bagel. She hadn't applied nearly enough cream cheese, but I was so hungry I didn't scold her for it. It's weird, being that hungry. It's not like lunchtime, when it's only been a few hours since breakfast and your stomach is popping and gurgling in history class. It's like the hunger has spread to your entire body and it's no longer about your stomach. In fact, your stomach doesn't hurt at all, but your limbs feel weightless and weak, and your jaw understands this and tries to chew as fast as it can.

I gulped down the orange juice. Every swallow seemed to make me thirstier, and I crushed the container trying to get the last sip.

Mom asked if I wanted anything else, but I didn't. The food and the orange juice had restored me, given me the strength to grasp the reality of the last eighteen hours. It took over the room, an invisible swell that wouldn't break for some time. Just carried me around in its arch wherever I went, drenching everything in misery.

"I was wondering"—Anita leaned forward and pressed her hands on her knees, directing a needy glance at Mom—"might I speak to TifAni alone?"

Mom knitted her shoulder blades together and stood up straighter. "I think that depends on what TifAni wants."

It was exactly what I wanted, but with Anita's support, my desire felt too powerful to yield. I said softly, so as not to hurt her feelings, "It's okay, Mom."

I don't know what Mom expected me to say because she looked very surprised. She collected the empty orange juice container and the napkins off my lap and said, primly, "That is perfectly fine. I will be right outside in the hallway if you need me."

"Do you think you can close the door behind you?" Anita called after her, and Mom had to struggle with the doorstop and she couldn't get it for an excruciating few seconds and I felt so bad for her. Finally she did, but the door dragged lazily behind her, so that I saw Mom when she thought I couldn't see her. She was looking up at the ceiling and then she wrapped her arms as far around her skinny body as she could manage and rocked back and forth, her mouth stretching out in a silent sob. I wanted to yell at Dad to hug her, goddamnit.

"I have the sense it's difficult for you to be around your mother," Anita said.

I didn't say anything. I felt protective of her now.

"TifAni," Anita said. "I know you have been through a lot. More than any fourteen-year-old should ever be expected to deal with. But I need to ask you a few questions about Arthur and Ben."

"I told Officer Pensacole everything yesterday," I protested. After I'd fled the cafeteria, so sure Dean was dead, I barreled down the same path Beth had taken, only I didn't scream like she did. I didn't know where Ben was, didn't want to call attention to myself. He had already put the gun in his mouth at that point, but I couldn't have known that. When I came upon the row of SWAT officers, crouched low, guns drawn on my nearing body, I thought they were aiming at me. I actually *turned around to go back into the school*. But one of them chased after me and ushered me through the crowd of googly-eyed bystanders and mothers hysterical in their embarrassing dog-walking tracksuits, screaming names at me and begging to know if their babies were okay. "I think I killed him!" I was saying, and the medics tried to put an air mask over my face, but the officers intervened, demanding details, and I told them it was Ben and Arthur. "Arthur Finnerman!" I shrieked when they asked, over and over, Ben *who*? Arthur *who*? I couldn't even remember Ben's last name.

"I know you did," Anita said. "And they are very grateful for that information. But I'm not here to ask you about what happened yesterday. I'm trying to assemble a clear picture of Arthur and Ben. To try and understand why they did what they did."

I was suddenly nervous about this Anita character. "Are you the police? I thought you were a psychiatrist."

"I'm a forensic psychologist," Anita said. "I do occasional consulting work with the Philadelphia police force."

That sounded more intimidating than the police. "So are you the police or not?"

Anita smiled, and the skin around her eyes collected in three distinct lines. "I'm not the police. But to be absolutely up front with you, I will be sharing whatever you say to me with them." She shifted in the small chair and cringed. "I know you've provided some very important information already, but I thought we could talk about Arthur. Your relationship to Arthur. I understand you were friends."

Her eyes moved back and forth over me, quickly, like she was reading a newspaper. When I didn't say anything, she tried again. "Were you and Arthur friends?"

I plopped my hands on the bed, helplessly. "He was really mad at me."

"Well, friends sometimes fight."

"We *were* friends," I said begrudgingly.

"And what was he so mad at you for?"

I fiddled with a loose string in the hospital blanket. I couldn't get into the whole story without getting into that night at Dean's house. And I couldn't get into that, not ever. "I stole this picture . . . of him and his dad."

"Why did you do that?"

I pointed my toes, trying to stretch out the irritation. It was like when Mom asked too many questions about my friends. The more she dug, the harder I wanted to hold on to all the information she was so desperate to get. "Because he said some really mean things to me and I was just trying to get back at him."

"What did he say?"

I pulled harder on the loose string, and a little family of threads bunched up in response. I couldn't tell Anita the awful things Arthur said to me because then I'd have to tell her about Dean. And Liam and Peyton. Mom would kill me if she ever found out what happened that night. "He was mad because I started hanging out with Dean and Olivia and those guys."

Anita tipped her head once, like she understood. "So he felt betrayed by you?"

I shrugged. "I guess. He didn't like Dean."

"Why not?"

"Because Dean was mean to him. He was mean to Ben too." And suddenly I had the map in my hands, the one that would lead me out of this mess unscathed. I had to guide everyone in my direction with swift surety, otherwise they would dig, dig, dig. All the way back to that night in October. I said, generously, "Do you know what Dean and Peyton did to Ben?"

Curiosity simmered in Anita's dark eyes. I gave her everything.

❧

Anita seemed very satisfied with the information I provided her, and thanked me for being so "brave and candid." I could go home now, if I wanted to.

"Is Dean in this hospital too?" I asked.

Anita had been collecting her things to go, but she paused when I asked this. "I think he might be. Did you want to see him?"

"No," I said. Then, "Maybe. I don't know. Is it bad?"

"My advice?" Anita said. "I would go home, be with your family."

"Do I have to go to school today?"

Anita regarded me strangely. It was another important look, but I didn't realize why until later. "The school will be shut down for some time. I'm not really sure how they are planning to finish the semester out."

Anita hadn't built up any traction in her new sneakers, and they squeaked on the shiny hospital floor as she walked away. Then Mom was back, this time with Dad, who looked like he would rather be anywhere else but where he was, stuck with us two crazy broads.

❧

I was surprised how sad it made me to leave the hospital, to see the people hurrying to work, the men in their dry-cleaned suits, the women driving their kids to the public school, cursing because they missed the light at Montgomery and Morris Ave and now they were going to be late. Knowing that when you're gone the grind will go on. No one is special enough to stop it.

Dad drove because Mom was too shaky. "Look!" She held out her bony, trembling hands as proof.

I climbed into the car, the leather cold and hard beneath my thin hospital scrubs. Those scrubs would remain in my wardrobe until college. They were my favorite thing to lounge around in when I was hungover. I only threw them out when Nell pointed out how creepy it was that I'd held on to them.

We looped around the Bryn Mawr Hospital parking lot until we found an exit. Dad rarely came out this way, and Mom pestered him the whole ride home. "No, Bob, left. *Left!*" "*Jesus*, Dina. Relax." When the road ran away from the scenic towns, and the highlights changed from cute little boutiques and luxury car lots to McDonalds's and no-frills strip malls, a sort of panic scooted into the elaborate labyrinth of my emotions. What if class never resumed at Bradley? There would be nothing left tethering me to the Main Line. I needed Bradley. Too much had happened to return to Mt. St. Theresa's, to that spectacularly middlebrow life.

"Am I going back to Bradley?" The question seemed to settle heavy on Mom's shoulders. They sagged even further down right in front of me.

"We don't know," Mom said at the same time Dad said, "Of course not."

Mom's profile was stern as she hissed, "Bob." Mom was a good hisser, it was a gift she passed along to me. "You promised."

I righted myself, leaving a rhombus-shaped smudge on the glass where my forehead had been sulking. That Dove bar had been no match for my shiny T-zone. "Wait. What did you promise?"

The way no one answered me, the way they both continued to stare straight ahead, made me even more nervous.

"Hello?" I said, louder. "What did you promise?"

"TifAni." Mom pressed her fingers on either side of her nose, dulling the oncoming headache. "We don't even know what the school is going to decide to do. What your father promised is that we will wait to hear from the administration before we make a decision."

"And do *I* get a say in this decision?" I admit, I said it like a real snot. Dad swerved left and flattened the brake pedal to the floor. Mom swung forward, and the seat belt squeezed a mannish grunt out of her.

Dad turned and pointed his finger at me. His face had sprouted all sorts of mangy purple veins. He shouted at me, "No, you don't! You don't!"

Mom gasped, *"Bob."*

I slunk into the car's corner. "Okay," I whispered. "Please, okay." The skin beneath my eyes had rubbed off raw, and it felt like someone had flung rubbing alcohol in my face when I began to cry. Dad realized he was still pointing his finger at me, and, slowly, he lowered his hand and tucked it between his legs.

"TifAni!" Mom twisted half out of her seat to get her hand on my knee. "Oh my God, you are white. Sweetheart, are you okay? Daddy didn't mean to scare you. He is just so upset right now." I always thought of Mom as beautiful, but suffering made her ugly and unrecognizable. She sobbed a few times, her lips searching for something to say to comfort me. Eventually, she managed, "We are all just so upset right now!" We sat there for a while, waiting for Mom to stop crying, the car rocking like a cradle as the traffic thundered past.

❧❧

There was another standoff when we got home. Mom wanted me to rest in my room. She had a bottle of pills from Anita in case I had a breakdown, and she would bring me whatever I needed—food, tissues, magazines, nail polish if I felt like giving myself a manicure. But I needed TV. I needed to be reminded that the world was still here, normal and stupid as ever with their talk shows and campy soap operas. Magazines could do that too, transport you to a silly world, but once you completed the quiz on the last page and found out that yes, you are a control freak and it's driving men away, the spell was broken. I required a permanent passport to Fluff City.

Dad headed straight for the master bedroom. Twenty minutes later he emerged, shaved and wearing khakis and that ugly yellow button-down I worried about on the rare day he came to pick me up from school.

"What are you doing?" Mom asked.

"I'm going in to the office, Dina." Dad opened the refrigerator and grabbed an apple. He bit into it, his teeth peeling back the flesh the way that knife had in Arthur's back. I looked away. "What do you think I'm doing?"

"I just thought we should be together today," Mom said, a little too brightly, and I suddenly ached for a storied Main Line family with brothers and sisters and aunts and uncles nearby, for the house to be alive with generations of our great name.

"I would if I could." Dad held the apple between his teeth as he pulled his coat out of the hall closet and shrugged it on. "I'll try to be home early." Before he left he told me to feel better. Thanks, Dad.

Our thin house rocked on its foundation when Dad

slammed the door. Mom waited for it to right itself before she said, "Okay, if you'd prefer to lie on the couch that's fine. But I'd prefer that you didn't watch the news."

The news. It hadn't even occurred to me to tune in to it before Mom brought it up, and now it was all I wanted to watch. I focused my eyes on her, challenging. "Why not?"

"Because it will be very disturbing for you," Mom said. "They're showing images of—" She stopped and pressed her lips together firmly. "You don't need to see that."

"Images of what?" I pushed.

"Please, TifAni," Mom begged. "Just respect my wishes."

I said I would even though I didn't, and went upstairs to shower and change into clean clothes. Then I came right back downstairs, intending to put the news on, but Mom was rummaging through the refrigerator. The house was designed with a large window in the middle of the kitchen, so that you could sit at the table and watch the TV in the living room. I didn't feel like hearing it from Mom about how I disrespected her wishes, so I turned the channel to MTV.

A few minutes later, I heard Mom padding around in the kitchen, muttering something about how we had no food in the house. "TifAni," she said, "I'm going to make a run to the grocery store. Is there anything you want?"

"That tomato soup," I said. "And Cheez-Its."

"What about drinks? Soda?"

She knew I stopped drinking that stuff when I started running. Mr. Larson said anything but water would dehydrate us. I rolled my eyes and gave her a barely audible "No."

Mom came around to the front of the couch, looking down at me like I was a body in a casket. She found a blanket and shook it in the air. It landed on me, the perfect trap. "I hate the idea of leaving you alone."

"I'm fine," I groaned.

"Please don't watch the news when I go," she pleaded.

"I *won't*."

"I know you're going to," Mom said.

"Then why did you even tell me not to?"

Mom sighed and sat down on the smaller couch across from me, the cushions exhaling with her weight. She picked up the controller and said, "If you're going to do it, I'd rather you do it with me." Like it was my first time smoking a cigarette or something. "In case you have any questions," she added.

Mom switched the channel from MTV to NBC, and, sure enough, even though it was the time of day the *Today* show should have been testing the newest vacuum cleaners, the segment was dedicated to "Another School Shooting Tragedy." Matt Lauer was actually standing on the sidewalk in front of the old mansion, the part that had been charred by the fire in the cafeteria.

"The Main Line is one of the most affluent areas in the country," Matt was saying. "I've heard numerous times this morning that no one can believe it's happened here, and, for once, it's really true." The camera cut away from him to reveal an aerial shot of the school while Matt listed the grim body count. "Seven are dead, two of them the shooters, five victims of the shooters. One of the victims died in the blast in the cafeteria, the result of a homemade pipe bomb placed inside a backpack and left near what officials have confirmed was the table favored by the school's most popular students. Only one of the bombs detonated, while police believe there were at least five, and, had they all gone off, the carnage would have been much worse.

Nine students are in the hospital with severe but not life-threatening injuries. Some are believed to have lost limbs."

I gasped. "Lost limbs?"

Mom's eyes looked bigger with tears in them. "This is what I was talking about."

"Who? Who did that happen to?"

Mom brought a shaky hand to her forehead. "I didn't recognize some of the names so I forgot them. But there was one. Your friend Hilary."

I kicked at the blanket. It tangled in my legs, and I wanted to tear that fucking thing thread from thread. The orange juice felt like a citrus boil in my stomach. "What happened to her?"

"I'm not sure," Mom whimpered. "But I think it was her foot."

I tried to make it to the bathroom before I spewed that putrid green bile everywhere, I really did. Mom said it was fine, she could get the stain out with spot remover, no problem. The important thing was that I just rest. She gave me an Anita pill. Just rest.

I came to a few times to hear Mom on the phone. I heard her say, "That's very sweet. But she's resting at the moment."

I fell into black muck after that, so dense it took physical effort to wade out of it. I tried a few times before giving up, falling under again. It was nighttime when I finally punctured the murky glaze, when I could form the words to ask Mom who she had been talking to earlier.

"A few people," Mom said. "Your old English teacher called to see how you were doing—"

"Mr. Larson?"

"Uh-huh, and also another mother. They activated that call chain thing."

School was suspended indefinitely. Mom said I was lucky I wasn't a senior. "Just imagine, trying to send out your college applications in this mess?" She clucked her sympathy.

"Did Mr. Larson leave a number?"

"He didn't," Mom said. "But he said he would call back later."

The phone didn't ring again for the rest of the evening, and I spent the first night on the couch, blank faced in front of the TV screen, listening to Beverly, mother of four, rave that the ABtastic DVD was the only thing that had given her her body back, and she had tried *everything*. The lights stayed on too. Another thing about our house is that the second-floor hallway is completely open, so that you can come out of any of the four bedrooms and look over the railing, see me, a lump beneath a pastel acrylic throw. Dad stormed out of the bedroom a few times, raging about how the sliver of light beneath his door was keeping him awake. Finally I told him I'd take that petty torment over the grisly scene on repeat in my mind, and he didn't come out of his room again.

I dozed off just as the sun came up, and, when I came to again, the TV was off and I couldn't find the remote control anywhere.

"Daddy took it," Mom called from the kitchen, when she heard me flailing around. "He went out and bought you a bunch of magazines before he went to work though."

Usually, Mom would monitor the magazines I read. But she gave a long list to Dad and told him to buy them all, even the ones that promised to teach me how to "Set

His Thighs on Fire." It was a small peace offering, I knew, because they'd banned TV. I cherished those magazines, still have them in a box underneath my childhood bed to this day. They made me want to move to a city—any city—wear heels, and live a fabulous life. In their world, everything was fabulous.

It was some lazy time in the afternoon, Mom napping on the short couch, me stretched out on the long couch, studying a smoky eye tutorial, when the doorbell rang.

Mom sprung up and looked at me accusingly, like I'd made the noise that woke her. We stared at each other silently until the doorbell rang again.

Mom ran her fingers through her hair, fluffing it at the dark roots, and patted her fingers under her eyes, clearing out the mascara smudges. "Damnit." She shook her foot as she stood, trying to knock the sleep out of it. It didn't work. She hobbled all the way to the front door.

I heard the low murmur of voices. Mom saying, "Why, of course." When she returned to the living room, there were two frowning men in suits, that basement-couch kind of brown, by her side.

"TifAni." Mom was using her hostess voice. "This is Detective . . ." She pressed her fingers to her temples. "I'm so sorry, Detectives. I've already forgotten your names." Her voice dropped its pleasant tenor and she looked like she was going to cry again. "It's just been such a time."

"Of course it has," the younger, skinnier one said. "I'm Detective Dixon." He nodded at his partner. "This is Detective Vencino." Detective Vencino had that same complexion so many of my relatives sport for most of the calendar year. Without a summer tan, we take on a sickly shade of green.

Mom addressed me. "TifAni, can you stand please?"

I folded the page to my smoky eye tutorial and did as I was told. "Did someone else die?"

Detective Dixon's blond-white eyebrows clustered together. If they didn't bristle off his face haphazardly, it would be easy to mistake them for not being there at all. "No one has died."

"Oh." I examined my nails. The article I'd been reading prior to the smoky eye how-to had said that white spots on the nails were signs of iron deficiency, and iron is what gives you thick, shiny hair, so you didn't want to be iron deficient. No white spots. "My parents won't let me watch the news so I have no idea what's going on." I shot the detectives a look like, Can you believe it?

"That's probably for the best," Detective Dixon said, and Mom gave me this smug little smile that made me want to throw the magazine at her head.

"Is there someplace where we can all sit and talk?" Detective Dixon asked.

"Is everything okay?" Mom brought her hand to her mouth, embarrassed. "I'm sorry. I meant has something else happened?"

"Nothing else, Mrs. FaNelli." Detective Vencino cleared his throat, and the loose green skin on his neck wobbled. "We just want to ask TifAni a few questions."

"I already talked to the police at the hospital," I said. "And that psychiatrist."

"Psychologist," Detective Dixon corrected. "And we know. We just want to clear up a few things. We were hoping you could help." He arched his spiky eyebrows pleadingly. So many people who needed my help.

I looked at Mom, who nodded. "Okay."

Mom asked the detectives if they wanted anything—coffee, tea, a snack? Detective Dixon asked for coffee, but Detective Vencino shook his head. "No, thank you, Mrs. FaNelli."

"You can call me Dina," Mom said, and Detective Vencino didn't smile at her, the way most men do.

The three of us sat at the table while Mom poured coffee beans into the top of the coffee machine. We all had to raise our voices above the whirring grind.

"So, TifAni," Detective Dixon began. "We know about your relationship with Arthur. That you two were in a fight. At the time of the . . . incident."

I bobbed my head up and down: *yup, yup, yup.* "He was mad at me. I took this picture from his room. I still have it if you—"

Detective Dixon held up his hand. "We are actually not here to talk about Arthur."

I blinked, dumbly. "What are you here to talk about then?"

"Dean." Detective Dixon watched for any effect the name might have on me. "Were you and Dean friends?"

I traced my naked toe on the kitchen's hardwood floor. I used to slide across these floors in my socks, arms flung out, pretending to surf. Then one day a three-inch-long splinter punctured the fabric of my socks, lodged itself neatly into the arch of my foot, and that was the end of that game. "Not exactly."

"But you were," Detective Vencino jumped in. It was the first time he'd spoken to me, and up close I noticed his crooked nose, skewed left, like a lump of wet clay someone had pushed to the side before it dried. "At one point?"

"I guess you could say that," I allowed.

Detective Dixon glanced at Detective Vencino. "Were you upset with Dean recently?"

I glanced at Mom, straining to hear my answer above the blade's whine. "A little, yeah. I guess."

"Can you tell us why?"

I examined my hands, my healthy nails. Olivia would never have to worry about being iron deficient again. I suddenly remembered that she'd been wearing green nail polish when I'd seen her last, in Chem, hunched over her desk, furiously scribbling notes. Hilary had been wearing it too, must have convinced Olivia to try it, because Olivia wasn't the type to experiment with makeup. Or maybe it was to show their support for the soccer team. I dazed off, wondering, if you die with green nails, if you're not going through life bumping into things and washing your hair— all those everyday things that chisel away at the veneer— will the Sally Hansen persevere? The way your teeth and bones remain when the rest of you decays? Here is Olivia, her green fingernails all that's left. Detective Dixon repeated his question.

"TifAni," Mom called. The machine's motor shut off with a click, and the next thing she said came out loudly, with accidental emphasis. "Answer the detectives, please."

Like one of those bath toys that swells to four times its size in a warm tub, I fattened up with tears. I wasn't going to be able to hide what happened that night. Why did I think I could? I jammed a fist into an eye and rubbed. "There were a lot of reasons," I sighed.

"Maybe you'd be more comfortable talking about them if Mom weren't here?" Detective Dixon asked, kindly.

"I'm sorry." Mom placed Detective Dixon's coffee cup by his elbow. "Be more comfortable talking about what? What is going on?"

The windows at the Ardmore police station were opaque inky squares by the time the lawyer arrived, introduced himself as Dan under the sallow hallway lights. Detective Dixon insisted we didn't need a lawyer, and he was so nice Mom almost believed him, but she changed her tune after she called Dad at the office. The lawyer came recommended by Dad's co-worker whose daughter had been arrested for a DUI over the summer. Neither Mom nor I was impressed. He was a schlubby guy in a suit with pant hems that collected in bunches around his ankles like the bulky neck of a bulldog.

Dan ("No competent lawyer can be named Dan," Mom hissed) wanted to hear the entire story from me first, before the detectives joined us in the frigid interrogation room. They really do lower the temperature, try to make you feel as uncomfortable as possible so you would confess sooner, the detectives home in time for dinner.

"No detail is unimportant." Dan rolled up the sleeves of his dress shirt, a royal blue eyesore that seemed the product of a buy two, get one free sale at Jos. A. Bank. He'd taken off his coat and hung it on the back of the chair, not noticing when the left shoulder slipped, the right shoulder clinging on with all its might. "Everything from the beginning of the school year. Every connection you had to everyone involved in this. Everything."

Even I couldn't believe how well it had all started out for me, that I was ever sought after by the likes of Dean or Olivia, how badly and how swiftly my good fortune had spoiled. I rushed through the details of the night at Dean's, burning bright as I recounted how I'd come to with Peyton, doing, you know, to me. "Performing oral sex?" Dan asked, and under the unrelenting fluorescent lights I must have looked sunburned. "Yes," I mumbled. I went through the list, the way I'd drifted through the night, coming to at various points with Peyton first, the others who followed. I told him what happened afterward, the night at Olivia's, the cut on my face that wasn't from her dog. I was wary of involving Mr. Larson in the whole thing, but Dan said no detail was unimportant.

"Did Mr. Larson . . ." Dan cleared his throat. He looked as embarrassed as I did. "That night in his apartment?"

I stared at him for a second before I understood what he meant. *"No,"* I said. "Mr. Larson would never do something . . . like that." I shivered to show my disgust.

"But Mr. Larson knew about the rapes? He could corroborate this story?"

That was the first time anyone had ever referred to what happened to me in the plural. The rape(s). I didn't know those other things could be considered rape. "Yes."

Dan made a note in his little notebook. His pen stilled. "Now, Arthur."

Was he depressed, was he on drugs? ("No," I said. "I mean, yeah, but just pot." "Pot is a drug, TifAni.") Did he ever say anything that, looking back, could have been his way of warning me about what he was planning to do?

"I mean"—I shrugged—"I knew he had that gun. The one he had in the cafeteria."

Dan didn't blink for so long I almost waved my hand in front of his face and yodeled "yoo-hoo" like in the commercials. "How do you know that?"

"He showed it to me. In his basement. It was his dad's." Dan still hadn't blinked. "It wasn't loaded or anything," I stressed.

"How do you know?" Dan asked.

"He pointed it at me. As a joke."

"He *pointed* it at you?"

"He let me hold it too," I bit back. "He wouldn't be dumb enough to let me hold it and not tell me it was loaded. What if I . . ." I stopped talking, because Dan's head dropped to his chest, like he had fallen asleep on an airplane. *"What?"*

Dan's chest muffled his voice. "You touched the gun?"

"For, like, two seconds," I said, quickly, trying to fix whatever it was I'd broken. "Then I gave it back." Dan still didn't look at me. "Why? Is that bad?"

Dan jammed his hands on either side of his nose, supporting the weight of his head. "It could be."

"Why?"

"Because if they find your prints on the gun, it could be very, very bad."

The overhead light shuddered and crackled, like it had sizzled a bug on a swampy summer night, and I realized what Dan meant. Had Mom known this too? Did Dad? "Do they think I'm *involved* in this?"

"TifAni," Dan said, his voice high and astonished. "What, exactly, do you think you're doing here?"

After Dan and I had our "powwow," as Detective Dixon put it, like he was my football coach and I was the quarterback with the entire town's expectations on my burly shoulders, I was allowed to use the restroom and see Mom and Dad. They were sitting on a bench, outside the interrogation room. Dad had his head in his hands, like he couldn't believe this was his life. Like if he could just fall asleep he might wake up somewhere else. Mom's legs were crossed, her stockinged foot half out of one of her flirty heels. I'd told her not to wear them here, but she'd insisted. She'd tried to make me put makeup on ("Maybe a little mascara before we go?"). I'd turned the lights off in the kitchen and gone and waited in the car, leaving her alone, blinking into the dark.

Dad stood to shake Dan's hand as we approached.

To Mom I said, "Do you know they think I had something to do with this?"

"Of course they don't think that, TifAni," she said, her voice shrill and unconvincing. "They're just covering all their bases."

"Dan says they have my fingerprints on the gun."

"Could have, *could*." Dan's shoulders jumped a little as Mom shrieked "What?"

"Dina!" Dad barked. "Lower your voice."

Mom pointed her finger at Dad, her acrylic nail shaking in rage. "Don't you dare tell me what to do, Bobby." She drew her hand back, making a fist and sinking her teeth into her knuckles. "This is all your fault," she whimpered, squeezing her eyes shut, tears worming paths through the thick layer of foundation on her face. "I told you! TifAni needed those clothes. So they wouldn't single her out, and look, that's exactly what they did!"

"This is my fault because I wouldn't pay for *clothes*?" Dad's mouth was open, his molars black. Dad hated the dentist.

"Please!" Dan whispered, loudly. "This is not the place to make a scene."

"You are un*believable*," Dad muttered. Mom only tossed her stiff, hair-sprayed hair back, settling into herself again.

"I don't know if they have her prints," Dan said. "But

TifAni shared with me that Arthur showed her one of the guns that *we think*"—he held up his hands like a cop in traffic telling the southbound lane to stop—"was used in the crime. And that he let her hold it."

The way Mom looked at me, sometimes you just have to feel bad for parents. For all the ways they think they know you. The mockery their kids make out of them when they find out otherwise. Before I'd told Dan about that night at Dean's, I asked if he was going to have to share this with my parents. "Not if you don't want me to," Dan said. "This is privileged client information. But, TifAni, the way this thing is going. It will come out. And it's better they hear it from you first."

I shook my head. "I can't ever tell them this."

Dan said, "I can, if you want me to."

Heels clicking against the speckled linoleum floor announced Detective Dixon's arrival, and we all waited for him to speak. "How you folks doing?" He glanced at his wrist, even though he wasn't wearing a watch. "Let's get going on this, huh?"

I didn't know what time it was, but when I sat down next to Dan, Detective Dixon in the seat across from us and Detective Vencino tucked into the corner, my stomach moaned impatiently.

The table, smudged like Arthur's glasses always were, was empty save for a cup of water (mine) and a recording device occupying the center spot. Detective Dixon pressed a button and said, "November fourteenth, 2001."

"It's actually November fifteenth." Detective Vencino tapped the face of the watch he *was* wearing. "Twelve oh six."

Detective Dixon corrected himself and added, "This is Detective Dixon, Detective Vencino, TifAni FaNelli, and her lawyer, Daniel Rosenberg." The discovery of Dan's full name gave me a lot more confidence in him.

With the formalities out of the way, I told my story again. Every last vulgar detail. It's a certain kind of hell, confessing your most humiliating sexual secrets to a room full of hairy middle-aged men.

Unlike Dan, Detective Dixon and Detective Vencino didn't interrupt me with questions. Which made me think it might be okay to leave out certain parts, but when I tried, Dan gently prodded me. "And it was Mr. Larson you ran into at the Wawa that night, remember?"

When I finished, Detective Dixon stretched in his chair with a loud yawn. He stayed like that, legs splayed apart, arms behind his head, staring at me for a long while. "So," he said, finally, "your story is that Dean, Liam, and Peyton assaulted you that night at Dean's house? And that Dean did again, that night at Olivia's house?"

I looked at Dan, who nodded, before answering him. "Yes," I said.

"See, TifAni, I'm not following." The way he was slumped into the wall, Detective Vencino's chest curled over his little potbelly. There wasn't one part of him that wasn't covered in itchy-looking black hair. "I guess what I'm not understanding is if Dean, *assaulted* you"—there was his rude laugh—"why would you even want to save him from Arthur?"

"I was trying to save *myself*."

"But Arthur was your friend," Detective Vencino said, condescendingly, as though I'd forgotten. "He wouldn't try to hurt you."

"He *was* my friend." I stared at the table so hard it blurred. "But I was afraid of him. He was mad at me. I'd taken that picture of his dad . . . I don't think you understand how mad he was about that. I told you. He *chased* me out of his house."

"Let's back up a second." Detective Dixon shot Detective Vencino a warning look over his shoulder. "Tell me what you know about Dean and Arthur's relationship."

I thought of that yearbook in Arthur's room. Their smiling, earnest faces. Not a clue in the world how it would all turn out. "They were friends in middle school," I said. "Arthur told me that."

"And when did they stop being friends?" Dixon asked.

"Arthur said it was when Dean got popular." I shrugged. Story old as time.

"Did Arthur ever talk about wanting to hurt Dean?"

"No," I said. "Not really."

Vencino pounced. "What does 'not really' mean, TifAni?"

"No, okay? He didn't."

"Never?" Dixon prodded, gently. "Think back."

"I mean, it was the usual talking shit about him. But no, Arthur never said, 'I'm going to take my dad's gun into the school and shoot Dean in the nuts.'" The word "nuts" made me giggle. I hiccuped and succumbed to a fit of silent, painful laughter, the kind that spreads like wildfire at a funeral, when someone breaks the somber silence with a wet, Diet Coke burp.

"My client is exhausted," Dan said. "Maybe you ought to let her go home and get some rest. She's fourteen, don't forget."

"So was Olivia Kaplan," Detective Vencino said.

The sound of Olivia's name straightened me out. I rubbed my arms, prickly with goose bumps. "How is Hilary?"

"She's an amputee," Vencino said, and nothing else.

I took a shaky sip of water. The room had chilled it

even colder, and I winced when I swallowed, when the liquid skated by my lungs. "But will she be okay? Will she come back to Bradley?" I looked to Dixon to ask the question that I had been carrying around since I left the hospital. Maybe he actually had an answer. "Will Bradley, I mean, the school won't shut down or anything, will it?"

"Do you want it to?" Vencino replied, behind Dixon.

I didn't know how to make Detective Vencino understand just how much I didn't want that to happen. I couldn't return to my life just a few miles shy of the Main Line. Those few miles made the difference between Yale and West Chester University, moving to New York when you grew up and breaking ground for your own mini McMansion, hand stroking your belly, swollen like an overfed tick, as the baby kicked and kicked. I turned my hands up on the table. "I just want everything to go back to normal."

"Ah," Vencino said, holding up his pointer finger like he understood. "Well it can now, can't it? That you're rid of all the people who caused you so much distress?" A cyanide smile crawled onto his face, and he gestured at me with a sarcastic flourish, Vanna White presenting the shiny new Toyota Camry only the winner would take home. "Take her in, folks! Right here in our midst! The luckiest girl alive."

Dan glared at Vencino. "That's a little out of line, Detective."

Detective Vencino folded his arms across his chest. "Sorry," he spat, "I've got bigger fish to fry than worrying about TifAni FaNelli's feelings."

Dan sniffed at him, turning to address Dixon. "Do you have everything you need?" He patted my back. "Because

I think it's in my client's best interest to go home and get some rest."

Rest. That would never come easy, even when it was supposed to come easy, ever again.

❧

Out in the hallway, Dan asked for a moment alone with me. He told me he would be by the house in the morning, to have that "conversation" with my parents that I couldn't be the one to have. The following morning was Friday, and I would have preferred he wait until Monday, so I wouldn't have to spend the whole weekend cooped up with both Mom and Dad, who would no doubt be disgusted by me. But Dan said if we waited until Monday there was a chance the story could leak, and I wouldn't want my parents to find out from *The Philadelphia Inquirer*, would I? "Let's not delay the inevitable." Dan put his hand on my shoulder, and I stared at the floor, at his shoes made of such bad fake leather they looked rubber.

"You did good in there," Dan said. "Vencino is a bully. He's just trying to get under your skin. But you didn't rise to the occasion. That was good."

"But they think I planned this with Arthur or something," I said. "How could they think that?"

"They don't," Dan said. "Like your mother said, they're just covering all their bases."

"Am I going to have to come back here?"

"You might." Dan gave me that heartening smile people give you when the truth is something you don't want to hear, and you need to be brave.

❧

Mom made me take one of those Anita pills, to help me sleep. I wanted to save it for later, after Mom and Dad had gone to bed and I could flip through all of the news channels, on mute, the captions setting on, but Mom insisted I take it right in front of her. Like it was a fucking vitamin instead of a sleeping pill that they later found out is as addictive as heroin.

Within fifteen minutes, sleep started with those weird dreams that you jump awake from, thinking, *Well, that was strange.* I had what looked like a raspberry, a beautiful one, plump and jewel ripe, growing out of the crown of my head. I kept trying to cover it with my hair, but every time I passed by a mirror, I'd see its large bubble body in profile. Soon, more sprouted—one along my hairline, another by my ear. *I'm going to have get these removed, and it's going to be very painful,* I thought. This is the point at which I'd normally leap awake, but that Anita pill blunted the instinct, so I just twitched, once, and then deep into the rabbit hole of the bizarre and terrifying I went.

I was in a crowd of people. They were my classmates, that much I knew, only I didn't recognize any of them. We were standing at the edge of a dock, and the colors were dull brown and yellow, old timey, as though from an illustration of New York at the turn of the twentieth century. It started as a whisper, "Arthur is alive," and grew to an excited hush, making its way over to me. "Arthur is alive?" I demanded of no one in particular.

There was a push in the crowd, all of us on the move, trying to find Arthur. I struggled to elbow my way out, but I was part of a formidable unit. I knew if I could just break free, I'd be able to find him. We weren't going to find him like this.

And then I was out, and Arthur was in front of me, laughing. A sweet laugh, like he was watching *Friends* and something Chandler said had amused him. Chandler had always been his favorite.

"You're alive?" I gasped, and Arthur kept laughing.

"Hey!" I pounded my fists on his chest. "You're alive? How come you didn't tell me?" I pounded harder, anything to make the delirious laughter stop. This wasn't *funny*. "How could you not tell me?"

"Don't be mad." Arthur held my fists still, smiling at me. "I'm here. Don't be mad."

I woke with the bad feeling first. The disorientation followed—I just woke up, how could something bad have already happened? For a split second, giddiness took over, like it does on a Saturday morning, when you think you have to get ready for school and then you realize, *ahhhh*, it's the weekend. Weekends would lose their magic for a while. Everything did.

There was the sound of food cracking on the stove and the time on the TV box read 12:49 P.M. Dan had said he was coming by this morning. Had he? Did he share all the lurid details with Mom and Dad while I writhed and sweat, just a few feet away?

The blanket had bunched around my torso, leaving my legs and feet exposed. I rolled onto my side, and the warm, starchy stench of an overheated and immobile body rose up in the air. "Mom?" I called out, anxious for her response. It would tell me how angry she was.

I heard Mom's bare feet on the kitchen floor, and then nothing as she crossed over into the carpeted living room. "You're up!" She clasped her hands together. "That pill really knocked you out, huh?"

There was no way she knew. "Did Dan come by?"

"He called, but I told him it would probably be better to come this afternoon, since you were still sleeping."

I swallowed, and my tongue stuck to the roof of my mouth for a beat too long. I swallowed again, panicked, trying to get it to unstick. "Where's Dad?"

"Oh, honey," Mom said. "He went into the office. Something big is going on. He might even have to work this weekend."

"He will?" I'd never known Dad to go into work on the weekends. Not ever.

Mom misinterpreted my relief for yearning. "I'm sure he'll be home early."

"What time is Dan coming over?"

"Soon," Mom said. "Maybe you should shower?" She held her nose and and waved her hand back and forth, teasingly. "You smell a little ripe."

I could smell like Olivia right now, I almost said. *Rotting.* I came this close.

❧

I've never been able to take fast showers. "What are you doing in there?" Dad would pound on the door and ask on school mornings. I don't know what I "do" in there—what everyone else does, I guess, it just takes me longer.

I'd taken two showers since Tuesday, and combined they were shorter than my usual one. I kept hearing noises, kept pushing the curtain aside, so sure I was going to see Arthur's ghost standing there, a strapping angry puff of air.

I turned off the water before I even rinsed off all the foamy suds on my back. "Mom?" I called, loudly. Whenever I spooked myself, sometimes the best remedy was just hearing Mom's annoyed cry back. "Don't *yell*, TifAni."

I called for Mom again, really bellowed this time. Still nothing. I wrapped myself in a towel and dripped my way across the bathroom floor, pulling the door open and shouting, *"Mooooom!"*

"Jesus Christ I'm on the phone!" Her voice told me everything.

I crept into my room, the carpet turning a shade darker with each soggy footstep. I picked up the phone from the receiver and pressed it against my ear. I'd begged for my own phone. When I got it, I'd covered the handle in pink glittery stickers like Rayanne from *My So-Called Life*.

I picked up to Dan, in the middle of saying ". . . indication she'd been on the outs at school?"

"No." Mom sniffed. "She'd had a sleepover at Olivia's recently."

"I think that was the night Dean attacked her," Dan said. "She slept at Andrew Larson's house."

"Her cross-country coach?" Mom wailed. Dan and I listened to her blow her nose. "I don't even know who this girl is anymore." I gripped the fold of my towel tighter. *This girl.* "How could she do this?"

"Teenagers don't always make the smartest decisions, Dina. Try not to be too hard on her."

"Oh please," Mom snapped. "I was in high school once. You don't have a body like TifAni's and go to a party with all boys and drink too much and not know exactly what you're doing there. TifAni knew better. She knows what this family's values are."

"Even so," Dan replied. "Kids make mistakes. TifAni has had to make up for hers in the worst way imaginable."

"And so the police know all about this?" Mom was beside herself, no doubt thinking, laughably, how humiliating this was for a family such as ours, with all our *values*.

"TifAni told them last night."

"And so, what do they think? That TifAni planned this, this *massacre* with the other school outcasts to exact her revenge?" Mom released a single "Ha!" As though this were the most preposterous thing in the world.

"I think that is one possibility," Dan said, and I could picture the impact that had on Mom's face. That Dan didn't find this preposterous at all. "The problem is, they don't have a single piece of evidence to prove that theory."

"What about that gun? The one TifAni touched."

"I haven't heard anything about that," Dan said. "Let's hope that never comes to fruition."

"But what if it does?"

"Even if it does, it's hardly enough evidence to charge TifAni with a crime. And if Arthur showed that gun around, it's plausible there would be other kids' finger-prints on it, and I'm sure, with that, a story to corroborate TifAni's."

Mom exhaled loudly into the phone. "Well, I appreci-ate your calling me," she said. "Hopefully this ridiculous speculation all dies down soon."

"I'm sure it will," Dan said. "They're just dotting their i's and crossing their t's."

Mom thanked Dan again and said good-bye. I didn't hang up until I was sure I was the last one on the line, and the phone made a wet popping noise as I pulled it away from my ear. I wiped it on my towel before placing it back in the receiver with a careful click.

"TifAniiiiii!" Mom's voice went ragged as my name wrapped the house in her call. I didn't answer, just let the water droplets gather around me on the carpet in my bedroom—turquoise colored, Mom had let me pick that.

It would get mildewy—she always nagged me about leaving damp towels on the floor—and it would be just one more reason for her to hate me.

෴

Mom told me I was not the daughter she raised. I cried, but her mouth never stepped out of its tight line. After that, we settled into a seething silence. There was still no word about when school would resume, and I spent my days on the couch, TV dazed, getting up only to eat or shower or go to the bathroom. Being the recipient of the silent treatment meant there was no one to tell me to turn off the news.

Seven days after the shooting, Bradley was no longer the top news story, and when it was mentioned, there weren't any new developments, just tearful interviews with parents and classmates who had been close to the blast in the cafeteria—but not so close that they weren't alive and well for the camera, gesturing wildly with their still intact limbs. Occasionally, a news reporter would mention that police were investigating the possibility of others being involved, but no names or further details were given.

So on Monday afternoon, when Detective Dixon called and told Mom we needed to come back down to the station immediately, and to bring our lawyer, I was angry that Katie Couric hadn't prepared me for the development that was about to come next.

Dan met us at the station, wearing his same limp suit. If Mom and I had been on speaking terms, I would have asked her why Dan dressed so poorly when he was a lawyer and probably made a lot of money. My little knowledge about lawyers came from the movie *Hook*, Robin Williams as the overworked, well-paid attorney who never had time for his children.

Dad was still on his way to the station when Dan and I were ushered into the interrogation room by Detective Dixon and Detective Vencino. This time, Vencino was holding a thick file folder and sporting a sly, knowing smile.

"TifAni," Detective Dixon said, as we sat down across from one another. "How have you been?"

"Fine, I guess."

"Well, that's good to hear," Vencino snipped. Everyone ignored him.

"We understand you've been under a lot of duress over the last few days," Dixon said, his tone, his body language, his bizarre eyebrows, everything about him amicable. "And we'd like to give you the opportunity to come forward with any important information that maybe, just, slipped your mind last time we spoke." He brought his fingers to his head and demonstrated how this important information could disappear from one's head in a poof of smoke.

I looked at Dan, the meanly lit room highlighting how vulnerable we both were. Whatever was in that manila folder matched Vencino's agenda. "Let's not be coy, Detectives," Dan said. "TifAni has been honest with you. I'd say you owe her the same courtesy."

I frowned at my lap, frantically searching my mind, unsure if that was the truth.

Dixon stuck out his lower lip and nodded, like this was a possibility, but he had to be convinced first. "Let's let Tif-Ani answer," he said, and all three of them looked at me, expectantly.

"I don't know," I said. "I did tell you everything I thought was important."

"You sure about that?" Vencino asked. He waved the manila envelope at me like I should know what was inside of it.

"*Yes*. Honestly, if I left something out I didn't mean to leave it out."

Dan gave my hand a reassuring little pat. "Why don't you just tell us what we're doing here?"

Vencino brought the file down on the table with a loud thwack. The force flung the front flap open, and a pile of colored Xeroxes reminded me. Slowly, *with intent*, Dixon spread the copies of the Bradley yearbook pages out on the table for Dan and me to see.

Vencino pinned each picture to the table with a yellow, ragged fingernail and read the things Arthur and I had written. "Chop my cock off." "Choke me with it." "RIP HOs." I wrote that last one. Mr. Larson had told us to compose a Halloween haiku on an illustration of a grave, beneath the words "RIP Farmer Ted." It had seemed like such a kiddie assignment at the time, but it had stuck in my head. Later, I'd jotted it down on Olivia's picture and Arthur had giggled, insidiously, when he read it.

"This is your handwriting, is it not?" Dixon asked.

Dan regarded me sharply. "Don't answer that, TifAni."

"We don't really need her to," Vencino said and nodded at Dixon. Another file had materialized in his hands.

Notes. The ones Arthur and I used to pass all the time, even when we weren't in class and could have just said whatever it was we were writing out loud. Some were about nothing . . . what a lemming Headmaster Mah was and what a slut Elisa White had become. I'd left my prints in the color of the ink, the same shamrock green as in the pages of the yearbook, my intent, laughable now, to proclaim my allegiance to Bradley. Not that they needed

the green to even know it was me. I'd attended a Catholic
middle school with nuns who didn't know how to explain
the sexual overtones in literature, and so it was eschewed
year after year in favor of grammar and cursive classes. My
perfect penmanship slanted and rolled across the pages of
the yearbook, my DNA in every graceful loop.

Did you see Hilary's hair today?

*It's so gross. Take a shower, sweetie pie. Her pussy
must smell so rank. If she even has one. There were
all these rumors in middle school that she was
really a man. A hermaphrodite at the very least. I
can't believe Dean banged her.*

**Dean and Hilary? When? I'm pretty sure
she's a virgin.**

*Oh, come on. Everyone knows about that. Dean
will put it anywhere. (No offense.) He's going to be
one of those guys who marries an ex–Ms. America
but bangs the fat waitresses at T.G.I. Friday's
on the side. The world would really be better off
without him. Raise your hand and ask to go to the
bathroom if you agree.*

**You are never going to believe what just
happened in the bathroom right now.**

*You better tell me fast, we have three minutes until
the bell rings.*

Paige Patrick was taking a pregnancy test.

And another note. A different day. This one dated at the top, because I started it and I was taught to put the date in the upper-right-hand corner of everything, even a stupid, hastily scribbled note.

> October 29, 2001
> Today Dean bumped into me in the hallway and called me a wide load. I'm seriously thinking about transferring. (I wasn't! I just liked to say this to get Arthur to remind me of all the reasons why Bradley was superior to Mt. St. Theresa's, which he would, happily: "Oh, you miss soccer mom training camp?").
>
> *You say this at least once a week. You're not transferring. We both know it. I'll just kill them all for you. How's that sound?*
>
> Swell. How are we doing it?
>
> *I have my dad's gun.*
>
> What happens if you get caught?
>
> *I wouldn't get caught. I'm wicked smart.*

I didn't know how to make the detectives understand. This was how we spoke to each other. We were all young and cruel. One time a freshman JV soccer player choked on an orange slice on the bus ride to an away game, and, instead of helping him, or even displaying the least bit of alarm, Dean and Peyton and all the guys laughed at the way the blood rushed to his face and his eyes bugged out of his head (the assistant manager finally realized what was going on and performed the Heimlich maneuver). For weeks afterward, the guys regaled us with this story, over and over, the veins in their necks straining with their laughter while the poor kid who choked on the orange stared at the lunch table, trying not to cry.

"I'm almost positive that when we look in your school notebooks we will see this is your handwriting, and that you use a green pen." Detective Vencino patted his paunch, satisfied, like he'd just eaten a great meal.

"Well, you're going to have to get a warrant to search TifAni's things to be able to do that. And if you had that, you would have used it by now." Dan leaned back in his chair and smirked at Vencino.

"It was just a joke," I said, softly.

"TifAni!" Dan warned.

"Really," Detective Dixon said. "It's better if we hear it from her. Because as we speak, we are getting that warrant."

Dan blinked at me, trying to decide. Finally, he nodded. Sighed, "Tell them."

"It was a joke," I said again. "I thought he was *joking*."

"And were you?" Detective Vencino asked.

"Of course I was," I said. "I didn't ever think something like this would happen. Not in a million years."

"I know it's been a few years since I've been in high school"—Vencino began to pace—"but, little girl, you better believe we never made jokes like that."

"Did you two ever discuss this . . . plan . . . verbally?" Detective Dixon asked.

"No," I said. "I mean, I don't think so."

"What is this 'I don't think so'?" Vencino demanded. "Either you did or you didn't."

"I just . . . didn't pay attention to it," I said. "So yeah, he could have joked about it, and maybe I did too, but I didn't make, like, a mental note of it or anything because it wasn't something I took seriously."

"But you knew he had one of the guns used in the attack," Dixon said, and I nodded. "How did you know that?"

I glanced at Dan, and he gave me the go-ahead. "He showed it to me."

Dixon and Vencino looked at each other, so astonished that for a second neither of them appeared angry at me anymore. "When was this?" Dixon asked, and I told him about that afternoon in Arthur's basement. The deer head. The yearbook. The way he'd pointed the gun at me and I'd fallen on my bad wrist.

Detective Vencino shook his head in the corner, shadows darkening his face like a bruise. Muttered, "Little fucking punk."

"Did Arthur ever joke"—Dixon bunny-eared that word—"about hurting anyone else?"

"*No*. I thought he wanted to hurt me."

"See"—Vencino tapped his grimy fingernail against his chin—"that's funny because Dean is saying just the opposite."

I opened my mouth to speak, but Dan jumped in. "What is Dean saying?"

"That Arthur offered the gun to TifAni. Told her now was the chance to shoot this—and excuse my language, but these are the types of kids we're dealing with here—cocksucker's cock off." Vencino scratched a patch of skin under his eye and grimaced. "He says TifAni reached for the gun."

"I never said I didn't!" I exploded. "I was going to use it on *him*, not Dean."

314 Jessica Knoll

Dan warned, "TifAni—" at the same time Dixon slammed his fist down on the table, sending a few copies of the yearbook pages into the air, where they hovered, still as a picture, before slicing back and forth through space, not even hitting the floor for some time after Dixon shouted "You're a liar!" His face was heart-attack red, the way only a natural blond's can get. "You've been lying to us from the moment we met you." He had been lying too, fooling me with his friendly mask.

By the end of it all I just assumed no one ever told the truth, and that was when I started lying too.

❧

The news informed me that Liam's funeral was the first, a full ten days after the fact. A few hours later, an e-mail went out to the Bradley "family." That's what they started calling us after this. The "Bradley Family." And even I, black sheep that I was, received the message.

Mom received it too, and she asked me if I needed to go shopping for a black dress. My laugh was my way of calling her demented. "I'm not going to that."

"Oh, yes you are." Her lips pulled in thin as a slice of grass.

"I am *not* going," I repeated, more fiercely this time. I was sitting on the couch, my stockinged feet on the coffee table, hair and lint stuck all over them. It had been three days since the interrogation, and I hadn't showered, hadn't put on a bra. This skank stank.

"TifAni!" Mom cried. She took a deep breath and brought her hands to her face. In a reasonable tone she said, "We did not raise you like this. This is the decent thing to do."

"I am not going to the funeral of the guy who raped me."

Mom gasped. "Don't you speak like that."

"Like what?" I laughed.

"He's dead, TifAni. He died a horrible death, and while he may have made some mistakes in his life he was just a child." Mom pinched her nose, sniffed back the snot. "He did not deserve that." Her voice went up high and weepy on the last word.

"You never even *met* him." I pointed the controller at the TV and turned it off, the grandest statement I could make. I kicked off the throw covering my hairy legs and glared at Mom as I passed her on my way up the stairs, to my bedroom, which I hadn't stepped foot in for the last two days.

"You are going or I won't pay for you to go back to Bradley!" Mom called behind me.

The morning of Liam's funeral the phone rang. I snatched it off the hook. "Hello?"

"TifAni!" My name was spoken with surprise.

I twirled my finger in the cord. "Mr. Larson?"

"I've been trying to call," he said, hurriedly. "How are you? Are you okay?"

The line clicked and Mom said, "Hello?"

"Mom," I snapped. "I've got it."

All three of us were silent for a moment. "Who is this?" Mom asked.

There was the unmistakable sound of a man clearing his throat. "It's Andrew Larson, Mrs. FaNelli."

"TifAni," Mom hissed. "Hang up the phone."

I hooked my finger in the cord tighter. "Why?"

"I said, hang up the—"

"It's okay," Mr. Larson said. "I was just calling to see if TifAni was okay. Good-bye, TifAni."

"Mr. Larson!" I shrieked, but it was only Mom there, raging over the dial tone. "I told you to stop calling! She is fourteen years old!"

I screamed right back. "Nothing happened! I told you nothing happened!"

≈

You know what the sick part is? Even though I was dreading Liam's funeral, even though I was so mad at Mom for making me go, I still wanted to look pretty for it.

I spent an hour getting ready. I curled my eyelashes for forty seconds each, so that they stuck straight up in wide-awake surprise. Dad had to work (sometimes I think he was just sitting in an empty office, scowling at his powered-off computer), so it was just Mom and me, not speaking in her bright cherry BMW with the heat that worked only when her foot pumped the gas pedal, so that we shivered in unison every time we stopped in front of a red light.

"I want you to know," Mom said, as she released the brake along with a plume of deliciously warm air, "that I don't condone what Liam did. Of course I don't. But you have to take responsibility for your part in this too."

"Just stop," I pleaded.

"I'm just saying. When you drink you put yourself into situations where—"

"I *know*!" We merged onto the highway, and the car was silent and warm after that.

The church I used to attend at Mt. St. Theresa's was beautiful, if you're into that sort of thing. But we weren't going to a church for Liam's "memorial service" (no funerals, everyone had a memorial service). Liam was a Quaker, and we were going to a meeting-house.

My confusion was so great it actually dulled my irritation with Mom long enough to muse, "I thought Quakers lived in their own communities and didn't believe in, like, modern medicine or whatever?"

Mom bit into a smile, despite everything. "That's Amish."

The Quaker meetinghouse was a single-level clapboard home, a faded, somber shade of white behind the oak arms that flapped around it, red and orange leaves clinging to random bark veins. Even though we were forty-five minutes early, there was a long line of shiny black sedans waiting in the muddy grass, and Mom was forced to park at the top of the hill. She tried to hold my arm as we climbed down, but I pulled away from her and stormed ahead, the rhythm of her high heels behind me unsteady and satisfying.

But as we neared the entrance, I saw the crowd of people, the TV cameras, and my classmates, in groups hugging and comforting each other. It was enough to make me lose my nerve and slow down so that Mom could catch up with me.

"What a scene," Mom breathed. Faced with the women in chic black pantsuits, gumball-size pearls around their necks, Mom clasped her large cross pendant self-consciously. The fake diamonds were dull, despite the bold blast of the late morning sun.

"Come on," Mom said, forging ahead. Her high heel stuck in the grass, and she boomeranged backward. A few frosted hairs caught in her pink lip gloss, and she spat them away. "Goddamnit," she muttered, working her shoe out of the mud.

As we came up on the edge of the crowd, a few classmates paused, eyes wet and wide on me. A few even stepped away, and what gutted me most was that they didn't do it meanly. They did it nervously.

The meetinghouse wasn't even half full yet. It would be packed to capacity and then some, but for now, there was a spectacle to be made outside, in front of the cameras. Mom and I hurried inside and found seats in the back of the meetinghouse. Right away Mom hunched over, searching beneath the pew ahead of her for a kneeler. When she didn't find one, she slid forward in her seat, making a swift sign of the cross and pressing her palms together. She squeezed her eyes shut, and her plastic-looking eyelashes crunched on her cheeks.

A family of four—the daughter, Riley, a junior at Bradley—entered the pew to the left, and I had to nudge Mom to open her eyes. She was blocking their way.

"Oh!" Mom slid back into the pew, turned her knees to the side to give the family room to make their way in.

They sat down, Riley nearest to me, and I nodded solemnly at her. She was a member of school council, always up at the podium at Monday's morning assembly, talking about how much money the car wash raised over the weekend. Her mouth was the largest feature on her face, and, when she smiled, her eyes retracted, like they were hiding from her lips.

Riley nodded back, the corners of her big mouth poking into the sides of her face. In my peripheral vision, I saw her lean toward her father, mumble something in his ear. There was a domino effect: now the father slanting toward the mother, and the mother toward the younger sister, who whined, "Why?" The mother whispered something else, a warning, a bribe, however their family operated, and the girl stood, eyes rolling and legs still slightly bent at the knees, and she shuffled out of the pew, her family following.

This happened a few more times. Classmates either recognizing the Judas in the back pew and not even bothering to stop, or getting up and moving when they noticed me. The pews were filling in fast, and like in a crowded movie theater, families and cliques of friends were having to split up in order to get a seat. I studied every person who entered, worried it could be Hilary or Dean. I knew they were in the hospital, that they would be for a long time, but still I looked for them.

"I told you we shouldn't have come," I whispered to Mom, triumphant. She knew nothing.

Mom didn't answer, and I looked over at her. Two pink circles had fought their way to the surface of her cheeks.

Eventually, some nice old people came by. Asked if these seats were saved. "They're all yours," Mom said gallantly, like she'd been holding the spots just for them.

Within minutes, attendees were forced to stand around the outside of the meetinghouse, pressing their ears against air-conditioning vents to hear. I can personally attest to the fact that half the students at the funeral had not spoken more than a few words to Liam since he started at Bradley that September. Strange, but I felt a sort of special bond with him. I knew what Liam had done was wrong. I found something like forgiveness for him my freshman year of college, at the sexual assault seminar every incoming student was required to take.

After the initial presentation by a local police officer, one girl raised her hand. "So if you've been drinking it's rape no matter what?"

"If that were true I would have been raped hundreds of times in my life," replied the pretty senior moderating the talk, so proud of herself when the room tittered. "It's only rape if you are too drunk to consent to it."

"But what if I say yes but I'm blacked out?" the girl pressed.

The senior looked at the police officer. This was where it always got tricky. "A good rule of thumb," the officer said, "and we're telling the men this too—you know what a blacked-out person looks like. You know when someone's had too much. That should guide your partner more than a yes or no."

I silently begged the girl to ask the next question. "But what if he's blacked out too?"

"It's not easy," the police officer admitted. She gave us all an encouraging smile. "Just do your best." Like it was mile-time day in gym class or something.

I think about that sometimes. Wonder if Liam was so bad. Maybe he just didn't know what he was doing was wrong. There comes a point where you just can't be mad at everyone anymore.

I had never been to a Quaker service before, and neither had Mom, so we'd looked it up on the Internet and found out that there is no formal service. Rather, people just stand and speak when they feel compelled to do so.

So many people stood to say nice things about Liam while his parents, his little brother with his same disquietingly blue eyes, clutched each other in the corner. Every now and then, Dr. Ross would start in on a low, slow howl that crescendoed, reaching either wall of the meetinghouse, exiting through the pipes and vents so that the people outside stepped away, the metal magnifying the sound like a microphone. Long before the Kardashians made it public knowledge on television, I knew what it looked like when someone who had gone overboard with the injectables cried. Turned out Dr. Ross, the wealthy, highly sought after plastic surgeon, was no different than the slithery housewives who came to see him, willing to try anything to reverse the damage they'd done when they were trying to pin down a husband in the first place.

He could barely contain himself as people stood to say how unique Liam was, how funny and good looking and bright. Bright. Now there's a word parents always use to describe kids who don't get good grades, either because they don't work for them or because they aren't, in fact, bright. In that moment I decided, no matter what happened, that I wasn't going to futz around and wait to find out which one I was. I'd put in the work. Anything to get out of here.

❧

After the service, we filed out of the meetinghouse, packs of crying girls three or four deep, the sun winking callously in their blond hair.

The graveyard was directly to the left of the meetinghouse, and all were invited to the burial after. Since Mom and I had sat so close to the entrance, we were in the inner loop of the circle that formed around Liam's grave. I sensed someone at my shoulder as the rest of the crowd gathered. Then I felt the Shark's sticky hand in mine and I squeezed gratefully.

Liam's father was holding a silver vase, which at first I thought was going to be for flowers to mark Liam's place, before I realized Liam was inside the vase. I hadn't been to many funerals in my life, but the few I had attended, everyone had been buried in a casket. Three weeks ago Liam was talking about how much he hated onions on his hoagie. I couldn't reconcile how a person could go from complaining about onions to turning in the incinerator, crumbling to ash.

I saw Mr. Larson on the other side of the circle. I sneaked a glance at Mom to make sure she wasn't looking and gave him a half wave. He half-waved back. There was a blond woman next to him, who had always been faceless and beautiful whenever I remembered her. Now I knew her name: Whitney.

When enough black dress shoes covered the soggy grass, Dr. Ross passed the vase to Mrs. Ross. You'd think the wife of a plastic surgeon would look like one, but Mrs. Ross presented typical mom. A little chubby, and all oversize tops to conceal it. What would she have done if she knew the way Liam behaved that night at Dean's, if she knew he'd taken me to Planned Parenthood for the morning-after pill? It wasn't impossible to imagine her sighing and saying, "Oh, Liam." Just as disappointed in him as Mom is in me.

In a clear voice, Mrs. Ross said, "This may be where we mark Liam's time with us, but I don't want you to think this is where you have to come to think about Liam." She held the vase close to her chest. "Think about him always." Her mouth puckered. "Anywhere." Dr. Ross picked up his arm and smashed Liam's blubbering brother into his chest.

Mrs. Ross stepped back and Dr. Ross wiped one elegant hand down his face and croaked, "It was an honor to be his father." He took the vase from his wife, and his face became inhuman again as he sprinkled his oldest son in the grass.

Mom didn't give me any shit when I turned the radio to Y100. After all that, she was grateful to have a spunky daughter to annoy her.

It took some time to get out of the parking lot. I'd overheard a few kids saying they were going to Minella's for food, and I mourned that too. That I would never again be part of some rambunctious group taking up two booths, the owners rolling their eyes but also secretly pleased that theirs was the place high schoolers came to get their grilled cheeses.

We finally pulled onto the road, a winding single-lane carved into green horse country, the houses more subdued here. We were a little ways from the true heart of the Main Line, from the sprawling old estates with the maid's Honda Civic parked next to the dashing Audi in the driveway. A gray mist pressed down, blurring the view from the window. Mom said, eyes in the rearview mirror, "That car is driving awfully close."

I blinked away the long-distance strain and looked in the side-view mirror. I didn't drive yet, so I didn't really have a concept of what was too close and what was normal. I recognized the car, a black Jeep Cherokee. It belonged to Jaime Sheriden, a soccer player and a friend of Peyton's.

"It's a little close," I agreed.

Mom bunched up her shoulders, defensively. "I'm going the speed limit."

I pressed my cheek against the cool glass and looked beyond the side-view mirror again. "He's just trying to drive fast to impress his friends."

"Moron," Mom muttered. "After everything that's happened, the last thing this school needs is a car full of more dead teenagers."

Mom kept on going the speed limit, her eyes slicing sideways every few seconds. "TifAni, they're seriously too close." She checked one more time. "Do you know them? Can you signal to them or something?"

"Mom, I'm not signaling to them." I pressed myself closer to the door. *"God."*

"This is very dangerous." Mom's knuckles were white on the wheel. "I'd pull over, but I'm afraid to slow down in case they—oh!"

Both Mom and I lurched forward as the lip of Jaime's vehicle bumped us from behind. The wheel spun frantically under Mom's hands, and it steered us right into the gummy, pockmarked field. By the time Mom stilled the wheel and slammed on the brakes, we were thirty or so feet off the road, our tires dunked halfway in the muck.

"Goddamn assholes!" Mom gasped. She brought a trembling hand to her chest before turning to look at me. "Are you okay?"

Before I could tell her no, I wasn't okay, Mom smacked the center console with an open hand. "Assholes!"

There was talk that I should consider other options for high school. But the idea of starting over somewhere new, of having to find my ranking in a new pecking order, all of it made me want to lie down and take a long nap. Maligned as I was at Bradley, I found comfort in knowing where I stood, that I could just go to class and eat lunch with the Shark and go home to study, focus on chiseling my tunnel out of there. At one point Mom mentioned homeschooling, but she quickly retracted the offer because she said she was at the point in her life where her body was changing ("*Mom,*" I'd groaned), and, for some reason, I had the ability to press her buttons in a way nobody else could. Feeling's mutual, I almost told her, but decided against it, on account of the button pushing and all.

The school balked when Mom told them I was coming back. "I'm surprised," Headmaster Mah said, "that TifAni would even want to come back. I'm not sure it's the right decision for her." He paused. "I'm not sure it's the right decision for us."

There wasn't enough evidence to charge me with any crime, but that didn't stop the court of public opinion from trying me. There were the notes and the yearbook ramblings, my prints that turned up on the gun along with the killers'. Anita, who I'd trusted, had determined that I showed little emotion for my dead classmates, and that I seemed excited to return to school now that my "problem peers" had been extinguished.

The most damning claim came from Dean, who insisted Arthur handed me the gun and told me to kill him "just like we'd planned." Of course Arthur never said that, but no one was going to doubt the popular, six-packed soccer star, paralyzed from the waist down, his promising future wrenched from him at the starting line of what would have been a charmed life. The media sniffed around, wailed for a few weeks about how terrible it was that not all parties responsible for this tragedy would be brought to justice. Plump housewives with gold-plated crosses hidden in their heavy cleavage came in from all the over the country to lay cheap drugstore flowers on Dean's front lawn, then went home to write grammatically incorrect hate mail to me: "Your going to be judged for what you did in the next life."

Dan took Headmaster Mah to task, said the school would have an even bigger lawsuit on their hands than the one they were currently battling if they didn't allow me to return. Some parents were suing. Peyton's led the charge. The sprinklers in the old part of the cafeteria had never activated. Had they worked, they could have prevented the fire from spreading to the Brenner Baulkin Room. The coroner determined that Peyton died from smoke inhalation, not the gunshot wound. With medical attention and plastic surgery, Peyton could have lived a relatively normal life. Instead, he was still conscious when the fire swept into the room, his raw face absorbing all that smoke like a hunk of bread in hot soup. I'll never not hate myself for leaving him there.

Dean was shipped off to a boarding school in Switzerland, a few miles from a progressive hospital specializing in experimental treatments for spinal cord injuries. The goal was to get him to walk again, but that never happened. Dean found the upside though. He wrote a book, *Learning to Fly*, that became an international bestseller. One speaking engagement lead to another, and Dean found himself a famous and well-regarded motivational speaker. I go to his website sometimes. There is a picture on the homepage of Dean, leaning forward in his wheelchair, embracing a pale bald child in a hospital bed. The grossly staged empathy on Dean's face reminds me what I might have been capable of doing if Arthur had actually handed me the gun.

Hilary didn't return to Bradley either. Her parents moved her away to Illinois, where her father's side was from. I wrote her a letter once, and it was returned to me, the envelope pristine and unopened.

To Anita's point, it was kind of unbelievable that everyone who had made my life so miserable was gone when school resumed for the spring semester. The cafeteria wouldn't be rebuilt for another year, and, in the meantime, we ate lunch at our desks. A lot of pizza was ordered in, and no one complained about that.

That first month after Bradley resumed, I dry-heaved every morning before school. But I needed to build up my loneliness tolerance, was all. The loneliness became like a friend, my constant companion. I could depend on it, and only it.

I worked hard like I promised myself I would at Liam's memorial service. Junior year, we took a trip to New York City, to visit tourist hot spots I would later despise, like the Empire State Building and the Statue of Liberty. At one point I was climbing off the bus and I bumped into a woman in a crisp black blazer and pointy, witchy shoes. She had a bulky cell phone pressed against her ear and a black bag with gold Prada lettering hooked around her wrist. I was a long ways off from worshiping at the Céline, Chloé, or Goyard thrones, but I certainly recognized Prada.

"Sorry," I said, and took a step away from her.

She nodded at me briskly but never stopped speaking into her phone, "The samples need to be there by *Friday.*" As her heels snapped away on the pavement, I thought, *There is no way that woman can ever get hurt.* She had more important things to worry about than whether or not she would have to eat lunch alone. The samples *had* to arrive by Friday. And as I thought about all the other things that must make up her busy, important life, the cocktail parties and the sessions with the personal trainer and the shopping for crisp, Egyptian cotton sheets, there it started, my concrete and skyscraper wanderlust. I saw how there was a protection in success, and success was defined by threatening the minion on the other end of a cell phone, expensive pumps terrorizing the city, people stepping out of your way simply because you looked like you had more important places to be than they did. Somewhere along the way, a man got tangled up in this definition too.

I just had to get to that, I decided, and no one could hurt me again.

CHAPTER 15

I used to hold down the doorbell to annoy Arthur. Over the *ding-dong-ding-dong-ding-dong* I would pick up his muttering path through the house. "Jesus *Christ*, Tif," he'd huff, when he finally wrenched the door open.

Today I knocked. I don't think I could stand to hear the loop of that bell ever again.

The camera was behind me, my bra bulge directly in the shot. Barely seven hundred calories a day, and still I had that little lump of skin protruding beneath the harness of my bra. How was it possible?

Mrs. Finnerman opened the door. Age and loneliness had converged on her, like allied countries during wartime. You get one side, I'll get the other. There was gray in her hair that would never be tended to, extra skin pulling the corners of her mouth low. Mrs. Finnerman had always been short and formless (Arthur's heft came from his father). It seemed especially cruel that a person who had to deal with what Mrs. Finnerman had to deal with was as naturally weak and defenseless as she was. Jell-O muscles, legally blind, prone to debilitating headaches and sinus infections.

Sometime in the spring of freshman year, when things finally settled enough to reveal what life would be like now that it had a big fat line drawn through it—before the slaughter, after—I received a letter from Mrs. Finnerman. Her handwriting appeared unstable on the page, like she'd been a passenger in a car flying down a potholed road when she wrote it. She wanted me to know that she was so sorry for what I'd had to do. She had no idea the rage and the hatred simmering in Arthur, her own child—how could she not have known, she berated herself over and over.

Mom forbade me from writing her back, but I did anyway ("Thank you. I would never blame you for what he did. I don't hate him. Even miss him sometimes"). I folded the piece of paper in half and slipped it under her door on an afternoon I noticed her car wasn't in the driveway. I wasn't strong enough for a tête-à-tête just yet, and I sensed Mrs. Finnerman wasn't either.

After I graduated college, Mrs. Finnerman sent me the occasional card, and an odd sort of relationship developed. She reached out when the news trickled down that I'd gotten engaged, and when she read an article she liked in *The Women's Magazine*. She ripped out one in particular, "Does Facebook Make You Sad?" Sent it in an envelope along with an article from *The New York Times*, titled "The Depressive Effect of Facebook." She circled the date on each—mine written in May 2011, the *Times*'s version on February 7, 2012. "You scooped the *Times*," she wrote. "Brava, TifAni!" It was the cheery correspondence of old friends, and that was a mistake, because Mrs. Finnerman and I weren't friends. This would be the first time we'd seen each other since before the shooting.

I smiled shyly. "Hi, Mrs. Finnerman."

Mrs. Finnerman's face wadded up like a wet paper towel. I stepped forward, unsure, and she frantically fanned her hand at me, waving off my hug. "I'm all right," she insisted. "I'm all right."

The coffee table in the living room was piled high with photo albums and old newspapers. The choice placement of a coffee mug altered a headline in a yellowed copy of *The Philadelphia Inquirer*, POLICE THINK GUNMEN DID WORK ALONE. Mrs. Finnerman picked up the cup and the word "not" reappeared, righting my fate.

"What can I get you to drink?" Mrs. Finnerman asked. I knew she drank only green tea because I'd come across her stash once, stoned and searching for a jar of Nutella.

"Yeah," Arthur had said as I marveled at it. Green tea seemed very exotic to someone like me. Mom drank Folgers. "My mom is really anti-coffee."

"Tea is fine," I told her. I hate tea.

"Are you sure?" Mrs. Finnerman's bulky glasses slid forward on her nose, and she pushed them back with her index finger, just like Arthur used to do. "I have coffee."

"Maybe coffee then." I laughed a little, and to my relief Mrs. Finnerman did too.

"Gentlemen?" Mrs. Finnerman addressed the crew.

"Please, Kathleen," Aaron said. "Like I said, pretend we aren't even here."

For a moment I thought Mrs. Finnerman would unravel again. I held my breath, bracing, but she surprised everyone by throwing up her hands. "Like I could do that." She laughed, wryly.

Mrs. Finnerman disappeared into the kitchen, and I

heard cupboard doors clapping open and shut. "Milk and sugar?" she called.

"Just milk!" I called back.

"What's it like being here again?" Aaron asked.

I looked around the room, at the faded fleur-de-lis wallpaper and the harp hulking in the corner. Mrs. Finnerman used to play, but now the strings peeled back like split ends in need of deep conditioner.

"Weird." As soon as I said it, I remembered Aaron's instructions from earlier. I should answer his questions in a complete sentence, since they would edit out his voice and what I said had to make sense on its own. "It's very strange to be back here."

"Here we go." Mrs. Finnerman stepped carefully into the room, handing me a mug so misshapen it had to be handmade. I caught the engraving on the bottom, "To: Mom, Love: Arthur 2/14/95." There was no handle, and I had to transfer the cup from hand to hand every few seconds, when the heat became too much for one side to tolerate. I took a scalding sip. "Thank you."

Mrs. Finnerman was rooted to her spot beside the couch. We both looked at Aaron, desperate for direction.

Aaron indicated the open seat beside me. "Kathleen, why don't you sit next to Ani on the couch?"

Mrs. Finnerman nodded her head and muttered, "Yes, yes." She walked around the coffee table and settled into the far end of the couch. Her knees pointed at the front door, away from the kitchen. I was closer to the kitchen.

"It will help the shot if you can scooch in a little closer." Aaron pinched his fingers together to show us what he meant.

I couldn't look at Mrs. Finnerman as I "scooched" to-

ward her, but I imagined she had the same polite, morti-
fied smile on her face as I did.

"Much better," Aaron said.

The crew waited for us to say something, but the only
sound was the hush of the dishwasher running in the
kitchen.

"Maybe you could go through the photo albums?"
Aaron suggested. "Talk about Arthur?"

"I'd love to see," I tried.

As though programmed by the two of us, Mrs. Finnerman leaned forward robotically and picked up a white
photo album. She swept away a whisper-light dust bunny.
It caught on the edge of her pinkie and reattached itself to
the laminated cover.

The album creaked open on her lap, and Mrs. Finnerman blinked down at Arthur, maybe three years old. He
was mid-scream, clutching an empty ice cream cone.
"We were in Avalon here," Mrs. Finnerman murmured.
"A seagull swooped down"—she swished her hand
through the air—"knocked the whole scoop right off the
cone."

I smiled. "We used to go through ice cream by the carton here."

"I know how he did it." Mrs. Finnerman flipped the
page, forcefully. "But not you. Tiny little thing that you
are." There was something menacing in her voice. I didn't
know what else to do but pretend I didn't notice.

"Oh, this." Mrs. Finnerman brought her chin to her
chest and sighed longingly at a picture of Arthur curled
around a yellow Lab, his face burrowed in her buttery fur.
Mrs. Finnerman tapped the dog's snout. "This was Cassie."
Her smile was all lip. "Arthur *loved* her. She slept in his bed
every single night."

The cameraman moved behind us, his long lens closing in on the picture.

I reached out to hold the page down, to deflect the glare obscuring my view, but Mrs. Finnerman brought the album to her chest and tucked her chin over its leather ledge. A tear rolled, clung to the edge of her chin. "He sobbed when she died. Sobbed. So he couldn't be what they say he is. He *had* emotions."

What they say he is. A psychopath. Incapable of experiencing true human emotions, only mimicking those he observed in others: remorse, grief, compassion.

A lot of time and energy went into dismantling the dynamic between Arthur and Ben, identifying the leader of the pack. Understanding their motives would bring closure to the community, and the information could prevent a recurrence at another school. The country's most renowned psychologists examined the evidence collected in the aftermath of the attack on Bradley— Ben's and Arthur's journals, their academic records, interviews with neighbors and friends of the family— and every single one arrived at the same conclusion: Arthur called it.

I arranged my face to signal sympathy, like Arthur had done for me so many times. "Do you know what I remember about him?"

Mrs. Finnerman plucked a tissue out of a box on the coffee table. Her face went maroon as she blew into it. She folded the tissue in half and wiped her nose. "What's that?"

"I remember that he was kind to me on my first day of school, when I didn't know anyone. I remember how he was the only one who stood up for me when a lot of people turned on me."

"That was Arthur." His name trembled on her lips. "He wasn't a monster."

"I know," I said, not sure if this was a lie or not.

The thing that everyone said Arthur was—I do believe it. But the report Dr. Anita Perkins submitted to the police acknowledged that even psychopaths can show flickers of real emotion, genuine empathy. I like to believe he experienced some for me, even though Dr. Perkins rated Arthur using the Hare test, a twenty-item inventory of personality traits and behaviors used to detect psychopathy, and Arthur scored off the charts.

So much of what Arthur did for me, the protective brother act and even that nonsense he sputtered at the end, the knife handle extending from his chest perfectly parallel to the floor, "I was only trying to help," was either an imitation of kindness or careful, chilling manipulation. Dr. Perkins wrote that psychopaths are particularly skilled at identifying a victim's Achilles' heel, and profiting from it in a way that suits their purposes. When it came to pulling off the ultimate con, forget Nell, Arthur was my original study.

Ben was depressive, suicidal, not necessarily predisposed to violence the way Arthur was, but not opposed to the idea either. He and Arthur had traded violent fantasies about taking out their idiot classmates and teachers all through middle school. It was always a joke for Ben—Arthur was just waiting for something to happen that would make him seriously consider turning fantasy into reality.

That something was Kelsey Kingsley's graduation party. The humiliating thing that Dean and Peyton did to Ben in the woods that drove him to his first suicide attempt. According to Arthur's diaries, he broached the idea of an attack, "a Bradley Columbine," when he visited Ben in the hospital not two weeks after his ragged wrists landed him there. In his diary he wrote how he had to wait for the nurses to change shifts, when they would finally have a few moments of privacy, and it was so annoying. ("What are we, two helpless fucking babies?") His father had a gun, the beginning of their arsenal. Arthur could get a fake ID, pose for eighteen—he looked older than his age already. There were instructions on the Internet for building a pipe bomb. They were smart, they could really do this. His instinct told him that Ben had snapped, turned a corner he would never retrace, and it was spot-on. Ben had nothing to lose because he wanted to die. If that was going to happen, he might as well make those guys pay for what they did to him.

The media narrative concluded that Arthur and Ben were bullied—for being weird, for being fat, for being gay. But the police reports tell a much different story, a truth that has nothing to do with bullying, the cause du jour. Although it's widely accepted that Arthur was gay, Ben wasn't. That thing Olivia said she saw, Arthur giving Ben a blow job at the Spot? That was a lie—desperate, stupid teenage gossip that tragically, *ironically*, made the fire dance higher. The rumor infuriated and hurt Ben, and Arthur pounced. "I promised him Olivia," Arthur wrote in his diary, the first blithe mention of a hit list. Only Arthur didn't care about a hit list, not really. The attack wasn't just about getting back at his tormentors, or about revenge, it was about his contempt. He was after anyone who was intellectually inferior to him, which was everyone, in his mind. He proposed the idea of a list only to tantalize Ben. His goal had been to take out the entire cafeteria with his bombs—the Shark, Teddy, the sweet

lunch lady who built his sandwiches, cheese layered between the roast beef and ham, just how he liked it—we
were all fair game. He hid out in the empty dormitory
rooms on the third floor of Bradley, waiting for detona-
tion so he could go downstairs and savor the carnage
before he ended his own life. The cops would shoot to
kill anyway, and a psychopath's worst nightmare is relin-
quishing control. If he was going to die, it would be on his
terms. He started shooting when he saw that only one of
his amateur bombs went off, inflicting "minimal"damage.

There was a part in Dr. Perkins's report, which was
available for the public to read, that I started in on and
only when I realized it concerned me did I double back
and reread the first few paragraphs. It was like seeing a picture and not recognizing yourself caught in the frame—
who is that salty girl frowning in the background? Doesn't
she know it gives her a double chin? The meta-moment of
experiencing how the rest of the world sees you, because
the salty girl is you.

Dr. Perkins classified Arthur and Ben's "partnership"
under the dyad phenomenon, a term criminologists
coined to describe the way murderous pairs fuel each other
with their bloodlust. Between a psychopath (Arthur) and
a depressive (Ben), the psychopath would most definitely
be in control, but as a psychopath craves the stimulation of
violence, a hotheaded partner can provide an invaluable
service: riling him up for the slaughter. Arthur and Ben
planned the attack for six months, and for almost that entire
time Ben was confined to a mental rehabilitation center,
putting on a show for the doctors and nurses to convince
them he was no longer a threat to himself. In the meantime, Arthur found himself a new cheerleader, someone
whose pain and anger padded the void of violence. This

sidekick kept him on a low simmer until he finally had the opportunity to boil over. She didn't name me, but there was no one else it could have been. Sometimes I wonder what would have happened if I hadn't set Arthur off the last time I saw him in his room. If he was gearing up to tell me about his plan. Ask me to be a part of it.

"This was at the shore too." Mrs. Finnerman smoothed a wrinkle in the plastic. I was surprised to see Mr. Finnerman, elbows draped over the back of a bench on the boardwalk, roily black curls springing out of his tan chest. Next to him, Arthur standing, pointing to the sky and shouting something, Mrs. Finnerman's flimsy arms anchored around his legs to keep him from falling.

"How is Mr. Finnerman?" I asked, politely. I have the picture that immortalizes one of his most intimate moments with his son, and still I've never met the man. He surfaced on the Main Line when everything happened, of course, but faded away shortly after the funeral. The funeral. Yes, killers need to be buried too. Mrs. Finnerman humiliated herself calling rabbi after rabbi, desperate to find someone who would be willing to perform the service for Arthur. I don't know what Ben's family did. No one does.

"Oh, you know," Mrs. Finnerman said. "Craig's remarried, so." She took a sip of cold tea.

"I didn't know that happened," I said. "I'm sorry."

"Yes, well." There was a speck of tea in the valley of Mrs. Finnerman's upper lip. She didn't brush it away.

"You know," I said, "I have a photo of Arthur and Mr. Finnerman too."

The living room suddenly burst with light, the sun pushing a cloud out of the way, and Mrs. Finnerman's pupils retracted. I'd forgotten her eyes were blue. "Excuse me?"

I risked a glance at Aaron. He was guiding a microphone around the room, oblivious to what I'd just triggered.

I clasped my hands around the coffee mug, lukewarm now. "I have this picture . . . um, Arthur used to keep it in his room."

"The one with the seashells?" Mrs. Finnerman wanted to know.

"Of Arthur and his dad." I nodded. "Yeah."

All the softness in Mrs. Finnerman's face was gone. Even her wrinkles didn't look so much like folds of skin as they did hard cracks in a pane of glass. "How do you have that? I've been looking for it everywhere."

I knew I had to lie, but it was like someone had taken an eraser to my mind. I couldn't think of any way to answer her that wouldn't upset her. "We got into a fight," I admitted. "I took it. It was mean. I was trying to upset him." I stared into my cold cup of coffee. "I never got a chance to give it back."

"I'd like it back," she said.

"Of course," I said. "I'm so—" I stopped at Mrs. Finnerman's scream.

"Ow! Ow!" She flung her mug on the table, newspapers absorbing the remainders of her foggy yellow tea. "Ohhhh!" Mrs. Finnerman clawed at her temples, her eyes crunched shut.

"Kathleen!" Aaron cried at the same time I did. "Mrs. Finnerman!"

"My medicine," she moaned, "by the sink."

Aaron and I rushed into the kitchen. He made it to the sink first, pushing aside dish detergent and sponges. "I don't see it!" he called.

"Bathroom!" came her strangled response.

I knew where the bathroom was, and I beat Aaron this time. On the sink's counter was a small orange prescription bottle, the instructions curved around the label: "Take one at the first sign of pain."

"Mrs. Finnerman, here." I shook a pill into my hand, and a member of the crew offered her his bottle of water. She put the pill on her tongue and drank.

"My migraines," she whispered. Rocking back and forth, her fingernails white on either side of her head, she began to weep. "I don't know why I thought I could do this." She held her head tighter. "I never should have agreed to this. This is too much. It's just too much."

"Can I give you a ride back to the hotel?" Aaron offered in Mrs. Finnerman's driveway.

I motioned to the street. "I have my car, thanks."

Aaron squinted at the house, slanting in evening's gray limbo. It had been beautiful and bright once, but that was long before even Arthur lived there. I tried to imagine it as the Bradley girls would have seen it fifty years ago, traveling from all over the country to receive a top-notch education that they would never put to use once husbands and babies took priority. "Not to take anything away from you," he said. "But I think it must be harder for her than it is for anyone."

I watched the wind snatch a leaf off a branch. "Not at all. I've always said that. It's like, at least everyone else died nobly, in a way."

"Noble," Aaron repeated. He nodded once the word made sense. "People do love a good victim."

"It's a privilege I'll never enjoy." I frowned, feeling sorry for myself. "I know it sounds so self-pitying, but I feel cheated by that." I didn't admit that to Aaron, but I did to Andrew last night, sitting on the edge of his childhood bed. His parents had left for their shore house. They liked to drive out late on Friday night. Less traffic then. Why didn't I come over for one drink before I went back to my hotel? That's what I suggested when we tumbled into his car, the stairs from the Athletic Center still challenging our lungs. Andrew turned to answer me and furrowed his brow.

"What?" I demanded.

He reached for me. "You have something in your hair." He pinched a section between his fingers and pulled, tugging various coordinates in my scalp that seemed to blur my thoughts, obliterate my conscience. "It's like wood chips or something. From the underside of the desk."

After the vodka in Andrew's kitchen, after the tour of his house that ended in his old bedroom, Luke came up again. And again I tried to explain what he did for me, how he was evidence that I was a good, decent person. "Luke Harrison wouldn't marry a murderess skank," I said. "He fixes me." I looked down at my hands, at my stunning armor. "I just want to be fixed."

Andrew sat next to me, his thigh warming my own. There are times I'm on the subway and it's so packed I can't escape the legs on my left and right. New Yorkers rage about this forced physical contact, but I secretly savor it, so soothed by the heat generated between bodies I could fall asleep on the shoulder of a stranger. "Do you even love him?" Andrew asked, and my eyes fluttered, fighting exhaustion, as I thought how to answer him.

I feel anger and hatred and frustration and sadness like they're physical fabrics. This one's silk, this one's velvet, this one's crisp cotton. But I couldn't tell you what the texture of loving Luke is anymore. I slipped my hand into Andrew's, watched him turn my engagement ring around. "I'm too tired to answer that."

Andrew guided me onto my back. A few tears leaked into my hairline, and I made a great honking noise as I attempted to breathe through my nose and failed. I was so nervous and hot a thermometer would have deemed me too feverish to go to school. Andrew felt my skin, boiling, tacky with sweat, and left me for a moment to turn off the lights and struggle with the window. I heard the rhythm of outside, shivered gratefully when the chill reached me several seconds later. "The cool air will help," Andrew promised. I wanted to kiss him again, but then he tucked around me and draped his large arm across my body. I was still wearing my shoes when sleep exploded over me, rare and dazzling as a meteor shower.

Yangming was always the special-occasion dinner place. New Year's Eve, birthdays, that sort of thing. Mom took me and the Shark there after high school graduation. Dad didn't go, said we'd probably enjoy it more if it was just "you gals."

Andrew's BMW was wedged between two SUVs in the parking lot, and I had that feeling this place always gives me, rarer and rarer these days, when I pushed open the door to the restaurant and saw the nicely dressed crowd of middle-aged parents, smelled that savory air, pickled with salt and fat. Like I couldn't wait for the next thing to happen.

After I'd left Mrs. Finnerman's house, I called Mom and

apologized, told her I really wasn't up to going out to dinner after all.

"I'm sure it was a tough day," Mom said, which was more than Luke had said to me in the last twenty-four hours. All I'd gotten from him was a one-line text asking how everything was going. "It's going fine," I wrote back. His silence made me bold.

"Good evening." The maître d's eyes crinkled pleasantly at the sight of someone like me. "Do you have a reservation?"

I didn't ever get a chance to answer him. Because I heard a voice speak my name high with surprise, and I turned to see Mom and my aunt Lindy, both dressed in black dress slacks, busy patterned scarves knotted around their necks, and bracelets that tinkled every time they sipped on their water. A mom's nice dinner uniform.

Mom and I just stared at each other while I concocted a lie to tell her. I was lucky she was standing where she was, with the bar behind her. Lucky she couldn't see Andrew in the far corner, waiting for me. I'd texted him after I'd texted Luke, inviting him to "take advantage" of our reservation. Three little dots appeared immediately after I hit send, then disappeared. This happened two more times, before Andrew finally settled on his response. "What time?"

❧

"I had no idea this place does takeout," Mom said, after we'd been seated. She flipped a page of the menu. "That's good to know."

I smoothed my napkin in my lap. "Why? They're not going to deliver to you or anything."

"It's so far," Aunt Lindy complained. She tapped her

acrylic nail against her empty glass and scolded the busboy tidying up the table next to ours. "Water?" Aunt Lindy
was Mom's younger sister. She was thinner and prettier
than Mom growing up, and she wasn't gracious about it.
Mom has the upper hand now, what with Aunt Lindy's
daughter marrying a cop and her daughter marrying a
Wall Street guy.

"Lin," Mom said, "believe me, it's worth the drive." Like
she was old hat in this place.

Mom had decided to keep the reservation even after I
backed out. I don't suppose it had anything to do with the
fact that Luke had left his credit card on file to pay for the
dinner. I fumbled around for a bit before telling her I'd decided to just swing by and order something to go. I'd eat
back at my hotel room.

When she told me Dad wasn't interested in coming, I
muttered, "How out of character for him." Mom sighed
and asked me not to start with her.

Aunt Lindy laughed suddenly. "Spicy veal ravioli?" She
made a face. "Doesn't sound very Chinese."

Mom gave her a pitying look. "It's fusion, Lin." Beyond
Mom's shoulder, I saw Andrew stand and motion to me.
He walked along the perimeter of the restaurant, toward
the hostess station and bathrooms.

"Will you order the lemongrass shrimp for me?" I
bunched up my napkin and tossed it on the table. "I need
to use the bathroom."

Mom scooted back and pulled out the table for me.
"But what do you want for an appetizer?"

"Just pick a salad," I said over my shoulder.

I tried the bathrooms first. I even swung open the door
to the men's room, pretending like I'd mistaken it for the

ladies'. A mustached father drying his hands informed me where I was. I called out Andrew's name and left when the man repeated himself, angry this time.

Mom and Aunt Lindy were sitting with their backs to me, so I hurried toward the front door. Outside, the air smelled so much like nothing I wasn't even sure if I was breathing. It took a second for the night's objects to focus before my eyes, and then I saw Andrew, leaning against the scuffed-up trunk of his car, like he had been waiting for me there all along.

I apologized to him with my arms. "She blindsided me."

Andrew shoved off the trunk and met me by the restaurant, underneath some scaffolding where the streetlights couldn't reach. He wiggled his fingers, witchily. "Mother's intuition. Like she knew you were up to no good."

I shook my head and laughed to show him how wrong he was. I didn't like Andrew referring to us as "no good." "No. She just really likes a free dinner at Yangming." I backed into the restaurant's brick siding as Andrew came up on me.

He brought his hands to the sides of my face, and I shut my eyes. I could have fallen asleep right there, standing up, his thumbs stroking my cheeks and the odorless breeze teasing hairs across my face. I layered my hands over his. "Just wait for me somewhere," I said. "I'll meet you wherever. After."

"Tif," he sighed. "Maybe it's for the best."

I held on to him tighter and tried to keep my voice light. "Come on."

Andrew sighed, and his hands slipped out from underneath mine. He cupped my shoulders in a brotherly way, and I started to splinter up a little inside. "We could have done something we couldn't take back last night," he said. "But we didn't. Maybe we just walk away from this now, before we do something we regret."

I shook my head and measured out my tone carefully. "I won't ever regret anything with you."

Andrew hugged me to him, and until he said, "I might though," I actually thought I had convinced him.

The door to the restaurant opened, releasing a shriek of laughter. I wanted to scream at everyone inside to shut the fuck up. It's never harder to stay in control than when everyone else is having a good time. "We don't have to do anything," I said, hating how desperate I sounded. "We can just go somewhere. Have a drink. Talk."

Andrew's heart ba-bummed in my ear. He smelled like a date, all cologne and nerves. I felt his sad sigh on the top of my head. "I can't just talk with you, TifAni."

Somewhere, that windshield finally shattered whole. I only knew how to strike, and I planted my elbows in Andrew's chest and pushed. He hadn't been expecting it, and he gasped, whether the wind was knocked out of him or he was just startled, as he stumbled away from me. "Of fucking course you can't." I waved him off. "I actually needed a friend. But you're just another guy who wants to put it in the Bradley slut."

Under the streetlamps now, I saw Andrew's face all pinched up with hurt and I immediately hated myself. "TifAni," he tried. "My God, you know that's not true. I just want you to be happy. It's all I've ever wanted for you. But this"—he pointed between us—"this won't make you happy."

"Oh, even better!" I laughed nastily. "Someone else to tell me what will make me happy. Exactly what I fucking need." *Don't do this. Don't say this.* But I couldn't stop. "I know, okay?" I took little steps toward him until we were kissing close. "I *know* what's best for *me*."

Andrew nodded kindly. "I know you do." He wiped a tear off my face, and it only made me cry harder. Would that be the last time he ever touched me? "So do it."

I gripped his hand to my face, leaking tears and snot all over him. "I can't. I know I won't."

The restaurant door yapped open, and Andrew and I broke away from each other as a couple, fed and happy, trotted down the stairs. The man waited for the woman on the street, slung his arm around her shoulders when she caught up with him. She pretended like she didn't notice my glassy eyes as she passed by, but I knew by the look on her face that she had. Knew she was thinking, *Couple's spat, glad it's not us tonight.* I would have killed for us to have been a couple, fighting about how Andrew's been working too much, how I spend too much at Barneys, anything other than what we were really doing here.

We waited for them to walk to their cars, listened to the doors slam shut. Hers first, his another few seconds later. He'd opened the door for her. I hated them.

Andrew said, "I never meant to upset you, TifAni. I hate seeing you like this." He thrust his arms in the air, angry at himself. "I let it go too far. I should never have done that. I'm sorry."

I wanted to tell him I was sorry too, that this wasn't what I meant to happen either. But I couldn't make the words come out, just more lies and excuses. "I think I gave you the wrong idea about Luke." Andrew pushed his hands at me, tried to stop me from explaining, but I pressed on. "It is not easy for someone like me to be happy. This is as close as I'm going to get and it's pretty great—"

"I didn't mean to imply that—"

"So don't you dare," I cry-hiccuped embarrassingly, "feel sorry," another hiccup, "for me."

"I don't," Andrew said. "I never did. I'm *bowled over* by you. You cared for Peyton. You held Peyton's hand. After what he did to you. You don't even know how amazing you are. You should be with someone who sees that."

I picked up the collar of my shirt and acted like I was just drying my face, but I wasn't. I was hurling quiet sobs into my protective mask. I heard Andrew's nice dress shoes take a step in my direction, but I shook my head and gave a muffled warning not to come any closer.

He waited for me, a full body's length away, while I destroyed my shirt. I couldn't ever return it to the fashion closet now; I was going to have to act like I lost it or something. Strategizing this new lie was the only thing that could calm me down. Was the only thing that dried me up inside and gave me the strength to clear my throat and say, just barely composed, "My mother's probably wondering where I am."

Andrew nodded at the pavement. Like he'd been watching it the whole time, giving me my privacy. "Okay."

I at least managed to get off a pleasant-sounding good night before I turned and took the stairs. Andrew waited behind me again, making sure I got inside safely. I didn't even deserve him anyway.

❧

"There you are!" Mom said as I squeezed myself between two tables and into the booth. "I ordered you the most boring salad they have." She dunked a crispy noodle into orange sauce and bit into it. "I know you're on that crazy diet."

"Thanks." I snapped my napkin over my lap again.

Aunt Lindy noticed my face first. "You okay, Tif?"

"Not really." I tossed a crispy noodle into my mouth without dipping it into anything and munched. "I mean, I did just spend the afternoon with the mother of the boy I murdered, so that may explain why I'm a little blue."

"TifAni FaNelli," Mom gasped. "You do not speak like that to your aunt Lindy."

"Okay then." I popped another noodle into my mouth. I wanted to shake the entire bowl down my throat, anything to fill the raging hole of hunger. "I'll speak like that to you."

"We came here to have a nice dinner," Mom hissed. "If you are hell-bent on ruining it, you can just leave."

"If I leave, so does Luke's credit card." I chewed noisily and gave her a crushing smile.

Mom managed to fit a calm veneer over her panic about Aunt Lindy witnessing such a scene. Surely my cousin would never embarrass her mother like this. She was marrying a man of the *law*. Mom turned to Aunt Lindy as though every bone in her body wasn't screaming at her to strike at me like a snake, and said Disney-princess-fucking-sweet, "Do you mind giving me a minute with TifAni?"

Aunt Lindy looked like she was sorry to miss this, but she unhooked her purse from the back of her chair. "I do need to use the ladies' room."

Mom waited until we no longer heard Aunt Lindy and her jewelry clanging through the restaurant like a goddamn marching band. She pushed away the hair that wasn't in her eyes in preparation for her lecture. "TifAni, I know you are under a lot of stress right now." She reached out to me, and I jerked away. Mom stared at the spot where my hand had been for a moment. "But you need to pull it together. You are *this close* to driving Luke away." She held her thumb and index finger a millimeter apart to show just how little breadth I had left.

It was impressive she knew to go there. So impressive it was suspicious. "And what would you know about that?"

Mom rocked back in her chair and folded her arms across her chest. "He called me. He was worried. He asked me not to tell you, but"—she leaned forward and her neck popped with stringy purple veins—"seeing how you're acting tonight, I think you need to hear it."

The idea that it might not be my call anymore, that I didn't have Andrew, that I might not have anyone, cinched that corset tighter. I shifted in my seat and tried not to look as concerned as I was. "What did he say exactly?"

"That you're not *you*, TifAni. You're combative. Hostile."

I laughed like it was the most absurd thing I'd ever heard. "I wanted to do the documentary and he doesn't think I should. He wants me to move to London and give up my shot at *The New York* fucking *Times*." I lowered my voice at Mom's glare. "And so now advocating for myself is being hostile?"

Mom lowered her voice to match mine. "It doesn't really matter if it's hostile or not, does it? Because it's more about how you're not acting like the person Luke fell in love with." She took a sip of the water the busboy had brought her while I was outside, battling Mr. Larson. "You better start acting like the old you if you want this wedding to happen."

We settled into our corners, our fierce silence only magnified by the merry, rambunctious room. I spotted Aunt Lindy on her way back from the bathroom. I'd gone with her and Mom to see the tacky little wedding factory where her daughter was getting married, the manager showing off how the lights in the "ballroom" could flash from neon pink to green to blue in tandem with the club music the house DJ was playing. Then she'd bragged about the menu, how it may have been a hundred dollars a plate for the surf and turf, but it was her only daughter and she would spare no expense. What a laugh. I'd jump for fucking joy if that was all my caterer was charging me, well, charging *us*. The memory made that thirst come over me again, the one that expert said could indicate a person wasn't getting a basic biological need met. Aunt Lindy gave me a tentative, questioning look, and I nodded at her to return while I drained my water glass, the ice cubes bumping up against my teeth in a way that always makes me cringe.

I signed the bill, and Mom reminded me to take my leftovers. "Take them for Dad," I offered, generously. I'd gone toe to toe with Mom, and I'd lost. "I don't have anyplace to store them in the hotel."

Out in the parking lot, both Aunt Lindy and Mom told me to thank Luke for dinner. I promised them I would.

"When do you head back to Manhattan?" Mom asked, doing that thing she does where she thinks she sounds in-the-know by saying Manhattan instead of New York.

"Not until tomorrow afternoon," I said. "I have one more thing to film."

"Well," Aunt Lindy said, "get some rest, sweetheart. There's no makeup like a good night's sleep."

My smile felt like a knife carving all the way around my

head. I nodded a good-bye to Mom, imagining the top half
of my head peeling off cleanly as an acorn squash halved,
ready for my disgusting, gluten-free dinner. I waited until
Mom and Aunt Lindy climbed into her cranky BMW. The
last time my parents had had the money to renew the lease
and trade in for the updated model was seven years ago. I'd
suggested something less flashy, not so expensive to maintain, and Mom had laughed. "I'm not driving a Honda
Civic, TifAni." For Mom, success wasn't working at *The
New York Times Magazine*, success was marrying someone
like Luke Harrison, who could provide all the things she
pretends she can afford.

I risked a glance at the even older version of Mom's car,
in the same spot where I'd left it an hour ago, only after
Mom and Aunt Lindy puttered out of the parking lot.

I walked past and pretended I didn't notice the New
York plate. There was a quick flash of movement from inside, and then the taillights saluted me in red. Andrew was
gone by the time I unlocked the doors of the Jeep.

Five years ago, Bryn Mawr College shaved down the trees
barricading the Spot from the road. Empty beer cans,
mouths ringed with decades-old teenage DNA, were collected and recycled, and the land was coiffed into a sweet
park with picnic tables and a swing set, a demure fountain
spitting water into the center. Sunday morning, I followed
the spindly tracks he left in the grass to their end, the cameras watching at my back.

He looked up at me, which I suppose he has to do to
everyone now. "Finny."

I snared my bottom lip in my teeth. Willed the location

to contain all that name called up before I spoke. "I can't believe you got me here, Dean."

Aaron urged me to sit on a bench. It would be better for the shot if Dean and I were the same height, and only one of us could even the disparity. I balked at first, but I gave in when I noticed Dean staring at the ground, the humiliation beading red in his cheeks.

We finally settled into our marks, the crew trained on us like an execution squad, but neither of us knew how to begin. Dean was the one who'd wanted to do this, had asked Aaron to ask me if I would be willing to see him. Which was what he had approached me about on Friday, as I left the studio on the first day of filming.

"What does he want?" I'd asked Aaron.

"He says he wants to apologize. Set the record straight." Aaron was looking at me like, *Isn't that great?*

I know I'd promised Luke I wouldn't talk about that night. I know I'd said I didn't even want to talk about that night. But with Dean willing to admit what they had all done to me, some vindication, finally, I suddenly realized how callously I'd been lying to myself. Of course I wanted to talk about it.

On Dean's level now, I raised my eyebrows at him, expectedly. I wasn't going to be the one to speak first. Dean attempted nostalgia, which just goes to show you how dumb Dean still is. "Remember how much fun we used to have here?" He gazed around, the yearning in his face an unintentional insult.

"I remember you inviting me to your house here. I remember going and being passed around like a gift bag." The sun jumped out from a cloud, and I squinted. "I remember that like it was yesterday."

Dean's fingers twitched like he'd been electrocuted,

then tightened in his lap. "I'm very sorry about how that all turned out."

"How that all turned out?" That's what I'd come here for? Some vague politician's apology skirting any real responsibility? My eyes turned to slits, a million crow's-feet everywhere, but I didn't care. "How about 'I'm sorry for taking advantage of you when you were fourteen years old and wasted out of your mind'? 'I'm sorry for trying to do it again at Olivia's house, and for slapping you across the'—"

"Stop filming this." Dean swung his wheelchair at the camera, his agility so shocking it silenced me.

The cameraman glanced questioningly at Aaron. "Stop filming this," Dean repeated, advancing on him in a slow smooth roll.

The cameraman was still waiting for Aaron to make the call, but he was just standing there, white-faced and dazed. It dawned on me suddenly that everything I'd just said to Dean had shocked him. Either Dean had glazed over the details of that night, or this was the first time Aaron was hearing it. *He wants to apologize. Set the record straight.* Aaron, I realized, had no idea how much Dean had to apologize for. "Aaron?" the cameraman asked, and Aaron seemed to come online. He cleared his throat and said, "Nathan, stop filming."

I addressed Dean's back with a sharp laugh. "Why do you even want to do this, Dean? If we can't say anything about *anything* that actually happened." I stood, the simple ability to do so a powerful weapon.

Dean maneuvered a turn. At least my albatross wasn't physical, wasn't a place where I was doomed to sit all my life. I understood, oddly, that it was almost worse for Dean that the end of his twenties hadn't attacked him the way it had others. He still had a good scoop of hair, still had that lithe definition to his upper body. One esteemed line crossed his forehead like a fold in an envelope, but that was all. At least if he'd withered under the weight of the years, it wouldn't be such a spectacular waste to be trapped halfway to the ground for all eternity.

Of course he was married to a bombshell, heels and a heavy lip at the breakfast table, glossy trimmings I still had to make myself resist, Mom's brash version of beauty ground deep into my bones. I'd heard her speak in a clip from the *Today* show—southern, on the crazy side of religious. Probably didn't believe in sex before marriage, or sex for anything other than procreation at that, which worked out well for Dean. I'm pretty sure he can't appreciate any of the lusty prowess we promise on the cover of *The Women's Magazine*. Arthur made sure of that much.

Dean checked over his shoulder at the crew. "This isn't being filmed, right?"

Aaron said, just a little bit testily, "Do you see a camera pointed at you?"

Then, "Can you give TifAni and me some privacy, please?"

Aaron looked at me. I nodded and mouthed "It's fine."

The cameraman pointed at the sky, bubbling over with clouds again. "We really should get this shot before it rains."

Aaron jerked his head, a signal to retreat. "We'll get it."

The crew trailed Aaron, his long strides widening the distance between us. Dean waited until the crew collected by the road before turning on me. One vein jumped in his jaw, twice, then rested.

"Can you sit?"

"I prefer to stand, thanks."

Dean rocked on his wheels. "*Ohh*-kay." The corner of his mouth curled up suddenly. "Are you getting married?"

My hand dangling by my side was right at his eye level. For once, I'd forgotten my emerald pride, all its magical, transformative powers. I spread my fingers wide and flat and looked down, the way girls always do when someone notices and asks. The excitement rushing in so fast it's like it's new again. The thing may as well have been a dead bug the way I regarded it. "In three weeks."

"Congratulations."

I tucked my hands in my back pockets. "Can you just get to it, Dean?"

"Tif, honestly—"

"I actually go by Ani now."

Dean stuck out his lower lip and repeated the name in his head, "Like the end of—"

"TifAni."

He turned it over to see how it fit. "Pretty," he concluded.

I kept very still to let him see how little his opinion mattered. The sky quivered, and one lone raindrop made a plea for urgency on Dean's nose. "Well, first, I want to apologize to you," Dean said. "I have wanted to do that for a long time." He held eye contact with me much too intensely, like a media coach had taught him, this is how you give an apology. "The way I treated you"—an exhale vibrated on his fat lips—"it was very wrong, and I'm so sorry."

I closed my eyes. Kept them shut until I'd generated enough power to swallow the ache of memory. Smoothed over, I opened them again. "But you don't want to say this on camera."

"I will say this on camera," Dean said. "I'll apologize for the wrongful accusations I made against you. Saying that you took the gun because you were in on this with Arthur and Ben"—I opened my mouth, but Dean held up a hand, the one with the silver band smiling around his own ring finger. "Tif—Ani, I mean—you can choose to believe this or not, but at the time I really did think you were involved. Imagine how it looked to me. You come running in and I know you and Arthur are friends and I know how angry you must be with me and he hands you the gun and basically tells you to finish me off and you *reached* for it."

"But I was terrified. I was begging for my life. You saw that too."

"I know, but it was all jumbled up to me," Dean said. "I'd lost all this blood and I was terrified too. All I knew was that he handed you the gun and you went to take it. Those cops, they came at me so sure you had done it. I was just, confused . . . and angry." He rolled in his wheelchair, meaningfully. "I was *angry*. Arthur and Ben were dead, and you were still alive to take my anger out on."

That was something Dan the lawyer had actually warned me about. That with the real villains dead, everyone was looking for a target, and I looked pretty right for it.

I reminded Dean, "But I'd never even met Ben."

"I know," Dean said. "I just, once I had some time to recover, and to think, I realized you didn't have anything to do with it."

"So why didn't you just come out and say that? Do you know the hate mail I still get? From your *fans*." The last word came out trembling with rage.

"Because I was angry," Dean said. "There's nothing else to it but that. Anger. And resentment. That you came out okay."

I laughed. All these people so sure I'd come out okay, and I only have myself to blame, for putting on the greatest show on earth. "Not really."

Dean looked me up and down. It wasn't a leer. He was simply making the most obvious observation. My casual, expensive clothes, my hair trimmed to $150 ends. "You look pretty okay."

Dean's legs slumped together in a V at the knees. I wondered if he set them like that every morning when he got out of bed. Another raindrop, more bulbous this time, docked at my forehead. "So why do we need privacy to say all this? Aaron said you wanted to set the record straight."

"I do," Dean said. "I'll say all of this on camera. I'll explain how I was confused and then too angry to rectify the situation. I'll apologize and you'll forgive me."

I simmered. "Yeah?"

"Yeah," Dean said. "Because you want to clear your name. And I can do that for you."

"And what do you get out of it?"

"Ani"—Dean steepled his fingers—"I've made a very good fortune out of my bad fortune."

Not far behind him was the black Mercedes, the driver in a spiffy suit waiting to chauffeur Dean to his next engagement. "You're a true inspiration, Dean."

"Hey"—he chuckled—"can you blame me for making the best out of it?"

The sun surfaced again. Found something like understanding and blasted it bright.

"I guess I can't," I said.

"It's a little serendipitous, actually." Dean leaned forward, like he was excited to share this next part with me. "I was working on my latest book, which is all about the power of asking for forgiveness, and here, this project comes along."

I went stiff. "Like it was meant to be."

Dean laughed into his useless crotch. "You're sharp,

Ani. You always were. I hope your husband appreciates it."
He sighed. "My wife is so fucking dumb."

"Fiancé," I corrected him.

Dean shrugged, like it didn't matter. "Fine. Fiancé." He
looked behind him again, checking to make sure no one
could hear but me. "It will be very . . . impactful . . . for
my *fans*"—a little smile, for my benefit—"to see us come
to some sort of peace. But I also think people will understand why it took me so long to get to this point, and why
I was confused at first. I didn't set out to ruin your good
name, I was *traumatized*. I'm man enough to admit that
now. But . . . the, ah, other stuff. There's not really much of
an excuse for that, is there?" He paused for a moment, as if
considering whether or not to tell me the next thing. "My
wife is expecting, did you know that?"

I stared at him numbly.

"Biologically mine." He looked up at me, squinting
beneath the temperamental sky. "It's amazing the things
they can do these days." His voice took on a tenor of
amazement. "All it takes is a noninvasive surgery, a lab
and a petri dish, and voilà, I'm a family man, exactly what
my community wants for me. And they foot my bills, so
I'm happy to oblige, even though kids . . ." He made a
face I had made many times before. For a moment, he
just studied the road, considering what his life would be
like with a child he could never chase after, could never
teach to play soccer. He cleared his throat and looked at
me again. "But the other stuff, I don't see them giving a
pass on that."

"No," I agreed. "It's pretty scummy."

"That's a private apology." Dean tilted his head. Gauged
my face and added, "And it *is* an apology. I am very sorry
for that."

I stared him down. "I want you to answer something though."

Dean's jaw ticked again.

"Did you guys plan it? That night at your house?"

Dean had the nerve to look offended. "We weren't diabolical, Ani. *No*. It just—" He looked at the empty road again and thought about how to put it. "There was a little bit of competition. Who gets the new girl. But when we went to my room, I didn't even know that what happened with Liam happened. I didn't even know that until the next day."

I took a step toward him, so shocked I wanted to shake the rest of his secrets loose. "You didn't know about Liam?"

Dean winced at himself. "But listen, I knew about Peyton. But I . . . I didn't *know*, I didn't think that was bad. I don't know"—he shrugged—"that wasn't sex to me. I didn't understand how what happened with Peyton and me could be bad." Off my look, he added, quickly, "But I do now."

The sun blasted us again, one quick lash before darting behind a moody cloud. "What do you know now?"

Dean pierced his eyebrows together, like I was a teacher who had asked him a difficult question and he wanted to get the answer right. "That it was wrong."

"No"—I pointed my finger at him, the line a downward diagonal—"I want you to say it. What it was. If I'm going to play along, I deserve to hear one of you finally call a spade a spade. Tell me what you did to me."

Dean sighed and considered my request. After a moment, he admitted, "What we did to you . . . it was rape, okay?"

The word ripped my stomach apart like cancer. Terrorist attack. Plane crash. All the things I'm terrified will get me because I slipped out of Arthur's fingers half a lifetime ago. But still I shook my head. "No. None of this distancing language. 'It was rape'—I know those tricks. I want you to say what you did to me. What you all did to me."

Dean examined the ground. The fold in his brow softened as all the fight went out of his face. "We raped you."

I rubbed my lips together, tasted something deliciously metallic. The moment felt impossibly sweeter than when Luke proposed. "And that night at Olivia's—"

Dean cut me off with a resigned nod. "I know. I hit you. There is no excuse for that. For any of it. All I know is I felt lied to. Led on by you. And it infuriated me. It was like I blacked out from the anger. I'm still so grateful that Olivia's dad broke the whole thing up, or, I don't know what . . ." He stopped, because the raindrops had roused the crew from their waiting place.

"Hey! Guys?" Aaron called. "If we want to do this, we have to do it now."

We got the shot moments before the sky found its release. Did I sell out? I don't see it that way. But only because there is still something else I've kept to myself all of these years, a reason to cut Dean a little slack. I may wonder what I would have said if Arthur came to me and asked me to be a part of his plan, but I don't wonder as much about what would have happened had Arthur actually turned the gun over to me. Because if I'd gotten my hands on it, I think I just might have blown that motherfucking cocksucker's cock right off. Arthur would have gone second.

CHAPTER 16

There are two keys on my key chain plus a New York Sports Club pass even though I haven't been a member since 2009. That means I have a fifty-fifty shot of getting the right key in the door. I can't remember a time I've ever gotten the right key in the door.

Luke thinks it's cute. He says it gives him the heads-up that I'm home. "So I can ex out of the porn windows," he teases. I've seen the porn Luke watches—girl with huge fake tits shouting yes, yes, yes, right there, some muscled moron plowing her, looks about as much fun as doing your taxes. Luke thinks I don't like porn, but I just don't like his porn. I need to see someone in pain. Pain is good. Pain can't be faked.

I pushed the door open with my foot. "Hi."

"Hi," Luke said from the couch, watching me struggle with a smile on his face. "I missed you."

The door slammed behind me and I dropped my bags. Luke opened up his arms. "Can I have a hug?"

The words "Can I have some help?" sat snippy on the tip of my tongue. The decision not to say them required some strength.

I walked toward Luke and curled up in his lap. "Aw," he said. "You okay, babe?"

I tucked my face into his neck. He smelled like he needed a shower, but I'd always liked him a little dirty. Some people have a good natural scent, and Luke was one of them. Of course he was. "I'm exhausted," I said.

"What can I do for you?" Luke asked. "How can I help?"

"I'm hungry," I said. "But I don't want to eat."

"Babe, you look amazing."

"No," I said. "I don't."

"Hey." Luke forced his fingers underneath my chin, tilted my head up so I was looking at him. "You are the most beautiful girl I've ever seen and you are going to be the most beautiful bride. One more cheeseburger isn't going to change that. A million cheeseburgers couldn't change that."

Now was the time to ask. I'd caught him in a moment of Ani-infatuation, a rarity these days. But before I could, Luke's expression became serious. "So," he said, "I have to talk to you about something."

It was like I was riding a roller coaster at the exact moment the car inched over the summit and plunged to the ground below. The change in force jumbled all my organs, my lower abdomen throbbing as though my heart had tumbled there. Had Mom been right?

"The London offer came through," Luke said.

I repeated what he'd said in my head, trying to adjust, trying to identify the emotion ricocheting from my free-falling kidneys and liver and heart. Was it disappointment? Relief? Resignation? "Oh," I said. "Oh," I said again, stumbling into something like curiosity. "When?"

"They want us to move over the holidays. So I'm there for the start of the new year."

I leaned away from him, transferring my weight in a way that made Luke grimace. He shifted beneath me, trying to get comfortable again. "Did you already tell them yes?"

"No," Luke said. "Of course not. I said I had to talk to you first."

"When do you have to give them an answer by?"

Luke frowned, considering. "I think I should let them know in a week or so."

The ligaments in Luke's legs tensed beneath me, bracing for my meltdown. I suddenly realized the leverage I had if I could keep my cool. It meant accepting a decision that made me sad, but the other option made me afraid, and I was so tired of being afraid. "I need to talk to LoLo," I said, imagining the meeting in her office, her chemically calm face incapable of expressing what a massive mistake she thought I was making. "Maybe she'll hook me up with a job at the UK brand."

Luke smiled, surprised. "I'm sure she would." He added, generously, "She loves you."

I nodded, all agreeable Ani. Fiddling with a button on his shirt I said, "I actually have to talk to you about something too."

Luke's golden eyebrows twitched.

"The production company wants to film the wedding." I rushed the next part before Luke could butt in and object. "They just felt really moved by my story, and it's kind of cool because they also offered to basically be the videographer and put together a wedding video for us. For free." WASPs love the occasional freebie.

Aaron had approached me after Dean wheeled up the ramp and into the handicap cave of his private car. I'd been so brave. So fearless. I slunk in on myself as he piled on the praise. "You really are emerging as this sort of tragic hero," Aaron said. "I think it could be so powerful to end the movie on your wedding. Your happily ever after. So long deserved."

I didn't disagree. This ending was the easy one.

I realized that I must have told Aaron I'd discuss his idea with Luke at the same time Luke was telling the partners he'd discuss London with me, both of us having something we wanted that only the other could make possible. I wondered if Luke exited his meeting, pep in his step, picturing the sleek modern flat the company would put us up in, dismissing the possible killjoy in the whole scenario, me. *She'll be no problem to convince,* he probably thought, as only a person whose life has been one endless loop of pass-go-and-collect-two-hundred-dollars thinks.

My meeting with Aaron had ended much differently. I waited to react until I was alone in the Jeep. *Our* Jeep, I reminded myself, grimly. I gripped the steering wheel so hard my teeth chattered, and then I was slumped over the center console, wailing my resignation into the leather that smelled faintly of skunk, like one of Luke's friends spilled a beer a very long time ago and never bothered to clean it up.

Luke scratched an ingrown hair on his neck. "For free?"

There was a give in his voice, and, for a moment, buyer's remorse crept in. Why not just let him say no? Why not just fight and cry and say, "I can't do this," and really mean it this time? I spoke loudly, over that possibility. "For free. And you know they'll do a good job. A really good job."

Luke stared at the naked white wall above the TV, thinking. I'd been meaning to get to Brooklyn Flea, find something "eccentric" to hang there. "I just really hate the idea of our wedding being in that documentary though."

"It really will be just a few minutes at the end," I said, the lie ready and waiting. "We'll get a say in the final cut."

Luke bobbed his head around, considering. "And you trust them?"

I nodded, meaning that at least. Aaron had surprised me after I decided to stop despising him. "I do. I really do."

Luke tilted his head back, the brown leather couch puckering beneath the full weight of his skull. His parents had bought us these couches. I'd gone from sharing a Diet Coke–and-pizza-grease-stained futon with Nell to these couches, the leather like butter, Mom said the first time she visited us, running her French tips along their creamy skin. Sometimes the transition seemed too much, too quick. There had to be an in-between, and it seemed unfair that I had skipped it. Like something I could be punished for later.

"Luke." Now I released the tears that had been building since I nosed the Jeep onto the West Side Highway, the sudden, disorienting panic that where I was headed was no longer home snowballing as the West Village became Tribeca. "This weekend was so good in so many ways. I really feel like, for the first time, everyone is on my side. Dean is on my side. I saw Dean. I think they want to—"

"You saw *Dean*?" Luke's head snapped upright. I stared at the couch, at the way it held his skull's imprint tight. "I thought you weren't planning on talking about what happened with him." Luke brought his thumb to his mouth and chewed on it angrily. "I knew those producers were going to manipulate you." He wiped saliva on his shirt and pounded his thigh with a tight fist. "I knew I should have gone with you."

A tingle, electric and wild, sparked all along my spine. Never in my life did I think I would feel the need to defend

Dean Barton. "I saw Dean because I wanted to see Dean," I snapped. "And relax. We didn't talk about the rape."

That word stopped Luke cold. I'd never said it out loud. Not to anyone.

"His story changed," I said, rushing to fill in the uncomfortable silence, confirming what I've always suspected about Luke: He doesn't think it was rape. He thinks it was an unfortunate incident, something that happens when hornball kids get together and drink too much. "He doesn't think I had something to do with it anymore." Remembering the picture I had promised to return to Mrs. Finnerman, I swung my legs over the arm of the couch and stood, making my way to the bookcase in the corner. I crouched in front of the bottom shelf for the folder where I store all things Bradley—news clips, memorial service cards, the image of Arthur and his father, laughing at the drab Jersey ocean, pastel seashells lining the memory.

"He said that?" Luke asked behind me.

I shook the folder, trying to locate the picture. "He *told* me that. He apologized for ever saying so. On camera."

Luke peered over the surface of the coffee table to see what I was doing. "What are you looking for?"

"That picture," I said. "Of Arthur and his dad. I promised Mrs. Finnerman I'd give it back to her." I dumped all the contents onto the floor. "It's not here." I pushed through it all, one more time. "What the *fuck*?"

"You probably moved it and forgot," Luke said, suddenly helpful. "It'll turn up."

"No. I would never have moved it." I eased one leg across the other on the hardwood floor and sat.

"Hey." Luke got up off the couch, and there was that sound, like peeling a sticker off a piece of paper. I felt his hand on my back, and then he was next to me on the floor, collecting the file's contents. "It will turn up. Stuff like that always does when you're not looking."

I watched him neatly file away my tragedy. The care on his face gave me the courage to try one more time. "Aaron understands how invasive it could be to have the cameras there. He really is going to just look like the videographer."

Luke sealed the folder shut. "I just don't want, like, an entire camera crew at our wedding."

I shook my head and held out two fingers. "That's it, that's all they need."

"Two guys?"

"I told them the same thing." *See, Luke, we're on the same page.* "They promised me, two. No one will be able to tell the difference between them and a regular videographer." I didn't mention the part about everyone having to sign releases. I just needed to get him to a yes.

Luke balanced the bulk of evidence in his lap. "This is going to make you happy, isn't it?"

I needed tears again, but just enough to make my eyes gleam. No track marks on my cheeks—that would be overkill. "This will make me really happy," I croaked.

Luke dropped his head to his chest and sighed. "Then we have to do it."

I flung my arms around his neck. "I want a cheese-burger now."

It was just the right cute, quirky Ani thing to say because Luke laughed.

"You are ridiculous," Nell said when I walked into Sally Hershberger Downtown. "Fucking eat something already."

I chose to take it as a joke and went to do a little spin for her, but Nell seized a crumpled magazine from the pile on the coffee table and glared at Blake Lively on the cover. I sat down next to her in reception, stung. The prepubescent model behind the front desk asked if we wanted coffee. "A latte," I said.

"Skim?" she asked.

"Whole milk."

"Still doesn't count as food," Nell muttered.

My hairstylist appeared before us. "Oh my *Godddd*." Ruben pressed his hands to his face like Macaulay Culkin in *Home Alone*. "You have cheekbones."

"Don't encourage it." Nell flipped a page in *W* with so much force she tore it half out of the magazine. Nell and I just weren't talking about it. Any of it.

"Oh, please." Ruben shooed her away. "It's her *wedding*. We can't have fucking Shamu walking down the aisle." He offered me his hand. "Come on back, gorgeous."

Ruben said I should do big Brigitte Bardot hair now that my face was so slender. "You can't do that on porkers." He twisted my hair into wet knots all over my head. "Just makes them look bigger." Ruben had never suggested Brigitte Bardot hair for me before I'd gotten down to 104 pounds.

Mom said she didn't even know why I was bothering to get my hair done in New York when the second I got to Nantucket the humidity would undo it all. I told Ruben that, and he pshawed. "Your mama doesn't know anything about anything."

Luke had left for Nantucket earlier in the week, but I didn't have the same liberty at *The Women's Magazine*. When I requested Friday off in addition to the two weeks I needed for my honeymoon, the managing editor balked.

But LoLo stepped in and made it happen. She approved of my honeymoon choice—eight days in the Maldives and three in Paris. I still hadn't talked to her about London, even though Luke had given his answer to the partners, and it was a go.

"Fabulous," she said. "And the Maldives are sinking, you know. So run, run, before it's too late."

Ruben had a tan bald head and glasses that sloped on the end of his elegant nose. He never pushed them up, the way Arthur used to. Just squinted over their tortoiseshell ledge as he fed sections of my hair through a round brush, twisting and turning at the bottom until the ends coiled like peppy ribbons securing a Christmas present.

Nell glanced at her watch. She had wandered over with my latte twenty minutes ago, handing it off to me with a slight, apologetic smile. I guess she figured I was going through with it and there was no point in continuing to punish me. "It's almost eleven," she said. Our flight was out of JFK at 2:00, and we still had to get back down to my apartment to collect my luggage.

Ruben worked some product into my hair, whipped off the black robe, and planted a loud kiss on the top of my head. "I want pictures," he said. "You are going to make the most gorgeous bride." He held his hand over his heart, and I watched him tear up in the mirror. "Ugh!" he cried. "Just the most gorgeous bride."

Nell and I tore into my apartment, shimmying the wet off our coats and umbrellas. It had started to rain on our way downtown, and getting a cab was going to be difficult now.

"Seriously," Nell said. "We have to go."

I was going through the fridge, tossing anything that would spoil over the next two weeks.

"I know," I said. "I have to trash this stuff though. I can't come back to a smelly apartment. Drives me crazy."

"Where's your trash room?" Nell grabbed the garbage bag out of my hands. "I got it. Just get everything together."

The door slammed behind Nell, and then I was alone. I dropped to my knees, pushing through the cleaning supplies we keep in the cabinet beneath the sink. I found a box of clean garbage bags and wedged it loose. A row of bottles shifted, and something fell, rattling as it spun. The object was a seafoam green blur only until it sputtered, ran out of gas, and went silent on its side. I pinched it between my fingers and studied it, wondering how long I had before Nell returned to the apartment and caught me on the ground, shaking like a wet dog.

"The first time I ever heard of Ani was in an e-mail my brother sent me on November sixth, 2011." The speech in Garret's hand fluttered as he brought it closer to his face to make out the words.

" 'I'm bringing a girl home for Thanksgiving,' he said. 'Her name is Ani and it's pronounced "Ah-nee." Not "Annie." If you screw it up, I'll kill you.' "

The room vibrated with pleasant laughter. Oh, those Harrison boys.

Garret glanced up from the paper in his hands. "I think you know when two people are meant for each other when you see that they're better people together than they are when they're apart."

A hum of agreement.

"Ani is one of the sweetest girls I've ever met, but let's just say it, she's a little kooky." There was robust laughter at that, which shouldn't have surprised me as much as it did. Wasn't that the personality I'd meticulously crafted for Luke? Adorably quirky? The razor-sharp spokes that sliced through every now and then, the thing that kept him on his toes, the extra little bonus? "And I know that's what my brother loves about her. It's what we all love about her."

I looked at Nell. She mouthed "Sweetest girl he's ever met?" and rolled her eyes. I looked back at my soon to be brother-in-law and hoped no one else had noticed.

"And my brother." Garret laughed, and the crowd did too. They knew he was gearing up for something good. "Well, not many people can keep up with my brother. He's the last one at the bar and the first one on the surfboard in the morning. You get out there, and he's been riding the waves for an hour and he'll want to stay out an hour longer than you do and you're like, dude, you made me take a Jameson shot at three in the morning, I *can't*." Garret covered his forehead, like he had a headache. "God bless you for putting up with that, Ani (Annie), excuse me, Ani (Ah-nee)." The laugh track was at full volume now, and, with Herculean effort, I joined in.

Garret waited patiently for the room to quiet down. A smile ate up half his face as he continued. This was going well. "But that's what's so great about Luke and Ani. They don't 'put up' with each other. They love each other unconditionally, inhuman amounts of energy and all."

Luke's hand found my own, gnarled into a claw, as though a paralysis had settled into the bones. My whole body creaked as he pulled my hand into his lap. With my other, I churned the discovery I'd made in our kitchen. I'd kept it close since I left New York, considering what to do with it, how to play it. Nell had badgered me the entire flight. "Jesus. What's *wrong*?" "You know how much I hate flying," I'd said to the window.

"My brother needed someone like Ani. Someone to show him what it's really all about, this life. Family, kids, stability." He smiled right at me. "She's it."

I rubbed my cheek on my shoulder, against a nonexistent itch.

"And to that point, Ani needed someone like my brother. Someone to be her rock. Someone to calm her down when she starts to *spin*"—there was a strong, almost hostile emphasis on that word, and a knowing wink at Luke—"out of control." *When she starts to spin.* I felt like I was standing outside of my body as I understood, with piercing clarity, that Luke made fun of me, of my rabid terror, of my silly, hard-earned phobias, over beers with his brother and friends. "She's ridiculous," I realized I could hear him say, and everything in me ached with that raw, ruthless exposure.

"I'm so excited to see where these two go in life," Garret said, the joy inflected in his voice jarring against my sudden decision, final and terrifying. "Well, and, to crash at their amazing London flat." Everyone laughed. "And, Ani, when it's time for a new little Harrison, at least we know Luke is no stranger to that three A.M. thirst"—more laughter and bile bubbled in my throat. I cleared it out and raised my glass with Garret and everyone else. "To being better together, than you are alone."

"To being better together, than you are alone." My voice was a part of this chorus too. Glasses clinked, the sound a delicate bell—*no! no! no!* I drained my champagne, all of it, even the angry curdles at the top.

Luke leaned in and kissed me. "You make me so happy, babe." I held on to my smile with all my might.

Someone tapped Luke on the shoulder, and he turned, began to chat about the honeymoon. I put my hand on his knee—funny, that would be the last time I could ever touch him like that—said, "I'm just going to use the bathroom."

I waded through the room, the perky pleasantries. "Hello, hello, hi." "You look stunning!" "Thank you!" "Congratulations!" "Thank you!" "Hi, hello, hi." "Lovely to see you." Lovely. When did I start saying that terrible word?

The wedding coordinator had pointed out the one-stall bathroom in the back of Topper's, the restaurant charging us thirty thousand dollars for the rehearsal dinner. "Usually just for staff," she'd said. "But you and Luke should feel free to use it tonight if you need some privacy." She'd winked, and I'd stared at her, horrified.

I locked the door behind me. There was no overhead light, just a white porcelain lamp on the counter, the light fuzzing through the shade golden and dreamy, like I was playing a part in an old movie. I lowered the toilet seat, carefully and quietly as a bench in church. I sat, the skirt of my size zero Milly dress collecting the DNA of all the brides who had sat here before me. I'd never be thin enough to wear it again.

My Bottega Veneta clutch made a smacky, kissy noise as I snapped it open. I dug around until I found the green seashell, ribbed and faded between my fingers.

It was some time before there was a knock on the door. I sighed and stood—*Showtime, ready?*—cracking it open just wide enough to reveal the eyes, nose, and lips of Nell. It was an entirely different light out there.

She smiled, and the corners of her mouth disappeared from the narrow frame. "Whatcha doing?"

I didn't say anything. Nell reached through the door and thumbed away a black tear.

"What was that, anyway?" she said. "You're the sweetest girl Garret's ever met? Has anyone here ever *met* you?"

I laughed. One of those horrible cry-laughs that juggles all the phlegm in your chest.

"What do you want to do?" Nell asked.

She listened patiently while I told her, then whistled low. "What a shit show this is going to be."

Nantucket suffers from a temperature inversion, which occurs when cold air is trapped under hot. This is what creates the ever-present fog, the Gray Lady, that cloaks the island, even on a clear day when there's not a cloud in the sky.

Of course, you realize it's a clear day only once the ferry barrels through the thick of it. You look forward and see the blue hanging over the land, crisp and bright as a screen saver on a projection screen, then glance over your shoulder and there's only a wall of groggy mist. It was all behind me when Nell appeared at my side and pushed a cold beer into my hands.

"I think the car rental place is within walking distance from the ferry," she said.

Beer gurgled in the bottle's neck. "It is." I wiped my mouth with the back of my hand. "It's right there."

"And you're sure you don't want to fly?"

"I couldn't stand to be in an airplane right now," I said.

Nell pressed her back against the ship's rail. "So when are you going to ask?"

I shielded my eyes with my hand and studied her. "Ask what?"

"If you can move in, while you get back on your feet." She smiled. Out of the gray, her teeth were so bright they seemed the closest thing to invisible. "It's like 2007, redux. Only this time we won't have rats."

I warmed my shoulder against hers. "You don't know how much I appreciate this."

Nell had done what I asked her to do at the entrance to the bathroom, and, a few minutes later, Luke had nudged the door open with the toe of his Prada loafer. "Ani? You okay? I can't find Kimberly and the music on the slide show isn't—"

Everything on his face went dark and different when he saw the seashell pinched between my fingers. I didn't even wait for him to lock us in before I asked, "What did you do with that picture of Arthur and his dad?"

Luke turned and shut the door behind him, slowly, like he would do anything to delay what was going to happen next. "I didn't want to upset you more than you already were."

"Luke, tell me now or I'm going to—"

"Okay." He pushed his hands at me. *"Okay."*

"John bought coke while he was in New York that weekend. I told him it was stupid. You know how I feel about that stuff." Luke gave me a meaningful look, like his hard line on drugs would somehow absolve him of whatever he had done.

"His fiancée wanted it too. When we got back to the apartment, he needed a picture to do it on. I don't know how that stuff works, but he said they always do it on a mirror or a picture frame."

"And you gave him the picture of Arthur and his dad?"

"I didn't want to give him a picture of *us*!" Luke said, like he'd had only two choices, like we didn't have a million pictures all over the apartment of our annoyingly photogenic friends.

"What happened to it?"

"Someone knocked it over." Luke mimed the crime, flicking his hand in the air. "It broke. I threw it away."

I searched his face for any sign of remorse. "Even the picture?"

"If you saw the picture without that stupid frame you would have known something had happened. You're . . . you're so *sensitive* about that kind of stuff. You get so *mad*." Luke brought his hands to his chest, like he needed protection from me. "I just thought it was better. And better for you. To move on. Why would you want to hold on to something like that anyway?" He shuddered. "It's creepy, Ani."

I cupped the seashell in my lap, gingerly as you would an injured baby bird. "I can't believe you."

Luke got on his knees in front of me, just like he did the day he proposed, the day I was so sure was the happiest of my life. I pulled back when he tried to brush away the mascara tracks on my cheeks. "I'm *sorry*, Ani"—even with this, he managed to make himself sound like the victim, St. Luke who has to put up with me, with my spins, my *kookiness*, my morbid neurosis—"but please. Let's not let this ruin the night."

Outside, one of Luke's friends shouted at another friend that he was a fucking pussy. I held on to the shell as if it was a stress ball. Squeezed so hard I heard the crack in its armor. "This isn't what's going to ruin the night." I let him wipe away a tear, the last time he'd ever touch me. Then I told him what would.

CHAPTER 17

Oh, it was a mess. The Harrisons, my parents, Nell, Luke, all knotted into a clot of varying alliances, fighting for individual best interests. Ultimately it was decided that Nell would call a cab, take me back to the Harrison estate, where I would gather my things before the rest of the family returned home, and we would get a hotel room, leave first thing in the morning. Mrs. Harrison's face was an odd mix of anger and sympathy as she discussed these arrangements with me, her tone very matter-of-fact, much to her credit.

Mom couldn't even look at me.

It would be Thanksgivings and Christmases at the FaNelli household from here on out. The same fake frosted tree Mom propped against the wall every year, strung with bubble-gum-colored lights and nothing else. The only thing to drink some acidic bottle of Yellow Tail Shiraz. I was prepared for this, I was.

I don't remember the car ride to the Harrisons'. The packing. Checking in at the three-star hotel by the ferry. One of Nell's pills wiped it all away.

It was well past midnight by the time we pushed open the door to our king-size room. My stomach arched into an impressive back bend, and I found the phone. Woozily dialed room service. "Good evening," the answering machine taunted. "Room service is available from eight A.M. until eleven P.M. A complimentary breakfast will be served in the—"

"It's closed." I tried to slam the handset into the receiver but missed. It crashed to the floor, unflinching and hard as a dead body. "I'm so hungry!" I wailed.

"Okay, kooky." Nell seemed to move as though she were on wheels. Smooth and graceful and determined. She was on the phone with the front desk, making a dignified request. Then she was ordering grilled cheese, chicken fingers, fries, ice cream sandwiches. I ate it all. I think I was still chewing through a French fry as I dozed off. The sleep was a liquid I kept poking my head out of in the night, gasping for air until Nell's pill pushed me back under. But I slept. I slept.

I'd gone and messed up my story line in the documentary too. A month or so after I made the decision that I would "regret for the rest of my natural-born life" (that was Mom), I met Aaron and his cameraman in a small sound studio a few avenues east of Rockefeller Center.

I had a new job too. I was now the features director at *Glow* magazine. It was a big title, but the brand didn't have nearly the same clout as *The Women's Magazine*. It certainly didn't have the prestige of *The New York Times Magazine*, which LoLo reminded me we were close to, couldn't believe I would give up now.

"They're offering me thirty thousand dollars more." I showed off the flat plane of my ring finger. "I need it. I owe a lot of people a lot of money. I can't wait."

"I'm loathe to lose you," she finally concluded. "But I understand." On the day I boxed up my desk, she told me I would be on her masthead again one day. When I teared up, she said, "Remember that article you wrote about how the worst thing you can do to your career is cry in the office?" She winked at me before charging down the hallway, bellowing at the digital director to get her those cover line numbers already.

I thought I would hate going about my day without that fantastic weight on my finger, the way it communicated to everyone to stay away, because all the boxes in my life were checked. I'd be lying if I said a part of me doesn't miss that emerald's wicked little glint, but I don't mind it as much as I thought I would. When a guy asks if he can take me out to dinner, I hope maybe he's someone who can eventually love me exactly the way I am, as Garret and so many others believed Luke did. Maybe he wouldn't fear my bite, my *kookiness*, maybe he'd get past my thorny bristles to see there is sweetness here. Would understand that moving on doesn't mean never talking about it, never crying about it.

"You remember what to do, right?" Aaron asked.

"Say my name, the age I will be when this comes out, and how old I was at the time of the attack." I had introduced myself as Ani Harrison the last time I was on camera, the name I was so relieved would be legally mine by the time the documentary aired. I had to film a second take to correct the error, wearing exactly what I'd been wearing on the day we first caught my story in the forever of the camera. Everything would be streamed together, so that it appeared as a single take. No mention of the way my past and present had collided into one another like tectonic plates in an earthquake, producing a fissure that re-formed the course of my life. I couldn't borrow those clothes from *The Women's Magazine* anymore, and they were not cheap to buy.

Aaron gave me a stubby thumbs-up and nodded at his assistant. I saw the gesture as it was really meant to be now—sweet, never smarmy.

Around the time I should have been toasting on a beach on my honeymoon, I'd gotten a call from Aaron that changed everything.

"You were right," he'd said.

I'd been waiting in a long line for coffee, but I gave up my spot and stepped outside, huddling in an alleyway for privacy.

"I went through the film. You and Dean were both miked up. The camera recorded your conversation."

I'd pressed the phone closer to my ear and released a long, triumphant breath. It had been good for me to hear Dean use that word. "Rape." Therapeutic, really. But that wasn't the only reason I'd asked him to say it. I've filmed enough segments for the *Today* show to know that the camera can pick up almost anything if your mike is on— that bitchy comment about Savannah's silly pink dress, that nervous pee in the bathroom right before you go on camera. Dean should have known this too, given his current *celebrity*. I wasn't sure what, if anything, I would do with his admission, but I wanted it just in case I decided to defy Luke and talk about that night. Now that the Harrison name was no longer mine to sully, I'd made my decision. "So we can use it, right? To back up my story?"

"I'd be lying if I said this doesn't make me excited as a director, because this is a real scoop," Aaron had said. "But as your friend"—my mouth had shimmied at the word—"it's an even sweeter get. You deserve for your truth to be told. I just—" his sigh cut him off "—I just want to be sure you're prepared for the backlash—I imagine people will be pretty outraged."

The back door of the coffeehouse swung open and an employee tossed a bag of trash into the Dumpster. I waited for him to disappear back into the kitchen. "Of course they will," I agreed, magnanimous as could be. "It was a terrible thing they did to me."

"That wasn't what I—" Aaron stopped when my sarcasm registered. "Right," he said. Then again, his voice full of understanding and indignation on my behalf, *"Right."*

The clapboard snapped at everyone to be quiet, let me speak. Aaron nodded at me: *Go.* I sat up straighter and said, "I'm TifAni FaNelli. I'm twenty-nine years old, and I was fourteen years old on November twelfth, 2001."

Aaron said, "Again. Try it with just your name."

The clapboard sounded one last time.

"I'm TifAni FaNelli."

ACKNOWLEDGMENTS

Thank you to my parents, for celebrating my weirdness and creativity as a child, even when I did bizarre things like ride my tricycle around the neighborhood in a frilly slip and princess veil and all the neighbors stared. Thank you for encouraging my imagination endlessly, for investing in my education and prioritizing it the way you did, even when it meant making sacrifices in your own life. Thank you for showing me through your own example of hard work and dedication what it means to be ambitious and to have a strong work ethic. I am truly the luckiest girl alive to have you two as parents. I would not be where I am without you.

To my rock-star agent, Alyssa Reuben, at the Paradigm Agency, for keeping after me for years and years to write. And when I finally did, got the book, got TifAni, knew exactly how I could make it better, and did so unbelievably right by me that I still wake up some mornings wondering if this is real life. Thank you for believing in me before I believed in myself.

To my best friend, Cait Hoyt, for forcing her friendship on me when we were just babies starting out in New York.

What would I do without you? You are the most special snowflake of them all.

To my editor, Sarah Knight, for being the first to swoop in on the book, for articulating my thoughts before I even thought them myself, for pushing me to attend to my words with a "gimlet eye" when I was running out of steam, and for making me see that I could not let them "get away with it."

To my film agent, Michelle Weiner at CAA, who told me that getting a movie made is like pushing a boulder up a mountain. Thank you for pushing. Also for the beautiful jewelry recommendations.

To my publicist, Kate Gales, for paying attention to the details like it was her own wedding and making me feel like I was in such capable hands, and to my marketing manager, Elina Vaysbeyn, for all her behind-the-scenes hard work. To everyone at Simon and Schuster for all their rousing words of encouragement and support in e-mails that I plan to frame and hang over the grand desk I will one day write from: Carolyn Reidy, Jonathan Karp, Mary-sue Rucci, and Richard Rhorer.

To my mentor, John Searles. I know that word makes you cringe, but there's no other way to put it. You hired me at *Cosmo* as a wide-eyed twenty-three-year-old totally in awe of your writing career. Thank you for your endless support and encouragement, for telling me I could do it, for listening to me bitch and moan about doing it, and for making me laugh when I officially entered "fork" territory.

To Kate White for teaching me to go big or go home, to ask for what I want, and how to suss out people's sweet spots. I will carry your advice with me for my entire career.

To Joanna Coles and Joyce Chang, two inspiring editors in chief who have encouraged, motivated, and challenged me in all the best ways.

I'd also like to thank my brother, Kyle, for all his love and support, for talking up the book to anyone who would listen, and for being such a bright spot in my life. I knew this is exactly who you would become and I am so proud of you.

Thank you to my in-laws: Barbara for being my number one fan and fastest reader/updater ever, and Andy and Natalie, who no doubt broke some presale orders record, for all your love and support from across the pond.

And special thanks to Dave Cullen, author of the eye-opening book *Columbine*, for providing so much insight into the psyches of those responsible for the attack on Columbine High School.

To my own set of "annoyingly photogenic" friends who are kind and loving and nothing like the characters in this book, who have been so excited and supportive of me and have tolerated me babbling on and on about this after one too many glasses of wine for the last year—thank you.

Bringing up the anchor: thank you to my husband, Greg, the best manager a girl could ask for, for letting me be the "talent." Thank you for being a good sport when I would banish you to the bedroom so I could take over the living room to work. Thank you for talking me up to anyone who would listen, for being my first preorder, for your unbridled pride in me that's made me love you even more.

ABOUT THE AUTHOR

Jessica Knoll has been a senior editor at *Cosmopolitan* and articles editor of *Self*. She grew up in the suburbs of Philadelphia and graduated from the Shipley School in Bryn Mawr, Pennsylvania, and from Hobart and William Smith Colleges in Geneva, New York. She lives in New York City with her husband.

WHAT I KNOW
Jessica Knoll

Why I'm coming clean about the real rape informing my novel, *Luckiest Girl Alive*

Originally published in *Lenny Letter* on March 29, 2016

The first person to tell me I was gang-raped was a therapist, seven years after the fact. The second was my literary agent, five years later, only she wasn't talking about me. She was talking about Ani, the protagonist of my novel, *Luckiest Girl Alive*, which is a work of fiction. What I've kept to myself, up until today, is that its inspiration is not.

Since the book was published last May, my list of unsuspecting supporters has expanded. The list includes critics and editors, publicists and Hollywood executives. It might even include you, if you are one of the thousands of readers who reviewed the book on Amazon and Goodreads, or who reached out to me on Facebook, Twitter, and Instagram. You probably didn't realize you had acknowledged what happened to me when you acknowledged what happened to Ani, partially because I've never publicly discussed that flashpoint in my life and partially because *Luckiest Girl Alive* is not a memoir or even a roman à clef.

Or maybe it's because I have been so adamant about the fact that I am not Ani FaNelli, despite a few toothless parallels to my own life: Ani is twenty-eight in the book; I was twenty-eight when I wrote the book. Like Ani, I grew up in the suburbs and attended a tiny private high school where, surrounded by old-money Ivy League strivers, I was a bit of an outlier. In adulthood, Ani writes about sex for *The Women's Magazine*; I was an editor at *Cosmopolitan* for the first five years of my career. (Also, it's a reference to *Bright Lights, Big City*, which is one of my favorite books.)

Still, it is as though people sense a deep connection between Ani and me, especially those who ask about my dedication, which reads:

To all the TifAni FaNellis of the world, *I know*.

It means I know what it's like to not belong, I waffle in response to readers, usually women whose albatrosses I can sense, just as they sense mine. What I don't add: *I know what it's like to shut down and power through, to have no other choice than to pretend to be okay*. I am a savant of survivor mode.

I've spent the past year throwing bum grenades like that and running for cover. I dodge left by pointing to all the ways in which my fictional protagonist and I differ. Ani's heritage is Italian; mine is German. Ani is planning a wedding in Nantucket; I got married in New Jersey (which, if you've read the book, you know would not have flown with Ani). I've been running and I've been ducking and I've been dodging because I'm scared. I'm scared people won't call what happened to me rape because for a long time, no one did. But as I gear up for my paperback tour, and as I brace myself for the women who ask me, in nervous, brave tones, what I meant by my dedication—*What do I know?*—I've come to a simple, powerful revelation:

everyone is calling it rape now. There's no reason to cover my head. There's no reason I shouldn't say what I know.

I know that before I was old enough to drive, I liked A Boy. I know that I went to a party at which the ratio of guys to girls was not in my favor, where I drank, flirted with A Boy, was dazzled by A Boy, drank some more, and slipped away from the waking world. I know I came to on the floor of a bedroom, A Different Boy's head between my legs. I remember A Different Boy from a flare of coherence earlier, trying to help me walk when my anesthetized legs failed me.

I know that the pain is what woke me next. That I was moaning "Ow," over and over, before even opening my eyes. This time A Boy was there, his shoulders rising and falling above me in an excruciating rhythm. I went under again, coming to on my knees in the bathroom, staring into a toilet full of blood. I know I was too young to understand. I thought I must have cut myself.

I know that next, I tasted something disgusting, and that months later, on a morning when I could no longer face my sniggering peers, I skipped the first few periods of the school day. I wandered around town, idling before a Chinese restaurant that had just set out fresh trays of food. I piled vegetable lo mein onto a plate even though it was ten a.m. and I wasn't hungry. Like Ani, I figured out food sometimes has to substitute for compassion.

I know I bit into what must have been a pocket of pure MSG. It burst in my mouth, salty and foul. I froze, a stitch of memory opening, realizing that was the only way to describe what I tasted that night.

In the morning, I know I woke facing a bare back. There was a nauseating moment where I had no idea where I was and whom I was with, but that if it had to be anyone, at least let it be A Boy. Please let it be A Boy. Then he turned over. He wasn't A Boy. He was Another Boy, A Third Boy, one I didn't like or find the least bit attractive. He laughed about how hungover he was, how crazy the party had been, how the reason I couldn't find my underwear was because it was downstairs. I had cut my hand on a broken bottle, evidently, and I'd left a murderous smear of blood on the wall as I stumbled around in front of everyone wearing nothing from the waist down—because I'm a *party animal* like that. I know I laughed, because laughing was easier than tending to my heart, which felt like a hot coal in my chest, on fire with shame.

I know I visited a clinic to get the morning-after pill. I know I was fifteen years old and aching for guidance and protection, for someone to release the mute button on my voice. The doctor, a woman, listened to me describe the events of the evening sixty-five hours prior—just made it!—and I know that when I asked if what had happened to me was rape she told me she wasn't qualified to answer that question.

I know my classmates called me a slut. (Plus a teacher, a cruel wisp of a woman, whom I have just described using the appositive in a nod to how she chose to explain the grammatical tool to the class: "For example, 'Jessica, a cheap mallrat.'") No one called it rape. Well, not no one. I would be remiss if I didn't mention the two boys who came close, who had left the party early that night. One put his head in his hands when he found out what happened and said he should have stayed. If he had stayed, he wouldn't have let this happen to me. The other told me that there are some things in life I should never be expected to forgive. One of those boys died before we graduated high school and the other before I graduated college, and I must acknowledge that they were the only ones to comfort me when it wasn't the cool thing to do. I must acknowledge their fine memories, which they deserve.

I called it rape, once. In a drunken confrontation with A Boy. The next day, terrified the herd might come after me even hungrier (*trash slut* had appeared on the inside of my locker just days before), I called A Boy and apologized. I apologized to my rapist for calling him a rapist. What a thing to live with.

From then on, I submitted to my assigned narrative. What was the point in raising my voice when all it got me was my own lonely echo? Like Ani, the only way I knew to survive was to laugh loudly at my rapists' jokes, speak softly to the mean girls, and focus on chiseling my tunnel out of there. I know that once I was free, I became obsessed with reinventing myself. Not because I didn't want anyone from my past to find me, just the opposite, in fact. I was sure that with the right wardrobe, a glamorous job, and a ring on my finger before the age of twenty-eight, I could transcend my reputation. That if everyone from my past could see me so put together, so accomplished in New York City, so *settled down*, my voice would finally be worth hearing.

I know that I am very, very angry. I learned in therapy that anger is easier to feel, that when it's present, it is near impossible to experience other, more anguishing emotions. My anger is carbon monoxide, binding to pain, humiliation, and hurt, rendering them powerless. You would never know when you met me how angry I am. Like Ani, I sometimes feel like a wind-up doll. Turn my key and I will tell you what you want to hear. I will smile on cue. My anger is odorless, colorless, and tasteless. It's completely toxic.

I know that I made the mistake of thinking that living well is the best revenge. That I figured out, eventually, that the appearance of living well is not the same thing as actually living well. And even if it were, revenge does not beget healing. Healing will come when I snuff out the shame, when I rip the shroud off the truth. If I were a victim of the other horrific crime in my book, I would talk about it openly. I wouldn't pretend like it hadn't happened to me, like I don't still hurt about it, like I don't still cry about it. Why should this be any different?

I'm trying, but I'm rusty at speaking the truth. The day I pitched this essay, a woman approached me at a book event in New Jersey. "You said you did some research for your book," she said. "Did you interview a rape victim?"

I told her I had researched the other major event in my book.

"So how did you—" She stopped. "I mean, it was just so real. What you said about not screaming until it was over? Until you knew you were safe?" I started to internally chant *Oh fuck, oh fuck, oh fuck* at the same time tears sprang to her eyes. I'm also rusty with compassion. I've been conditioned to prefer an economy-sized bag of chocolate-covered pretzels to that. "Because that almost happened to me," she said.

Fuck it. "Something similar to what happened to Ani happened to me," I responded for the first time ever, and she grabbed my wrist and held it tight, blinking tears, while I smiled brightly, insisting in a foreign falsetto, "I'm fine! It's fine!"

I'm not fine. It's not fine. But it's finally the truth, it's what I know, and that's a start.

Pocket Books
Reading Group Guide

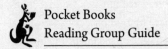

LUCKIEST
GIRL ALIVE

Jessica Knoll

TOPICS & QUESTIONS FOR DISCUSSION

1. Ani tells the reader "I'm no plucky heroine." Do you agree? Why or why not? Did your opinion of Ani change as you learned more about her past? If so, why?

2. During the course of the book, the way that Ani is identified changes. At varying times, she is TifAni FaNelli, Tif, Finny, and Ani Harrison. What do these names indicate about her and how she relates to herself and others?

3. Why do you think Ani agrees to participate in the documentary about the Five? What was her role in the tragedy? How has it shaped her as an adult?

4. When describing Arthur for the documentary, Ani remembers how "he was the only one who stood up for me when a lot of people turned on me." Why is it so important that she shares something positive about him? Discuss Ani's friendship with Arthur. Why do you think he defended her? What was your first impression of Arthur? Did your feelings about him change? If so, why?

5. Ani says the word "fiancé" does not "bother me so much as the one that came after it. Husband. That word laced the corset tighter, crushing organs, sending panic into my throat with the bright beat of a distress signal." Discuss why it is so important to Ani to be married before the documentary airs. Do you think, as Ani does, that her engagement ring is a symbol of status and legitimacy? What compromises, if any, must Ani make for the sake of her engagement? Do you think the compromises are worth it? Explain your answer.

6. What were your initial impressions of Dina FaNelli? After learning what happened to Ani at Dean's party, Dina "told me I was not the daughter she raised." What values did Dina impart? Do you think she was a good mother? Why or why not?

7. During Ani's junior year of high school, she takes a trip to New York City with her classmates. How is this trip a watershed moment for her? Contrast the reality of her life in New York City with the vision of her future that she had then. Has she achieved the success she dreamed of? How does Ani measure success? Does this change by the novel's conclusion? In what ways?

8. Although Ani initially distrusts the documentary director, Aaron, she begins to think of him as "kind, rather than leering." What causes Ani to change her mind? Do you think Aaron has her best interests at heart? Ani's burgeoning trust of Aaron ultimately leads her to wonder "if that had been the reality all

along, and, if it was, what else I'd read wrong." Many of the characters in this book struggle to distinguish their perceptions from reality. Are there any who are particularly adept at it? If so, who are they? Discuss how they manage to do it.

9. Explain the significance of the title of the book. When Ani is called the "'luckiest girl alive,'" the phrase is used derisively. Who describes her as such and why? By the conclusion of the book, did you think Ani was lucky? If so, in what way?

10. What do you think led to the tragedy at Bradley? Could it have been prevented, and, if so, how? What role, if any, does Ani play in the tragedy?

11. After Luke meets Ani's parents, he says "I can't believe I'm the one who got to save you." Discuss Luke's relationship with Ani. Do you think he did save her from her past? Why is he so reluctant to speak with Ani about it? Did you think Luke and Ani were well suited?

12. Discuss the structure of the book. What's the effect of alternating between Ani's current life and her freshman year at Bradley? Did learning about Ani's past help you better understand her current actions? Did your feelings about Ani change as you learned more about her? If so, how?

13. Ani tells Andrew Larson that she is wary of participating in the documentary because "'I don't know what the bent is. I know what the editing process can do.'"

Are Ani's reservations justified? Many of the characters edit their versions of events, often to fit self-serving narratives. When Ani is interviewed by Dr. Anita Perkins, Ani "had to guide everyone in my direction with swift surety, otherwise they would dig, dig, dig." What effect does Ani's distortion of the truth have on her life and the lives of those around her? Are there other characters who are lying by omission? Who are they and what are their motivations?

14. Why is Ani desperate to be friends with Hilary and Olivia? What sacrifices is she willing to make to keep their friendship? Contrast Ani's friendship with Hilary and Olivia with her friendship with Nell. Do you think that Nell is a good friend? In what ways?

ENHANCE YOUR BOOK CLUB

1. *Luckiest Girl Alive* has been compared to *Gone Girl*. Megan Abbott praised Knoll's writing, saying "With the cunning and verve of Gillian Flynn but with a febrile intensity all its own, Jessica Knoll's *Luckiest Girl Alive* is a debut you won't want to miss." Read both books, then compare and contrast Ani FaNelli and Amy Dunne.

2. Jessica Knoll has worked as a senior editor at *Cosmopolitan*. You can read some of her articles at http://www.cosmopolitan.com/author/10la00/jessica-knoll/. Do you think that job helped her create Ani? If so, how?

3. Ani's assigned summer reading for Mr. Larson's English class is *The Catcher in the Rye*. Read that novel with your book club and discuss how Ani and Arthur both react to it. Do you agree with their interpretations? Why or why not? Have your book club discuss if there are any parallels between Ani and Arthur and Holden Caulfield.

4. After the tragedy at Bradley, Dina does not want Ani to watch the news reports about it. Discuss how the media portrays tragedies. Are Knoll's descriptions accurate? Does the media's portrayal of the events affect Ani? In what ways?

Mother Daughter Book Club Guide

Introduction

I thought *Luckiest Girl Alive* would strike a chord with readers in the same stage of life as Ani, women who were just coming into their own professionally, on the cusp of Big Life Decisions, about marriage and when and if to have children. That did happen. But the book resonated with another group of women, too. On my book tour, I met so many mothers who told me that they had been the ones to discover my book, passing it along to their teenage and twentysomething daughters after finishing it. "This book is required reading in my house," one woman, a mother of a twelve- and fifteen-year-old, told me.

Sensing that there was a conversation to be had here, we've put together a reading group guide designed specifically for mothers and daughters. My hope is that it spurs a dialogue around the complicated issues facing teens and young women, particularly when it comes to consent. Ani was not able to talk to her mother after her assault, but if the lines of communication had been open between them, her story might have ended differently.

Topics & Questions for Discussion

1. From the beginning, we know that Ani's life was changed by The Bradley School. While high school is transformative for many teenage girls, how is this particularly true for TifAni FaNelli?

2. How do fourteen-year-old TifAni and her peers exert power over the world around them? How does this change for Ani as an adult?

3. What's in a name? How do TifAni's many nicknames (Tif, Ani, Finny) signal different stages of her transformation?

4. Sexual violence is a very serious problem that affects millions of women and men. In the United States, one in five women and one in fifty-nine men have been raped in their lifetime. Most victims first experienced sexual violence before age twenty-five. Do you think TifAni's parents talked openly to her about sexual abuse? What are some of the conversations you have had with your parents/children about sexual abuse?

5. What do you think are the similarities and differences between conversations about sexual abuse had with teen girls versus conversations with teen boys? Would Liam have had a conversation with his parents about the meaning of consent?

6. Describe Ani's relationship with her body as a teenager and as an adult. What does having the right body, the right clothes, the right hair mean to Ani? What does this mean to you?

7. Do you think the social pressures placed on Ani today are more or less fraught than they were when her mother was a teenager? Why or why not?

8. How does Ani's relationship with her mother affect her attitudes toward the possibility of becoming pregnant or having children?

9. Why do you think TifAni doesn't confide in her mother after the first incident at Dean's house? What would you have done in TifAni's place?

10. What could the adults—the parents, teachers, and administrators—in The Bradley School family have done differently? Do you think they could have affected the outcome for TifAni? For Arthur?

11. Compare the female friendships in *Luckiest Girl Alive*: Ani's adult relationships with Nell and Moni, Olivia and Hilary's friendship, Ani's relationship with Olivia and Hilary, Ani's relationship with the Shark. What do they have in common? How are they different?

12. How did you react to Ani's recounting of her experience of "the awful tie that would always bind" her to her classmates? Do you think Ani was brave? Selfish? Why?

13. TifAni's high school experience carried over into her adult life—her career choices, her relationships, etc.—as did the dangers of having internalized her abuse. What are some of the effects of her not getting help?

14. Following Liam's service, how does Ani find a way forward? Why does she choose to finish high school at Bradley?

15. During the first discussion of *The Catcher in the Rye* in Mr. Larson's class, Arthur doesn't think Holden Caulfield is a reliable narrator. Do you think Ani is a reliable narrator? Do you believe her version of events? Does it matter? Why or why not?

16. Do you think Ani gets her happy ending? Does she get her closure? Why or why not?

Turn the page for a sneak peek at Jessica Knoll's
latest bone-chilling thriller

THE FAVORITE SISTER

Coming in May 2018 from Simon & Schuster

PROLOGUE

Kelly: The Interview
Present day

Aman whose name I do not know slides his hand under the hem of my new blouse, connecting the cable to the lavalier mic clipped to my collar. He asks me to say something—sound check—and for a crazed moment, I consider the truth. *Brett is dead and I'm not innocent.*

"Testing. Testing. One. Two. Three." I'm not just dishonest. I'm unoriginal.

The sound guy listens to the playback. "Keep your hair off your left shoulder as much as you can," he tells me. I haven't had a haircut in months, and not because my grief has bested my vanity. I'm hoping viewers are better able to see the resemblance to my sister. I have nice hair. Brett had beautiful hair.

"Thanks," I reply, wishing I could remember his name. Brett would have known it. She made a point of being on a first-name basis with the crew—from the gaffer to the ever-rotating harem of production assistants. My sister's specialty was making underappreciated people feel appreciated. It's a testament to that quality that we are all gathered here today, some of us prepared to tell heroic lies about her.

Acoustics isolated, I take my seat before Camera A with the grim poise of a fallen soldier's widow. The small room is as cozy as a Christmas card—fire going, over-stuffed chairs. This is my first time in Jesse Barnes's apartment, and I was dismayed to discover that while richly appointed, it is not much bigger than my one-bedroom in Battery Park that atrophies my savings on the fifteenth of every month. Jesse Barnes has a hit reality show on a prestige cable channel and all she has to show for it is nine hundred square feet. New York does not have the real estate for any more success stories.

Jesse emerges from her bedroom and frowns at me. "Better," she says, meaning my outfit. I agonized over what to wear for this interview, scouring the flash-sale sites, until finally giving myself permission to shop the full price racks at Ann Taylor. Not Loft. When you are going on TV to talk about your little sister, dead at twenty-seven, you spring for the core product.

I showed up for the interview fifteen minutes early (location one, Jesse's living room), feeling spruce in a starched white button-down and black pants that hook above my belly button. Jesse barely glances at me and calls over her stylist with an excoriating sigh, like she was expecting me to disappoint her. My grieving big sister costume has since been reimagined with the help of a pair of large ripped jeans and sneakers, though we kept the fitted button-down *for contrast*, rolling up the sleeves and knotting it at the waist. *This is an intimate fireside chat in my living room, not a network interview with Diane Sawyer on a soundstage*, Jesse told the stylist, speaking about me as though I were not standing right next to her. She noticed but did not comment on the price tag, still attached to the interior seam of the rejected pair of black pants by a small brass safety pin. Diane Sawyer actually wanted to interview me on a soundstage for half a million dollars, but I said no, for Jesse, and I'm a single mother wearing clothes I'll try to return tomorrow.

Jesse Barnes sits down across from me and does a very confusing thing. She smiles at me. All morning, she has oscillated between picking me apart and ignoring me, which is not an easy thing to do in such tight quarters. Jesse Barnes knows what really happened and that's why she's hot and cold on me. She needs me, that's for sure, so you would think she would smile at me more. The problem is that I need her too.

"You feel okay about this?" she asks, sounding almost nervous. All around us, yellow sandbags moor light stands, their naked bulbs too bright to look at directly. *It's like we're preparing for a natural disaster*, I thought the first time I saw them, not too long ago.

"I do," I tell her with the confidence I've learned to fake as a mother. *What's my father's name?* I don't know. *What if a man comes to my school with a gun?* That will never happen.

"Let's make this quick for both of our sakes," Jesse says, raising her phone to her face to brush up on her interview questions, one combat boot bobbing. *Jesse dresses like a goth lesbian Audrey Hepburn*, Brett told me before I met her for the first time, and then she actually repeated the witticism to Jesse's face, as though to prove to me that unlike the other women, Jesse was her friend and not just her boss. Jesse and I were on our way to friendship before Brett died, our one inside joke igniting a streak of insecurity in my sister that had remained mostly contained since she became famous. This fear that we might regress to our childhood roles—me the golden child, Brett the reprobate—was a fire that nothing could put out entirely. *At least you didn't have the shitty childhood*, she would say whenever something bad happened to me in adulthood, as though I had no right to complain about needing a root canal now because I was Mom's favorite growing up. What Brett never understood was that Mom favored me because she could control me, and that made for a shitty childhood in its own right. I was the *yes* daughter, and for the record what that got me wasn't love. What that got me was a lowering limbo bar, until I couldn't bend any deeper. So I snapped.

"We're good, Jess," Lisa says. Lisa is our showrunner and the only person in this room who wasn't enamored with Brett while she was alive. Well, besides me. Don't get me wrong—I loved my sister, but I saw her too.

There are the last-minute preparations: a dab of Vaseline in the bow of my lips, a spritz of hairspray from the on-set hairdresser, smile check—no breakfast in our teeth. The set clears, leaving only the main players. It is not the most ideal of circumstances, but not even a year ago, I could only dream that Saluté would be promoting *The Kelly Courtney Interview Special* on the sides of MTA buses.

Jesse begins. "Kelly, I want to thank you so much for agreeing to share your story with the Saluté community." She is speaking in a gentle lilt, but her eyes are dark and hard. "Let me start by saying how profoundly sorry I am for your loss. I know I speak on behalf of the entire Saluté family when I say we are all grieving." She pauses long enough for me to thank her. "That grief, as I'm sure you know, is a tornado of emotions. Hurt, shock, confusion, *anger.*" A bead of Jesse's spit lands just below my eye. I wipe it away and realize it looks like I am wiping away a tear when Jesse clucks. "How are you holding up?"

"I'm hanging in there." I picture my fingers monkey-gripping the edge of a rooftop, cartoon clouds separating me from the gawkers on the street below: *Am I really going to do it?* Something Stephanie must have thought. How many times?

"I noticed you're wearing your sister's ring," Jesse says. "Can you share the significance of that with the people at home?"

My right hand flies to my left, shielding the gold signet as though Jesse has threatened to take it from me. "The women had these rings made after the first season of the show," I explain, my thumb brushing the letterpressed metal. Like everything of Brett's but her shoes, the ring is too big on me. On cold days I have to wear it on my thumb. "They're inscribed *SS,* for Standing Sisters."

"What does Standing Sisters signify?"

That the lethal casting process you subjected them to every year didn't bring them to their knees. Production was notorious for toying with the women between seasons. They brought in new women, younger women, smarter women, richer women, put them on tape, and sent them to the network to consider. Potential "new hires," all under the guise of keeping the cast fresh. But they also made sure the old women heard about it, that they knew *no one* was irreplaceable. If they wanted to come back, they had better dance for their dinner. And the old women would do anything to come back. No one ever left the show of her own accord, despite what previously axed *Diggers* have claimed in the press. You were fired or you died, and honestly, dying might be better. Once you were fired, it was over anyway.

It was a point of pride for Jen Greenberg, Stephanie Simmons, and my sister that they were original *Goal Diggers* who withstood every between-season casting gauntlet. They had these rings made to congratulate themselves and, let's be real, to assert their authority over the newbies like me.

"The rings are our promises to each other that as women, we will raise each other up," I revise.

"As women, we *must* make this commitment to one another," Jesse says with the vigor of someone who believes herself, "especially when the world is designed to keep us down. And I have to give it to you, Kelly, because after what happened to Brett, I think most of us would understand if you wanted to back off, sell your share in the company, and hand over the reins. Instead, you've taken complete creative control and doubled your revenue, all while raising the most thoughtful, caring, and enterprising teenager I've ever met. You're not just standing. You're thriving."

The mention of my daughter gets my heart going at a primal pace. *Keep her out of this*, I think, unfairly, since I'm the one who brought her into *this* in the first place.

"Kelly," Jesse continues, "the network faced a great deal of flak when we announced that we were not only moving forward with airing season four as planned, but that we would be sharing the footage of that day uncensored. But as a show dedicated to the empowerment and advancement of women, we felt it was our responsibility to lay bare the truth of domestic violence. I know, as your friend, you agreed with Saluté. Would you talk to me a little bit about that?"

Even though I know we are not and never will be "friends," the word sends a warm spike through my middle. To be a part of Jesse's orbit is a fantastic thing. I'm sorry this is the way it had to happen—of course I am, I'm not a monster—but I shouldn't have to feel guilty about it either. Everything Jesse just said about me is true. I have revitalized the company. I have doubled our revenue. I have raised an exceptional daughter. I deserve to be here, maybe even more than Brett ever did.

"I think of it like this, Jesse," I answer. "That if what had happened to my sister had happened to me, I wouldn't want the truth *censored*"—this verbal mirroring is met with an almost imperceptible nod of approval from Jesse—"just because it makes people uncomfortable. We should be made uncomfortable by domestic violence. We should be traumatized by it. It's the only way we are ever going to be motivated to do anything about it." My voice has intensified, and Jesse reaches out and catches my hand in hers. The gesture produces a clapping sound, as though we have high-fived.

"Why don't we start from the beginning?" she suggests, her pulse electric beneath my fingertips. *She's not nervous,* I realize. *She's excited.*

My mother always told me to make my own money so that a man could never tell me what to do. (Like my father ever told *her* what to do.) But here I am, doing that, or trying to at least, just to take orders from a woman who would not hesitate to hit me harder than any man ever could if I do not do as she says. I do not have independence. I do not have desirable options. What am I to do but to start from our version of the beginning?

If you loved *Luckiest Girl Alive*, don't miss Jessica Knoll's highly anticipated second novel,
THE FAVORITE SISTER!

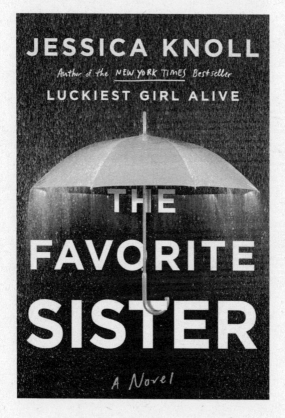

Pick up or download your copy today!